"Before Overman learned to walk, he learned his limits. Enduring sure-targeted bias reinforced by genetic fiat, Overman is doomed. He can only claw from destiny once he is visited by the sins of an entire people. This remarkable achievement is the seminal victory within Bruce Ferber's brutally funny, *Elevating Overman*. Frailty abounds in this searing examination of our lesser selves. With hints of Philip Roth, the cultural byplay will bring out the self-hatred in us all – and turn it on its head. *Elevating Overman* deserves a place in the Jewish-American canon."

—Roy Teicher, former *Tonight Show* writer,
Los Angeles Times columnist

"Ira Overman knew his world was narrow and petty, but after a dramatic Lasik surgery he sensed "it was about to become narrow and petty in bold new ways." It's well worth going along with him for the ride. *Elevating Overman* is funny, sad, and very, very engaging."

—Charlie Hauck, **author,** *Artistic Differences,*
creator, seven network TV series,
New York Times Contributor

"If Woody Allen, SJ Perelman, and Phillip Roth had a son.... that son and his three fathers would love this book! A great read! Outrageous, funny, sad, and wildly original!"

—Billy Van Zandt, writer/producer
of a ridiculous amount of TV comedies,
widely popular playwright,
and author of *"You've Got Hate Mail"*

"Bruce Ferber has come out of the gate with balls. His dysfunctional creation Ira Overman ponders why "volumes have been written about bad things happening to good people," but nothing about when good things happen to someone like him. Ferber's novel makes one think, "What would happen if Holden Caulfield suddenly got everything he wanted?" Okay, besides a bevy of hot ladies...Loaded with laughs, *Elevating Overman* makes you read late into the night when you have a court appearance the next morning. "What is going to happen to this jerk?" Is what your brain says as it continues to turn the page. Thankfully, the answer is happy, funny, sexy and utterly original."

Dwight Slade, **standup comedian,**
Winner *Boston Comedy Festival*

elevating

Overman

a novel

bruce ferber

Fulcourt Press

Permission to reprint previously published material may be found in the acknowledgements section at the end of the book.

Library of Congress: 2012936867

Fulcourt Press ISBN: 978-0985322106

Cover and Interior Design: AuthorSupport.com

Author photo: Paul Harris

www.bruceferber.net
Twitter: @BruuuceF

In loving memory of Jenise and Sam

For Lyn, Aaron, Sarah, Bea, Vy Vy, and Anthony

But by my love and hope I be-
seech you: do not throw away the
hero in your soul! Hold holy your
highest hope!

—FRIEDRICH NIETZSCHE,
"Thus Spoke Zarathustra"

For many minutes, for many hours,
for a bleak eternity, he lay awake
shivering, reduced to primitive terror, comprehending that he had won
freedom, and wondering what he
could do with anything so unknown
and so embarrassing as freedom.

—SINCLAIR LEWIS, *"Babbit"*

A mole digging in a hole
Digging up my soul now
Going down, excavation
I and I in the sky
You make me feel like I can fly
So high, elevation.

—U2, *"Elevation"*

ignitiOn

one

To Overman, everything in life was a negotiation. In his dealings with women, the grueling battle of give and take was a foregone conclusion, cruelly validated by the indelible scars left in its wake. At the office, there was the ever-nagging question of whether the size of the paycheck justified the level of abuse. When purchasing a car, it was the time-honored test of wills between buyer and salesman, the exhaustive parrying back and forth that ultimately left both parties spent and irritable. If negotiation was indeed such an integral part of the human experience, why then, Overman concluded, should it be any different with eye surgery?

The Lasik coupon he found in the Pennysaver advertised "FDA approved, Life-Changing Vision Correction" for $299 per eye, which immediately told Overman he could close the deal for $500 out the door. But now here he was, seated across from Dr. David Gonzales of the Clearview Vision Center listening to a quote of $1999 for the pair including a five-year extended warranty. The doctor seemed enthusiastic about slicing open Overman's corneas, cheerfully adding that the fees could be paid in monthly installments with absolutely no money down.

Overman shook his head. "If it says $299, how can you charge me a thousand dollars each?"

Dr. Gonzales nodded sympathetically, eager to clarify. "Ira, I really don't think you'd be happy with a $299 eye."

Overman pondered the meaning of this remark, wondering if there was any sort of lemon law that applied to this procedure, and if so, how that would work. It was also conceivable that the warning had been issued because Dr. Gonzales himself, with his thick, coke bottle lenses, had opted for the bargain basement Pennysaver deal and wound up paying dearly. Apparently this was not the case. The doctor went on to explain that his astigmatism, paired with a family history of glaucoma, made him a poor candidate for Lasik surgery. The $2000 treatment, he continued, bought one the identical surgery but with the peace of mind that any complications would be fully covered for five years.

Overman smiled and said he understood perfectly. He took his wallet out of his back pocket, removed a wad of cash and slapped it on the doctor's desk.

"I'm a gambler. I'll take the best you can give me for $450."

Fifty bucks later, Overman and Dr. Gonzales shook hands and agreed on the terms. Two eyes Lasiked, one hundred dollars below the advertised Pennysaver price, no extended warranty. A Pyrrhic victory perhaps, if he went blind. But those were the wages of fear, paranoia and decades of perceived victimhood.

Overman hadn't always been a miserable soul. Misery had slowly attached itself to him barnacle upon barnacle, culminating in the formation of a sublimely dysfunctional individual. As he walked over to the microwave to nuke his Healthy Choice Fettuccine Alfredo with Bacon, he imagined himself a modern-day Ratso Rizzo, drifting further away from reality while trapped in a dwelling fit for squatters. If only he could be more like Ratso, he thought, who somehow managed to look at the glass, no matter how filthy, as half-full.

The dinging of the oven signaled him to remove the paper tray and plunk it down on the dinette table, no plates necessary. That was his wife's thing. The perfect place settings, the recipes out of Bon Appetit, the remodeled kitchen with its requisite Holy Grail, the Granite Counter. What was it about granite that made it an object of worship among the upwardly mobile? And what was it about kitchens? Back when he was married, it occurred to Overman that most of the people he knew with fancy kitchens went out to eat all the time. Then they would take their friends back to the house to show off their gourmet kitchens.

Divorced Overman deals with food as fuel, not fetish. He shovels it in, the fettuccine sweet and congealed, the bacon limp and chewy. And yet, a healthy choice. All things considered, it is a moment of triumph. For the first time since toddlerhood, Overman is consuming a meal without wearing glasses. He had often noted that while people don't need eyeglasses to eat, they rarely act on that option. Oddly enough, they instinctively put on glasses when they're not hearing well, even when lip reading doesn't enter into the equation. The glasses become the thing one reaches for when searching for comfort. While Overman could never picture himself finding comfort in anything, he suddenly felt the urge to look around. Just because he had always been terrified of the unknown didn't mean he had to stay that way. The known was so mediocre and shitty, what did he have to lose?

In truth, the eyeglasses obscured Overman's growing collection of wrinkles and crow's feet, and the absence of spectacles actually made him look older than his pre-Lasiked self. But the surgery was less about vanity than a desire to shed unnecessary weight in his life, even if it was only that which rested on his nose. As he scarfed down the gluey noodles, Overman couldn't help but notice that his newly unencumbered pupils not only saw better, but saw differently. While his peripheral vision had understandably improved, so, surprisingly, had his awareness. Every disgusting nook and cranny of the apartment now looked like it was being presented in IMAX

3-D. The startling images beckoned him to focus on them with a yogi-like acuity. The mildewed carpet had far more texture than he had previously thought. The hole he had kicked in the drywall exposed curiously gray fiberglass insulation that had gone unnoticed for years. The "mid-century" cottage cheese ceilings were cheesier, richer, undoubtedly masking a history of secrets Overman dared not contemplate.

It was a strange sensation. As he continued to process visual stimuli, he recalled the advertisement's claim that the surgery would be "life-changing." Had the $500 eyes purchased from Dr. David Gonzales of the Clearview Vision Center altered his relationship to the world around him? Cleaning up the table and going off to brush his teeth, he considered this far-fetched possibility. He faced himself in the bathroom mirror and saw more wrinkles, but no sign of any change afoot. Still, as Overman climbed into bed and got under the covers, he felt that something was brewing. Yes, his world was a narrow and petty one, but his sense was that it was about to become narrow and petty in bold new ways.

The alarm clock blasts Overman out of his dream. In it, he is being ripped off by the contractor who is re-modeling the house he will eventually lose in the divorce. Flawlessly mimicking real life, his soon-to-be ex-wife seems to have no problem with a forty-two thousand dollar bathroom fixtures charge, and to top it off, is winking conspiratorially at the contractor. Overman is ready to threaten a lawsuit when he realizes he's semi-conscious and due at work in forty-five minutes. He leaps out of bed, grabbing from his closet the standard-issue cotton blend white shirt, permanent press slacks and synthetic tie that have long been the *couture de rigueur* of his current profession. He accessorizes the look with a personal touch, Elevator shoes purchased online to prop up his sagging 5 foot 6 inch frame. Whatever embarrassment Overman already felt about his diminutive stature was formalized the day he received his lifted loafers in plain brown packaging, sent that way to hide its contents from snickering mailmen or inquiring neighbors. The stealthy nature of the delivery clearly branded him as a lowlife, indulging in some sort of abhorrent, illegal foot porn.

In a matter of moments, Overman is in and out of the shower and racing downstairs to the subterranean parking garage that houses his "E" Class Mercedes sedan. As he waits for the rusty security gate to open, he marvels how his is far from the nicest car parked here. How can people live in such a shitty apartment building and drive $100,000 automobiles? Auto leasing knew a good thing when it met Los Angeles.

The drive from old-school mid-Wilshire to Nouveau McMansion-happy Calabasas could take anywhere from a half-hour to three times that depending upon traffic. Today Overman was cruising comfortably, having successfully erased from his consciousness the sales meeting that would occupy most of the morning. How many more ways could his boss continue to sell German cars to Jews? To be fair, it wasn't just Jews. All manner of conspicuous consumers descended upon Calabasas, that proud Southern California bastion of white flight. But the fact that Overman was an intrinsically guilty Jew made him feel extra guilty each time he sold a Mercedes Benz to one of the tribe. The congregants of Temple Alhashem were undoubtedly his best customers; a living testament to the amount of energy Overman expended diverting them from the BMW dealer down the street.

Mostly he just hated his job. How did a once young man with such promise become a middle-aged hawker of zero down financing? After graduating from Columbia with honors, he had worked as an entertainment executive for the studios, segueing into positions with various management firms and talent agencies on both coasts, garnering ever more generous stock option grants and lavish expense accounts. Now he struggles to keep his eyes open as self-important gasbag Hal Steinbaum enumerates the latest sales incentives being offered by Steinbaum Mercedes of Calabasas. "We'll pay off your trade, no questions asked!" "Complimentary maintenance for 36 months!" "Free, All-You-Can-Eat Sunday Barbecue, with 16 oz. Stein-baums of beer!"

The fledgling sales guys, or Green Peas as they are known in the trade, seem to get off on these depressing pep rallies, filing out of the conference room with renewed determination and amped-up testosterone. Overman feigns his usual smile and pads back to his corner desk, away from the hubbub. He will pick up the phone and good-naturedly badger the couple who looked at the CLK convertible last Saturday, review his list of customers with leases about to expire, make a few cold calls from the leads handed out at last week's meeting.

Overman looks up from his desk to see Douchebag-of-the-Month Rick Crandall flirting with Maricela, the receptionist with the insanely round ass. Crandall is a white trash middle-aged lifer with a tired wife and two ADHD kids. Maricela, a hard-partying and even harder-bodied twenty-six year-old, is best known for the ornate and provocative "tramp stamp" tattooed above her coveted rear bumper. She has a steady boyfriend, but is also aware of her power over all things male. On the surface she may be a lowly receptionist, but for all intents and purposes Maricela runs the dealership. It is common knowledge that Hal Steinbaum himself begged her to accompany him to Cancun one weekend when his wife was out of town. And that when Maricela turned him down, she somehow wound up with a raise rather than a pink slip. The unspoken truth is that every guy on this lot is her bitch. Maricela is at all times the model of grace and composure as she cheerfully answers the phone: "It's a beautiful day at Steinbaum Mercedes."

When has it ever been a beautiful day at this shithole? Overman asks himself. On the other hand, how could you blame the messenger? The poor girl didn't make up that greeting, she was instructed to recite it by some dopey middle manager without a creative bone in his body. Overman has nothing against Maricela. She has always treated him kindly, although, to his chagrin, like some benign grandfatherly eunuch. Conversely, he has been nothing but polite and gracious, which could not be said for the rest of the esteemed sales force. Overman admired her assets as much as the next guy: he just had enough class not to drool all over the showroom floor. At least that's what he told himself. In truth, the respectful distance he kept was rooted in a lifelong fear of rejection and being exposed for the lonely, horny train wreck he had honed to perfection.

Overman studies Maricela as she works the phones. She has an effortless, inviting smile, chatting with the ease of someone who has yet to experience despair, know anybody with cancer, or even gain a few extra pounds. He thinks about getting to work, but instead contemplates for the gazillionth time whether or not she's fucked Rick Crandall or anyone else at the dealership. How could she say no to the boss and then bang one of his puerile protégés? Then again, she's the one in control of the company pheromones. She can do whatever she wants. For all Overman knew, she was blowing Gene Cantalupo in Pre-Owned, who fucked his way through Nissan of Rancho Cucamonga. Picturing the two of them together made him want to throw up.

He tries to get to work, but an Einsteinian equation, profound yet elegant in its simplicity, invades his already cluttered brain. Based on the massive amount of fantasizing, plotting and planning at Steinbaum Mercedes, one of these degenerates had surely banged or *would* bang the exquisite Maricela.

Overman manages to regroup, and is about to dial a number when he hears Maricela laugh from across the room. As he stops to savor this primal, unrestrained thing of beauty, he sees that she's looked up and caught him staring. He feels himself starting to blush, but Maricela doesn't chuckle or grimace or avoid his gaze. She gamely stares back, openly and without judgment. Overman keeps looking at her. Maricela doesn't blink. Should he turn away? He tries, but he can't. Overman is focusing with an unconscious intensity, a wild current coursing through his veins. He feels his body start to convulse, his blood pressure rising like the price of bathroom fixtures in his dream. Fearing a seizure or worse yet, a spontaneous public ejaculation, Overman manages to get up and stumble toward the water fountain. He bends down and lets the cold stream splash all over his face, now drenched in sweat. The sleeve of his poly-cotton shirt comes in handy, a surprisingly quick drying agent. Overman takes two deep breaths and starts to regain his composure when he feels a tap on his shoulder. He turns to find himself face to face with the magnificently sweet-smelling Maricela; her bare midriff only inches away.

"Excuse me, Mr. Overman."

"Please. Ira," he managed, his pulse racing.

"Ira," her lips formed the two simple syllables of his name in a way that really did make it a beautiful day at Steinbaum Mercedes. "I don't know what it is, but something about you seems… different."

I've been the same asshole my whole life, he thinks to himself. Then he remembers that there has, in fact, been a change. "No glasses," Overman informs her, pointing to his naked face. "I had Lasik."

The young woman can't take her eyes off him. "I… I don't know why but when you looked at me just now, something happened."

"No kidding?" Overman asks lamely, an impressively speedy erection in the making.

Maricela nods her head. "Even though I've seen you like a gajillion times before, I felt like I really saw you for the first time. And you really saw me."

Nothing new about the latter, Overman thinks to himself. He's studied every inch of this girl in the office and reviewed his findings in the shower for as long as he can remember.

"Does that sound stupid to you?" she asks adorably.

"Not stupid at all." Overman has no clue what she's talking about. At the same time, he's smart enough to recognize that he's scoring points and must get them on the board while the getting is good. He tries to think of something insightful to say, but draws a complete blank. As he wonders how any man could be this pathetic, Hal Steinbaum appears out of nowhere and grabs Maricela by the arm, dropping a roll of Mentos on the floor in the process.

"Just the girl I want to see. I got a laydown who's about to get reamed for two g's over sticker. Come in my office and watch how it's done."

Maricela follows him, her eyes not wavering from Overman as she goes.

What just happened? Overman wondered. It was as if he had telepathically communicated his needs and desires to this young woman and she now wished to respond in kind. But why would a smoking hot twenty-six year-old be interested in a poorly preserved middle-aged relic? Maybe it was a nasty joke set up by one of the Green Peas. Then again, maybe it wasn't. What if the Lasik surgery really did make him handsome and desirable? Overman checked his reflection in the showroom window and quickly nixed that theory. Still, on the off chance that this beautiful girl was trying to make a connection, it would be a ray of sunshine in a life that had thus far wallowed in every conceivable shade of gray. While highly unlikely, for now he would allow himself to bask in the possibility that things could get better. Maybe he wouldn't have to spend the rest of his days feeling like some stray dog at the pound, marking time before his incineration.

It turns out to be a productive afternoon. With Maricela busy at her station, Overman uses his newfound energy to sell a fully loaded S-class, lease a CL, and have a relatively cringe-free telephone conversation with his ex-wife. The erstwhile Nancy Overman had been happily re-married to internist Dr. Stan Belzberg for thirteen years, which she felt compelled to bring up nearly every time they spoke. Today they needed to go over the details of their daughter Ashley's high school graduation party, which would of course be held at the Recurring Nightmare House. The one he never got to live in because by the time it was built, he had already lost it in the settlement. But today none of that mattered. Overman offered to buy centerpieces for the tables and assist in whatever way he could. Nancy was taken aback, wondering aloud if Overman had finally found a mind-altering medication that worked. If so, her husband could surely get him free samples of whatever SSRI he was taking.

"The pharmaceutical companies love Stan," she crowed.

Why should they be any different from the medical supply outlets, the blood work technicians and everyone else to whom Stan had ever said two words? Overman thanked Nancy for the offer, but told her he didn't need any pills.

Relieved to be finished with this conversation, the car salesman shoves the phone back in its cradle and looks up to see Maricela waving at him as her boyfriend enters to take her out. Overman is momentarily crestfallen but quickly recovers, seeing this as a positive. After all, to be crestfallen one first has to have reached some manner of crest, a feat he had inarguably accomplished. He waves back, Maricela smiles, and Overman feels certain that his life has somehow changed overnight.

He picks up the phone and dials Jake Rosenfarb to see if he wants to hit some tennis balls. Maybe lovely Rita, the Rosenfarb better half, who trades her husband blowjobs for jewelry, will let him out tonight. He's been kicking Overman's ass for months, but tonight the Mercedes salesman extraordinaire is firing on all cylinders, recharged by his blossoming relationship with the receptionist. He will even spring for the post-victory beer and sandwiches so he can tell Rosenfarb about the portending revelatory moment with Maricela.

Rosenfarb answers his cell phone. "Yello?"

Why do people say "Yello?" Overman wonders.

Rosenfarb is out in the field, installing electric blinds in some yenta's pool house. He's had his own window treatment business for twenty-four years and loves to boast about being his own boss. Overman knows the real story: his clients treat him like shit and after that, he goes home to get abused by Rita.

Rosenfarb says he wants to play. Rita has her book group tonight and it is imperative that he gets out of the house. It's either that or listen to twelve Botox survivors in a gated community discuss Oprah's latest selection, something about women suffering in Afghanistan. They agree to meet at the courts at 7. Overman surmises that even though Rosenfarb might lose, it will still be more enjoyable for him than listening to that phony whining about the injustice of wearing burqas. Who are they kidding? If Prada designed them, the entire book group would snap them up.

Overman gets onto Valley Circle and sees the 101 choked with traffic in his direction. It has been such a refreshing, renewing day up until now. If only there were an alternate route. But there really is no other way to travel from the West Valley to mid-Wilshire. He creeps down the ramp and onto the freeway. Overman moves a lane to the left, hoping that as he gets into the flow of traffic, sluggish though it may be, he will be able to relax and reflect on the positive events of the day.

Almost immediately he is behind an anxious eighty year-old of indeterminate gender and being tailgated by some yahoo in a Roto Rooter van. He crosses one lane to the left and gets honked at by a teenager whose text messaging he has rudely interrupted. For no apparent reason, the guy in the left lane driving the Ford F-150 gives him the finger. Now he's behind a meatpacking truck and a cloud of diesel exhaust. It is putting a serious crimp in his evening. All cars come to a standstill. Overman wishes he could have his own HOV lane that would whisk him home. It would give him the space to breathe in his recent good fortune and imagine more positives in the Overman future. His eyes close for a split second, mid-reverie. When he re-opens them, traffic appears to be easing up.

The meat truck in front of Overman moves to the right lane. The tour bus ahead of the truck goes left. The Taurus just beyond the tour bus inches to the right. The Corolla in front of the Taurus moves left. Overman starts to pick up speed. He's cruising. It's turning out to be a decent drive home after all, Overman regaining the indescribable feeling he had at work. Why shouldn't he feel good? He wouldn't be the first person on earth to turn around his life and change for the better. There were countless stories about gang leaders and career criminals, who, against all odds, became productive members of society, achieving professional and personal goals they had never dreamed possible. Even at a beaten down fifty-five, Overman believed he still had a shot.

A mile or two later, the car salesman realizes that the traffic jam is still very much on: it's just his lane that is clearing out. One by one, each car gets out of the way for his Mercedes and he is breezing his way home. The notion of a beautiful twenty-six year-old being interested in him was one thing, but parting the 101 like some low-rent Moses? Rosenfarb will never believe this. He didn't believe it himself. Otherworldly phenomena were for psychics and movie franchises, not bottom-feeding car salesmen. More likely, this was one of those positive state-of-mind deals where a person is able to block out the annoying stuff, turning negative encounters, e.g. traffic jams, into the illusion of pleasurable ones like lanes clearing. Yet the notion of positive thinking was as foreign to Overman as Kabbalah or Voodoo. He felt at once exhilarated and nauseous. The unknown was navigable, but now that it had morphed into the bizarre and unexplainable, he was no longer on such firm footing.

As Overman arrives home and pulls into his parking space, he realizes he is hyperventilating. He has never before experienced anything supernatural, spiritual or lucky. Religion left him cold. To Overman, clinging to ancient beliefs was a tasteless cocktail of quaintness and science fiction. Naturally, he had heard over and over again about his "bad karma," which he had surely earned from the poor life choices that flowed out of him like water. But as Overman had observed, existence for most people was, by necessity, secular and mundane. The bulk of it was spent going to work, paying bills and trying to keep the kids away from STDs and crack pipes. If God spoke to humankind in dreams, visions, or via the burning bush, and there were revelations to be had, he had never seen evidence of it.

He stumbles out of the car, now enervated from his startling brush with the fantastic. Apparently the unexplainable could be quite exhausting. It dawns on him that if he can't get his energy back, Rosenfarb will kick his ass as usual. Perhaps then things would go back to normal. The receptionist would forget him, he'd have to wait in traffic like everybody else and Ira Ethan Overman would resume his uneventful march toward death. He was deeply conflicted, excited by these strange new developments, yet spooked as to why they were happening to him of all people.

Decked out in color-coordinated Nike tenniswear, Rosenfarb was working his hamstrings as Overman sauntered up to the court. The window man always liked to make a big show of how limber he was, then follow it up with the acid aside that Overman did not stretch enough. This never failed to rile the nerves and send Overman into an early tailspin, an important gambit because Rosenfarb hated to lose. Who could blame him, really? After a day of client and spousal battery, what could be worse than being defeated by an out-of-shape car salesman whose entire being reeked of defeat? Rosenfarb would drop maybe a few sets a year, but they always played two out of three, and only once in the last seven years did Overman win a match. Now Jake was hopping up and down like one of those ingénue Sharapova types. In a few moments he'd be grunting ecstatically with every stroke. He looked like a dope but felt like a champion. Overman shook his hand and took his racquet out of his bag.

"Aren't you going to stretch?" Rosenfarb asked, by now a parody of himself.

"I stretched at home," Overman lied, fooling no one.

They began their usual warm-up, half-volleying at the service line. Rosenfarb recounted his day, not bothering to ask whether Overman wanted to hear about it.

"Hunter-Douglas didn't have the Duettes ready, but *I* look like the schmuck."

You only look like the schmuck if you *are* the schmuck, Irma Overman used to say. It certainly seemed true in the case of Rosenfarb. Wait till I tell him about my day, Overman thought, deciding it would probably be best to save his Maricela bombshell for later.

They move back to the baseline, warming up groundstrokes and taking serves. Rosenfarb hops around again, preening like a moron. He spins his racquet, Overman calls "up" and like clockwork, the "W" on the grip faces down. Rosenfarb elects to serve, swaggering back to the baseline like the cock of the walk.

Rosenfarb's serve is much like everything else in his distorted worldview. He thinks of it as a gorgeous, searing weapon when it is, in fact, a pedestrian stroke that meanders over the net. When Overman effortlessly returns the serve, Rosenfarb counters with an unspectacular shot back, Overman tries to put it away, Rosenfarb hits another mediocre shot, then Overman hits it out or into the net. More often than not, such is the pattern. Consumed by boredom, Overman succumbs to Rosenfarb's tedious style of play and makes an unforced error. Meanwhile, Rosenfarb feels like Roger Federer. It is beyond annoying, but literally the only game in town, because Overman doesn't have anyone else who wants to play with him.

"These go," Rosenfarb announces, holding up the ball. "Have fun."

Like he ever wanted Overman to enjoy himself. Like Overman ever knew how.

Rosenfarb tosses the ball in the air and hits a decent serve to Overman's famously weak backhand. Overman focuses on the ball and drives it back to Rosenfarb. Rosenfarb steps around his backhand and hits a pussy forehand. Overman steps around that and blasts an inside out forehand down the line.

"Love-15," Rosenfarb calls out, proceeding to serve to the ad side.

Again to the backhand, Overman drills it back to Rosenfarb's feet, leaving him helpless.

"Love-30," says Rosenfarb, starting to get annoyed.

He double faults and it's Love-40. The window man serves and volleys, Overman easily lobs it over his head and wins the game.

And on it goes. Overman scores every point and wins 6-0, 6-0. Rosenfarb insists on a third set, and once again loses every point.

Three golden sets, as they are known, but rarely experienced in the world of tennis. Rosenfarb looks like he's about to kill himself. An exhausted Overman manages to spit out a few words. "Imagine what the score would've been if I'd stretched." Adding insult to injury wasn't necessary: it just felt so good.

"I've never lost every point in a match," Rosenfarb sputters in disbelief.

Even though the outcome was just desserts for this preening diva, the man had become so unraveled that Overman couldn't help but feel sorry for him. "Don't be so hard on yourself. There's a reason this happened. It has nothing to do with you."

Rosenfarb doesn't know what to make of this. Is Overman saying he actually anticipated this lopsided victory? That overnight, he was somehow transformed from plodding, unathletic *schlub* to grand slam level player?

"This isn't about tennis," Overman says, trying to console him.

"Stop patronizing me, Ira," Rosenfarb snorts.

"I'm not. Something has happened to me."

"You're making it worse. Just shut up."

"Fine. I'll meet you at Jerry's, the one across from Cedar's.

Jerry's was the deli, Cedar's Sinai the hospital, both overpriced as far as Overman was concerned. Thank God he didn't have any more children being born and only had to deal with fifteen-dollar pastrami sandwiches. Rosenfarb ate light anyway, always pretending to be on some ludicrous diet Rita heard about in her Pilates class.

Rosenfarb is already seated when Overman arrives. His face is ashen, a shocking contrast to the forced conviviality that had always been Rosenfarb's stock-in-trade.

"You all right?" Overman asks.

The waitress, a young, lip-plumped Kim Basinger lookalike, comes over to take their order.

"No, I'm not all right, you prick," Rosenfarb snaps. "What the fuck happened out there?"

The waitress offers to come back in a few minutes but Rosenfarb says he needs food and brusquely asks for the triple-decker corned beef and Swiss.

$18.75, Overman silently notes to himself. "I'll have the blintzes." He smiles at the waitress, patting his paunch. "Just what I need, huh?"

She scurries away, convinced that Rosenfarb is some kind of loose cannon.

"What the fuck, Ira? You're too cheap to buy performance-enhancing drugs. I don't get it."

"I'm not on drugs," Overman replies. "It's hard to explain. I don't fully understand it myself."

"Do you know what my record is against you? 232-1." Only Rosenfarb could hold on to a stat like this. "That's matches. Maybe you've taken 10 sets off me since we've known each other."

Overman explains that this unlikely result is part of something bigger. "I'm telling you, Jake. There's been a change. I suddenly have this new focus, this new power, if you will."

"You? Power?" Rosenfarb scoffs. "Ira, you've been fired from practically every job you've ever had, your wife left you, your kids barely speak to you and you live in a place where plants grow out of the carpet. What kind of power could you have?"

"I won every point tonight, Jake."

"I had a hard day at work. Don't make it into more than it was."

"Ever since my Lasik surgery—"

"Which I believe you had done at the 99 Cents Store," Rosenfarb interrupts.

"— I'm able to make things happen. I think about something, I feel this rush through my whole body that saps me of all my energy, but then the thing I want to happen, happens." Overman recounts his bonding with Maricela, followed by the parting of the 101 south on his drive home.

Rosenfarb finds all of it absurd, as implausible as Rita having sex just because she feels like it. "So what are you telling me? You had bargain basement eye surgery and now you have special powers?"

"I just feel like a different person."

"From car salesman to magician," Rosenfarb laughs. "Hey, you've got all this power, maybe you're a superhero. Why take the freeway home when you could fly? You know, I've always suspected you were from another planet."

What a supreme dick, Overman thinks, now glad he slaughtered the guy on the tennis court. He wished there were a way to shut this asshole up once and for all. An idea suddenly occurs to him. It would have seemed crazy yesterday, it might be crazy now, but it was worth a shot.

"Do you think I could get a date with our waitress?" Overman asks.

Rosenfarb sees the curvaceous Ersatz Kim Basinger approaching, bearing corned beef and blintzes.

"In what universe do you think that could be an option, Overman?"

Overman doesn't dignify the remark with a response, choosing instead to focus on Kim as she rests the plates in front of them.

"Will there be anything else?" she asks.

"Spicy mustard for me. Anything for you?" Rosenfarb snickers at Overman.

"Nothing, thanks, it looks great," Overman says, looking deep into her eyes. "Do we know each other from somewhere?"

"I don't think so," Kim smiles back. She starts off then quickly turns back. "You know there is something about you that seems familiar..."

"Let me guess. He looks like your old fart Uncle Larry," Jake chortles, thrilled to have added his ever-extraneous two cents.

"No, not really," Kim replies, moving away to take another order.

Rosenfarb gives Overman a knowing, "you stupid shit" nod. "Ira, I think maybe you need to see a new therapist. Rita's been very happy with hers."

And a lot of good that's done her. Was it the therapist who came up with the whole sperm swallowing for diamonds arrangement, Overman wonders?

Kim returns to the table wielding a brand new squeeze bottle of spicy mustard. "Here you go, sir," she says, placing it in front of Rosenfarb. She then looks at Overman and produces a hand-written note. "My phone number. In case you ever feel like getting together." Kim smiles seductively at Overman and heads back toward the kitchen.

Rosenfarb is convinced that Overman and Kim pre-arranged this as a practical joke.

"When have I ever been that clever?" Overman asks, a valid point on any given day.

But Rosenfarb cannot deal with what he has witnessed with his own eyes and ears throughout this evening. It is as if everything he has gleaned over a lifetime has been rendered false in one fell swoop. "I don't know what you think you're up to Overman, but we'll settle this on the court next week." He stands up and motions toward Kim, hoisting the gargantuan corned beef triple-decker in the air. "I'll take this to go."

Having left his friend a discombobulated mass of Ashkenaze jelly, Overman had much to contemplate on the ride home. He ruminated on the fact that there had been volumes written on the subject of bad things happening to good people, but were there any texts that addressed when good things happened to someone like him? If an all-loving, merciful God couldn't prevent pain and suffering but was nonetheless responsible for Good, what had a weak, soulless, unremarkable man like Overman ever done to deserve the gifts he had been given today? Granted, it was only one day and things could turn to shit tomorrow, but at the very least, he had been thrown a major cosmic bone, for which, even in his mystified state, he was thankful.

There are certain individuals for whom high school is a Defining Moment. On some level that could be said of Overman, for it was in the halls of Long Island's Lakeview South (there was no lake anywhere and the only view was of a shopping center) that young Ira perfected the art of blending into the woodwork, thereby avoiding blame or arousing ire. While his neighborhood friend Jake Rosenfarb was an inferior student with no discernable talent, he made the most of his subpar skill set. Rosenfarb was unafraid of talking to girls, something Overman was never able to master, even into adulthood.

Jake had a simple opening line that seemed to work every time.

"You nervous about the test?" he'd inquire of Sharon Kramer, the pouty brunette from World History class with the best rack in Lakeview North or South. She would confide that although she knew the material, she worried that it wouldn't translate to the testing environment. Rosenfarb would then admit his own academic insecurities, suggest studying together, and three chapters later would be exploring globes Vasco Da Gama only dreamed of.

In the fall of their senior year, Rosenfarb claimed to have gone around the world quite a few times with Nancy Morrison, a spirited redhead from his economics class, who, according to Lakeview legend, had an insatiable sexual appetite. Many years later, by the time she became Nancy Overman, she had had her fill of fleshly pleasures and considered any sort of physical contact an unnecessary annoyance. The fact that his best friend had deflowered his wife was not a pleasant thought for Overman, yet it seemed right in keeping with the path his entire life had taken. After all, he didn't have to pursue Nancy. He made his move knowing full well that a bothersome past would inform a troubled future. This was to be cemented when the Overmans and Rosenfarb ended up in Los Angeles together.

Ultimately things evened out, which is not to say that life got better for Overman, but worse for Rosenfarb and Nancy. Jake wound up marrying a gold-digging interior decorator and Nancy became stepmother to the spoiled, druggy kids of her new internist husband. And Overman was free. Alone and miserable, but free.

Back in high school, Rosenfarb was a decent athlete, better than Overman of course, but not varsity material in any sport. Still, the jocks liked his vapid affability and always invited him to parties. Occasionally he would drag Overman along – never a problem because rarely did anyone notice Ira skulking in the corner. There was one particular soirée where the guys on the basketball team had some girl all tanked up in a bedroom. Rosenfarb had taken off early to console Sharon Kramer on her recent B minus, leaving Overman alone to pick through the Fritos and onion dip. Suddenly, someone was elbowing him, directing him upstairs.

He walked into a bedroom and discerned what seemed like a bizarre tribal ritual, but was, in fact, a contemporary adaptation being performed by plastered suburban high school kids. Overman knew Janie Sweeney from English class. Amiable and shy with a solid grasp of English literature and zero self-esteem, she was sprawled on her back in a semi-conscious haze. What Overman witnessed before him was nothing like the anonymous, mass-marketed porn he had come to know and love. These were his frothing classmates, pounding the poor drunken girl who had written that brilliant paper on the Brontë sisters. Overman started to panic. What would happen when the other guys finished and they turned to him? If he didn't participate he would be branded as weak, gay, or a potential snitch.

He tried to tiptoe out of the room when a huge hand slammed the door shut. The next thing he knew all eyes were on him. Overman was on deck, a late-inning addition to the lineup in a new sport the Lakeview boys had created for their own amusement.

"You know, I'm not feeling that well," Overman managed to squeak out.

"That's 'cause you've never seen a pussy before," countered Marty Merkowitz, the point guard and ringleader of the party. "Unzip your pants and get over here."

Merkowitz had been in his Bar Mitzvah class. How does a person go from the *bima* to orchestrating a gang rape? Overman wondered. There was no time to ponder the hows and whys. They were all waiting for him. It was Overman's move.

He awakens to a new dawn, having been blessed with a good night's sleep for the first time in as long as Overman can remember. Uncharacteristically pumped and looking forward to the workday, he considers trying to access his would-be telepathy to clear the freeway on the drive to Calabasas. Then the Ghost of Overman Past warns him not to attempt too much too soon. He enters the dealership with guarded optimism, throwing off a casual "hi" to Maricela, anxious to see the reaction on Day Two of his Pennysaver-induced Life Change. The open, inviting smile the receptionist flashes his way leaves no doubt in his mind that the streak is continuing.

People around here had better start getting used it, Overman thinks to himself. I am no longer the invisible irritant who demands to be ignored. I have Lasiked my way into something greater, the potential of which has yet to be fully realized. He turns to see Hal Steinbaum coming his way, wielding a can of Diet Coke. What does this idiot want now? Overman wonders. If he bugs me, maybe I can will some sort of illness on him. Nothing serious like say, tuberculosis, but maybe a cold. Flu, if he really gets on my case.

"Nice job moving that 450 SL," Steinbaum exclaims, slapping Overman on the back.

"Thanks, Hal," Overman says, thinking it's about time this *putz* acknowledged his accomplishments.

"There's hope for you, yet!" Steinbaum barks, laughing as he works his way toward Maricela's desk. "How's my girl this morning?" he salivates.

Steinbaum is so damned obvious that Overman imagines buckets of drool dripping out of his mouth as he addresses the receptionist. What Overman can't imagine, however, is where his fantasy will lead. In the middle of Steinbaum's weak attempt at flirting with Maricela, his mouth literally starts to foam. He takes out a handkerchief to dab it, but there is too much saliva for the

Mercedes dealer to soak it all up. The car dealer is gushing as his junior salesmen step over one another wielding boxes of tissues, each wanting to be the first to express his concern for the boss. Maricela stifles a giggle as Steinbaum excuses himself and scampers off to his office. Overman is in shock. Could he possibly have willed such a thing to happen? Was the ability to embarrass assholes like Steinbaum an additional perk of his discount metamorphosis? Or had he simply anticipated that which was about to happen? The thought of it being his doing leaves him ecstatic, but winded.

He thinks about asking Maricela to lunch. Hell, why not dinner? You can only do so much quality bonding over a Chinese Chicken Salad in half an hour. But she has a boyfriend. A buff, tattooed boyfriend, Overman reminds himself. What if she resented the forwardness of his even suggesting they get together? Perhaps the key to the connection they made yesterday was his lack of aggressiveness; the fact that he carried himself like the anti-Steinbaum. On the other hand, maybe the new perks gave him license to behave any way he wanted. It was possible that he could tell the boyfriend to go fuck himself and then, as just witnessed in the Steinbaum incident, watch that very thing happen before his eyes. It was wild, uncharted territory.

Overman decides to hold off on lunch or dinner invitations and take some time to consider the implications of what is unfolding. He also recognizes that whenever these inexplicably good things happen to him, they take a substantial physical toll. Padding back to his cubicle, Overman feels like he has just done fifty push-ups. He then realizes that he has never done fifty push-ups in his life.

As he plops down in the cheap rolling office chair Steinbaum bought from some overstocked lot dot com, the phone rings, perhaps the SL buyer calling to take delivery.

"Overman, may I help you?" he brightens.

"Yes you may, you fat fuck."

"What do you want, Rosenfarb?" Overman's sure he's still pissed and is calling to arrange a re-match.

"I can't stop thinking about that waitress."

"What waitress?"

"What waitress? I'm sorry, I forgot who I'm talking to. Oh, now I remember. The broke, paunchy *schlamazel* who can apparently land any young chick he wants."

"You mean the waitress from last night?"

"With the lips," Rosenfarb reminds him. "She was incredible. Can I have her number?"

"Jake, I don't know if that's such a good idea."

"You never were one for sharing."

"I wasn't going to call her. I did that to make a point," Overman informs him.

"You weren't even going to call her and still you don't want to give me the number? How do you sleep at night, Overman?"

"What about Rita?"

"You despise Rita."

"But you don't. Do you really want to see this waitress?"

"No. I just wanted to see if you'd give me the number. And now I have my answer. Nice talking to you."

Rosenfarb hangs up on him. What a piece of work this guy was. Overman might assume the friendship was over if he didn't know better. Beating this head case at love three sets in a row guaranteed that Rosenfarb would continue to be part of his life, like it or not.

The phone rings again. "Overman," he answers curtly. Better to get this over with.

"Hi," says the sweet familiar voice on the other end.

"Hi," says Overman, looking up. He sees Maricela smiling at him as she talks into the phone.

"I didn't want to come over there because Hal might follow me. Are you doing anything after work?"

"After work?" Overman stammers. "Let me check my calendar." He shuffles through a day planner that has never been written in. "What do you know? I happen to be free tonight."

"I thought maybe you could come over to my place, have a glass of wine—"

"I'd love to, but…don't you have a boyfriend?"

"Yeah. I really want him to meet you."

There is a long pause. This was not how it was supposed to go, according to the calculations of a man reborn. Thus far, the unique experiences that had recently come his way had been trouble-free. This one was the most exciting, yet had a giant wrench thrown into it.

Maricela sees Overman staring into space. "Is there a problem? Do you not want Rodrigo to be there?" she asks, seemingly willing to cut the boyfriend out of the picture.

"Oh, no, I'd love to meet Rodrigo," Overman sputters, immediately thinking what an idiot he is because she gave him the out.

"Great. I'll email you the address. Come by around 8."

While Overman deliberated on what his evening might bring, Jake Rosenfarb pulled into the driveway of his Laurel Canyon home, relieved to be away from the screamfest to which he has been subjected for most of the day. He had long ago learned that if his upscale Los Angeles clientele weren't one hundred percent happy with their new plantation shutters, they would become as angry as if they were actually being enslaved on a plantation. It made no sense, but these people seemed to blame their inner unhappiness on subcontractors. All he could think about now was getting in the house, plopping down on the family room sofa and pouring a single malt scotch.

Rosenfarb is barely through the door when he sees a frowning Rita standing in their brand new $350,000 kitchen, arms folded as if she is about to scold him.

"Hello darling," he musters, girding himself to hear what he's done wrong now.

"Take me out to dinner. I don't feel like cooking."

"Honey, I had a horrible day. I just want to relax," Rosenfarb pleads.

"You'll relax at the restaurant. How about sushi?"

"I don't want sushi."

"Italian. We'll go to Angelini Osteria."

"Too noisy. And I don't feel like Italian."

"Fine. Let's get you a steak."

Rosenfarb didn't want a steak. No food sounded appealing to him, but Rita was determined to get out of the house. He tried to think of what would be the fastest possible dining experience. She quickly rejected the In 'N Out Drive-Thru. Rita had to sit down and be waited on while his head throbbed. Suddenly, it dawned on him.

"Jerry's Deli."

"You went there last night with Overman," Rita says, confused. "You still have the leftover sandwich in the fridge."

"Which I would be glad to eat, but you want to go out."

"I don't think they have anything for me," Rita informs him.

"Their menu is thirty-two pages long. I'm sure you'll find something."

Rita reluctantly agrees. Rosenfarb knows exactly what he is looking for and it's not on the menu. He is obsessed with Corned Beef Kim Basinger, partially because of her attractiveness, more so because she is attracted to Overman. Suddenly his headache is gone and he informs Rita that he wants to change into something more comfortable.

A half-hour later, peacock Rosenfarb in his $250 Nat Nast silk bowling shirt is tearing his hair out as his wife puts in the world's most complicated salad order with Corned Beef Kim, who seems to have no recollection of him whatsoever.

"No onions, no dressing, extra spinach, light beets, double jicama…" etc, etc.

The waitress looks even more stunning than last night, prompting Rosenfarb to inquire as to whether she recommends the rye bread or the bagel chips to complement his matzo ball soup.

"They're both good," she replies, not tipping her hand.

Unsurprisingly, Rita has an opinion or two of her own. If he gets the rye bread, he'll want to butter it, and he doesn't need the cholesterol. The bagel chips are dry and less fatty but sometimes they're burnt. "Are the bagel chips burnt?" she asks Kim.

Kim doesn't think so, promising to do her best to find some unburnt ones.

"The rye bread might be safer though," Rita re-considers, as if the bagel chips were somehow irradiated with nuclear contaminants.

"I'll bring you both and you can decide," says Kim, the perfect hostess, wanting to get away as quickly as possible.

"That was nice of her," Jake comments.

"She's just lazy. Wasting the company's money. If she were my employee, I'd fire her ass. I'm going to wash my hands."

Rita gets up to go the ladies' room. Rosenfarb's chance to make his move. As soon as his wife is out of sight, Jake intercepts Kim on her way to another table.

"Excuse me, don't you remember me from last night?"

Kim's expression is as blank as white roll-up shades.

"Jake Rosenfarb. I was with another gentleman—"

"Mr. Overman," she smiles, apparently delighted at the thought of him. "Do you think he'll call me?" she inquires hopefully.

"I don't know. Can I just ask you one question?"

"Sure. Seeing as how you're a friend of his, you can ask me anything you want."

"Why?"

"Why what?"

"Why does a young girl like you want to hear from Overman?"

"It's nothing specific," she sighs. "There's just something about him. He's special."

Rosenfarb bursts out laughing. "Darling, your triple-decker corned beef and pastrami with cole slaw is special. But Ira Overman? Please."

"Why do you find that so hard to believe?"

"Maybe because I've known the man for over forty years and I've never once seen or heard of him doing anything evenly vaguely special."

"Perhaps the fact that he doesn't broadcast it is a sign of his humility," Corned Beef Kim reasons.

"Look, I don't mean to burst your bubble—"

"You seem kind of threatened. And jealous."

"I happen to be a very successful entrepreneur. More successful than he is, I'll have you know."

"I'm not interested in your tax return," she replies. "Here's the deal. When Mr. Overman looked at me, I sensed a certain power."

Power. There was that word again, the one Overman had used — only this time it had been seconded by a complete stranger. Rosenfarb is sure he has entered some sort of alternate universe. He feels as if he is driving through a thick fog, straining to find the white lines and praying he doesn't topple over the guardrail.

The waitress blasts the window dresser out of his queasy reverie. "Mr. Rosenfarb, a handful of men are extraordinary, and then there's the rest. Maybe you can learn from him," she finishes, going off to take an order for stuffed derma.

Rita returns from the ladies' room to see the same ashen expression that Overman saw when he entered Jerry's the night before. "You look like shit," she informs her husband. "Did you eat a bad pickle?"

Rosenfarb shakes his head, wondering what kind of pickles Overman has been eating.

The Overman E350 is driving Topanga Canyon Boulevard. Not anywhere near the expensive, woodsy, former hippie haven, but far north, deep in the bowels of the West Valley. Maricela Flores lives in Chatsworth, an odd mishmash of horse ranches, estates and business parks with a smattering of smaller single-family houses and inexpensive apartment buildings. He finds a liquor store and realizes he needs to stop. Sure, she's got wine, but Overman needs to bring something out of politeness. How did he get involved in such a thing, he asks himself? He is going to spend an entire evening with a twenty-six year-old girl and her boyfriend. Plus, he has to be polite and shell out money for that privilege.

Overman surveys the vodkas, thinking a classy cocktail might serve as a nice icebreaker for the evening. He can score a gallon of

Gordon's rotgut on sale for eighteen bucks or a petite but stunning bottle of overrated Grey Goose for twenty-eight. That Overman spends more than ten seconds thinking about it speaks to his dreadful instincts. But tonight, in honor of being invited into a beautiful young woman's life, boyfriend or no boyfriend, he comes to his senses and the Grey Goose wins out. He throws in a tin of Altoids, two of which he pops in his mouth while glancing at the condoms he might be purchasing had he not expressed his eagerness to hang with Rodrigo. What is he thinking? Maricela is young enough to be his daughter. Overman pulls a wad of cash out of his wallet and checks his look in the mirror behind the register. He determines it best to lose the tie and ballpoint pen before knocking on Maricela's door.

The Mercedes fits neatly into a space in front of Le Monde Garden Apartments on billboard-infested DeSoto Avenue. Despite its location on a busy, ugly thoroughfare, Overman can't help but notice how much nicer the place is than his. And Maricela's just a receptionist. With no alimony or child support, he reminds himself. He works his way over to the apartment buzzer. 303. Flores. No boyfriend's last name. She lives there alone. Promising, unless the boyfriend is some sort of professional freeloader. Overman presses the buzzer.

"Who is it?" bellows the ominous voice that could only belong to the imposing Rodrigo.

"Hi there. It's Ira. Ira Overman. From Steinbaum Mercedes."

"Who the fuck is Ira Overman?" he hears the boyfriend ask.

"One of our salesmen," Maricela says. "I told you. We're having wine with him."

"I ain't havin' wine with no fuckin' salesman—"

"Come on up." Maricela cheerily buzzes him in.

Overman considers making a run for it, but it's too late. Maricela has stuck her head out the window.

"I'm glad you came, Ira."

"Me, too." I am so fucked right now, he thinks, sorry he ever agreed to such foolishness. "Are you sure this is okay?" he asks. "'Cause I've got a million things to catch up on at home."

"Name one," Maricela snaps.

She's got him. Even if he could think of something it would sound ridiculously phony.

"I suppose I could stay a little while." Overman takes the longest three-floor elevator ride of his life. He is expecting that when the door opens, he will find himself face to face with Rodrigo and a machete. But what he sees instead is Maricela smiling at him in a tight black tank top and low-rise jeans that expose a stomach so flat there is nothing left to crunch.

"Hi." She gives him a kiss on the cheek and a full-on hug, smelling like the sweetest wildflowers he could ever imagine. Having never actually smelled a wildflower, imagination is his only frame of reference. Maricela takes Overman by the hand and leads him through the open door to her apartment. Rodrigo is in the kitchen, guzzling a beer.

"Rodrigo, say hello to Ira,"

The boyfriend nods disinterestedly.

"I've heard a lot about you," Overman offers with car salesman-like geniality.

Rodrigo doesn't bother looking at him, grabbing a jacket off the chair. "I'm going out," he announces, heading out the door.

"Nice meeting you," Overman calls out.

"As you can see, I have horrible taste in boyfriends," Maricela confesses.

"Everybody has their issues," Overman offers.

"He's a pig. That's his issue."

Outside the office, Maricela is as direct as Overman is phony.

"I brought you something," he says, thinking it best to drop the subject of Rodrigo.

Maricela's eyes light up as she is presented with the elegant Grey Goose. She is in love with the hand-painted bottle, and its contents happen to be her favorite premium vodka. She caresses the glass with a tenderness that more than justifies the $27.95 price tag. Overman starts to envision what those hands might do with human flesh, but wisely thinks better of it.

There are no mixers in the house so they decide on shots with Pabst Blue Ribbon chasers, ironically the lagerly equivalent of the Gordon's rotgut he left on the shelf. Overman pours and they head for the sofa. As Maricela's body moves, it generates more molecules of lilac or lavender or whatever that heavenly smell is.

"So," she says.

An ominous first line in that it is an invitation for Overman to dictate play. Where will he direct the conversation?

"So," he fires back, an ingenious deflection.

"Tell me something about yourself."

Now he is truly fucked. "Let's see," says Overman, having no clue which uninspiring facet of his being to lead off with. He downs his first shot hoping the liquor will produce something exciting, or at least help him summon the on-demand vulnerability that comes so naturally to his friend Rosenfarb.

Overman gives it his best. "Maybe this sounds crazy, but until yesterday, I felt like my whole life amounted to nothing. Now it seems like my luck is going to change."

Maricela smiles. "That's awesome. You know, I kind of saw that in your eyes after the Zero Downapalooza meeting."

"Believe me, it had nothing to do with Steinbaum and his inane gimmicks."

"Hal's an asshole," she nods. "You don't have to tell me."

It's official. This girl is much sharper than she lets on. In addition, she has now made Overman feel comfortable enough to share some choice biographical tidbits. He imparts how the Depression mentality of his parents turned him into a "people pleaser" who feared confrontation. This set the table for accepting jobs he didn't want, entering into relationships he wasn't excited about, adopting a nose-to-the grindstone mentality rather than seeking a more fulfilling life.

Maricela shares her story as breezily as she juggles responsibilities at the dealership. She grew up in Panorama City, California, one of seven children born to a Mexican father and Filipina mother. Dad drove a roach coach that stopped at construction sites to feed the Mexicans who were building homes for white people. Mom cleaned houses and brought the kids along whenever she could. Maricela was a happy child. She was a high school cheerleader who did reasonably well in school, then made her big mistake getting married at nineteen and not going to college.

"I was so naïve. I thought Jacob was going to take care of me. That we'd have babies and live happily ever after."

"Jacob?" Overman has to ask. "Jewish?"

"His dad was Jewish, his mom was black."

"What happened?" Overman asks, strangely high on the image of Maricela's rock hard body *davening* at High Holy Day services.

"Turns out Jacob was running a meth lab and they put him in prison."

She wasn't kidding about her taste in men. And this was the one she married.

"Thank God we didn't have kids," she sighs.

Overman tells her he has two: Peter, in his junior year at Brown, and Ashley, graduating from Harvard-Westlake and bound for Columbia in the fall. In his case, having children wasn't the mistake. Not being the father he wanted to be was the thing he'd always regret. "I never was the kind of dad they could look up to. I never achieved a greatness they could admire."

"I guess it all depends on how you define greatness. My dad drove a taco truck and we all looked up to him. He took care of us. He kept us safe."

Maybe it was as simple as that. Perhaps all the bullshit he had been fed about modeling success for one's children was just that. Bullshit.

"Sounds like you've been pretty sad most of your life," Maricela concludes.

"I have been," Overman concurs. "I guess happiness just doesn't agree with me."

"I think you're way too down on yourself."

"My mantra is 'Low Expectations.'"

Maricela lets out an irresistible belly laugh.

"I'm serious," Overman insists. "That's why I was so shocked when you came over and talked to me. I mean every guy in that place wants to—"

"No one in that dealership will ever come within striking distance, I guarantee you that."

Overman is impressed. She's smart *and* discriminating.

"I guess that's not totally true," she corrects herself.

"Cantalupo?" Overman blurts out, immediately regretting it.

"Fuck no. Are you kidding me?"

"Of course I was kidding," his laugh transparently fake.

Maricela clarifies. "What I meant was that right now you're next to me on this sofa which makes you technically within, you know, striking distance."

She giggles, throwing her head back in that adorable way. Overman laughs really loudly now, thinking he must sound like one of those cartoon hyenas. Regardless, he has to let her know he gets the joke.

For a split second he wonders if maybe it isn't a joke. Then Maricela grabs him with both hands and draws him into a ferocious kiss. Stunned by the unexpected outburst of passion, Overman breaks for a quick breath and a reality check.

"What about Rodrigo?"

"Fuck Rodrigo," she cries out, starting to unbutton Overman's shirt.

"What if he comes back?"

"He won't."

"How do we know that?"

"Your luck's changing. Remember?"

The girl had a point. Overman feels his pants being unzipped.

He starts to kiss her perfectly sculpted neck, lingering on its smoothness as he gently lifts the tank top. Discovering she is bra-less, his manhood springs to attention, much as it did in the hopeful days of youth, long before the decades of rejection. He cups his hands over Maricela's small, firm breasts, suddenly feeling something cold. He looks down to find himself staring at two gold nipple rings.

"Do they freak you out?" Maricela asks.

"No. I just don't want to hurt you," he responds, his first opportunity to say something gentlemanly in as long as he could remember. And never in his life did he imagine "gentlemanly" and "nipple rings" being part of the same thought process.

"The only thing you could do to hurt me is leave before you make love to me."

Overman's not going anywhere. He pulls down her jeans, revealing a lacy, pink thong that perfectly bisects the treasured orbs that the rest of the sales force has only dreamt about and blasted off to while having intercourse with their wives. And here was Overman, the treasure in front of his face. He begins by kissing the multi-colored butterfly tramp stamp, slowly moving his tongue down under the thong and all over her ass. He is so hard he feels like he is going to explode. Unable to wait another second, he pulls down the panty and dives in. As Overman furiously laps up her sweetness, he imagines himself a spectator, watching the event as it unfolds. Overman the spectator can't help but wonder why the beautiful young Maricela is giving her body to Overman the sorry, middle-aged lump. One hears all the time about younger women with older men, but in most cases, the man is either wealthy or good looking, rarely wears Elevator shoes and at very least, possesses some redeeming qualities. Overman can't think of anything in his character that that would entitle him to the joy of entering this gorgeous creature from behind. But that doesn't take away from the joy. Not for one minute. Filling her with his hardness, he will never forget this moment, witnessing the deepest, most soulful moan he has ever heard.

It is the final thaw of spring, the common lawns of the Queens apartment buildings morphing into one immense playground. The pent-up youthful energy stored over the particularly cold winter of 1958 explodes onto 71st Crescent, the Fresh Meadows cul-de-sac that Ira Overman calls home. Here he is king of the world, an entity in its prime. It is only later in life that he comprehends the poignancy of reaching one's prime at five years old. At this moment he is completely absorbed in the wonder of his universe: a place where friends appear instantly from across the hall, where trucks arrive each day delivering milk, selling ice cream, even hawking carnival rides. There was no greater pleasure for young Overman than the ride truck pulling in to the crescent. Most people had to go to fairs or amusement parks to get this kind of dizziness in-duced, but Overman got it brought to his doorstep. For a nickel, he could get a nauseating spin on the tilt-a-whirl and be up in his room five minutes later.

They lived in a small two-bedroom apartment but Overman had everything he needed. He got to spend quality time glued to the wood black and white console, spellbound by the venerated Mickey Mouse Club. For some reason there was no Mouseketeer named Ira, giving the boy his first inkling that he might be differ-ent from the Donnies, Bobbies and Richies of the world. But by and large, he felt a kinship with the happy, big-eared gentiles who sang and danced their way through each episode. At the end of every show came the highlight: the commercial for the Mecca to which he was determined to one day make his pilgrimage, the hal-lowed ground of Disneyland. Tomorrowland and Tinkerbell and spinning teacups. If such a place indeed existed then the world of-fered limitless possibilities. After turning off the TV set, Ira always felt whole, imbued with Mouseketeer spirit and a renewed sense of purpose. To his young mind, this was a life in full.

How did this pleasant, ordinary beginning take its plunge toward mediocrity? Overman perseverated on this question throughout his fifty-five years. Most likely, the fall had been set in motion by Irma's second pregnancy, followed in quick succession by the announcement that Saul had put down a deposit on what was to be their own single-family home. Ira would never forget that morning. The excitement in the apartment was electric, both parents regaling him with images of the earthly paradise the family would soon inhabit. Irma and Saul described a mystical, utopian subdivision on the North Shore of Long Island, filled with parks and shopping centers, speaking of it in the celestial terms Ira reserved for Disneyland. Their enthusiasm was infectious, convincing Ira that Long Island would be a glorious way station between Queens and Anaheim, the homeland where he would ultimately settle amongst the Mouseketeers.

The incredible journey takes place on a crisp March Saturday morning. An exuberant Ira is about to dash outside and twist his body around the monkey bars when Saul and pregnant Irma inform him that they are going to pile in the Plymouth and drive out to see the new house. The boy's heart starts to pound, bursting with anticipation. If 71st Crescent had a tilt-a-whirl, his new Long Island wonderland might have its own rollercoaster. Maybe a little steam train that stops on Main Street, where friendly shopkeepers offer candy and cupcakes to all the kids in the neighborhood. Twenty-five minutes from now, he would get to see it all.

Saul pulls off the Long Island Expressway at the Lakeview exit and heads down a two-lane country road toward the Melvin Terrace subdivision. There's not much to see as far as Ira can tell. A few houses, a pond, a cornfield. No tall people in animal costumes. In fact, no people at all. Saul turns left on Melvin Terrace Lane, which will no doubt reveal the kingdom of pleasure they will soon call home. Ira had never seen a palm tree in Queens, but perhaps they had them on Long Island at Melvin Terrace.

Minutes later, the family gets out of the car and Ira finds himself looking down at a dirt pit, surrounded by other pits and lots in the more advanced stages of framing.

"Isn't it fantastic?" his father beams. "This is all going to be ours."

No trees at all. No train. No sidewalks. Nothing.

"That's the backyard," Saul cries, proudly pointing to more dirt.

Irma explains that no one else will be living in their building since it is, after all, a house. There will be other kids moving in across the street and next-door, but the only one on the other side of the hall will be his new brother or sister. Irma seems to like this idea as much as Ira hates it. This was not the interim pre-Disney lifestyle he had pictured.

Ira is mute and sullen in the back seat as they head home to Fresh Meadows. No one seems to notice, Irma wrapped up in her ideas for wallpapering the kitchen, Saul mulling over which type of grass to plant for his lawn. None of it makes sense to Ira. As far as he can tell, the apartment community of Fresh Meadows is far more like Main Street, U.S.A. than Melvin Terrace. Why leave an enclave brimming with friendly faces for big dirt lots where families were confined to their own pits? He knew the dirt would eventually be filled with houses, grass and sidewalks, but to what end? Perhaps as he grew older he would understand why people placed such great value on putting distance between themselves and others, and furthermore, why they felt the need to change what was already working. There was so much young Overman didn't understand. This didn't bother him nearly as much as the sinking feeling that as he grew into adulthood, he would enter a whole world he would never understand.

No surprise, Long Island and Overman are not easy partners. Everything about the place fills him with uneasiness and dread. His six year-old stomach, bloated from the huge breakfast Irma force-fed him, is churning as she walks him to school for his first day. He knows no one. The tilt-a-whirl truck has been cruelly eradicated from his life. There is no reason for being. He is the Jean-Paul Sartre of the Melvin Terrace first grade.

As they approach MT Elementary, Ira tells his mother that he doesn't feel well. She assures him it's a case of first day jitters and that all will be well once he meets his teacher and settles in. They arrive at the classroom and he is introduced to a perky young woman named Mrs. Jarvis, who assures Ira that he will have a great time and love school. As she leads him by the hand into the class-room, he looks through the window and sees his mother leaving, limply waving goodbye.

"Ira, would you like to meet your fellow classmates?" Mrs. Jar-vis smiles.

Overman nods, suddenly feeling his face turn a whiter shade of pale. Before he or anyone can fully comprehend what is happen-ing, Ira is vomiting all over Mrs. Jarvis. The cereal, eggs, bagel and cream cheese have been melded and reborn in projectile form. The class half-laughs, half-gasps, Mrs. Jarvis doing her stoic best as she tries to smile through the puke. She tells the class she's going to get some paper towels, but not before Overman vomits yet again. The good news is, he no longer feels bloated. The bad news is that she has left him alone with his new peers. She is gone only a minute and he survives without incident, but this is the first impression that the children of Long Island have of Ira Overman, an impres-sion that will follow him throughout his public school career.

The vomit story indeed went on to become lore, affording each student the opportunity to embellish it with charming apocryphal additions like: "And then he peed on her." Nevertheless, by the time Overman reached the fifth grade, he had more or less come to terms with suburban life. One reason for this was that he had finally found a subject he deemed worthy of his time and effort: Glorietta Zatz-kin. Even at ten years old, Glorietta possessed an undeniable femi-ninity, potent enough to be recognized by the boys and envied by the girls. And the fact that she lived down the block from Overman gave him a leg up. For the record, he had been the first to point out that Estelle Zatzkin, Glorietta's mother, had huge breasts, which he declared a harbinger of magnificent things to come. In November of 1963, much to the chagrin of other potential suitors, Overman was lucky enough to be assigned an art project with Glorietta. He worked as slowly as possible, attempting to stretch out the assignment as long as Mrs. Jarvis could bear. The two of them were happily painting and gluing away when the news came in. President Kennedy had been shot. Glorietta let out a whimper and threw her arms around him. Overman held her tightly, genuinely sad about the president who seemed like a cool young guy, yet also cognizant that he would never be in this position if not for the assassination attempt. "It's going to be all right," he told her. He had heard somewhere that women liked you to say that.

"You really think so?" she sniffled.

"Uh-huh," he assured Glorietta, clutching her ever more tightly.

Thirty minutes later, word arrived that President Kennedy had been pronounced dead. Glorietta gave him the "you're so full of shit" look that would become painfully familiar to him over the next forty-five years. He was just trying to be comforting. What else could a person say in that situation? Besides, someday, probably a few presidents down the road, Glorietta would remember who she instinctively went to for consoling; whose arms enveloped her calmly and soothingly, in spite of the fact that he was full of shit.

When Overman arrived home, his mother was at the kitchen table, crying. She was one of the many women in Melvin Terrace who lived under the spell of JFK. As far as Irma was concerned, Kennedy was an icon who could do no wrong, the only drawback being that he wasn't Jewish. Why was it so important that everyone be Jewish? Ira wondered. Irma's Polish mother, his Grandma Gussie, actually believed that everyone in America *was* Jewish. She called JFK President Kaufman, Ed Sullivan was Ed Solomon; even Mickey Mouse was Mickey Weiss.

Ira's little brother Steven sat on his mother's lap and tried to wipe away her tears. Ira agreed with Irma that it was a horrible tragedy, but his mind was elsewhere. He was picturing Glorietta Zatzkin with Estelle Zatzkin's breasts. How if she already had those breasts, they would have been pressed up against him in school to-day. Suddenly, Overman was getting an erection. The president had been shot dead and he had a boner. And to add insult to injury, his mother noticed, letting out a reflexive, "Oh my God!"

Ira slinked off to his room, waiting for dinner and the end of another awkward day in an increasingly peculiar life.

The Belzberg home sits high on a perch in the hills, west of La Cienega, but east of Doheny where the more mansion-like residences are situated. It is an ideal house for entertaining, a u-shaped structure on one level, built around a central pool with a grassy area just beyond it that overlooks the entire city. On a clear day one can see all the way to the ocean, and at night the lights twinkle like some magical Never Neverland. Perhaps when Overman bought the property, he had subconsciously channeled his childhood vision of a utopian Disneyland. This was to be his refuge, the sacred space to which he could always return after a hard day's work as a vice-president of some grateful corporation. As he trudged up the drive carrying a couple of centerpieces, he reluctantly admired how lovely the garden looked. Nancy always had a knack for hiring good landscapers. The idea of putting her own hands in dirt never occurred to her.

Overman opens the door and is greeted by Stan.

"Ira, glad you could make it."

"It's my daughter's graduation party," Overman reminds him. "What do you mean you're glad I could make it?"

"Don't be so sensitive. I was just being polite."

Stan takes the two centerpieces and Overman goes to the car to get more. The guy who is living in his house is glad he could make it. How patronizing is that? Does he have any idea who he is talking to? He thinks he's dealing with the old Overman, the Overman whose wife he stole, whose life he stole. But *this* Overman's life has meaning, and a power that he is only beginning to understand. This Overman is irresistible to women and has had the best sex of his life with a knockout barely older than his children. This Overman is on a roll.

Nancy marches out to the car to retrieve a couple of centerpieces. "Hello, Ira." She gives him a brittle kiss on the cheek. "These are very nice."

"How's Ashley?" Overman inquires about the daughter who hasn't spoken to him in eight months.

"Why don't you ask her yourself?" Nancy responds, never missing a chance to up the dysfunctional ante.

"I will. I just brought it up because I hope she's happy."

"If you wanted her to be happy, why were you such a shitty father?"

The old Overman might have let such a comment slide. Those days were over. "It's our daughter's graduation party. Can you find a way to not be a castrating bitch for one day?"

Then the unthinkable happened. Nancy, having never seen this assertive side of her ex-husband, said something he couldn't ever remember hearing out of her.

"I'm sorry, Ira. You're right."

If it all ended tomorrow, he would die with a smile on his now un-spectacled face. But the way his fortune was turning, Overman wanted to go for more, whatever that meant and however it played out. The main thing was not to revert to old patterns. As he and Nancy rounded up the rest of the flowers and set them on the tables, he contemplated for the umpteenth time how he had made such a horrible mess of things. The truth was, he *had* been a shitty father. But he never wanted to be. He had expressed to Nancy his reservations about having children, but she steamrolled right by them, writing off his doubts as an immature case of the jitters.

"You're just afraid of the responsibility," she reprimanded him. "It's time to grow up."

Overman hears Stan regaling one of his friends with tales of the free cruise he and Nancy took, courtesy of the nice folks at Pfizer. The shameless internist had it down to a science. Send me to the Mediterranean; I prescribe Lipitor instead of Zocor, Zoloft instead of Prozac. The little pills that cost people thousands of dollars had sent the Belzbergs around the world two and a half times over. Through the sliding glass doors, Overman sees Ashley giggling with a few of her friends. Does he march out and say hello, casually wave, or wait for her to come inside? As he weighs the options, he feels a tap on his shoulder.

"Hi, Dad." Peter is there with his new girlfriend, an adorable Asian who at first glance seems far too well adjusted to be at this gathering. "This is Kiana."

"Pleasure to meet you, Kiana," Overman says, shaking her hand.

He is on speaking terms with his son, the only problem being that they have nothing to say to one another.

"What's new?" Peter asks, feigning interest. Overman tries to think of an appropriate response, never his strong suit.

"I had Lasik surgery," Overman offers, pointing to his naked face.

"Why?" Peter asks incredulously. His father had never been one for changing appearances and hated to spend money on anything.

"I thought it might turn me into a superhuman stud," Overman announces. Why the hell not? He can say whatever he wants. No one takes him seriously anyway, and on the off chance he really had become superhuman, he'd be able to deal with whatever consequences there were.

Peter looks at him like he is out of his mind, just the way Peter always looks at him. Kiana laughs politely, thinking it's some sort of joke that Jews tell.

"I take it you two met at Brown," Overman interjects, moving past his outrageous declaration.

"Yes," says Kiana. "We're both pre-law."

"Just what the world needs: more lawyers," Overman laughs.

Peter and Kiana don't find this funny.

"Nice seeing you, Dad," Peter says, ushering Kiana over to the buffet.

Overman shakes his head. And this was the one who was talking to him. He sees Ashley on the patio. As she turns her head to greet one of her friends, his eyes make contact with his daughter for a split second. She quickly looks away. How did it come to this? How did a well meaning, if unremarkable man land in such a place? He was never malicious toward his children: he simply lacked the tools to be a competent parent. Did that warrant such a bitter estrangement?

Overman is struck by the urge to make things right, to repair years of miscommunication and no communication with some grand, sweeping gesture. He wonders if there is something awesome he can do, the paternal equivalent of clearing the left lane. If gorgeous Maricela could suddenly be attracted to him out of the blue, might not Ashley Overman want to repair the dismal relationship with her father? Perhaps all it would take was looking into her eyes, just like when he looked at the receptionist or the waitress at Jerry's. Then again, what if he only had one kind of look and his own daughter mistook it for something depraved and incestuous? Trying it would be a risk, to be sure.

"Overman, you sly asshole!" a familiar voice cries out.

Rosenfarb is on his way to greet him when the window man is stopped by his former lover, Nancy Morrison Overman Belzberg, who kisses him full on the mouth right in front of Mrs. Rosenfarb. Rita doesn't give a shit as long as Nancy's husband continues to supply her with free samples of Zoloft. Overman wonders how much the doctor has been told about Nancy's history with Jake. He also knows it's a matter of moments before Rosenfarb comes over to hassle him about a re-match or the waitress or some other stupid thing, so he takes the opportunity to slip outside and talk to his daughter.

Ashley and her friends seem to be involved in some kind of group text messaging.

"Hi honey," Overman, says boldly, the "honey" perhaps too presumptuous in light of their eight-month chill.

"Hi Dad," she responds curtly, immediately going back to her cell phone.

Overman won't be deterred. "I don't mean to interrupt, but when you get a second, I'd like to talk to you." Not only was this more than he had said to his daughter in eight months, it was delivered with the same assertive quality he had employed with Nancy.

Ashley looked up. "Sure."

He couldn't be positive, but despite her monosyllabic answer, it appeared as if they had connected. Ashley starts to make a move, possibly in his direction when Rosenfarb yanks him by the arm and pulls him aside.

"We have to talk."

"Why do we have to talk, Jake?"

"Because there's something wrong with you. In a good way," Rosenfarb clarifies. "That waitress thinks you're special. She thinks you have power."

"She's young. She doesn't know anything," Overman replies, trying to get rid of this garden pest he has been foolish enough to call a friend.

"I considered that, but then I opened my mind to the other possibilities." He takes a deep, portentous breath, then stares at Overman. "What if, Ira? What if?"

"What if what?" Overman is completely flummoxed.

"I can't talk about it here," Rosenfarb whispers. "You and I need to have a meeting," an oddly formal tone to his pronouncement.

"What kind of meeting?"

"We need to discuss what your plan is. Map out the future."

"What the fuck are you talking about?" Overman asks. "What do you have to do with my future?"

Rosenfarb has gone from annoying to certifiable. "I'll tell you all about it at the meeting. Tomorrow. Lunch. I'll come out to Calabasas. My treat."

While well versed in his friend's legendary *noodging* skills, Overman accedes, just to get it over with. He looks for Ashley but she has disappeared into a different group of friends. Rosenfarb remarks to Overman that Nancy is looking really good. "I always loved her vagina," he sighs, as if remembering a favorite wine he used to sip as a young man.

This "meeting" was bound to be unbearable. The only positive was that agreeing to Rosenfarb's demand bought Overman some breathing room for the rest of the afternoon. He would still have to make conversation with Nancy and Stan's friends who treated him like some sort of leper unless they needed a deal on a car, but to the new Overman, this was amusing rather than insulting. Krakauer the stockbroker, Morganthal, the entertainment lawyer, Gerstein, the dermatologist: they had all become the people they were destined to be and weren't going any further. Overman, on the other hand, had been re-hatched. His future was *tabula rasa*. For all he knew, he could now will a mole to be removed, rather than having to pay Gerstein eighty bucks a pop. He makes a mental note to try that sometime.

Overman picks at the buffet, keeping an eye on Ashley, waiting for an opening. As he examines some sort of wild mushroom puff, she enters from the patio. She is by herself, and from the looks of it, has come in to see him.

"Enjoying the party?" she asks.

"Oh yeah, this is great," he replies, doing his best to appear enthusiastic.

"I'm happy you came," Ashley smiles.

"Me, too." Overman takes a deep breath, then goes for it. "Listen, do you think maybe we could have dinner one night?"

"Absolutely. Right after I get back from Israel."

"Israel?"

Ashley explains that she is going on her birthright trip, an expedition available to any Jewish child under the age of twenty-six for the purpose of embracing his or her roots. Overman doesn't have a problem with this. He has heard that stringent safety precautions are taken to protect young American tourists. What strikes him, however, is how out of the loop he has become. His daughter is about to leave the country and he had no prior knowledge of it. No one consulted him, asked for any input whatsoever. But why would they? He had allowed himself to drift apart from his children, letting it go far enough that he was embarrassed to call them after having been out of touch for so long. And this was the price.

"You're going to have a great time," Overman tells her, figuring it's the right thing to say.

"I hope so. Anyway, I should get back to my friends."

"Is that Jennifer Marcus?" Overman asks, indicating a blond girl on the patio.

Ashley nods that it is.

"I haven't seen her since she was nine. How's her dad? I always liked Charlie."

"He's a prick," she informs him.

"Maybe that's why you and Jennifer stayed friends all these years," Overman postulates. "Because of your lousy fathers."

"He tried to touch my boobs when I was sixteen. I'm sure you never did anything like that," Ashley says, walking back out to the patio.

Overman is shocked to hear this about Charlie Marcus. Charlie was a respected ophthalmologist, known for his political activism and philanthropy. He was the husband every wife wanted, the father every kid looked up to. And it turned out he was some form of Closet Merkowitz. Overman decides to interpret this news as an opportunity to pat himself on the back. Yes, he has been a crappy parent, a social ignoramus, a selfish boor, but he never tried to feel up an underage girl. Life was good.

The Kennedy assassination might have marked a turning point for the country, but to Overman, it would be remembered as The Day of Losing Glorietta Zatzkin. Of course he had never "had" her in any sense of the word. They were in the fifth grade, partners on a few school projects and happened to live around the block from one another. He harbored a serious crush, but so did every other boy at Melvin Terrace Elementary. Whether or not Glorietta realized the extent of their group lust was conjecture, but regardless, she remained a nice, bright and polite young girl who had simply decided that she was no longer interested in Ira Overman. She never said anything mean or ignored him. As far as he knew, she never talked behind his back. She just had a way of letting him know that there would be a line of demarcation between them, and the line seemed more pronounced with each passing day.

This saddened Overman, particularly when after the sixth grade, Glorietta returned from summer camp having developed the luscious breasts that he himself had prognosticated. As he walked through the halls of Lakeview Junior High School, guys came up to congratulate him about being the first to make the call.

"You were right, Overman. She's totally stacked," said Tommy Oshefsky, who had the desk next to his in homeroom. "I wish I lived around the block from her."

"What's her cup size?" Jimmy Rizzoli asked Overman, like he might actually have access to such information.

Overman made up a number just to drive them crazy. "I'm guessing she wears the kind of bra than makes them look smaller, so I'd have to go with 36 DD."

In truth, Overman was the one being driven crazy, less out of lust than confusion. What was it about him that was putting her off? Did he smell? Was he ugly? He didn't have buckteeth or an overbite like Tommy Oshefsky. He wasn't hairy and chubby like Rizzoli. Ira wanted answers but had few places to turn. If he asked any of his peers, they would then know that he wasn't as tight with Glorietta as he used to be, which could only serve to lower his standing with kids who weren't very high on the ladder to begin with. So Ira went with the only option he could think of.

"Who could not like you?" Irma Overman barked, shoving milk and cookies in his face. "I'm not saying somebody doesn't like me," Ira replied. "I'm just asking if somebody didn't like me, what about me wouldn't they like?"

"It's the Goldstein boy, isn't it?" Irma blurts out. "Jerry Goldstein. I never liked him and I'm not crazy about the parents either. The country club and the Cadillac and the fancy patio furniture—"

"It's not Jerry Goldstein. And that's not the point—"

"Frankie Cosentino!" She's sure of it. "What do you expect? The father hangs a big lighted cross over their garage at Christmas time. Don't they know Jews live in this neighborhood?"

"Mom—"

"Drink your milk. Do you want me to talk to Frankie's mother?"

"No. I'm sorry I brought it up. I'll talk to Frankie myself," Overman says, just wanting to end this debacle. It would be the last time he ever went to his mother for advice.

As seventh grade progressed, Glorietta began to associate with a different crowd, all from outside the neighborhood. The boys were jocks, the girls destined to be cheerleaders. Glorietta would wave politely whenever she saw Overman on the street or walking to school, but it seemed eerily like the caste system he had read about when they studied India. And Ira was an Untouchable. Late at night, alone in his bed, he would reflect on what he could have done differently. What if instead of trying to comfort Glorietta, he had said: "I'm sorry, but the president is going to die a quick yet miserable death." Could that have helped his case? He thought not. The bitter truth was that Glorietta had dropped him because she knew she could do better. He couldn't fault her for wanting to improve her circle of friends. He just pined for the halcyon days before she realized that was an option.

Months later, Ira was in the driveway helping his father wash the latest Overman Plymouth when Estelle Zatzkin rounded the corner, walking the family's new miniature schnauzer. The sight of her prompted Saul Overman to jump up, say hello, and coo enthusiastically at Pumpkin Zatzkin. As far as Ira could remember, his father had never particularly liked dogs. But whatever he was saying now was making Estelle smile and Pumpkin pee. Estelle was looking particularly curvy this morning, her resplendent cleavage glistening in the morning sunlight. She spotted Ira rinsing out one of the wheel wells.

"Ira, come say hello to Pumpkin," she called out.

Young Overman dutifully marched over to pet the schnauzer. He liked dogs well enough, but seeing Estelle only reminded him of losing Glorietta.

"Pumpkin loves kids," Saul crowed, as if he gave a shit.

Estelle had just told him this and Saul wanted to keep the conversation going as long as possible, much like Ira did during his art project with Glorietta. Ira did not fault his father for sneaking peeks at the tiny beads of sweat that had made their home between Estelle's wondrous breasts. Yes, Saul had a wife and she was Ira's mother, but the cold hard fact was that the Zatzkin women were irresistible. All the men in the neighborhood envied her husband Murray, who, despite his modesty and lack of affectation, was one of the most prominent furriers in Manhattan.

"It's great to have Pumpkin in the neighborhood," Saul beamed. "Good girl," he said, scratching the dog's tailbone.

"Actually Pumpkin's a boy," Estelle corrected him." And he won't be in the neighborhood very much longer."

Ira sensed something. The axe handle was about to come down.

"We bought a house in Crestwood Knolls," Estelle informed them.

Ira's heart sank. Crestwood Knolls was a new development with properties starting at a half-acre. It couldn't have been further from Melvin Terrace in terms of status and attitude, but the crowning blow was that even though the homes were only two miles away, they landed in a different school district. Now, unless Ira happened to run into her at an inter-school basketball game or the local Baskin-Robbins, he would never see Glorietta again.

"Congratulations. You must be thrilled," Saul says, Pumpkin starting to hump his leg.

"We're excited. But we'll miss everyone here—"

Estelle looks down and sees the schnauzer wrapped around Saul's leg.

"Pumpkin!"

She bends down to give him a light whack, which in the process gives Saul and his son a view they will never forget. These were breasts that would not be out of place in Playboy. Or the Louvre.

"The good news is, we've sold our house to a lovely family. They have a son who's your age, Ira."

When the moving vans came, Overman spent the day at Howie Finkel's house, conveniently situated directly across the street from the Zatzkin's. Finkel was three years younger and always wanted to hang out with the older kids, so Overman figured he'd do him a favor. In return, he got to satisfy his strange desire to watch the Zatzkin furniture being moved, hoping for a glimpse of things touched by Glorietta. He had been in the house once or twice and could identify certain pieces — drawers she had opened, a dresser where she might have laid out a bra and panty set for the next day. It was his way of saying goodbye.

When the movers drove away, Overman felt a strange sense of relief. He no longer had to be visually reminded of the rejection on a daily basis. Soon, new people would be moving in and this, too, would help him heal. Every once in a while he would swing by and check out the house to see if anybody was living there. And then one day, the new kid rang the Overman's bell.

Irma opened the front door, revealing a courteous and friendly young man who said he heard there was a boy his age living there.

"Yes, our son, Ira. Nice of you stop by. And what's your name?"

"Jacob Rosenfarb," he replied. "Everyone calls me Jake."

Overman has a client at his desk when the dreaded moment arrives. Jake Rosenfarb struts in donning the Dolce and Gabbana sunglasses Rita insisted he buy in order to appear trendy. Rosenfarb's first stop is the reception desk. He wasn't about to drive all the way out to Calabasas without getting a generous eyeful of Maricela. She is wearing a white lacy bra that peeks out of her skintight pink tank top, displaying her high, firm breasts to delightful effect. To Rosenfarb, the thought of this taut, brown body wanting anything to do with Ira Overman seemed even more ludicrous than the waitress at Jerry's Deli. This one actually knew the man and his multiple deficiencies.

"May I help you?" she asks the leering window man.

Jake suavely removes the Dolce and Gabbanas. "I'm here to see Overman."

"You must be Rosenfarb."

Wow. Overman has told her about him. Maybe Ira wants to switch over to the waitress and donate the receptionist to him. The textbook definition of a *mitzvah*, if ever there was one.

"You're the guy he beat 6-love in straight sets," Maricela says, a little too loudly for Rosenfarb's tastes.

Rosenfarb scowls and marches over to Overman's desk. Overman has just sent his client over to financing.

"How're you doing, Jake?"

"I'm fine," Rosenfarb barks. "My car's out front. We're going to Malibu for lunch."

"Okay," Overman says, grabbing his jacket and following Rosenfarb out the door. "How come you want to go all the way to Malibu?"

As they approach Rosenfarb's BMW 750i (bought just to irk his Mercedes salesman friend), he sees that Jake is opening the passenger door rather than going to the driver's side. He tosses Overman the keys.

"You're driving," Jake announces.

Overman shakes his head. "Is this because you want Steinbaum to see me driving a BMW? Just so you know, he doesn't give a shit, as long as I'm closing deals."

"That's not the point," Rosenfarb assures him, explaining that he has something far more important in mind. "Take Malibu Canyon Road."

As they get off the freeway and Overman turns onto Malibu Canyon, Rosenfarb's motive begins to present itself. In front of them stands a blinking sign that reads: "Road Construction. Long Delays."

Rosenfarb knows his friend doesn't like to take a long lunch and the trip across the canyon is eighteen minutes each way with no traffic. If Overman is the powerfully changed man he claims to be, he will be able to clear the canyon and get them to Malibu without delay. If he can't deliver, he has to come clean about what is really going on.

"I can't believe you're doing this," Overman protests.

"You make certain claims, you have to be able to back them up," Rosenfarb explains. "You told me you cleared the 101 freeway."

"I said I *think* it happened. Maybe I imagined it. And even if I didn't, who's to say I can do something like that on demand?"

"I guess we'll find out, won't we?"

Overman is apoplectic. "Jake, whenever I've tried to will something to happen, it's taken everything out of me. It's debilitating."

"Are you saying I'm not worth it?" Rosenfarb asks, suddenly the wounded lover.

"What do you want from me?" Overman implores.

"I want you to make sense out of this. You owe me that much."

Why did he owe Rosenfarb anything? For reminding him in explicit detail how he was the first to enjoy Nancy's zesty, fruit-forward vagina? For screwing him out of an easy commission by buying a Beemer instead of a Benz? For being a sore loser at tennis? It was absurd. Still, there was a part of Overman that wanted to see if he could perform in front of someone else, even if that someone happened to be the unbearable Jake Rosenfarb.

He grips the wheel tightly, staring straight ahead at the grid-locked canyon and road maintenance vehicles in the distance.

"I don't see anything happening," Rosenfarb shouts, practically splitting his eardrum.

Nothing *is* happening, much as Overman tries to "will" it. He is stone silent as they creep along at five miles an hour, Jake starting to sigh with boredom. The more Overman concentrates, the more drained he feels.

"Yeah, well, I've always believed that a person can't be afraid to dream," Jake yawns. "This dream was a dud, so sue me."

Overman tries to conjure a clear lane to Malibu, but the car is barely inching forward.

"Why don't we play the Celebrity Game to pass the time?" Jake suggests. "I name a celebrity I've worked with, you guess the type of window treatments I installed."

"I don't think so, Jake."

"Morgan Fairchild. I'll give you a hint. Not a drapes gal."

"This is stupid."

"Not at all. You'd be surprised how quickly the time passes. The answer is 'vertical blinds.' Tom Selleck."

"I don't know, wood mini-blinds," one of the few window treatments Overman can identify by name.

"You are so wrong. Selleck hates blinds."

At that moment, a siren starts blaring, giant red fire trucks suddenly appearing in Overman's rear-view mirror. One by one, cars begin pulling over to the side of the road, the Rosenfarb BMW following suit. Then, as the two trucks pass in front of Overman, he gets back on the road behind them and within moments, the Beemer is sailing toward Malibu, hurling Rosenfarb into a sea of befuddlement.

"My God, Ira, you did it! I'll never doubt you again."

"There was a fire, Jake," Overman reminds his excited passenger.

"But there wouldn't have been one if you hadn't willed it."

"I didn't *will* a fire."

"Don't be modest. The self-deprecation thing gets old."

"Jake, why would I want to be responsible for a disaster that could cause millions of dollars in damage and potentially take the lives of innocent people?"

"Because you wanted to prove something to a friend."

"You've got to be kidding me."

"Thank you, Ira. Your generosity leaves me awestruck and humbled."

There is no turning back. No matter how many ways Overman tries to toss this off to coincidence, Rosenfarb is having none of it. There is no denying what the window man has just witnessed through his goofy, overpriced glasses, and as promised, he is going to reward his pal by buying lunch at Geoffrey's Restaurant, one of Rita's swanky haunts. He lets Overman know that had his claims of willpower been a crock of shit, Plan B was a fajita pita at the Malibu Jack-in-the-Box, Dutch treat. But the man behind the wheel, the long shot on whom Rosenfarb had doubled down, had delivered the goods and deserved to be recognized.

It is a balmy, sun-drenched afternoon, the perfect day to be sitting out on Geoffrey's patio overlooking the Pacific. Awash in his friend's lunacy, Overman decides to immediately stick it to Rosenfarb with a double Belvedere martini, coupled with their priciest ahi tuna appetizer. While waiting, he guzzles down two glasses of bottled water to replenish the fluids he burned up in his efforts to will the car through the canyon.

Rosenfarb can't bring himself to eat, drink or even order. He is lost in thought. "So who are you?" he asks his friend.

"What do you mean? You know who I am," Overman spits back.

"I know your alias," Rosenfarb continues. "But who are you really?"

Overman can't abide this idiocy. "Can we speak English, Jake? What are you talking about?"

As the waiter places the martini in front of Overman, the window man explains.

"Bruce Wayne was Batman. Clark Kent was Superman. Men-

achem Schneerson was *Moshiach* according to many people. Who
are you?"

"Let me get this straight. You think I'm some kind of superhero
who's been disguising himself as a failure for fifty-five years just to
fool people?"

"Do or do you not own a cape?" Rosenfarb asks, with McCar-
thy-like precision.

"Why? You think I can fly?" Overman laughs.

"That wasn't my question. Batman wears a cape, but he can't fly."

"Then what's the point of the cape?" Overman wants to know.

"He wears a cape because he's Batman and he wants to look like
a bat," Rosenfarb explains.

"But bats fly. If his name's Batman, he should fly."

"Batman doesn't fly. He dresses like a bat and uses powerful
gadgets, end of story." Rosenfarb is starting to get mad. As a child,
Jake collected comic books and was considered the neighborhood
expert on all creatures super and fantastic. A person could name any
superhero and Rosenfarb would bark out the character's assumed
identity, followed by a precise description of his or her powers.

"I'm trying to help define you," Jake tells Overman as the ahi
arrives, decoratively presented on crisp, greaseless wontons. "We
need to know where you fit in the scheme of things so we can figure out your next move." On a historical note, he informs Overman
that he is not the first Jewish superhero to arrive on the scene. Ira
is pre-dated by a character named Atom Smasher, real name Al
Rothstein, Blue Jay, AKA Jay Abrams, and Wiccan, the esteemed
William "Billy" Kaplan.

"Can I bring up one small point?" Overman interjects.

Rosenfarb nods, picking at his friend's ahi.

"These superheroes that you know so much about? They're fictional characters."

"So?"

"So I'm not a superhero. I'm a regular guy whose luck has changed."

Rosenfarb decides that this would be the ideal time to educate Overman on Jungian archetypes and how his new powers are modern incarnations of previous human experience. As he launches into a pretentious discourse on Celtic mythology and its contemporary equivalents, Overman's eyes glaze over. He can't help but wonder why, if Rosenfarb knows so goddamned much, he is installing blinds for a living.

Rosenfarb can tell from Overman's bored facial expression that he isn't making much headway with Joseph Campbell so he switches to a more brass tacks approach.

"Here's the bottom line, Ira. Superman could do a whole lot of great shit, but he had enemies who hated him, like Lex Luthor."

Overman reminds Rosenfarb that he already has scores of people who hate him, having nothing to do with the alleged supernatural powers his friend has ascribed to him.

"Fair enough," Rosenfarb admits. "But what if you have a kryptonite?"

"Huh?"

Rosenfarb explains the way it works. If you were able to do things normal humans couldn't, the possibility existed that some object or herb or chemical that was harmless to normal humans was now capable of hurting you. And it was imperative that Overman recognized this.

Overman shakes his head. "I've just got to ask—"

"Of course. You must have lots of questions," volleys Rosenfarb the expert.

"You're putting me in the same category as Superman—"

"No way. You can clear traffic. But you can't fly." Rosenfarb pauses for a moment. "Can you?"

"Rosenfarb!" Overman is fed up. "Just because you've read lots of comic books, doesn't mean I'm a superhero."

"Don't get bogged down in semantics, Ira—"

"It's not semantics. Have you ever met a superhero?"

"Besides you?"

"Yes, besides me."

Rosenfarb goes silent. Overman decides to make use of the precious available airspace.

"Have you had coffee with Atom Smasher? Have you golfed with the Fantastic Four?"

"Why would I? They're already a foursome—-"

"You know what I'm talking about, Jake. This is apples and oranges. Fiction versus reality."

Rosenfarb says that all he is trying to do is make sense out of an extraordinary situation. "I just think I can help you, Ira."

Overman can't imagine how. Rosenfarb lays it on the line. With power comes responsibility and decisions have to be made as to the hows, whys and wheres of using it. Rosenfarb's take is that based on his own vast knowledge of superheroes, their failures as well as successes, he is in a unique position to advise Overman on how to proceed.

"And what's in it for you?" Overman asks, curious to know what Rosenfarb has up his sleeve.

"You're my best friend. I'm here to serve."

"And?" Overman knows him too well.

"And nothing. I only wish for your success."

"That's very nice of you—"

"Because I know you're the kind of person who shares his success with others."

There it was. The window man wanted his piece of the pie. "And how exactly will I share my success, Jake," Overman wants to know.

"There's plenty of time to talk about that," Rosenfarb scoffs it off. "Right now we've got a lot of work to do."

As the waiter brings the check to the patio, a thought occurs to Overman. If he lets Rosenfarb pick up the tab, it is an implicit acceptance of the deal on the table. The broad strokes of the deal are that Overman is at the precipice of enormous change and will need help navigating the dangerous twists and turns in the road ahead. The fine print suggests that Rosenfarb's "guidance" is a euphemism for constant meddling with the ultimate goal of capitalizing on Overman's abilities.

"Why don't we split it?" Overman says, making an honest attempt to grab the check.

Rosenfarb, much too quick on the draw, will have none of it. "You'll get the next one. Heck, maybe you won't ever have to pay for meals again. You can just "will" the restaurant to comp you," Rosenfarb laughs.

It is a grim vision of the future. Something good finally happens to Overman and he's got Rosenfarb tailing him around like a dog, angling for dinners and free trips to Vegas. This guy was annoying enough at a party or on the tennis court. Overman decides to nip it in the bud before it gets out of hand. As soon as Rosenfarb stiffs the valet and they're back on the road, he states his case.

"Jake, you know I've been thinking—"

"Willpower Man," Rosenfarb interrupts, beginning to spitball superhero names. "Nah, too cumbersome. Maybe we need a 'the' name. You know, like the Hulk."

"Jake, I don't want any help with this," Overman states.

"I don't mind, Ira. Really, it's my pleasure to share my insights with you. Hey, here's a great idea: Over Man. You had the name all along." Then he thinks better of it. "Maybe it's not so good, because it has the negative connotation of implying that things are over."

"I appreciate your offering to help, but this whole series of events has been a very personal kind of—"

"Overman, you know nothing about superheroes," Rosenfarb snaps. "You need a sidekick," he declares, as if it some kind of legitimate occupation.

"A sidekick?"

"You're not prepared to do this alone."

"With all due respect, I'll be the judge of that," Overman replies.

"Jesus Christ, what's the matter with you? Batman, one of the greatest superheroes of all time had a sidekick, but Mr. Fancy Pants here thinks he can go solo."

"Superman didn't have a sidekick," Overman points out.

Rosenfarb reminds him that he is a far cry from Superman.

"That's like me comparing myself to... John Hampson for Christ's sake!"

"John Hampson?"

"The first American to patent Venetian blinds," Rosenfarb spits out, as if Overman is an idiot for not knowing this information.

"I'm just going to say it one last time. You're making a mistake."

"Duly noted," Overman assures him.

A tinge of paranoia creeps into Rosenfarb's disappointment. "You don't have another sidekick in mind, do you?"

"I have no other sidekicks," Overman assures him.

The rest of the ride to Steinbaum Mercedes is more than a little icy. That said, Overman is pleased because he has laid down the law, refusing to let this interloping bug put a damper on what is his and his alone. "How's Rita?" Overman asks, an admirable attempt at meaningless conversation.

"She's having her tits redone for the third time. I can't believe the amount of money I've spent on those things. Especially since I never get to go near them."

Overman feels a rush of sympathy for his friend. Yes, it could be a ploy to get him to reconsider, but the truth is that Rita knows no bounds in what she will take from her husband, giving little if anything in return. If he were Rosenfarb, he'd jump at the chance to be a sidekick, too. But he is not Rosenfarb and grateful for that.

"Thanks for lunch. I'll definitely get the next one," Overman says, jumping out of the passenger seat.

"Call me if you need anything," Rosenfarb pouts.

"Take care, Jake."

As Rosenfarb speeds off, Overman is sky-high. His elation has nothing to do with alleged superpowers. It comes from his successful deployment of a self-defense mechanism. An unlikely sexual encounter and the ostensible willing of a fire were one thing, but having the balls to impede a seasoned guilt monger like Jake Rosenfarb was in another league entirely.

The rest of the day unfolds, presenting Overman with a slew

of realizations. Realization Number One is that Maricela and Rodrigo are still together. When he picks her up at work she reacts as if there were never an Overman inside her. Yet she relates to Overman with a new warmth and understanding, as if they are the deepest of friends with an unbreakable bond. Overman rather likes this. While some men, after a night of marathon sex with a score like Maricela, might feel the need to continue the affair, Overman has stored it in his brain as a once-in-a-lifetime trophy: an unforgettable memory that will serve as his gateway to a life that matters.

Realization Number Two is that he feels like he can now sell a car to any customer he wants. It is just a matter of how much stamina he can muster to invoke the necessary willpower. Which leads to Realization Number Three: that he needs to get in shape so he can build strength. Realization Number Four is the proclamation first voiced by Rosenfarb: in the event that Overman actually has extraordinary abilities, where, when, why and how he chooses to use them will be of paramount importance.

On the way home, Overman checks in at the Jungle Gym to investigate some sort of fitness program. A clueless shill named Chuck tries to rope him in for three years at $250 per, but is sorely outclassed. Even the old Overman could browbeat this rank amateur down to a hundred a year, the new one closing the deal at a cool $79. From the gym, it's off to the comic book shop and the video store, where Overman stocks up on "Iron Man," "Batman 1-3," "The Incredible Hulk," the two "Spidermans," and as a nod to diversity, the poorly received "Hancock." While he firmly rejects Rosenfarb's superhero theory, he recognizes it as a possible learning tool. In fiction as in life, the powerful are faced with difficult choices, so it might be useful to see how pop culture archetypes approach moral dilemmas. The heroes naturally take the side of Good rather than Evil, their equally powerful nemeses skewing to the wicked and self-aggrandizing. While Overman never imagined himself using any of his "skills" for nefarious purposes, he knew there were gray areas and was curious to learn how others approached them.

Sitting down to study his fictional forbears, what is most striking to Overman is that virtually all these characters came from backgrounds far more dysfunctional than his own. Peter Parker was a nerd, mocked incessantly by his peers before becoming Spiderman. Bruce Wayne saw both his parents murdered before he turned into Batman. Iron Man's mother and father died in a car crash. By comparison, Overman's background seemed downright bucolic: the misfires of his life hadn't converged into a spectacular pile of shit until he grew into adulthood. The other universal theme he discovered was that the transformation from helpless to invincible inevitably led to vigilantism. Power was a natural breeding ground for revenge. Overman pondered whether this was where he might be headed. To be sure, there was a laundry list of bastards who should have treated him better: teachers who picked on him, bosses who fired his ass, friends who betrayed him. If he truly had superpowers, he could go back and serve justice one scumbag at a time. But would it even be satisfying to avenge their idiocy so many years later? It seemed like a lot of energy for precious little gain.

Overman chose to envision his future in more modest terms. It would be enough to sell a bunch of cars, put some money away, maybe move out of the shithole apartment and buy a condo. Nothing fancy, but enough to carve out a life. It never seemed to be enough for the heroes of those comic books and movies. Of course if it had been, the story would be over and the publishers and movie studios couldn't make any more money. Playing devil's advocate, Overman then reminded himself that his personal evolution was just starting to kick into gear. Limiting his options at this early juncture reeked of Thinking Small. No need to close the door on anything right now. Stay fluid, be open to the opportunities that present themselves. The first order of business was to keep selling cars and get in shape.

He is about to crawl into bed when the phone rings — not the cell, but the landline that has been dedicated to wrong numbers since the day public television took him off their call list, having finally realized that his fifteen-dollar donation was a once in a lifetime affair.

"Overman," he answers, as if it's the finance department buzzing him about a lease deal.

"Sorry to call you this late, Mr. Overman. This is Dr. Gonzales from the Clearview Vision Center."

The car salesman brightens. He never got to thank the man who was seemingly responsible for the Overman game-changer.

"Dr. Gonzales. I've been meaning to call you. I've been so pleased with your work."

"I know," Gonzales responds. "One of your friends has been calling me every day about Lasik surgery because he loves the job I did on you."

"Oh, no," Overman whimpers. He knows what's coming.

"The thing is, his vision is fine and there's no reason to do anything. But he won't listen. Can you give me any advice on how to handle Mr. Rosenfarb?"

"If I were you, I'd leave the country," Overman replies, only half-joking. Overman explains that the window man is imbued with the tenacity of a pit bull, a quality he unleashes whenever he has an idea, no matter how small or how stupid.

"He thinks that if I cut open his eyes, he'll be able to have sex with beautiful young women," Gonzales says, bewildered. "It's crazy."

"The man is ill," Overman avers. "My advice is not to take his calls and sit tight. Maybe he'll have some sort of breakdown."

"Are you kidding me?"

"I'm sorry for any trouble this has caused you." Overman hangs up, wracked with guilt for what he has thrust upon the poor doctor. He wonders if he can use whatever is in his arsenal to tame Rosenfarb, but he knows in his heart that going toe to toe with Jake requires a lot more horsepower than he currently has under the hood.

When the alarm goes off at 6, Overman springs into action. He throws his car salesman gear into a small duffle bag and by 6:45 is walking through the door of the gym. He waves to Chuck, now the embodiment of shame for the beating he took on the annual membership fees, then proceeds to the locker room to store his work clothes. It is Overman's first visit to a locker room since high school and he is quickly reminded why he never missed it. The smells were identical, that curious blend of soap and stench, and the sights had worsened considerably. This was Ira's introduction to preening fifty year-olds with shaved pubes standing in front of a mirror, admiring their pecs and appraising their junk. Gay? Maybe half of them. Self-absorbed? Across the board. This was, after all, Southern California, where youth was not permitted to go gently into that good night, but hung onto with a ferociousness that turned its worshipers into wannabes. For the first time in his poor excuse for a life, Overman felt glad that he was different. Unlike the posing guy with the bald genitalia, scrounging for a kernel of existential validation, the new, improved Overman felt like he possessed something singular. It didn't have to be stared at or paraded around, just sharpened and strengthened.

Overman brushes past Sir Baldy and makes his way out to the gym floor. He's going to start with the tricep bar that pitiful Chuck showed him how to operate. He sets the weight at a light twenty pounds to start. Overman's been told that at his age it's about reps, not how heavy he can lift. He does ten pulls then takes a break, using the opportunity to drink in the Jungle Gym scene. Lots of plastic tits, old guys with dyed chest hair, young moms trying to get back to their pre-baby weight, a former professional wrestler, a middle aged female ex-bodybuilder named Carla who seems to know everybody and won't shut up. After his second set of tricep pulls, she drops by to add him to her friendship circle. It turns out that after her bodybuilding career, Carla became a private detective. Upon leaving the gym, she will drive to City of Industry to spy on a beer distributor who's banging his secretary. She feels super fat and she shouldn't have had that onion bagel yesterday and she's single, no surprise. As Carla flutters off to pester someone else, the wrestler known as Bo arrives to introduce himself to Overman. He welcomes Ira with a quick survey of the landscape, pointing out which of the plastic-titted gym junkies are porn stars, which are actual junkies.

Moving on to the next machine, Overman tries to make sense of this strange world that has apparently embraced him with open arms. While he's able to finish his bicep sets without making any new acquaintances, it occurs to him that people seem to fancy their personal training in noisy, showy, social environs. While Overman knew he'd be working out amongst others, he pictured a parallel pursuit of individual goals rather than the yammering interaction before him. At the shoulder machine, he manages to clear his head. This was what he wanted: to concentrate on the business at hand and rid himself of the clutter that would fill up brain space as the day wore on.

The last time he exercised on a regular basis was when he joined the wrestling team as a freshman in high school. Wrestling was where they sent the slight and the puny, an apt description of fifteen year-old Overman, providing one was to add "pimply" to the mix. Clocking in at 5'3, 105 pounds, he couldn't be taken seriously for football or basketball, but ostensibly had the potential to shine at a sport where the requirement was to bulk up, yet go down a weight class. In Overman's case, it meant the 98-pound weight class. Getting there required rigorous workouts, dieting and staying after school for practice until it was dark outside. Since wrestling season fell smack in the middle of the frosty Long Island winter, by the time Overman had finished rolling on the sweaty mats and being humiliated in the group shower, he would find himself walking into the black night, wet hair hardening into icicles as he shivered his way home.

Conceding that listening to Carla, the private detective, yap about her onion bagel is preferable to the sweaty, frozen night walks of his past, he then spots, to the left of the barbells, a man who looks familiar and foreign at the same time. He's sure he has seen this face many times before, but the body, the clothes, the hair — they just don't add up. It is only after a fellow exerciser tells a lame dirty joke and the man laughs that Overman identifies him as Gary Sheslow, his ex-therapist. There is no mistaking the wheezy cackle of the legend whose most memorable line was, "We have to stop now." This *goniff*, currently hoisting two-pound free weights and sporting a hideous dye job, had accrued thousands of Overman dollars during a span of nearly twenty years, only to conclude that his client was hopeless and toss him out on the street. In Sheslow's defense, Overman had ignored or refused any piece of advice the therapist offered, precipitating a lengthy and expensive stalemate. The end had been unpleasant, to say the least. Sheslow denied Overman's request to refund his money, instead recommending a psychiatrist and daring his former client to sue him.

What would the dipshit have to say now? Here was Overman, poised to climb his personal Everest while Sheslow the Clown was dipping his head in Kiwi shoe polish. He is tempted to go over and broadcast this salient point, but Sheslow has made an unforeseen exit to the locker room. Overman is not so tempted that he wants to follow his former shrink, confident that their day of reckoning will come further down the line. The therapist is not gone a minute when Overman notices a pleasant-looking brunette lying down to use the leg machine. She looks familiar as well. He knows they have not met yet she somehow conveys the essence of a brunette from his past. As the young woman pushes the platform with her feet and both calves extend, it triggers the rush of an earlier Overman memory, hands-down the saddest moment of an adolescence that had been defined by the Sad Moment.

Janie Sweeney is on her back in an alcoholic fog. The cacophony of the male chorus eggs Overman on as Marty Merkowitz shoves him on top of her. The others pin him down and he is forced to unzip his fly in order to make his inauspicious presence known. Janie emits a slight, but unmistakable cry at the moment of entry, a whimper not unlike that of a small wounded animal. The sequence of events had lodged itself within him and tortured Overman throughout his subsequent years. Why didn't he get away? How come he didn't report the incident? Moreover, if it had affected him this deeply, how badly had it damaged Janie Sweeney? Janie's parents moved to New Jersey for the next school year and he never heard anything about her since. Not that he tried very hard to track her down.

As Overman picks up the five-pound free weights to do his lateral lifts, it dawns on him: on that fateful night when his good friend Rosenfarb abandoned him by the onion dip, he had been forced into penetrating another against his will. Since it was out of his control, didn't that make him a victim as well? He had never thought about it in such terms, but technically, Ira Overman had been raped.

However one chose to interpret it, Overman's first sexual experience with a woman was an act of violence and criminal behavior. Neither Spiderman nor Batman could boast that kind of dysfunction in their pasts. Overman wasn't proud of it. The mere thought of that sperm-filled night rendered him pale and lifeless. But the resurfacing and ongoing crystallization of this memory also made him want to exercise harder and toughen up. Nobody would rape Ira Overman ever again, not even figuratively.

There is a pristine pleasure in being able to radiate confidence after a lifetime of unhappiness and insecurity. When Overman marches through the doors of Steinbaum Mercedes that morning he is still pudgy, his hair still thinning, yet he carries himself as he supposes a superhero might: not boastful (that was Rosenfarb's domain) or unnecessarily talkative (Detective Carla's yammering was still ringing in his ears), but self-assured and businesslike. He realizes that the change he has undergone has yielded a dividend he's never before known: dignity. Working on a car lot, this quality was arguably in even shorter supply than superpowers. In fact, no salesman at Steinbaum had ever experienced such a thing in a co-worker. His new demeanor baffled the entire dealership. Not only did Overman refuse to kiss the boss's ass, he didn't seem nervous about meeting sales expectations in a recessionary marketplace.

A young couple walks in to purchase a car they clearly can't afford. The Garrisons have decent enough credit but should be using it toward something like a Ford Focus rather than a $50,000 automobile. Big fucking deal. Overman has done this dance a thousand times. Suck them in with zero down, put them into an upside-down monthly payment that gets higher as they "advance in their careers and have more disposable income." Nine times out of ten the buyer can't afford to keep up with the increases and winds up selling the car back at a loss or having it taken from him by the bank.

Even though he is far from a superhero, Overman feels obliged to consider: Would Spiderman engage in such deplorable activity if he worked at Steinbaum? Selling this car to these people would be tantamount to Batman taking candy from a baby while he's fucking the baby's mother. Overman is not desperate to close this deal. The deals would come when they were the right ones.

"Mr. and Mrs. Garrison, I really don't think it makes sense for you to buy a car from us," Overman says, within earshot of an incredulous Hal Steinbaum.

The Garrisons are naturally surprised. They thank him for his forthrightness and he is pleased. Overman then decides to amble over to say "hi" to Maricela, who looks exceptionally fetching this morning.

"Hey, how's everything going?" he smiles. It comes out naturally now. Sincere, completely unforced, they are friends and words flow as they are meant to.

"I'm good. It's nice to see you," she smiles.

"You and Rodrigo seem to have come to an understanding."

"I guess. He's a shithead but I'm working on him."

"People can change," Overman assures her, now having experienced the concept firsthand.

"Want anything from the Coffee Bean?" he asks. "I was thinking of driving over."

"A vanilla ice-blended sounds great."

"You got it," Overman winks, starting for the door.

"Ira."

He turns around.

She whispers. "I'm glad we got to make love."

"Me, too. You're incredible."

Her whisper becomes even softer.

"There's so much more I'd like to do to you."

"Oh Jesus," he moans, suddenly interrupted by a noxious whine that could only belong to Hal Steinbaum.

"Overman, get in my office."

"I was about to go to Coffee Bean. You want anything?"

"I want to rip you a new sphincter. You let those laydowns walk."

"They couldn't afford that car."

"Get in there," Steinbaum points, as if scolding a small child.

"I'm going to Coffee Bean. I'll talk to you when I get back."

"You walk out that door, you won't be coming back, Overman."

The gauntlet had been thrown down. If he had been faced with the identical scenario last month, he would have blown off the Coffee Bean run and followed Steinbaum back to the office with his tail between his legs. Not so in the current configuration of things. Now he asks himself: If the Incredible Hulk wanted an ice-blended, would he bag it in favor of being reprimanded by a moron? It seemed unlikely.

"I'll talk to you later," Overman says, blithely sauntering out the door.

Maricela, having witnessed the whole ordeal, calls Hal over to calm things down. He is fuming, but so accustomed to responding like a puppy dog to her every command that he rushes to her station.

"Just reminding you," she smiles, "you have an 11:30 call with the Finance department."

"Fuck Finance. Can you believe what an asshole that guy is?"

"Ira?"

"Who else?"

"I don't think he's an asshole at all," Maricela replies. "I respect him."

The boss shakes his head and starts to walk away.

Just before he is out of earshot, Maricela speaks up at a decibel level that is barely audible. "By the way, I slept with him."

Steinbaum's head snaps around. "What did you say," he roars, clearly beside himself.

"I slept with him," the receptionist repeats nonchalantly.

"You're lucky I'm a nice guy. I'm going to give you a chance to explain why you would mock me like this."

"I wasn't trying to mock you, Mr. Steinbaum. I'm sorry."

"Sorry. That's a little better. So what was the point of that nonsense?"

"No point."

"I see. Is there anything else you'd like to say for yourself?"

"I don't know. He gave me multiple orgasms?"

The man's head now looks as if it's about to implode.

Maricela smiles. "Oops."

Overman orders the two vanilla ice-blendeds with the authority of a man who knows what he wants, above and beyond his coffee-flavored beverages. His gorgeous "fuck you" to Steinbaum and doing something nice for Maricela had combined for an exultant one-two punch. Leaping tall buildings and teleporting might be awesome, but looking that asshole in the eye and saying "no" to his bullshit was huge in its own right. The power niche that Overman was creating for himself was a beautiful thing.

He carries the drinks into the dealership and is surprised to find Dora, the blond, dumb-as-a-post file clerk from Pre-Owned, seated at the receptionist desk.

"It's an awesome day at Steinbaum Mercedes," she informs the caller, apparently having done her own re-write on this timeless chestnut.

"Mr. Steinbaum wants to see you," she informs Overman.

"It's an awesome day at Steinbaum Mercedes, please hold," she chirps, moving on to answer the next call.

"Where's Maricela?"

"In Mr. Steinbaum's office, getting fired," she answers matter-of-factly. "It's an awesome day at Steinbaum Mercedes…"

The depths to which the wormy Hal Steinbaum would sink were staggering. On what possible basis could he terminate an employee who performed her admittedly simple job to perfection? Everyone loved Maricela and not just for her ass. When she said "It's a beautiful day at Steinbaum Mercedes," you almost believed her.

Overman storms into the scuzzbag's lair to find an expressionless Maricela seated across from Steinbaum, who's slurping another Diet Coke. He hands her the ice-blended and demands to know what's going on.

"What's going on?" Steinbaum repeats with a sick smile. "You want to know what's going on?"

"He doesn't like that I had sex with you so he's canning me." Maricela explains.

"Listen to this shit!" Steinbaum yelps. "She made up some crazy story about having sex with you just to humiliate me!"

"I didn't make it up. Everything I said is true," Maricela swears.

"I'm not an idiot, young lady. And no employee of mine is going to treat me as such."

Adding to his street cred as a consummate asshole, Steinbaum liked to sprinkle a little pomposity into his *schtick*, randomly employing phrases like "as such."

"I'm not treating you like an idiot. I'm only speaking the truth," Maricela replies. "Tell him, Ira."

Overman doesn't want to add fuel to the fire. The important thing now is to make sure Maricela gets to keep her job.

"Hal, I think there's been a misunderstanding," he offers, having no clue where he's going with this.

"So you didn't fuck her?" Steinbaum snaps. "I hate liars, Maricela."

"I don't think name-calling is going to solve anything," Overman counters, inching forward the negotiation. "Maricela may have exaggerated some of what went on between—"

"Exaggerated? You know that's not true!" she bursts out, insulted.

Christ. How do I protect her if she won't let me? Overman

wonders. She starts to cry. It occurs to Overman that now might be the time to dig into his recently acquired bag of tricks and see if there is anything useful in there. Could he utilize his willpower to save Maricela's job? Perhaps he just had to state his position firmly and Steinbaum would have no choice but to do the right thing. Regardless, if he did nothing, Maricela could wind up working for those scumbuckets at Marmelstein BMW or worse.

"Look, Hal, nobody wants to hurt anybody else's feelings. Maricela is a beautiful woman, a lovely person, an exceptional employee."

Maricela wipes a tear from her eye as Overman continues.

"The truth is that yes, we did sleep together. It was one night, it just happened, a connection between friends. More importantly, in no way did it affect our ability to do our jobs. It had nothing to do with you and we both continue to hold you in the highest regard."

Overman hated saying that last part. He feels like he needs a shower.

After an awkward moment of silence, Steinbaum announces that he is willing to strike a compromise. "Overman, you're going to call back that couple and send them over to Pre-Owned, and Maricela, you're going to dinner with me Saturday night."

A strange take on the concept of compromise, but consider the source.

"I'm not going to dinner with you," Maricela responds. And just in case the read-between-the-lines thing escapes him, she goes for the big finish. "And I am never, ever going to sleep with you."

"You can't fire someone for not sleeping with you," Overman reminds him.

"I can do whatever the fuck I want, Overman. I can find a million bullshit reasons to fire both your asses."

"But you won't," Overman asserts. "And do you know why you won't?"

"Educate me, you latte-drinking piece of shit," Steinbaum snorts, spraying Diet Coke across his Excel spreadsheet.

"You will not fire her ass because even *you* are not idiotic enough to terminate an employee whose personality and communication skills increase your sales productivity and whose emotional investment in your dealership protect you from every lying, cheating, sleazeball salesman who would happily fuck you over."

Boy did Overman like how that sounded. Forceful, commanding, dare he think it? Batmanesque. Apparently, some of this came through to Maricela.

"I love you, Overman!" she crows, as the dealership owner with the aspertame soul pops open another Diet Coke.

Steinbaum seems impressed with the Overman argument.

"Not bad. Now what about you? Why won't I fire your ass?"

Overman gets ready to tee it up. How he's been at this shithouse for eleven years, thrived as the dealership's most dependable closer, stayed when others left for management positions on other lots, stopped himself from fucking over Steinbaum even though he hated him more than any salesman there. Not particularly complimentary toward his boss, yet an accurate evaluation of what he, Overman, brought to the table.

"I'm waiting, Overman. Tell me why you think I'm not going to shitcan you right here, right now."

Overman clears his throat and prepares to deliver the speech. Somehow the words come out much differently than expected. It is not an angry Tourette's-like diatribe that spews from his lips, but rather a sober answer that communicates exactly what it is Ira Overman wants. At this moment, he has zero desire to placate his douchebag boss. What he wants is to re-frame the debate and end it.

"Hal, let it be said for the record that you are the lowest life form on God's great earth. You elevate the amoeba."

"I'd like to see how you ask for a raise," Steinbaum snickers.

"You won't get that opportunity because as of this moment, you will no longer infect or pollute my world with the putrid mind-vomit that oozes out of your poison spigot."

"Not look-ing go-od," Steinbaum singsongs. "Someone's gonna get shitcanned."

"It's not going to be me, Hal. You can't shitcan me because I quit."

And with a brisk wave of the hand to Maricela, Overman walks out the door, his career as a car salesman ancient history. It was time to start writing a new chapter, with no end-of-the-month margins, zero profit loss leaders or helpless laydowns. The fact that he was now unemployed was beside the point. Even if his new abilities were of no use to him financially, never again having to utter the phrase, "Are you leasing or buying?" would make him a happy man.

The freeway was open, traffic moving at a decent if not break-neck clip. No need for the man behind the wheel to run a test of his resources. Besides, even if he had a full tank's worth, Overman would bow to the hoarding instinct that had been graciously hand-ed down to him by his parents. String savers of the highest order, Saul and Irma covered, closeted, locked up and hid anything that was or wasn't of value. Though they were not holocaust survivors themselves, they knew people who were and deemed the victim mindset a good fit. Ira had even thought of stuffing wads of string in each of their coffins just in case those muckety-mucks in the hereafter wanted to overcharge them.

While recognizing the logic of being prudent with his new-found abilities, Overman had come to hate the hoarding gene, one of many fear-based character traits that had been carved deep into his psyche. He knew that if Saul and Irma were somehow watch-ing his life from their condo on the Styx, they would be appalled by what he considered to be his proudest moment. Standing up for what one felt was right, leaving a position that wasn't worthy of one's talents, sticking one's neck out to save another's job — this was for other people. *Goyim.* It certainly wasn't for Overmans.

How could anyone live this way? Ira himself had done it for fifty-five years and it had taken its toll. But now he had been given a second chance. Had it appeared so that he might become super-human? Or unabashedly human, able to see the world for what it was: a difficult, sometimes scary, other times exhilarating place that demanded to be met head on. Dice had to be rolled, hands needed to be played. Cowering, groveling, apologizing for mistakes one hadn't made — these non-starters needed to be eradicated and fast.

Overman decides that since he has the whole afternoon and in fact the rest of his life free, he should find a quiet, meditative place where new ideas might come to him. Powers or no powers, Overman still needed to make money. How exactly was he going to do that? Starting over required thought and strategy.

He stops at home to change out of the cheap car dog ensemble he will never again wear as long as he lives, vowing to burn every poly-cotton shirt he owns and donate the Elevators to Goodwill. The underground parking structure is empty, his neighbors hard at work selling falafels, taking urine specimens, whatever other unappealing jobs they did. He opens the door to the apartment, noting that it is even more revolting in the light of day. Overman is determined to get out. He fantasizes about flying to some Caribbean paradise, luxuriating in his private pod on Virgin Atlantic Airways. He wants another piña colada. Instead of asking for it, he wills the flight attendant to place it down in front of him. Why not? It could happen. This is, after all, the new Overman, the modest purveyor of positive results whose potential was still being mined. An outrageous thought occurs to him. The patented Rosenfarb "What if?" What if he actually had the power to travel to the Virgin Islands alongside the plane rather than on it? Overman? Flying? Insanity. On the other hand, it's not like he's ever tried, so who really knows?

Overman shakes his head. What am I thinking? I'm just working up to human and now I'm in a comic book, flying? Then again, maybe it was okay to open the box. Maybe that reflexive slap on the wrist came courtesy of Saul and Irma. Don't aim too high. Don't dare to think you can distinguish yourself and dream about soaring above the clouds. Hell, even if he couldn't fly, it wasn't a crime to fantasize about it. Just because his parents had made a career of setting their sights low didn't mean he had to go into the family business.

This insight continues to seep in as Overman drives toward the beach. Heading west on Olympic Boulevard, he decides to pull over and experiment. What did he have to lose? He gets out of the car, waits for the sidewalk to clear, then raises both arms in the air. The plan is to bend the knees and spring off the ground like that bullshit Hancock, jumping high enough to propel his poochy body into some semblance of airborne motion. He notes that should he happen to reach any substantial velocity, he might want to avoid flying into the precipitously close Bed, Bath and Beyond. He wonders what *is* this Beyond they are advertising? Perhaps he is about to find out.

Overman closes his eyes and takes a deep breath, all systems ready to take flight. As planned, he bends his knees and leaps skyward, but with less than optimum results. Within seconds, his body comes crashing down on the hard, unforgiving pavement, aggravating his sciatica in the process. Two things have become clear: One, that even if Overman has such potential, flying is not currently in his wheelhouse. Two, that as a card-carrying member of AARP, he has to know his limits and not behave like some eighteen year-old superhero on Spring Break. Overman dusts himself off and hobbles back to the car, deciding to make the Santa Monica Pier his next stop.

Overman brushed off his failed attempt at flight as an audacious experiment that was not yet ready for primetime. Meanwhile, completely unbeknownst to him, his recent string of successes was having a huge impact in the hills of Laurel Canyon. Rita, wearing sweatpants boasting the word "Juicy" spread across her ass, was pacing at the foot of the Rosenfarb Dux bed, howling into her cell phone.

"He's just sitting there, mumbling. I can't convince him to get up." She turns to bark at Jake. "Get the fuck up, you lazy piece of shit!"

Rosenfarb, eyes glassy and staring into the void, manages an attempt to "shush" her.

"Can you make out what he's saying?" asks the voice on the other end of the phone, none other than Pfizer's favorite son, Dr. Stan Belzberg.

Rita explains as best she can.

"He keeps mumbling crazy things about Overman. How he's some kind of hero, how he has sex with young girls..."

"Ooh, Jake's definitely not well," Belzberg sympathizes. "When did all this start?"

"I'm not exactly sure," Rita tells him. "I began to get alarmed a few days ago when clients started calling the house saying he never showed up for a job."

"That's not like Jake at all."

"And then, on Tuesday, a marshal comes to the door with a restraining order from Overman's eye doctor."

"His eye doctor?"

"Apparently, Jake has been going into the guy's office every day and demanding Lasik surgery that he doesn't need."

"I want to be able to drive in no traffic," Jake cries out in explanation.

"Shut up! I'm trying to talk to the doctor!"

"Would you like me to refer you to a psychiatrist?" Stan asks.

"I'd prefer a divorce lawyer," Rita counters, only half-joking.

Belzberg gives her the name of a $450 an hour Beverly Hills big shot who turns out to be in the same building as Rita's boob and liposuction guy. A seasoned multi-tasker, Rita brightens at the prospect of coordinating Jake's mental illness appointments with her own Botox injections. Belzberg ends the conversation with his signature crowd-pleaser: free drug samples of whatever she wants, whenever she wants it.

Rita throws down her iPhone and shoots bitch darts at Jake.

"Why are you doing this to me?"

"I'm not doing anything to you," he responds, a bit more alert.

"You are not working. You are not producing the income to run this household the way it needs to be run. You are babbling like a fool."

Her husband ponders this for a moment, then speaks. "You don't love me, do you, Rita?"

"What kind of a question is that?" she sneers.

The fog is starting to clear. Yes, he has been in an Overman-induced haze for some time now, but Rita's rancid verbal discharge has snapped him back to life. Slowly, but methodically, he rises from the bed.

"Good. You're up. Go to work," his wife instructs him.

This command does not sit well with Rosenfarb. "Don't tell me what to do."

"I'm trying to help you."

"You don't give a flying fuck about me, Rita. All you care about is your granite counters, your collagen and your Juicy pants, under which, I might add, there has been no juice whatsoever for ten years."

"Fuck you, Jake!" she screams, now totally unglued.

He refuses to engage any further and goes to retrieve a different shirt from the closet.

Rita decides it might be best to diffuse the situation. She tries to access the calm she feels in Pilates class, closing her eyes, then softly asking:

"Are you going to work now?"

Rosenfarb regards his wife with contempt. "I am leaving. Now ask me if I'm coming back."

"What is wrong with you?" Rita screams, loud enough for the whole neighborhood to hear. "You can't go anywhere, Jake. You're fucking psycho!"

Oddly, this brings a smile to Rosenfarb's face.

"Maybe I am, Rita, but let's see how *your* mental health holds up when you're cleaning your own toilets in the valley, on a pauper's plastic surgery budget."

"Are you threatening me?" she fumes.

"It's not a threat, Rita. It's a guarantee."

As Rosenfarb starts for the door, his wife picks up a table lamp and throws it at him, narrowly missing his head as it smashes to the ground.

"One more antique you'll be replacing with an item from Target," he chuckles.

"I hate your guts!"

"And soon you'll have the opportunity to do that in a one-bed-room apartment, abutting the freeway. Have a nice day, Rita."

Rosenfarb walks out the door, head held high. Would he really be able to leave her? Could he survive what would surely be the most difficult divorce since Henry VIII had to start his own church to get one? Probably not. But it was a great feeling to have pissed her off so royally. Her haranguing had thrown him back into the world. Yes, he was still thinking about Overman, but it was once again a functional obsession.

Overman strolls out on the pier, inhaling the salt air and cotton candy fumes from another lifetime. He and Nancy used to bring the kids here when they were little. He always loved watching Ashley and Peter play, how they'd squeal with glee as they bounced from ride to arcade booth and back again. He marveled at how they loved him unconditionally, only to learn later in life that they were too young to know better. And today he was walking on that very same pier: wife gone, children grown away from him, job an irritating memory.

Re-visiting this turf was like stepping into a Twilight Zone episode where life never changed for anyone but you. The rest of the world has been basking in a garden of earthly delight until you, the zombie, inadvertently trespass on these nice people's property. The townsfolk eye you with quiet suspicion. You, in turn, feel disconnected from the joy with which they were consumed until *you* showed up. You keep walking to the end of the pier, stare down at the ocean and prepare to jump, hoping against hope that when you emerge from the breakwater you will see a different sky, a re-tooled landscape, a new society that has never met you, yet warmly embraces you as family. When you actually do jump and climb back up onto the pier, you find your new society, but it is not the one you imagined. It is a world devoid of delight. Everyone is a zombie, just like you. You have missed your chance to dance unfettered, laugh until you cry, love so deeply you can barely find the strength to breathe. That was the life you passed up. It is no longer available.

Why did Overman choose to come here? What led him to a location that represented nothing but lost opportunities? It seemed that regardless of how his future turned out, some part of him knew that in order to create a happier existence, he needed to be in a place where he had once felt happiness. At least he had the good sense not to go to Venice Beach, where the brown, bikini-clad skaters stayed eighteen while he had become a dinosaur.

He decides to take a ride on the carousel, the safer, drier alternative to jumping off the pier. Mounting a regal white stallion, Overman notes that he easily has thirty years on the oldest mom aboard this merry-go-round. A graying, middle-aged man alone on a kiddie ride. Stranger sights have probably been seen, but the incongruity of this picture is not lost on Overman. Thankfully, it is a balmy, relaxed summer's day and nobody seems to give it a second thought. And it is only a minute or two before the creepy carnival music begins. Once the wheel is in motion, the other riders will be too occupied to notice the interloper in their midst.

As he starts to move, Overman notices the way he is sitting on his horse. Defying fifty-five years of slouching and *schlumping*, he revels in the phenomenon that is good posture. He might be going around in circles with little clue as to a purpose, but he is riding high, his physical and emotional spines both starting to uncurl.

What do I really want to do with my life? he muses. I once thought about running a record shop. It was just like Overman to have such a brainstorm just as the entire music retail business was tumbling into the toilet, having lost the war with digital downloads. A dumb idea, but so what? The point was to imagine any and all possibilities. What about a restaurant? There were only like twelve thousand of them in L.A. And he wasn't that into food anyway. He could go back to school. At fifty-five? That was just as likely as him returning to the entertainment industry to work for one of his kids' friends. He could teach. Not the best idea considering he didn't know anything worth knowing. Random thoughts start to spill out. Inventor? Bad with my hands, short on conceptual thinking. FBI agent? Cave under pressure, can't keep a secret. Librarian? Long, tainted history of unpaid overdue book fines. The ride ends with no answers. Yet it gives Overman hope. The juices are beginning to flow. For the first time in his life, he is tapping into a fluid stream of consciousness, determined to clean up and dispose of his tainted past.

After a shaky, but injury-free dismount, Overman heads toward the arcade where years ago he had helped his children hone their skeeball technique; where he had labored at the toy crane in the glass booth, struggling to pick up worthless little *tsochkes* he could've bought for a tenth of what he was shelling out. On the way, he spots another poignant reminder of cash gone by: the midway games offering prizes of large stuffed animals for tossing rings onto milk bottles, bouncing frogs onto plates, whirling whiffle balls into impossibly small holes.

At the whiffle ball stand he sees the Ghost of Overman Past: a Salvadoran father standing beside his wife and young child, all of whom desperately want to win the six-foot Kung Fu Panda but have little chance because they are so fucked, percentage-wise. Overman watches the dad blow dollar after dollar, his wife trying to pull him away from this foolishness as the kid bawls louder with each miss. Dad curses himself in Spanish, wondering why he can't, just once, succeed at what seems like a simple task.

It is painful for Overman to watch. After Dad's fifteenth consecutive miss, the former car salesman turns away, going off to forage for funnel cake. Overman's never tried one but he likes the name. It contains the word "fun," and paired with the word "cake," it's a no-lose proposition. Taking his first bite, he is impressed with both taste and texture, pleasingly donut-like yet subtly waffle-ish. While consuming empty calories certainly does not jibe with his new commitment to fitness, today has been a milestone, and if he chooses a deep-fried celebration, so be it. He'd do an extra set of ab curls in the morning.

Overman is blissfully wolfing down the sugary dough when he

hears the shriek. Salvadoran Mom is having a meltdown, desperate to pry her husband from the whiffle ball toss before he blows the entire week's pay. Dad will not budge. Overman walks back toward the stand and sees the neighboring booth operators laughing and whispering amongst themselves.

"How lame is this dude?"

"Serious loser."

Laughter and fist bumps all around.

Dad realizes he doesn't have any more money. One of the booth operators jokingly suggests he empty out the ATM. Dad's more than ready to oblige. As Mom makes a heartbreaking, but futile attempt to block the cash machine, Overman steps up to the stand and grabs a whiffle ball.

"Okay if I have a go at it?" he asks.

"We'll take anybody's money," the booth guy smirks.

Dad and blubbering son return to see Overman winding up. Mom tells them it's someone else's turn and time for them to go home. Overman focuses on the green hole in the upper right hand corner. If ever there were a time when willpower needed to be summoned, this was it. He focuses, aims and fires, proceeding to hurl a splitter right through the center. He's won on the first try, which has the net effect of sending father, mother and son into a fit bordering on hysteria. Overman tells the booth operator to hurry up and give the boy his panda. They must stop these people from killing themselves.

Arcade Jerk takes his time, electing to send a few text messages before retrieving Overman's prize. The wife now has both hands around the neck of her husband and the son is screaming bloody murder. Overman goes behind the counter and grabs one of the pandas himself, rushing over to present it to the little boy. Spiderman would be proud. This new suburban superhero had identified a troubled situation and insinuated himself into it, using his power for Good.

Unfortunately, his admirable intentions yield a strange and unexpected outcome. Just as Overman hands over the panda and the boy starts to smile, the father rips it away.

"We don't want it." He shoves the stuffed animal back at Overman.

"What are you talking about? Look how much money you spent trying to win one of these."

"That doesn't matter. We don't take handouts."

The boy starts to cry again.

"Look," Overman pleads. "There's nothing I can do with this thing. I won it for you. Let it make your son happy."

After processing his plea, the wife proceeds to put her arm around her husband. They have come together for a common purpose. "We don't want your charity, Mister."

Heads held high, the newly united couple and their screaming offspring walk off toward the corn dog stand. Overman recognizes that his suspicion had been right all along. The hero game wasn't as cut and dried as people thought. And he had just met his first gray area head-on.

His superheroic good deed roundly unappreciated, Overman now sat shuffling papers in the dismal overhead light of his kitchen, wondering if Batman had to pay monthly bills. That fancy car he drove burned an awful lot of gas. The cape and mask had to be dry-cleaned. Somebody had to go food shopping. Was that Alfred's thing? Who renewed the Lipitor? Overman wondered, cursing the bank statement in front of him. Surely the Green Hornet didn't have to pay a fee to his own bank in addition to the original ATM charge? Unfortunately, Overman was still very much of this world, saddled with an $800 car payment and $3600 outstanding in credit card bills while having accumulated barely $2000 in a low-percentage savings account. Deliberating what the next phase of his life should look like had to take a back seat to figuring out how to make money. He postulated that the best course of action might be to investigate temp jobs, where he could be exposed to different professions and working environments while figuring out the Next Act.

The wrong number landline rings. He decides to answer on the off chance that somebody somewhere owes him money and wants to settle up.

"Over Man," he announces, as if his true superhero moniker had indeed been given to him at birth.

"Have you heard from Jake?" screeches Rita, practically bursting his eardrum.

"No, is he okay?"

"He's gone insane, Ira. I blame you."

"Rita, calm down. What's going on?"

"Ever since the night he met you at Jerry's he's been a little off. And it's been nothing but downhill from there."

"Maybe it was that big sandwich," Overman hypothesizes, having little else to add.

"I don't know what you said to him, but when he left the house this morning, he told me it was for good."

"Come on, Rita. That's just Jake's sense of humor."

"Jake doesn't have a sense of humor."

She had him there. Not only did Jake Rosenfarb have terrible comic instincts, he had the unique gift of sucking the humor out of any situation with which he came in contact.

"If he leaves me, Ira, I'm coming after you."

"What are you talking about?"

"You're an accessory. Obviously something you said poisoned the beautiful life we had together."

Beautiful life? Jake's description of living with Rita made Bergen-Belsen sound like a vacation.

"Rita, believe me, I didn't say anything."

"That figures. Your friend reaches out to you and what do you do? You sit there like a lox." Rosenfarb logic at it's finest.

"He didn't reach out to me. He didn't say his marriage was in trouble. He didn't even talk about you."

"He didn't talk about me?"

"No."

After a rare pause, Rita sighs. "Is there another woman?

These crazy people are two peas in a pod. "Rita—"

"Like you'd fucking tell me."

"There's nothing to tell."

"You'd better watch your back, Overman," because you're already enmeshed in this.

Enmeshed? It's become Iran-Contra all of a sudden. "Rita, if I hear from Jake, I promise I'll talk to him."

"Don't you dare. You're in deep enough already." Click.

As Overman unplugs the landline, he realizes one more thing he did right in his life. He didn't marry Rita.

He also knows that it is only a matter of time before the indefatigable Jake Rosenfarb comes knocking at his door. Dealing with him had been the one constant in his life, and it had come with a steep price tag, monopolizing countless hours of therapy. While those sessions had been fruitless, the memory of them would be with Overman forever. He attempts to get back to bill paying, but the gas company check has to wait, as he is taken back to that exasperating moment in pre-heroic Overman history.

Gary Sheslow's look appeared to be one of concern, but Overman pegged it as some bastard form of psychological method acting.

"Tell me, how do you feel about your friend Rosenfarb having stolen your wife's virginity?"

"I'm dancing a fucking jig," Overman snapped. "How do you think I feel?"

"There's no need to get hostile with me. *I* didn't deflower her."

"Great answer, Gary. How much do you rake in a minute for dispensing these passive-aggressive pearls?"

"Ira. We can only make progress here if you're willing to put in the work."

"Right. I have to work. And what exactly is it *you* do? Sit on your ass and make up shit? How do I get that job?"

"If you have such little respect for the process, and me, why do you continue here?"

"Because I can't believe a person could spend all this money and get absolutely nothing for it. I keep hoping that one day you'll say something vaguely illuminating to amortize the expense."

"And it's worth it to you to keep coming back week after week, laying out more cash and feeling angrier each time you walk out unsatisfied?"

Overman explained his Warren Buffett-esque reasoning. "I'm a long-term investor. Leaving now would be like pulling my money out at the bottom of the market. You never want to do that."

"Fine," Sheslow sighed.

This was the gist of their therapeutic relationship. Nancy had been referred to Sheslow by one of her divorced friends and suggested that Ira accompany her for marriage counseling. Six months later, Mrs. Overman announced that she wanted a divorce, crediting Sheslow for helping them both realize that they had moved on. Except Overman hadn't moved anywhere. His problem had always been inertia and he resented Sheslow for not being professional enough to pick that up on Day One.

"You know, I think my problem is inertia," Overman proclaimed, a good six and a half years after the marriage had ended. "I don't want to be that way, but somehow whenever I think about changing my attitude I—-"

"Ira, can you hold that thought?"

"Huh?"

Overman looked up to see Sheslow flashing him that classic method-bullshit smile. "We have to stop now."

After a grueling two-hour workout during which he managed to tune out Carla's history on the pill, Overman reports for his interview at the temp agency. He tells an enthusiastic young lady named Sam that he is amenable to employment anywhere but in the entertainment industry, not that anyone there would hire someone his age anyway. To prove his point, Overman says he would prefer canning on the assembly line at a dog food factory to the filing job at Creative Artists Agency. Sam hates to break the news, but the dog food position has already been filled. On the upside, she explains that with low-level industry jobs, employers dare not risk age discrimination suits, so would he at least consider CAA?

Not a chance. It was in the agency business where Overman had suffered his most stinging career humiliation. He had been kind enough to mentor a wide-eyed kid named Morgan Schmeltzer, son of his music producer friend Simon Schmeltzer. In short order, the ambitious trainee went from being Overman's assistant to overseeing his department. When a group of the agency's young Turks started to assert their power, Overman was the first to be downsized, his former protégé uttering not a word on his behalf. Yes, someday Overman might revisit the studios that let him go, the talent agencies that unceremoniously ejected him, the clients who "moved on" to representatives who were better connected. But that would have to wait for when he was at full strength, at the top of his game. For now, he just needed rent money. Sam scrolls down her computer screen, reciting a number of "fabulous opportunities" which could conceivably blossom into a full-time career.

"This is great. Ira, how would you like to be a Wal-Mart greeter?"

Short of whoring at CAA, there is nothing Overman would like less. He doesn't mean to be difficult but he's had his fill of uniforms and phony cheeriness, thank you very much. This rules out the next job she was going to offer him with Honeybee Estates Homes. That stellar position required standing on a sun-baked corner of the San Fernando Valley, dressed in a bee outfit, singing the Beach Boys' "Wild Honey."

"Don't you have something kind of standard, you know, like stuffing envelopes?" Overman asks.

Sam seems taken aback, as if such a classless job choice is unworthy of a top tier establishment like the Temp-Right Employment Agency.

"Ira, first of all, everything's going green, and second of all, stuffing envelopes is a totally dead-end job."

"I'm fine with dead-end," he assures her.

"Mr. Overman," she demurs, using surname for emphasis. "I don't mean to be disrespectful, but don't you think that at your stage of life you should be thinking about a real career?"

"I am. If I'm stuffing envelopes in the White House, I get a feel for what the place is like in case I ever decide to run for president. If I'm stuffing at General Mills, I pick up valuable information in the event I want to start a cereal business. See what I'm saying?"

Sam doesn't have much faith in this argument, but her optimistic nature compels her to look for positives. "I wouldn't put my eggs in the president basket, but I do believe that if you pick the right place, someone could take you under his wing and let you grow with the company."

"Exactly," Overman agrees, wanting to end this silliness and punch his fucking time card, wherever that might be.

"But you can't just stuff envelopes. You have to make an impression. Let people know who you are, find common interests."

Jesus Christ. What did this thirty year-old know-nothing want him to do, sign a Networking Clause? Overman explains that he had enough of that in the entertainment business so he sure isn't about to start kissing ass with the managers of escrow companies or the foremen at Alpo.

She politely reminds him that the Alpo position is taken. He explains that he was using this as an example, much the way he had alluded to the White House earlier.

"Why does it matter to you if I just want to stuff envelopes?" he asks.

"Why? Because I care about my clients. This happens to be my career, and unlike *some* people, I take pride in what I do."

He can't believe this idiot is talking down to him. How did he pick the one temp agent who is personally invested in finding shit jobs for people with no skills?

"Look, maybe we just don't see eye-to-eye. Why don't I try another agency?" Overman starts to get up.

"Hold on."

Sam has found something she can live with. Filing, a bit of phone handling, some computer work, at a place in the valley called Cavanaugh Foster Financial. Twelve bucks an hour, starting tomorrow. According to her fact sheet, the employer has "hinted" at an opportunity for growth.

"Sounds great. Give me the address and tell me what time to show up." Overman stands.

Sam hands him the info and tells him one more thing he needs to know before reporting for work. Cavanaugh Foster requires that all men in the office wear ties. What did he expect with a name like Cavanaugh Foster? On the other hand, why not? Perhaps working at a stuffy financial firm would be a refreshing change from the bottom-feeding world of car salesmen.

Overman shakes Sam's hand, happy to be getting out of there. He is almost to the door when she calls out: "Ira?"

Overman turns to face her.

"Make an impression," she smiles. "Even those of us who aren't extraordinary can find a way to stand out."

Patronizing imbecile. This must be the reason sane people look for their drone work online.

"You know, Sam, I think you spend way too much time behind that desk," he informs her.

"I love my work," she chirps.

She reminds Overman of his junior high school math teacher Miss Hubbard, a young brunette as full of eagerness as she was lacking in charisma. Hubbard possessed, hands-down, the best legs in the district, energizing him to devote an entire semester to devising ways of getting her up from the desk so he and Rosenfarb might feast on those flawless calves and thighs. Professing arithmetical confusion he either didn't have or didn't care about, shuffling Miss Hubbard to the blackboard was the lone endeavor of his academic career at which he excelled — perhaps an early superpower, he is now beckoned to consider. Eyeing Sam, Overman suddenly wonders whether he still "has it." He spots a small fridge at end of the wall behind the low-wage headhunter and makes his move.

"Sam, I'm a little thirsty. Do you have a bottle of water for the road?"

"Of course. The last thing you want to do is show up for your interview all parched," she smiles perkily. The moment of truth: The ebullient Temp Queen could just as easily ask Overman to fetch it from the refrigerator himself.

Such is not the order of things in this changed, post-Lasik universe. Sam stands, turns around and bends down to retrieve the water, her lengthy and formidable pair of gams on full display. While they do not possess the subtle smoothness of the Hubbard calf-thigh combo, the smoothness of Overman's maneuver after a forty-year hiatus could not be minimized. He had succeeded without a hiccup, and moreover, without draining the energy that using willpower seemed to require. The adventure marched on, signposts pointing to a winning streak just beginning to gather steam.

The elliptical trainer and Overman have become fast friends. He likes the fact that it is both low-impact and far away from Carla, P.I, who mostly loiters by the weight machines spewing intimate details of her life story to the innocent and uninitiated. Revisiting his leg-viewing skills has inspired a disciplined work ethic in the new Overman, now on a crusade to build muscle and reduce body fat. He gives little thought to the job he will start in less than an hour, feeling that if he could handle Hal Steinbaum, he can deal with a couple of stuffed shirts like Cavanaugh and Foster. At the rate he's going, who can say what he won't be able to handle?

Overman arrives in the parking lot of the Cavanaugh Foster office in Studio City, which appears to be located in a mini-mall above a Do-It-Yourself Pet Shampoo shop called U Wash Doggie. Not exactly what he was expecting, but how refreshing to know that these British-sounding gents didn't put on airs. Office space was office space and these days one could make mega-deals from a laptop in a Winchell's Donut Shop. Which coincidentally happened to be located right next to U Wash Doggie. Pumped for a dull day of filing and phone answering, Overman ties his single Windsor knot and climbs the outdoor stairs, turning left and finding himself in front of a questionable-looking shiatsu massage center. Seeing one of the vertical blinds askew, he can't resist sneaking a peek. It seems that at this particular establishment, the ancient Japanese art of healing is defined as a large black woman sitting on the face of a scrawny white guy, who is gasping for breath. An L.A. moment if ever there was one.

At last arriving at the storefront suite of Cavanaugh Foster, Overman opens the glass door, triggering what sounds like a cowbell as he enters the shabby reception area. It is empty, save for a torn vinyl chair and wood-colored particleboard desk from the early '70's with an ancient computer monitor and phone on top of it. He hears a voice from the back, screaming into a receiver.

"I don't want the Buckaroo, I want the Sunset Renegade! I don't give a fuck if you don't have my size, make my size! You know how much business I give you people? Email me with a shipping date. If I don't hear from you by tomorrow, I'm taking it up with Tony!"

The caller slams down the phone and emerges from the back to greet Overman. He looks to be 6'3", maybe 240 pounds, and sports a western shirt, bolo tie, low-rise jeans and blue lizard cowboy boots. Overman pegs him for mid to late forties, his shaggy hair graying and reddened face creased from excessive sun exposure.

"Sorry about that. I'm trying to order a new pair of boots and these Tony Llama clowns keep yanking my chain. Dave Dobson," he says, extending his hand. The two men shake. Overman grimaces in pain as he extracts his limp hand from Dobson's vice-like grip.

"I must be in the wrong office," Overman explains. "Did Cavanaugh Foster Financial move to another space?"

"No sir. Been right here since we started the place in '98."

"Oh. Are Mr. Cavanaugh and Mr. Foster here?"

Dobson lets loose a good 'ol boy laugh with an eerie, Dukes of Hazzard-ish air about it.

"Never been a Cavanaugh or Foster. It's just the name of our outfit. Has a nice ring, don't you think?"

"Very nice."

"You must be Overman."

"Yes."

"You look a little confused. Jew?"

"Yes," Overman replies, not anxious to hear what's coming next.

"I work with a lot of your people in this business and I will be the first to say, the Yids know how to farm a dollar."

"Farm a dollar? I've never heard that expression before."

"Cultivation of wealth management. You folks have a natural feel for how to keep the assets moving, an eye for fiscal crop rotation, if you will."

Fascinated by the agricultural metaphors, Overman still feels he must speak up. "You know, I was expecting more of a…I don't know… financial institution. What exactly is it you do here?"

"We are a financial institution," Dobson lets him know in no uncertain terms. "We specialize in hard money loans."

As Overman suspected, this was the royal "we" coming from less than regal auspices. Cavanaugh Foster was a one-man shop headed by a displaced Texan who charged an average of 22% interest and six points on each loan. The clientele consisted of down-on-their-luck borrowers with horrible credit who needed cash fast and were incapable of obtaining loans from legitimate banks or mortgage companies. Having no other option, they agreed to Cavanaugh Foster's outrageous terms, offering up their homes as collateral in the event they couldn't come up with the payments. The loans were almost always short term, putting the borrower under pressure to pay them off in 30 to 120 days. And if somehow the money didn't come, Cavanaugh Foster would take hold of the property. As Dobson explained it, the loans were bankrolled by investors looking for quick, high returns. He could guarantee them 15% and keep the other seven plus all the points for himself. In the event the borrower reneged, the investor would share in the profits reaped from the foreclosure.

Overman had thought the automobile business was oily, but this was the true Beyond. Be that as it may, Dave Dobson seemed to love his work.

"This industry has been very good to me," he proclaims. "And I'm at the point in my life where I want to give something back."

"To the people whose homes you sent into foreclosure?" asks a naïve Overman.

"No, sir. To the hard working individual who wants to learn my craft from the ground up."

Bingo. That "hint" of career opportunity Sam had been so jazzed about. Apparently, if he "made an impression" on Dave Dobson, he himself could reap the rewards of sending desperate folks into bankruptcy.

"I'm late for a meeting," the burly Texan announces. He points to the decrepit desk and instructs Overman to make himself comfortable, use the computer, take any messages that might come in. Dobson has a lunch appointment as well so he won't be back until three. Overman asks if there's any filing he needs to do.

"Don't bother. I know where most of this shit is. Why don't you go through those cabinets and look at some of the deals we have going. I want you to start getting a feel for what we do around here."

The guy seemed to be serious about grooming him for greatness.

"Any questions, Overman?"

"Just one. Will anybody be coming into the office today?"

"Nope," Dobson says. "We don't get a lot of foot traffic since I rarely take my meetings in-house."

Small wonder, looking at this hellhole.

"Then why do I need to wear a tie?" Overman can't help but ask.

"That's two questions," Dobson roars heartily, Overman doing his best to laugh along. Dobson then strikes a more serious pose, explaining the theory behind the employee dress code.

"Appearance counts in any business. If you look serious about what you're doing, folks take you seriously."

"But there are no folks coming here to see me look serious," Overman reminds him.

"It's company policy," Dobson explains. "We can't set a bad precedent."

The man does not seem to connect the fact that one: he *is* the company and can do whatever he wants and two: precedent for what? There were no other employees. How this sacrosanct dress code accounted for a riveted cowboy shirt and blue lizard Tony Llamas was a whole other topic for discussion, but Overman wasn't about to get into it with a man who was almost twice his size, had a hydraulic handshake, and thought Jews grew money. Dobson grabs a giant Stetson and waves goodbye. Overman wishes him luck with his meetings.

For a brief moment, the new usurer-in-training thinks about going downstairs to inquire whether there are any jobs available at U Wash Doggie. At least that place contributed something of value to the world. But it was quiet here and with so little going on he would have time to plan his future. The old HP, beaten up though it was, would be able to help him move forward.

Since the boss suggested he look at some files, Overman figures he should attend to this first. He leafs through a deal in Waco where the developer was building a mixed-use complex "just a hop, skip and a jump" from the former Branch Davidian compound. Apparently he felt the site had tourist potential and where there was tourism, there was money to be made. When he ran out of funds to finish the complex, Cavanaugh Foster loaned him $300,000 at 27% interest and 5 points. The developer was never able to pay off the loan, so now Cavanaugh Foster and its investors owned a shitload of David Koresh-trodden dirt. Could it get any more depressing? Overman decides to take a break from the files and go to the computer.

Checking his email box, he sees twenty-six messages from Rosenfarb with subject lines like: "Where are you?" "Where the fuck are you?" "Why are you avoiding me?" "They say you quit your job," "Rita is a cunt," "Tennis re-match?" etc. etc.

Poor Jake. For someone who had boasted for so long about being on top of the world, he seemed to be heading into a tailspin. No doubt it aggravated him doubly to see his friend's trajectory on the rise. "A Star is Born," with an ex-car salesman and a window man. Overman can't bear to answer the emails. He's sure his voicemail box must be loaded with Rosenfarb messages, but he'd rather let it fill up than listen to the nagging.

Buried between Rosenfarb emails is one from Ashley. He opens it immediately, pleased that his daughter has contacted him from Israel. She writes that it has been the experience of her life, inspiring her to become more committed to Judaism. She suggests that perhaps they can have Shabbat dinner together when she returns.

"*Shalom* Ashley, I would love to," he swiftly types.

Overman found the Shabbat thing precious and antiquated, but if it means his daughter agreeing to see him, he will *daven* as asked. Aware of his poor record concealing indifference, his hope is that Ashley will at least give him an "A" for effort and as a result, welcome her father back into her life. What he will do once he's there is of course the bigger question. Just as he fumbles in the dark ascertaining the breadth of his transformation, he is flying without a net when it comes to parenting. Having been so removed for so long, it is like learning to walk all over again.

After reviewing a file and answering his important email, he thinks about what to do next. He glances at the ten most popular searches on Yahoo and has no idea what eight of these things are. It is a perfect case of synchronicity: the popular culture of the masses left Overman as cold as Overman left the masses. He surmises that this must change if he is to become an active participant in the world, be it as man or superman. Since the comic book heroes, by definition, served the masses, perhaps he of the real world could run his racket surreptitiously; doing random good deeds that didn't call attention to deed-doer. Let the *hoi polloi* have their Batman. He would be the boutique superhero, handpicking only the clientele he considered worthy.

At the moment, Overman is a mortal with seven-plus hours to kill. He plays some online poker where his willpower is apparently of little help. It seems he can only use it to stop playing, which is a blessing considering how quickly he loses $200. Before he knows it, he is back at the home page, trying to decide whether to click on "Global Warming and the Polar Bear" or "Easy Mexican Lasagna Casserole." He is about to push the lasagna button when, on a whim, he decides to go a whole other way. He'd burn up two minutes tops with the "sweet but spicy, south of the border" recipe, but this third option had the potential to get him through the entire day. He clicks on "People Search" and settles in for an afternoon of revisiting his less than illustrious past.

Once again dipping into the stream-of-consciousness, Overman searches for the first name that comes into his head: Glorietta Zatzkin, currently Glorietta Feinman of Boca Raton. He had googled her before, fishing, without success, for pictures of what she looked like now, thirty-seven years after she gave him what he had never imagined could be his. Why he kept searching for these pictures he wasn't sure. What good could it do to see perfection undone, youth withered away? Wouldn't he be better served remembering that one perfect night?

It was the spring of '71. Glorietta was on break from Earlham College in Indiana and visiting an art exhibition in Manhattan. She needed a place to crash and called Overman out of the blue. He graciously offered to share his dorm room uptown and having no other options, she accepted. Glorietta had smoked a joint at the gallery opening then gamely partook as Overman and his roommates hauled out the Boone's Farm Apple Wine and the bong. After listening to "Whippin' Post" thirty-eight times, Glorietta climbed into Overman's single bed with him. Astonished to have the longtime object of his lust so close against him, Overman was doubly stunned when she removed her shirt and began smothering him with her humongous breasts. The cruel irony was that he found himself unable to stay in the fortuitous moment. The Moment of Moments. No matter how hard he tried to concentrate, his focus kept drifting from her astounding body, to the image of the boys from Lakeview seeing this, to his father drooling all over Estelle Zatzkin, to Pumpkin humping him, to wondering why Glorietta dumped him as a friend from the seventh grade all the way until they graduated. He had so many things to ask her. But seeing as how she had just slipped his cock inside her, the questions would have to wait. Ira Overman was having real, honest-to-God sex with Glorietta Zatzkin. He was able to soak in his good fortune for roughly thirty seconds before the hottest babe Temple Emmanuel Hebrew School had ever known puked all over him and passed out, a fitting bookend to the now nearly Biblical First Grade Mrs. Jarvis Incident.

Glorietta actually remembered everything the next morning and apologized for seducing him, assuring Overman that she would never have done such a thing had she been in her right mind. She left the dorm and they never spoke again. Still, this didn't take away from his earth-shattering victory. With precious little else to hold on to, the night would forever live in Overman infamy.

He tries googling "Glorietta and Fred Feinman" thinking that perhaps adding her husband's name will yield a photo of the two at a fundraising event or some stupid costume party that somebody put up on the internet. No pictures to be found, instead the sad news that Fred Feinman of the Potlatch Company had recently suffered a heart attack and passed away. There were two kids, roughly the same age as Overman's. He feels awful. He wants to send a note or call Glorietta, but senses it would be awkward given what went down when they last met thirty-seven years ago.

"Jane Sweeney," Overman googles, aware that she may well have married and go by her husband's name. He finds pages of Jane Sweeneys, pictures of a few, none the Janie in whom so many had ejaculated but undoubtedly forgotten, one dark night long ago. Except Overman had not forgotten. Of the many mistakes he regretted, the incident with Janie was Transgression Number One. For all he knew, the woman had moved past it and was living a fine life, having vanished that horrible moment into thin air as quickly as most people vanished the memory of meeting Ira Overman. On the other hand, she could be dead, or stricken with leukemia, or homeless. She could be suffering from severe depression as a result of that one horrific night. What if this were the truth? Did he really want to know? What could be done about it now, so many years after the fact?

Overman shudders at the thought and prepares to look at another file when he masochistically types in the name "Martin Merkowitz." Within fifteen seconds, Overman is looking at picture after picture of the now grown head rapist, the one with the Bar Mitzvah portion from Leviticus.

"For the life of the flesh is in the blood: and I have given it to you upon the altar to make an atonement for your souls."

"Smirkowitz," as he was sometimes called, didn't look like he'd done much in the way of atoning. He was now the smiling CEO of a prestigious software company in the Silicon Valley with twelve hundred employees and offices in Tokyo, Seoul, and Beijing. He had a beautiful young wife, Daphne, who supervised the Merkowitz Foundation, a nonprofit that raised money for children with disabilities. And he had a secret that only Overman seemed to feel was worth exposing.

Overman shuts off the computer monitor and drops to the floor to do fifty push-ups. This would help get his head out of the past and his body into the future. He can't help but notice that the stronger he gets, the more he thinks about retribution. Like it or not, he is drawn to this key component of the superhero game. Overman gasps and wheezes as he hits his fortieth push-up. In the past, this would be a natural lead-in to patting himself on the back and going downstairs for a donut. But this time he is on a mission. He will struggle through the last ten push-ups even if they kill him.

Completing number forty-eight, Overman is on the verge of collapse when Dave Dobson struts back in to see his new employee on the floor.

"Exercising on company time, are we?"

"I'm sorry, Dave—"

"No problem. We're cool with it." Dobson informs him. "We believe that staying fit will help sharpen your lending skills. Oh, and we appreciate that you kept the tie on."

Big Dave grabs the folder he forgot and high-tails it out the door. Overman staggers up from the floor and takes his place back at the desk. He is about to pull another file out of the cabinet, but finds himself drawn back to the computer monitor and staring at the flawless image of Daphne Merkowitz. Whatever happened to bad karma? Conventional wisdom said that a person paid a price for his actions, which had certainly proved true in Overman's case. Yet Marty Merkowitz had hit the jackpot while Janie Sweeney had faded into oblivion.

Dobson calls in to say he won't be returning to the office today and Overman can leave at 4:30. After locking up, he trudges downstairs, overhearing a heated argument coming from U Wash Doggie. Apparently, some guy with a beagle was getting ready to wash his doggie when it was attacked and bitten by an irritable pit mix. The beagle owner is threatening to call animal control and have the pit taken away. The pit owner claims that the beagle's master wasn't watching because he was too busy checking out the ass of the blond with the Pomeranian. The Pomeranian starts to freak and pees all over the girl, who exits screaming with her yappy, crazed powder puff. Neither of the two guys is backing down. They are about to come to blows when the pit slips between their legs and goes back after the beagle.

Pandemonium ensues as the rest of the doggie washers grab their animals and race for the door. Meanwhile, the pit and beagle guys try to pry the dogs loose but the pit's jaw is locked in. Overman's natural instinct is to get in the car and drive the hell away, but something stops him. When Superman happens upon a dangerous situation, his obligation is to help. Why shouldn't a fifty-five year-old temp worker follow the same ethical road map?

Overman bursts into U Wash Doggie, energetic and focused, summoning knowledge he had no idea he possessed. Somewhere along the way, information had seeped into his brain about how to break up a dogfight. As the beagle yelps in pain, Overman grabs a pencil out of the pit owner's pocket and rams it right up the pit's asshole. The pit's jaw unclenches immediately, Overman removes the soiled, ironically designated Number Two Eberhard Faber and the violated dog goes to skulk in the corner.

"You guys need to pay better attention to your pets," Overman lectures them. "I believe this is yours," he says, holding the ass-injected pencil under the pit owner's nose. Overman gets back in the Mercedes, having performed his first superheroic public service. He felt great. Had a fantastic workout, landed a tolerable job, saved a beagle.

Euphoria proves fleeting. As soon as the Overman Mercedes turns onto Wilton Place, he sees the dreaded BMW parked outside his apartment building. Jake Rosenfarb is staking out the joint, waiting for him to arrive home so he can confront him with something guaranteed to be irritating, nonsensical or both. Overman reflexively cuts a hard right and parks around the block, proceeding to sneak through alleyways and back entrances to get to his apartment. He spends the rest of the evening in the dark, occasionally peeking out the corner of the living room window to see if Rosenfarb's BMW is still there. At four in the morning, Rosenfarb finally gives up and goes home.

The window man parks outside the building for an entire week. Overman gets his entrances and exits down to a science, dodging the relentless Rosenfarb at every turn. Somehow he manages to get to the gym every morning, put in his eight hours helping Big Dave rake borrowers over the coals, and make it home at night without ever having to deal with his stalker. How long this will continue is anybody's guess, Overman fully aware that he is squaring off against the most seasoned of badgerers. If history was any indication, a week of pestering constituted a mere speck in the Rosenfarb oeuvre. As in the past, it would take a disciplined and forward-thinking battle plan for Overman to keep one step ahead of his unrelenting pursuer.

two

lift Off

He was getting stronger by the day. Not only was fat being replaced by muscle, a new mindset had emerged. Encouraged by the success of the U Wash Doggie incident, Overman now felt comfortable interceding when he saw an injustice occur. In the past few days, he had stopped a mugging at a cash machine, a burglary in his own apartment building, and most notably, a hate crime at an orthodox wig shop. His approach was a judicious mash-up of willpower and burgeoning physical might, the latter attribute heretofore unfamiliar to any of his known ancestry. He was even getting to like Big Dave and, despite himself, developing a fascination with the hard money business. The flipside of being an avaricious usurer was that Dave lent money to people who might have lost everything had he not provided them with fast cash. And thus far, the two deals Overman witnessed had accomplished the dual tasks of tiding over the borrowers until their money came in and turning a profit for the investors. The loans were paid back in a timely manner, nobody went into bankruptcy, and Dave Dobson got to put thousands of dollars in the Cavanaugh Foster money market account for not doing much of anything. Overman had to admit that it beat roping in Mercedes buyers on their way to *Havdallah* services.

Big Dave was impressed with how quickly Overman learned the business and encouraged him to "take the bull by the horns." Unfortunately, Dave's spin on bull taking involved the sort of sales tactics of which Overman had had his fill. The mandate here was schmoozing, networking, endeavoring by whatever means necessary to find clients willing to invest in Cavanaugh Foster's sub-sub-sub prime loans. Dave explained that regularly re-vitalizing the investor base was the key to shoring up enough capital to close new deals. And in times when Long Term CDs were paying 1%, there were always takers.

"You must know folks who want to make more than 1%," Big Dave reasoned.

"I don't keep up with a lot of people," Overman informed him.

"Then re-acquaint yourself, my friend!" Big Dave cheerleads, slapping him on the back just a little too firmly.

Every year Dave put together a promotional sales dinner akin to what the money management firms do to sell people on financial growth opportunities. This year's event was to take place in December, held in a banquet room at Maury's Steakhouse.

"You'll be amazed at how receptive a crowd gets after a couple of martinis and a big rib-eye."

He explains that the idea is to go through your address book with a set goal. For example, last year Dave hosted twenty potential investors, this year, his goal is to attract twenty-five.

"What would be a number you feel you could come up with, going through all your contacts?" Dave asks Overman.

"I could probably get one guy to come. But he's stalking me," Overman explains.

Big Dave is convinced that someone with as much potential as Overman must be downplaying his abilities.

"You've got to know ten people who want to make money," Ira.

"I know lots of people. I just don't want anything to do with them," Overman explains.

"I'm gonna make a businessman out of you yet," Big Dave nods. "Your goal is five."

"That's impossible —"

"Not five investors, Ira. Five people. Who only have to agree to come to the dinner and hear the *spiel*. You think you can get five people to eat a free steak?"

"I'm sure I could, but I don't want to waste your money."

"You won't be wasting it. I'm willing to bet that if you get us five steak-eaters, we get at least one investor out of it. Can you deliver me five steak-eaters, Ira?"

Overman agrees to try. He's not quite sure why, but some part of him appreciates that anyone would take the time to groom him for anything, even a career at the bottom of the food chain. He likes Dave's enthusiasm. The cowboy bit is goofy but kind of charming. Overman figures that even though he's moonlighting while working toward the yet-to-be-revealed Main Event, he might as well throw himself into it.

Dobson gets ready to leave for a meeting with mortgage broker Jay Firestone, a longtime investor who's decided to dip his toe in the porn business. It seems Firestone has found a young starlet named Juicy Jones, whose claim to fame is ejaculating for distance. Explaining that she currently holds the North American record of thirty feet, Big Dave sees it as a chance to get in on the ground floor of a revenue juggernaut. He will be meeting them on the set of their latest movie, "Squirtz," a romantic triangle between Juicy and two Little People.

"Have you thought about bringing a change of clothes?" Overman asks, looking out for his new boss.

"Not necessary," Big Dave assures him. "Jay's got rain slickers for everybody on set. Want to come with?"

"No thanks," Overman responds. "I need to catch up on some things around here."

Dave is impressed with his hire's work ethic. "I like you, Overman. Has anyone ever told you that you're destined for greatness?"

"Never," Overman answers with total candor.

"Well, people are stupid. They can have brilliance staring them in the face and not get it worth shit. I know promise when I see it."

And with that, the Texan was on his way to watch a porn star squirt pussy juice on two midgets.

Overman gets back to the computer, having yet to complete his daily googling. He learns that Merkowitz is off to Italy to speak at a software convention in Rome. He signs up for My Space and Facebook in case Janie Sweeney has a page. No such luck. He makes a contribution of $25.00 to the American Heart Association in memory of Fred Feinman, anticipating a thank-you and eventual re-connection with Glorietta. He gets an email from Ashley recommending a book called "To Be A Jew," which he should be able to find at his local library.

And then, out of nowhere, he remembers that Janie's parents had both worked at the public library near the high school. Donovan Sweeney was the guy who ran the Great Books discussion group and his wife, Fiona, organized the free film screenings on Sunday nights. If he could track them down, they could provide him with Janie's phone number and/or email address and Overman could finally make amends.

With such unusual first names, finding the Sweeneys should be fairly easy, provided they were still alive. Overman goes to ZabaSearch.com and first clicks the state of New Jersey, their last known whereabouts. Finding no Donovan or Fiona statewide, he blows off the idea of writing to every "D" and "F" Sweeney in New Jersey, instead doing a search of the entire U.S. With one click he is led to Delray Beach, Florida, where the only Donovan and Fiona Sweeney in the United States now make their home. He excitedly starts dialing the phone number when he realizes that he might want to think through what he's going to say. He's an old friend from Lakeview High. But Lakeview was the scene of the crime. What if they had wiped the place out of their memory as a survival instinct? Overman considers a number of other scenarios: Their daughter is owed money in a stock settlement case and he needs to know where to send the check. He's writing a book on the Irish-American high school experience in the Long Island suburbs. He's from the IRS and regrets to say that he needs to audit their daughter's tax returns.

One idea seems worse than next. He decides to leave out the word "Lakeview" and present himself as an old friend who needs to get in touch with Janie about something that happened to a person they both knew. Vague, but truthful, because something important has indeed happened to him. Overman's hope is that even if the Sweeneys are reluctant to give out Janie's information they will still relay the urgency of his message.

He dials the number, and an older woman answers the phone.

"Hi there," Overman crows. "Is this Fiona Sweeney?"

A long pause on the other end.

"Hello," Overman jumps in.

"Mrs. Sweeney passed away two years ago."

Click. Overman reminds himself that people searches only provided the registered address of the party one was seeking. There were no guarantees that the information would be up to the minute. He takes a breath and gets ready to give it another try. This time he will ask to speak with Donovan Sweeney, crossing his fingers that the lady who answers doesn't hang up on him again.

As luck would have it, Donovan answers. After the introductory information is exchanged, Overman goes into his rap, first apologizing for mistaking the man's new wife for the dear, departed Fiona, then attempting to clarify who he is.

"You say you were a good friend of Janie's?"

"We were in a lot of the same classes."

"At which school?"

Overman fears what's coming and decides to attack it from a different angle.

"Melvin Terrace Elementary. We both had Mrs. Silvera in the third grade."

It is a brilliant ploy, conjuring up for Donovan the carefree days when his daughter was eight years old, well before the incident that would change her life. In a manner of minutes, Overman has learned that Janie is now Janie Leeds, a Professor of English at SUNY Binghamton in upstate New York, living in the nearby town of Endicott. She has a husband but no children, two dogs and a vegetable garden.

It sounded like she was happy. But was she really? The "no children" part was suspect. True, not everyone wanted to be a parent, and as Overman well knew, not everyone should be. The woman was obviously doing fine with her dogs and her broccoli, what point was there in dredging up the worst night of her life? Then again, what if that one incident had so traumatized her that she could never bear the idea of becoming pregnant? Or possibly worse, what if that sickening fusion of errant sperm to which Overman had contributed made her pregnant, forced her to get an abortion and resulted in her no longer being able to conceive? None of this would be knowable unless he contacted her.

"What did you say your name was again?" Donovan asks.

"Overman. Ira Overman."

"I don't recall her ever mentioning you. But it was a long time ago," Donovan concedes.

Overman thanks him for his time and tells him that he will be getting in touch with Janie shortly. After hanging up, it occurs to Overman that a phone call would be awkward and borderline inappropriate. How absurd it would sound, apologizing on the phone for participating in a schoolboys' assault that took place almost forty years ago. A letter or email might be better suited for the task, but Overman had little faith in his ability to craft what must be nothing less than a perfectly worded document, packed with emotion and begging forgiveness.

He needed to find a way out of this conundrum quickly because Janie would soon know that he was looking for her. Now that he had spoken with her father, dropping the ball would leave her in a limbo that could range anywhere from uncomfortable to inhuman. Overman imagined her thought process. The last one to deposit his sperm that night is suddenly looking for me. What does that animal want after all these years?

She cuts a lithe, graceful figure in jeans and flannel as she bends down to harvest the first of the summer's crop. It is a short growing season in the Southern Tier, a deceptive name for what is in fact, the southernmost part of northern New York State. Frost can make an appearance in mid-May and have its return engagement as early as September. This year, Janie has focused on herbs and tomatoes, the excess to be dried and canned for the winter. Up in the corner of the second floor, Garvin is ensconced in his study, where he spends Saturday mornings grading papers and reviewing lesson plans for the following week. Heathcliff the schnauzer and Nelly the lab hover close by, sniffing the soil for bones and the occasional buried tennis ball. The morning is crisp and cool, redolent with the exhilarating aroma of freshly grown fruit and belying the heat and humidity that will eventually claim the day. Janie breathes it all in, blessedly unaware of the rented Hyundai Sonata that is driving back and forth on her street.

When Overman finally parks, he sits there for a moment, taking in the result of where his impulse and conscience have led him. While his comic book compatriots might have strapped on a cape and flown non-stop to Endicott, Overman's options were decidedly less glamorous. At LAX, he purchased a standby ticket to Syracuse and after a two-hour layover, boarded a puddle jumper to Binghamton airport. Now he sits in a rental car beside a lovely, 1920's two-storey brick house, watching Janie Sweeney Leeds quietly bond with her surrounds in a way that seems preternaturally exquisite, miles from the landscapers Nancy hired to deal with anything outdoors and living. Overman admires Janie's long ponytail, brown but laced with just the right amount of gray, a suggestion of wisdom intertwined with earthy beauty. She is one of those women who is much more attractive in adulthood than she was in her youth. As she stands up to move her basket of tomatoes into the shade, she appears taller, more slender, radiating a sure confidence in her ability to work the land.

What will she say when she sees me? Overman wonders. While she has no doubt learned of his effort to track her down, the last thing Janie is expecting is for him to show up at her doorstep. She has probably been waiting for a phone call. Perhaps she has rehearsed her lines as often as he has rehearsed his. When Overman finally gets out of the car, he takes in the Southern Tier air, which seems unlike any oxygen he has breathed since his move to Los Angeles.

Janie is picking bunches of basil as he approaches, his arrival announced by the barking of Heathcliff and Nelly.

"Hi," he waves, shooting her a dumb-ass smile.

"Hi," she responds, apparently quite comfortable. "May I help you?"

She's not connecting the dots. True, Overman looks different so many years after the fact, but still, there was that phone call to Dad.

"Ira Overman. It's nice to see you again, Janie."

She looks confused. "I'm sorry. Do we know each other?"

"We went to school together. Didn't your Dad tell you I was going to get in contact? I called him in Florida to get your info."

"Oh. My Dad has a pretty bad case of Alzheimer's. We've been having pretty much the same conversation for the last ten years."

"I'm sorry," says Overman, who's sorry on two levels. He had come here as soon as he could under the assumption that she would have had time to prepare for this moment. And now everything was new and even more awkward.

"So remind me," Janie smiles. "Where did we go to school together? My family moved around a bit."

"We started out in the third grade at Melvin Terrace."

"Mrs. Silvera?" she asks.

Overman nods as her memory starts to kick in. They joke about the teacher's strong perfume, which had the irritating habit of lingering on the students' clothes when they went home. They reminisce about fire drills, the idiocy of "duck and cover," the feel-good lesson of trick-or-treating for UNICEF. Not wanting to offend, Janie refrains from mentioning that she still doesn't recognize him, but based on the generic quality of her conversation, Overman is not fooled. He moves on to anecdotes about junior high, throwing in his wrestling experiences for a little color, then working his way up to the denouement.

"We were at Lakeview High together until you moved." Overman lets out an unconscious sigh, having at last spit it out. He carefully waits for a reaction, studying her face for any kind of sign.

"Oh my God, Lakeview," she blurts out.

Jesus, what have I wrought? Overman wonders. Why was I determined to make this woman re-live her humiliating horror?

"I hated that we had to move," Janie says. "I despised the kids in New Jersey."

Overman is speechless. After the Neanderthals at Lakeview, what could the Jersey boys have been like?

"So you liked Lakeview?" Overman asks for clarification.

"Oh yeah, it was a blast, didn't you think?"

"Not really. If you remember, I was not exactly the most popular guy in school."

Janie apologizes for not remembering anything about him, which confirmed his point. But she's happy he looked her up just the same.

"It's always great to re-connect with your past," she says. "Do you mind if I cut this row of oregano? I've got a load of papers to grade today."

Overman says he doesn't mind at all and asks her some perfunctory questions about teaching. He tells her how much he admired her high school paper on the Brontë sisters and she seems pleased.

"So what brings you to town?" she asks, catching him un-awares. "Business? Vacationing in the area?"

What the hell is he supposed to say? That he came specifically to see her in order to apologize for something she obviously either doesn't remember or has blocked out? He's about to make up some story about re-visiting the Catskills out of nostalgia for his child-hood vacations when Garvin Leeds comes bounding out of the house to introduce himself. He looks to be nearly seventy and tells Overman that he's in his last year as Chair of the English Depart-ment at SUNY Binghamton. He's excited to hear that Overman is an old schoolmate of Janie's, and invites him for brunch. Overman figures why not? The woman he thought he had damaged for life has turned out to be a beautiful, vital force of nature, with a hus-band who worships her, animals that cling to her, vegetables that absorb her energy and thrive on it. And here he was, starting over at fifty-five. He might as well have something to eat.

Garvin pours Overman a glass of wine and peppers him with questions about his life and work. Overman reduces his answers to "two great kids," a former career in the entertainment business and a new venture having to do with finance, neglecting such phrases as "hard money" and "twelve dollars an hour." Like most people who have never thought of leaving the east coast, both Garvin and Janie are intrigued by the fact that Overman moved all the way to California. They knew people at UCLA, but still, the thought of picking up and settling in a place like Los Angeles was more alien to them than re-locating to France.

Garvin wonders if Overman keeps up with other people from high school. He mentions Jake Rosenfarb, of whom Janie has no recollection. Overman takes this as his cue to push the envelope a little further. For what reason? Why deliberately try to upset this lovely, happy, well-adjusted woman? Somehow he can't stop himself.

"I read that Marty Merkowitz became very successful. He's a big software guy in the Silicon Valley."

"Isn't that interesting?" Janie replies, Overman unable to read anything in her expression at the mention of the rapist.

Garvin asks if she, Overman and Merkowitz were all friends. Janie says that she wasn't at all close with Merkowitz, too sweet to mention that she still didn't remember Overman. Overman keeps pushing.

"Merkowitz was the point guard for Lakeview. Terrible basketball team. All Jews."

This gets a polite laugh. Against all his better instincts, Overman digs deeper.

"The team didn't win many games, but they loved to party."

He can't be sure, but thinks he detects a change of expression as Janie gets up to clear the table and prepare dessert. Garvin, obviously unaware of the Overman agenda, takes the opportunity to offer up a bit of his own academic past. Unsurprisingly, he spent his childhood buried in the classics and could barely throw a ball. He had heard all about the wild parties his peers were attending, but never got invited himself. Overman assures Garvin that his experience was nearly identical, the only difference being his shamelessness in tagging along.

"And then once I got there, I felt incredibly uncomfortable and participated in things I truly regretted," Overman laments pointedly. "If I could turn back the clock, I would change everything."

"Wow. I'm afraid to ask what you did," Garvin laughs.

"Let's just say I'm sorry for my behavior and leave it at that," Overman replies, satisfied that he's taken every opportunity to pound home his point. If Janie needed an apology, it was there for the taking. If she didn't, his remarks could just as easily be processed as vague generalities.

Janie doesn't respond as she brings her homemade apple pie to the table. Overman loves this woman and everything she represents. Projecting strength and dignity, she has clearly survived being degraded by morons, not the least of whom is receiving the first slice of pie. Overman wished he had the power to know what was going through Janie's head. If he could connect with Maricela in such a deep way, why shouldn't he be able to do the same with his ex-classmate? It occurs to Overman that the act of seeking sex is far easier than the act of asking forgiveness.

Janie asks Overman a few more questions about his kids, then volunteers that when she finally decided she wanted children of her own, she was already in her late forties and unable to have any. She and Garvin thought about fertility treatments or adopting, but the potential obstacles and expense seemed too overwhelming. For the first time, Overman detects a sadness in her, for which he feels a hundred percent responsible. He meets Janie's gaze, assuring her that having kids isn't all it's cracked up to be. It's the kind of line that elicits a knowing laugh from people who have had teenagers, but sounds patronizing to those who are childless.

Overman offers to help with the dishes, but Garvin will have none of it. That's his job, the least he can do to repay the talented cook who prepares his wonderful meals. He gives Janie an affectionate kiss on the forehead and heads for the sink. Overman takes the opportunity to thank husband and wife for their hospitality and says his goodbyes. Garvin gives him the warmest of handshakes, reminding Overman that he's always welcome in their home. Janie offers to walk him to the car and Overman accepts, basking in the glow of newly cemented friendship. It is only when they reach the driver's side of the Hyundai and he attempts to hug his hostess that he is thrown off guard, finding himself face to face with the steely stare of a woman who remembers everything.

"What is wrong with you? How dare you come here?"

"I thought you didn't remember me."

"Not at first. But then, as you kept spitting out detail after detail… I can't believe you would have the nerve to show up at my house."

"I had to apologize. I needed to tell you personally."

"Do you always have such bad judgment?"

"Actually, yes. But I didn't think this fell into that category. I thought it was important to make amends for having taken part in something reprehensible."

"Something I needed to bury. And I had done a damn good job of it until you kept pressing and pressing and pressing. Jesus Christ. I liked you so much better when I had no idea who you were."

"I understand," Overman nods, recalling the countless times he had stood on the cusp of friendship, only to be rejected once his peculiar personality had been fully revealed.

"What positive thing did you think would unfold here, other than you feeling less guilty for being a rapist? Did you think that saying you're sorry after thirty-seven years would change anything for me?"

Overman tries to answer as best he can. "I thought maybe you'd want to know that at least one of that group found his actions deplorable."

"What does that accomplish now?"

"I don't know," Overman admits. "I just wish there were something I could do to make it up to you."

"You could've not come here. But it's a little late for that." Janie starts to tear up, every sickening moment of that night coming back to her like some cruel, digital slideshow. "Garvin doesn't know anything."

"He shouldn't have to. It was a lifetime ago and you weren't responsible for what happened."

"I know I wasn't responsible, Ira," she responds icily.

"I'm sorry. I guess that's pretty obvious." Overman feels like a complete idiot.

Then, as if a plug has been pulled, she lets the tears fly. "I wanted to fight back, but my parents didn't want to press charges. They were old-fashioned and thought that when those kinds of things came out, it always looked worse for the girl."

"So they moved you out of town and the team got off scot-free."

"I never thought about what happened to them. I just tried to start over. I stopped having anything to do with boys until I was thirty. Then I would only date older guys, father figures who I thought could take care of me."

"Seems like you did really well with Garvin."

"He's wonderful. But I know he senses there are things I withhold from him. He's just too much of a gentleman to put me on the spot."

"Unlike yours truly. I'm sorry, Janie."

Finally she begins to soften. "I'll bet it took a lot for you to come see me."

"I'm trying to make some changes in my life," Overman explains. "And I felt I had to own up to my past mistakes. But now I realize that showing up at your door was selfish. All it did was make you feel worse."

Not disagreeing with him, Janie somehow needs to ask: "Do you think Marty Merkowitz ever had a second thought about that night?"

"I can't say," Overman replies. "Based on what I've read about the guy, he doesn't seem to be losing any sleep."

"Somebody should pin him down so he can see what it feels like to be violated by seven drunkards and a ninety-eight pound wrestler," she proffers, the first hint of a desire for vengeance.

"I'll see what I can do," Overman fires back.

Janie manages a nervous laugh. Overman says there's nothing funny about someone who commits a heinous crime and never looks back.

"Nobody said life was fair," she reminds him.

Overman nods. "It was great to see you, Janie," he says, instinctively moving to wrap his arms around her. The fact that her warm, loamy body does not reject him is the win he had been seeking. It is her silent acknowledgement of the risk he took in traveling three thousand miles, so many years after the fact, to make this apology. Janie watches as the rental car drives off into the Endicott morning. Shortly afterward, Garvin steps outside, detecting that his lovely wife has been crying.

"What's wrong, darling?"

"Nothing," she replies, seeing no point in re-opening the wound that had just stopped bleeding. "We were talking about people from our past."

Garvin is relieved. "I wish I could feel nostalgic about my past. These days, I'm just happy I can remember I had one," he chuckles.

Janie takes his hand and holds it tightly, wondering if her husband will ever know how much his love means to her.

A wistful Overman stretches out to soak up the pleasures of the old Route 17, gateway to the Catskill resorts of his youth. He considers re-visiting Kutsher's, then driving down toward the city to get a look at his old neighborhoods, followed by a jaunt into Manhattan for some celebratory sesame noodles. Part of his newly energized self wants to get on a plane to Rome and confront Merkowitz at the software convention. But he is due back in the office tomorrow and he doesn't want to let down Big Dave, who has a critical investor meeting with the owner of an Applebee's franchise.

Passing a billboard boasting fabulous nightlife at the new Mohawk Indian Casino, Overman is reminded of something in his research. One of his favorite superheroes, Nightcrawler, aka Kurt Wagner, had the ability to teleport himself to other locations in a matter of seconds. The fact that he was a German mutant with blue skin, three-fingered hands, yellow eyes, and a prehensile tail wasn't all that appealing, but the teleporting aspect was intriguing. Not only did it seem like less exertion than flying, one wouldn't have to deal with atmospheric conditions or worry about air traffic. Nightcrawler could only comfortably teleport two miles at a time, but it seemed to Overman that the guy was hampered by physical limitations and a violent family background, his mother having been a terrorist, his father a warlord. All Overman had to overcome was the "sky is falling" mentality of Irma and Saul, those holocaust-surviving poseurs. Up until this point, he had never considered mental transportation as a personal option, but the new order of the day was to dispense with self-editing and examine every possibility. If he were indeed able to teleport, would the Hyundai come with him? If not, who would return the rental car? Nightcrawler and the superhero population in general never seemed to be faced with such problems.

Overman spots a spiedie stand on the side of the road and pulls over to sample the local specialty. While he is still full from brunch, this Southern Tier treat is something he's heard about for years: grilled meat in a special marinade on Italian bread, basically shish kabob without the skewers and the vegetables. Waiting for his order, he gets excited about attempting to teleport, as well as the image of Rosenfarb shitting a brick should he actually be able to pull it off. As soon as the sandwich is ready, Overman carries it to the outdoor wooden picnic bench, poised to determine the best "teleport of call."

Taking a page out of Nightcrawler's playbook, he concentrates on places he has been before. Familiar locales were the only ones available to that particular superhero; perhaps it would work the same way for Overman. He returns to the idea of nearby Kutsher's, the premier vacation destination of his mundane childhood. Jews had a thing for entertaining the elderly, and it might cheer up the *alter cockers* to see one of their own teleport in for a fruit cocktail. Overman closes his eyes as he chews on the deliciously vinegary spiedie, recalling the Jewel of the Catskills' large, noisy dining room, bursting with starch and obesity. The sights and smells of this world-renowned citadel of mountainous, mediocre cuisine come back to him as if he'd been there only yesterday. A table full of *zahftig* Jewish widows has just finished their chopped liver appetizers when the waiter informs them that the kitchen has run out of *kishka*. Mrs. Kupferberg is not pleased, remarking that the Silverman table is filthy with *kishka*. As Overman remembers it, the young man gave a heartfelt explanation of why the Silvermans got the last of the coveted intestines. The resort's intestine supplier had a fire at the plant or some such thing. At the time it sounded credible to Overman, no subterfuge being waged on any level. However the stern and determined Mrs. Schecter didn't buy it, nor did her friends Mrs. Tanenbaum and Plutsky. But it was the tenacious Ruth Kupferberg who took matters into her own beefy hands. As Overman had learned early on, nobody puts Ruth Kupferberg in the corner.

"The food is supposed to be all-inclusive! American Plan! All-You-Can-Eat," shouted a visibly irate Mrs. Kupferberg.

The ladies grabbed their walkers and prepared to storm the kosher Bastille in search of the *kishka* they believed was being withheld from them by stingy management. Overman remembers the fear that ensued amongst the other diners. Sophie Tannenbaum wasn't so steady on her feet. What if she tripped and broke a hip while attempting to burn down the kitchen? There was additional talk of Ruth Kupferberg being even pushier than she had been last season when she famously browbeat a lifeguard into applying sunscreen to the numerous folds of her back, traumatizing the young man for life. The images were frighteningly real to Overman, much like the first time he saw his apartment after Lasik surgery. Was this a sign that he was on the brink of teleportation? Would he, in a matter of seconds, find himself face-to-face with a new generation of Kupferbergs and Plutskys? There was only one way to find out. Concentrating with all his might, Overman closed his eyes and imagined himself in the middle of the *kishka* fracas, in droopy arm's length of the enraged Ruth Kupferberg. Then his eyes opened, concentration blown, willpower disappearing into thin air. Something had gone amiss. Overman realized that if he wanted to teleport, familiarity and proximity couldn't be the only elements in the equation. When Nightcrawler attempted such a feat, he had been urgently motivated to get to his destination. Overman, on the other hand, while fascinated by the concept, was conceivably looking at an end result of slathering Coppertone on a chubby, unpleasant and perpetually famished *bubbe*. Where was the motivation in that? He had none. And without will, there could be no willpower. It had become clear that performing heroic acts was not a "Hey Ma, Look at Me!" proposition. Every positive result that had sprung from Overman's transformation had been initiated by genuine purpose, and it was likely that any future accomplishments would be governed by similar principles.

Despite the teleporting hiccup, as the plane touches down in Los Angeles, Overman is filled with a sense of momentum he has never before known. While his instincts in the past had been piss-poor, these days they were taking him to wondrous places and against all odds, giving meaning to a life that never seemed to have any. He returns to his shithole apartment and finds a message on the answering machine from Ashley, inviting him to Friday night Shabbat dinner at Nancy and Stan's. He had hoped for one-on-one time with his daughter, but the fact that she had followed through on wanting to see him was a good starting point. And the stronger he got, the less he was bothered by his ex-wife and her self-important excuse for a husband.

Thumbing through the mail, Overman wades through reams of home remodeling ads to discover a postcard from Dr. Gonzales, reminding him that he is due for his two month Lasik follow-up. According to the card, they will be checking for the healing of the corneal flap, near vision problems, any infection or complication possibilities, proper eye medications, uncorrected distance vision, and the possible need for surgical enhancements. Momentum notwithstanding, the thought goes through Overman's brain that whatever procedures were to be performed in the follow-up might erase the fringe benefits of the initial surgery. He thinks about blowing off the exam, sticking with the vision he's got and everything else that came with it. But there was a downside to that scenario as well. It was certainly within the realm of possibility that ignoring maintenance could diminish effectiveness, eventually reverting Overman to his original state. Either way it was a crapshoot. The old Overman with the inherited hoarding gene would have avoided the eye doctor at all costs, but this one knows that aspiring to any sort of hero-dom requires a dash of fearlessness. He is confident that Clark Kent never hid from his optometrist so why should he? Overman will visit Dr. Gonzales, trusting that it is all part of the adventure.

He's about to get into bed when Big Dave calls on the cell phone, just making sure that his star employee arrived home safely. Overman tells him that it was a very successful trip and that he is very much looking forward to coming to work in the morning.

"Bless you, Overman," Big Dave replies.

The re-energized Jew from Fresh Meadows has made quite an impression on his money-lending Texan mentor. "I got a little something for you. It'll be on your desk in the morning," Big Dave informs him.

"Thank you, Dave. That wasn't necessary."

"My pleasure, son," Dave counters, continuing to assume his parental role with a man almost ten years his senior. "See you mañana, hoss."

Overman kind of likes the "hoss" thing, but also wonders if he and his employer might be getting just a bit too chummy. How will Big Dave handle it when he ultimately picks up and leaves? He must make a concerted effort to keep it a business relationship.

Overman oversleeps, yet manages to get to Cavanaugh Foster by 8:45, fifteen minutes before the cowbell is to ring signaling the arrival of Big Dave. Having foregone his morning hair-brushing regimen, Overman's coif is of the Bozo variety. It turns out not to matter because the gift Dave has placed on his desk is a Stetson. Overman tries it on for size, just as the solicitous Texan bursts through the door.

"Hello, little man. Give us a hug," commands Big Dave, relieved to be reunited with his protégé.

Squeezing nearly every last breath out of Overman, it doesn't look as if the plan to keep it all business is going to pan out. As soon as the winded Ira manages to gather whatever remaining oxygen he can, Dave launches into a summary of his weekend. He didn't want to get into it on the phone last night, but Luanne, the former Dallas Cowboys cheerleader to whom he has been married for eight years, took off to the Turks and Caicos with a rival hard moneylender. Unbeknownst to Dave, Luanne and Deke Summers had been having an affair for seven years and now they have decided to become a committed couple. Stupidly, Dave had not asked her to sign a pre-nup and since he and Luanne had become California residents, she would be entitled to half of everything he owned. But before getting into "all that messy paperwork," she said she needed a little vacation.

"You think you know people," Dave bemoans. "They come into your life, they seem to be good, honest folks who know the value of loyalty. And then they just let you down. My first two wives were exactly the same."

As Big Dave gives Overman another hug, it becomes apparent that Overman is not going anywhere until his boss is at least marginally back on his feet. He wonders whether he should call the Applebee's guy and postpone Big Dave's meeting this afternoon. He is still in the big man's vise grip when the cowbell rings once again and what he assumes is a random walk-in enters. Until the walk-in opens his mouth.

"Jesus Christ. Overman?"

The voice is unmistakable. How could this be? Overman looks up to see the sad mug of the ubiquitous Jake Rosenfarb.

"What is this, 'Brokeback Mountain II'? Since when are you a fag?" Rosenfarb demands to know.

Big Dave quickly releases his employee and grabs Rosenfarb by the collar.

"Hey, don't get yourself in a bunch," Rosenfarb gasps. "I'm just saying, Marvel tried the gay cowboy superhero with the Rawhide Kid. Didn't work worth shit."

Dave is not enjoying any of this. "He is not a fag. I am not a fag. And I do not appreciate you barging into my offices unannounced."

"How the fuck did you find me, Jake?" Overman asks, incredulous.

"I don't know. I wasn't even looking for you."

"Who is this intruder?" Dave demands.

"He's the stalker I was telling you about," Overman reminds him. "The guy who claims to be my best friend but won't leave me alone."

"So that's how you feel about me?" asks Rosenfarb, a picture of hurt. "Now I'm a stalker?"

"You parked outside my apartment for a month."

"You actually saw me and you didn't let me in? Unbelievable!"

"I needed some space," Overman soberly confesses.

"Needed space? You sound like a woman. How far do we go back, Ira? You want to just toss me away like garbage?"

Dave has had enough. "Sir, why did you follow my assistant to his place of employment?"

"I didn't," Rosenfarb explains. "I had no idea he'd be here, much less be embracing another man."

"Then what are you doing in this office?" Dave inquires.

"I owe people money and I need a loan."

Big Dave's demeanor turns on a dime. "That makes perfect sense. Step into my office, young man. Any friend of Ira's is a friend of mine."

As Rosenfarb follows Big Dave into the back, Overman is dumbstruck by the myriad ways Rosenfarb keeps re-entering his life, a virus that refuses to be eradicated. He picks up bits and pieces of the conversation coming from Dave's office. Rosenfarb's threat to banish Rita to an apartment by the freeway has evidently not come to fruition. Instead, Rita has thrown Jake out of the house and withdrawn all the money in their joint checking account. Rosenfarb still has assets but not much in the way of liquidity. The banks won't approve a loan because unbeknownst to Jake, Rita ran up their credit cards and they are all over their limits. Dave offers him a fast fifty g's for thirty days at 22% interest and 5 points. Jake, obviously desperate, takes the deal. He shakes Big Dave's hand and marches out of the office, without a word or glance to Overman.

"Jake —" the usurer's apprentice calls out, wanting to settle this before it gets even further out of hand.

But Rosenfarb is gone, a result Overman would welcome if he could be assured it were permanent. But he knows the truth all too well. A malignant tumor can be surgically removed, but once the cancer has metastasized it is destined to return in even more horrendous ways.

Big Dave walks out to Overman's desk to thank him for bringing in such a terrific client.

"I had nothing to do with it," Overman reminds his boss. "It was pure coincidence."

Big Dave is having none of it. He wants to believe in Overman as much as Overman wants to extricate himself from Rosenfarb. Happenstance is not about to get in the way.

"What say I take you out to lunch today, hoss?"

"That's not necessary," Overman responds, trying his best to re-frame the paradigm back to a business relationship.

"I know it's not necessary. I just feel like buying you a steak."

"That's really nice of you, Dave, but I'm working on getting in shape," Overman says, patting his shrinking belly.

"Don't be a pussy. You're having a steak."

"Fine," Overman caves, not wanting to get into an argument.

"And no 'petite' filets, mind you," Dave states firmly. "I'm trying to bring you to the big boy's table. Take advantage of it."

All Overman can think about is what it will feel like later in the day when he will have to contend with a belly full of fatty animal flesh. Never had there been a superhero with digestive problems, in no universe a masked man suffering from Irritable Bowel Syndrome. If Overman were ever to join their ranks, his kryptonite would surface in the form of saturated fats and cream sauces.

As the various bits of his new life begin to coalesce, Overman finds himself in an oddly comfortable groove, hitting the gym every morning before going off to collect twelve dollars an hour from his affable, money-grubbing boss. Not a peep from Rosenfarb, which has no doubt contributed to Friday's swift arrival. Dave, in a particularly effusive mood, invites him out for a drink after work, but Overman must pass because he is due at his ex's for Shabbat dinner. After explaining to Dave as best he can, what that is, Overman gets the distinct impression that Dave wants to go to the dinner more than he does. That said, he knows his presence is important: *Shabbat* is his gateway to another stab at parenthood. He even went out and bought himself a nice shirt for the occasion, as if to celebrate his re-birth as a father.

At five o'clock, Dave wishes him a "Merry Shabbat" and Overman is on his way. Driving toward the property that should have been his, he searches for a way to decompress before having to make small talk with Nancy and Stan. He decides to access the recent memory of Janie Sweeney in her bountiful garden: an image symbolizing all that was good in the world. As a sense of calm begins to set in, Overman opens the glove box, taking out the *yarmulke* he remembered to bring along. No karmic stone to be left unturned, he soon discovers that the inside of the skullcap is embossed with the words: "Bar Mitzvah of Jonathan Rosenfarb." The Son of Rosenfarb saga comes reeling back with nightmarish familiarity. Rita had insisted on having the Bar Mitzvah reception at the Beverly Hills Hotel, which translated into years of backbreaking shutter installations for poor Jake. Then, adding insult to injury, the minute Jonathan left for college he chucked Judaism and became a Hindu or Buddhist, joining a cult and cutting off all contact with his parents. Everybody had their shit, even the overbearing Rosenfarbs.

Overman parks his car and rings the bell, primed and ready to *daven*. Ashley answers the door, duly impressed by the sight of her father in his anticipatory *yarmulke*. She hugs him warmly, informing Overman that there is to be a surprise guest at the dinner table. Nancy greets her ex-husband, noticing the change in his bearing.

"You look trimmer, Ira."

"I've been working out," Overman tells her.

"Is there anyone special?" she teases, which wouldn't seem so inane if she actually gave a shit.

"No, I'm doing this for bigger reasons," Overman answers.

"Atta boy," shouts Stan, coming over to shake his hand. "He's working out because he cares about his health. That's the kind of attitude we doctors love to see."

Bullshit, Overman thinks. All Stan wants to see is a proliferation of drug sales so he can hop on the next cruise.

"So who's the surprise guest?" Overman wants to know.

The words are barely out of his mouth when his brother Steve emerges from the back room. Dr. Steven Overman, gastroenterologist, remained close with Nancy after the divorce, bonding with Stan over mutual concerns like HMOs and the prospect of lower incomes as the health system collapsed. Steven always stayed with the Belzbergs when he came to Los Angeles, occasionally picking up the phone to call Ira right before he went back to New York and there was no time to get together. The brothers had drifted apart since Ira migrated west, never having been all that close to begin with. Steve was one of those people who mapped out his destiny at a very early age, never straying from the path until reaching his desired goal. He had no understanding of, or patience for, someone like Ira, a man who made bad choices, then spiraled downward from show business to car sales to "God knows what?" Steven was the baby of the family, the Good Son, the one who became a doctor. Most significantly, he was the heir to Saul and Irma's tradition of regarding Ira as a second-class

Overman, as if first-class was something to write home about. Steven had a nice and intelligent wife who for some reason never accompanied him to his conferences on the west coast. He was very comfortable staying with Nancy and Stan, the three of them regaling each other with tales of expensive vacations, fine wines and vintage automobiles. Good *shabbos* indeed.

Ashley lights the candles and tells everyone how special it is that they are able to spend this Shabbat together. She then announces that she'd like to go around the table and have each participant talk about one thing that happened this week for which he or she is thankful. Overman hates these kinds of surprises. They remind him of those stomach-churning pop quizzes in school with the added embarrassment of having to present one's answers aloud to other people — other people who look down on him.

Steve decides to kick it off. "I am thankful to my good friends Nancy and Stan for welcoming me into their home."

No mention of his brother, the reason he knows these people in the first place.

"I am thankful to my wife for preparing this beautiful meal," Stan smiles, clasping Nancy's hand like he's in some ancient Jewish Kodak commercial.

Nancy speaks next.

"I am thankful to have Ashley home safe and sound."

Applause all around. A cheap shot, Overman thinks. So fucking obvious. But he doesn't really need to worry about that, because he has prepared for this moment. While Nancy, Stan and Steve sit there looking pleased with themselves, Overman clears his throat, ready to play the enlightenment card. He speaks in a soft but firm tone.

"An ancient *Midrash* says: 'There was a Monarch who prepared a special wedding canopy. It was intricately carved and adorned; the only thing missing was the bride. So, too, the world was created intricately and majestically, but the only thing missing was Shabbat.' Tonight I am honored to help fill in the blank by joining my wonderful daughter at her Sabbath table."

"Daddy that was so beautiful!" Ashley pronounces.

The others look at Overman, stunned.

"What the fuck do you know about *Midrash*?" Nancy barks.

"I've been reading —"

"Yeah, right," Steven sneers. "If you knew how to read you wouldn't be selling used cars for a living."

"I don't think he's doing that anymore," Stan adds.

"I never sold used cars," Overman clarifies.

"I think you're all missing the point," Ashley interjects. "Daddy was pointing out to us how lucky we are to have the gift of Shabbat. And I, for one, would like to thank him for that."

His daughter begins to applaud. Not wanting to be viewed as spoil sports, the others follow suit.

"Daddy, would you like to say the *motzi*?"

"Of course, darling."

Ira says the blessing over the bread, luxuriating in the petty contempt of the others as they watch him earn the respect of his daughter. He asks to bless the wine as well, after which he turns to his brother.

"So how are things in the bowel and colon business, Steve?"

Steven is not used to this kind of boldness from his older sibling. "Since when are you John Q. Jew?" he snaps, dismissing the original question.

"I'm not particularly religious," Overman explains. "But this is something Ashley cares deeply about and I think we owe it to her to honor that."

None of the adults is prepared for this kind of confidence from the man they wrote off more than two decades ago. Even Ashley is surprised by the ease with which her father has set a new tone. The difference is, while the others react with disdain and cynicism, she is moved by what she sees before her.

After dessert, Ira offers to help Ashley do the dishes in the hope of spending a little private time with her. As father washes and daughter dries, she is pleased to learn that much like her own recent metamorphosis, Daddy has also been re-evaluating how he wants to live his life.

"I know I haven't been the best father," he says, handing her the crusty kugel casserole.

"You weren't that bad," she lies, trying to make him feel better.

"I never felt like I understood how to do it. But I'm going to try to have a closer relationship with you. Which won't be easy since you'll be going off to college."

"You can always fly out and visit," she reminds him.

I can't fly, he thinks to himself. I can't even teleport like Nightcrawler.

"Who's Nightcrawler?" inquires a confused Ashley.

Apparently Overman has uttered this last sentence aloud. "One of your mother's relatives," he chuckles, going for the amusing save. "Nobody you know."

"So will you come visit?" she asks sincerely.

"Of course, sweetheart." Overman is thrilled that his daughter wants his company.

"That makes me happy," she smiles, handing her father the dry brisket dish to put away. "Daddy?"

"Yeah, hon?"

"Do you believe in any kind of Higher Power?"

"Yes, I do," Overman, responds with certitude.

"Wow. I never knew you even thought about God."

"You didn't say anything about God. You said 'Higher Power.'"

"How is that different from God?"

"I've recently come to believe that even the unlikeliest of people have vast, untapped power. The trick is to identify it, then figure out how to use it."

"That's really deep," she nods admiringly at her dad.

At which point Steven enters the kitchen, desperate for a bottle of Gas-X. Shabbat dinner has evidently not sat well with the Earl of Intestines. In keeping with the arc of the evening and his recent fortune in general, Overman's digestion has never been better.

"What else do you want to do differently? Ashley asks, as her uncle trots off to the bathroom.

"Everything," Overman responds. "I'm going to be a new man."

"Ambitious," Ashley acknowledges, suggesting that the High Holy Days are always a good time to start. "Atonement followed by renewal is one of the keystones of Jewish life."

Overman tells her that even though it didn't coincide with the Jewish calendar, his renewal has already begun and is gathering considerable steam by the day. If all goes according to plan, Tropical Storm Overman could well be Hurricane Overman by *Erev Rosh Hashanah*.

At 10:30, a sanguine Overman is coasting down Doheny Drive with all the windows open, sucking in as much jasmine and eucalyptus as his lungs can manage. He has left three sour and confused Jews in his wake while reclaiming a foothold on fatherhood. The happiness this gave him was so gratifying that the prospect of teleporting seemed trivial by comparison. The progress he had made in human relations and personal growth had given him a clear perspective on what truly mattered and little by little, the pieces were falling into place.

The crispness of the air is yet another reminder of Overman's trip to Endicott. Crossing Sunset Boulevard, he recalls the warm welcome he received from Garvin Leeds, the husband who loved Janie Sweeney as Overman wished he could love (and be loved by) a spouse. Garvin's generous smile conveyed both delight and respect for the soul mate he had been so blessed to find later in life. What's more, Overman was certain that should Janie ever choose to share the whole of her experiences with Garvin, he would process them with compassion and insight, taking their marriage to "the next level," as people liked to say. While it was understandable why Janie had not, thus far, chosen to re-hash the harrowing incident from her past, Overman wondered if acting on his own selfish impulse to confront her might ultimately impel her to open up to Garvin.

The old brick home had a window air conditioner in the master bedroom that hadn't worked in eight years. For the purpose of saving energy and money, Janie and Garvin Leeds had elected not to replace it, choosing instead to muddle stoically through the humid summers as the house's earlier residents had done without recourse. Certainly not the most comfortable way to live, Janie found it nearly impossible to sleep through the nights of July and August. Sometimes she'd awaken to find her whole body drenched in sweat, other times a bad dream would jolt her so sharply that her screams would rouse her husband from his snoring trance. In either case, Janie was doomed to remain awake until the morning light made it official. Tonight she had been restless to begin with. Then, just as her eyes were closing, the whine of the New York Susquehanna and Western freighter put a quick end to any hope of drifting off.

She found herself staring at the ceiling, thinking about Ira Overman's visit and the memories it rekindled. For as much alcohol as she had consumed that night long ago, she never forgot the oppressive, claustrophobic upstairs bedroom in which she'd been raped. Decades later, Janie could still smell the musty, overstuffed furniture, the bulky curtains, the sweat of the seven inebriated schoolboys who assaulted her and went on with their lives. Of course there was the ringleader, Merkowitz, but oddly enough, the foot soldiers in Merkowitz's army were the ones who truly haunted her.

Overman was literally forced into the sex act. But were the others like regular Germans, just following orders? How had the

aftermath of that night played out for Anthony Saldo? Dennis
Geoghan? Seth Hammer? Was Michael Herzog able to have normal relationships with women after he had followed Merkowitz's
directive to jerk off all over a high school girl's face? Did Kevin
Royce ever regret having taken the number two spot, his introduction to the act of lovemaking a bloodied hymen broken by
someone else? It had taken Janie her entire adult life to work
through the fallout and she considered it a miracle that she had
emerged as healthy as she had. Obviously it was something Ira
Overman needed to resolve; certainly the episode must have resonated with some of the others.

It saddened her that she could not talk about this with her
husband. While she knew that Garvin would not judge her for
having been a victim, she was less sure how he would react to her
having withheld this information from him for all these years.
She glanced at the man who looked every bit his seventy years,
envious of the half-snore, half-wheeze that had delivered him to
the restful state she was incapable of visiting anytime soon.

She thought about Overman coming to apologize to her and
how she would never even try to right a wrong from nearly forty
years ago. It seemed crazy, like digging up old bones that had
been left to decompose undisturbed. And yet, Overman's excavation had reawakened more than just the bad memories within
her. She kept wondering about cause and effect. Overcoming a
complete emotional shutdown, the rape victim had survived and
even prospered. But what of the rapists? They were kids. Kids who
never got caught. There were plenty of adults in the world who
could convince themselves that their crimes or sins never happened, or were somehow committed by someone else. The O.J.
Simpson approach to a double murder rap. Were the Lakeview
boys a team full of O.J's, or did a conscience lurk somewhere in
the cracks? Did they agree to erase the entire incident by taking a
vow of eternal silence? Or was it simply relegated to old news that
had faded into oblivion? In one way, Janie couldn't believe that

she was allowing herself to revisit any of this. In another way, it offered a fascinating peek into the mechanics of human interaction, the battle of rationalization vs. accountability.

The more Janie thought about it, the more clearly she understood that Overman had reopened the book because he could no longer live with himself without having closure. And for her part, while she had survived the most horrible of feelings, she now yearned to know if the others had ever bothered to feel anything.

Overman gets back to the Wilton apartment parking garage, failing to notice that the chatty Armenian neighbor from next door has pulled in at the same time. Daderian or Zakarian or something like that. Looked to be in his thirties, worked as a lab technician at Valley Pres.

"Hello, Mr. Overman. What brings you out this late?"

None of your fucking business, Overman thought. Not to mention that he hated that this guy knew his name. "I had dinner with my daughter."

"I didn't know you had a daughter."

That's because there is no reason for you to be given this information, dickhead. "Analyze any good stool samples tonight?" Overman asks, deciding to go toe-to-toe in the obnoxiousness department.

"That is joke?" the neighbor asks, stone-faced.

"Isn't that what you do? Analyze stool samples?"

"I don't talk about what I do," the man responds.

"Yet you want to know all about my personal life?" Overman shoots back, hating himself for getting sucked into this. Luckily, it doesn't seem to register with the neighbor, who's on to bigger and better subjects.

"If you ever want to play poker, I have a regular game Thursday nights."

"Won't do you any good. I don't have any money."

"Maybe you can win some at the game."

"What's in it for you?"

He flashes a weird, I-Have-Bodies-In-My-Freezer kind of grin. "I like making new friends."

"Me, not so much," Overman responds, quickly opening the door to his apartment and double-locking it behind him.

There were no two ways about it. Overman needed to get some money so he could move out of there. He considered the possibility of using his willpower for monetary gain. If, like the comic book superheroes, he didn't have to worry about trivialities like bills, he could focus on good deeds, employing kind of a Robin Hood/Chabad business model. His conservative estimate was that achieving financial solvency would enable him to give back to society tenfold. But how would he go about it? Perhaps the energy he had expended trying to teleport might be better used to will hard, fresh cash out of ATM's. There were banks on practically every corner, any one of which could be the ticket to Overman's freedom.

It is not lost on the aspiring hero that entertaining this Raskolnikov-like notion of criminal behavior comes right on the heels of celebrating Shabbat with his daughter. Visions of Saul and Irma creep into his thoughts; the way they accessorized their old-world victim *weltanschauung* with the proselytizing of obvious ethical concepts. Even as members of the invisible lower middle-class, his parents believed that it was never okay to get a free ride. One had to earn one's keep and earn it honestly. And if one was lucky enough to do so, he was not permitted to flaunt success in the face of the less fortunate. Showiness was unseemly in whatever form it took. Overman figured he had the showiness problem licked by going the Robin Hood route. But the act of willing cash that didn't belong to him was a whole other matter. Even if he could make it happen it would pose a complex series of moral dilemmas. Whose money would he actually be removing from the bank? For all he knew he'd be taking from the accounts of people who were just getting by. You couldn't really run a Robin Hood-type operation if you didn't know whose money you were stealing. He had to give Saul and Irma credit: somewhere in course of being ineffectual, unhappy people, they had instilled in their son a basic sense of right and wrong.

Overman considers the possibility that he might one day make a decent living working for Big Dave. Like it or not, at this moment in time, Dave Dobson is an integral part of whatever weird trip Overman is on. And who, save for the hard moneylender, had ever believed in him from the get-go? The Big Man was an Overman fan, no questions asked, having signed up without any prior knowledge of a post-Lasik awakening. Overman imagined that if life operated like a comic book and he truly was a Batman-style hero, Dave would be a good candidate for the sidekick role. Yes, he was larger than life and you never wanted to be overshadowed by your Number Two, but at the same time, someone with his personality would allow Overman the under-the-radar anonymity he so highly valued. Big Dave would fit comfortably into the role of Attack Dog, leaving Overman free to do his chosen Good Deeds Du Jour. And unlike the needy, neurotic Rosenfarb who had begged for the job, Dave's unflappable presence would give him the capability to honestly assess the potential up and downsides of joining the Overman team. As far as their roles being reversed with Overman in effect, becoming the boss, he saw Dave as a pragmatist who would be able to work with whatever hierarchy was best for business. Which got him to thinking: What do you pay a sidekick?

As the 80's clock radio strikes 1 a.m. and he is nowhere near falling asleep, Overman thinks about calling Maricela. She had left numerous messages for him after his dramatic departure from Steinbaum, but he had not returned them, thinking a clean break would be best. The flipside of the coin was that he had not had any physical contact with a woman since their supercharged encounter, and he had many times pictured the sinewy contours of her miraculous body.

Was it permissible for a hero to jerk off? While it seemed beneath a legend like Batman, it felt perfectly natural to Overman. Tonight though, he craved the real thing. He longed to hear her voice. So much had happened to him since they last spoke that he wanted to share his positive frame of mind at the very least. But it was late and as far as he knew, she was still dating or living with Rodrigo. No good could come of her cell phone ringing at this hour. Then again, if Maricela went to sleep, she probably turned off the ringer and he could leave a casual message saying "hi" or that he was just wondering how she was doing. Or he could simply call the number, hear her warm, breathy greeting on the voicemail ("Hi, this is Maricela, tell me everything,") and just hang up. She'd eventually see his missed call and phone back if and when she felt like it.

Overman decides it's all too much work, the quicker and easier choice being to bite the bullet and beat his meat. He turns out the light and strokes himself, figuring that even after such an exciting night, he can get the job done in five minutes. He closes his eyes and imagines her smooth brown body lightly grazing his lips. He begins to inhale her, kissing the velvety skin with the gratefulness of a man who has been to the depths of hell, but somehow managed to claw his way back up to the pearly gates. He is able to evoke every intoxicating smell and taste of that night, his engorged member throbbing as Fantasy Maricela opens her mouth to take in all of him. The talented receptionist is smiling and sucking at the same time, her eager head bobbing and weaving, the wild herbal scent of her long black hair permeating the air. Solo Overman is writhing on the bed, ready for blast-off.

The phone rings. He desperately wants to ignore it, but feels obligated to check the number in case it is Ashley or Peter or someone who truly needs his help. He will be really pissed if he looks at the caller ID and sees the name "Jake Rosenfarb."

There is no name on the ringing phone, but rather an area code that he has come to recognize as Endicott, New York.

"Hello," Overman answers, still breathing heavily.

"Ira, are you all right? I'm sorry for calling so late."

It was Janie Leeds, née Sweeney. She sounded distraught.

"It's fine, Janie. What's going on? It must be four in the morning there."

"I know. I just can't stop thinking."

He knew exactly what she meant. His apology for reprehensible actions of his past had reopened a wound that had never been treated.

"Tell me what's on your mind," he jumps in.

"I don't know. I keep trying to imagine who those guys turned into. What they look like now. Do they have children? Are they all still alive?"

Overman listened intently as she talked about the secret she had kept inside for so long. He loved the sound of her voice. While it wasn't flirtatious and sexy like Maricela's, it had a calmness about it, even when she discussed matters that were obviously so painful to her.

"Do you want me to find these people, Janie?" Overman asks, point blank.

"What good would it do?"

"I don't know," Overman answers honestly. "I had no idea what would happen when I went to see you, but some good and I guess some not so good, came of it."

"I feel like a crazy person," Janie tells him. "Why not leave well enough alone?"

Overman points out that if she's still feeling the need for answers, things are not really "well enough." He suggests that they keep talking in the days ahead. Between the two of them, they should be able to come up with some kind of game plan.

"Have you said anything to Garvin?" Overman asks.

"No. I don't want to bring him into this. He's so happy with who he thinks I am."

"He loves who you are, no matter what happened."

"Ira, I withheld a major life experience from my own husband. How do you think he's going to feel about that?"

"I think he's an understanding guy."

"He is," Janie admits. "I wish I could tell him, but I'm not there."

"Maybe in time."

"Thanks for being a friend, Ira."

"My pleasure."

"Good night."

"Good night, Janie."

Overman hangs up the phone, his former need for self-flagellation now subsumed by the overwhelming depth of his feelings. Reaching back into his less than illustrious past and attempting to right this wrong has changed everything.

Saturday morning turns out to be rush hour at the Clearview Vision Center. Overman can barely find a parking space and the waiting room is packed. He checks in with the frazzled receptionist and parks himself between an overweight postal worker sporting a "Luis" nametag and a pretty blond woman reading Us magazine. She looks to be in her late forties but is dressed like a teenager, breasts decidedly aftermarket, nipples sprung to attention as if ready to serve their country. Fake though the look may be, Overman no longer feels he is in a position to judge the remodel of any individual. While he himself had not undergone cosmetic reconstruction designed to increase his sex appeal (e.g.: a penile implant), by electing Lasik surgery he had nonetheless fiddled with the elements, altering his God-given structure. The results had been exemplary, so who was to say that someone else's tummy tuck or butt lift wouldn't yield similarly positive results?

Overman's attention is suddenly diverted by the music playing in the background. Is this song choice deliberate or sheer coincidence? Could he really be sitting here at Clearview Vision Center listening to Jackson Browne croon: *"Doctor my eyes, tell me what you see, I hear their cries, just say if it's too late for me..."*

There were more important things to consider. For example, if Luis and the blond had already had their Lasik surgery and were also there for follow-up exams, wasn't it possible that they, too, had been graced with newfound powers? Neither looked particularly heroic, but Overman was self-aware enough to realize that even now, in his trimmed down and bulked up form, the same could be said of him. He figures it couldn't hurt to strike up a conversation while he waits for his name to be called. The no-brainer is to start with the blond, then if she turns out to be a cold fish, move on to Luis.

"I never liked that whole 'Brangelina' thing," he opines, pointing to the magazine headline. "It sounds like an Italian raisin bran."

The blond laughs, a raspy, throaty, almost masculine guffaw. Her name is Tiffany and she's more than willing to talk. Yes, she has had the surgery already and is indeed there for a follow-up like Overman.

"How did the Lasik affect you?" Overman asks, not wasting any time.

"It was great. What a thrill not to have to wear glasses after all these years."

"Did the surgery make you feel different in any other ways? Your mind? Your body? I only ask because it's had an enormous effect on me." Overman wasn't about to go into specifics, unless, of course, Tiffany did first.

"My mind and body have been completely changed," the blond affirms.

Overman brightens. A burgeoning superheroine perhaps? What a plus it would be to have a contemporary with whom to compare notes. He is thrilled by the prospect, mind racing as he wonders whether Tiffany can teleport and if so, how far? "What did the Lasik surgery do for you?" Overman asks excitedly.

"The Lasik just made me see better," she says. "The other surgeries are what changed my life."

Tiffany, it turns out, is not a superheroine but transgender, having lived for forty-two years as Thomas O'Grady, a truck driver hauling big freight between Atlanta and Amarillo. After an extended series of hormone treatments in Los Angeles, Tiffany physically became a woman last spring and married a fellow trucker.

"Then I decided I wanted a better look at my new self, so I had the Lasik. Probably more information than you bargained for, huh?"

"Honestly, yes," Overman admits. "But I admire you for having the courage to make that change."

"I didn't have a choice. This was the person I was destined to be."

If that were true, who was Overman destined to be?

"Tiffany O' Grady," the receptionist calls out.

"It was nice meeting you —"

"Overman. Ira Overman."

They shake hands and Tiffany goes off to her appointment. Overman can't help but notice that this ex-man has a great ass. Four out of five guys would stare at it if she passed by. He looks around to see that four out of five *are* staring. All except for Luis the postal worker. What was his story? Or her story. At second glance, there was no way this *schlub* could ever have been a woman, and if by some chance he is a superhero, this is the greatest disguise of all time. Overman doesn't really feel like striking up a conversation, but in the interest of continuing education, he fires away.

"Crazy the way stamps are always going up. Not that I blame you —"

Turns out Luis doesn't speak any English, initially a relief to Overman. Upon further examination it just seems weird. How can you work for the United States Post Office and not speak any English? It made no sense, but neither did the price of first-class postage rising every year.

"Ira Overman," the receptionist calls out, before he has any more time to obsess on such questions.

As she leads him toward the back, Overman asks if the office is still being harassed by Jake Rosenfarb. The receptionist says she is new, the latest in a revolving door-full of phone answerers. Overman is sure Rosenfarb is to blame for the rapid turnover, which is only confirmed by the exhausted look on Dr. Gonzales's face.

"I shouldn't even be talking to you," are his first words to Overman.

"I am so sorry," Overman says. "He's annoyed me for forty-four years, if it makes you feel any better. "

"It doesn't," Dr. Gonzales lets him know.

The doctor orders his patient into the chair and begins a barrage of questions as to how well Overman has been seeing and if there has been any blurriness or discomfort. Overman says he has no complaints whatsoever, only accolades for the procedure that has transformed his life. Paying little attention to his glowing, big picture review, Gonzales goes about the business of putting drops in Overman's eyes. As Overman submits to the doctor's ocular intrusions, he cannot ignore the elephant in the examining room: Would the introduction of saline or whatever liquids were being dispensed somehow change the balance, altering or even reversing whatever magical equation had been created by the initial surgery? He also considers the possibility that the modifications to his eyes have had nothing to do with his change of fortune, their convergence the result of some rare cosmic coincidence.

"Okay, now I'm blurry," he tells Gonzales.

"You're supposed to be."

"Doctor, has anyone reported any unusual side effects from Lasik surgery?" Overman asks.

"Like the ability to date waitresses at Jerry's?" Gonzales shoots back, obviously up to his ass in Rosenfarb buffoonery. "Generally, that's not included in our service."

"I understand," Overman nods, his eyes stinging. "I'm just curious to know if anyone has had experiences that go beyond seeing or not seeing better."

"What happens in people's personal lives is not my business," the doctor maintains. "As long as they like my work and don't hit me with frivolous lawsuits, that's all I need to know."

"I understand. But when you ask a patient how he or she has reacted to the procedure, has anyone given you really strange answers?"

"Sure. One guy said that after Lasik, he could communicate with the dead."

"Really?" Overman's interest is piqued.

"He also claimed to be Jesus Christ. I think he's in a state facility somewhere."

Overman notices the blurriness starting to go away. He feels strong and confident, hopeful that his new abilities will still be intact.

After the doctor gives his stamp of approval, Overman marches out of the examining room on a mission. He wants to know as soon as possible whether his willpower has dissolved as quickly as it appeared. On his way out of the office, he spots a drop-dead gorgeous Asian woman in the waiting area. She looks to be Chinese or Vietnamese, in her early twenties, even younger than Maricela. He weighs the notion of striking up a conversation to see whether he still has the goods to land such a prize. Then, realizing that he could again wind up sleeping with someone barely older than his daughter, his recently developed conscience gets the better of him.

Overman leaves the office and heads for the parking garage, mulling over his next move. His thoughts drift to the various superpowers in the comic books he's been studying. What about becoming invisible? Wouldn't that be a hell of an addition to the portfolio? Sure, it sounded ridiculous, but as he had learned in his research, it was not at all uncommon, even amongst the lowest tier of superheroes. Overman's personal favorite was a character named Invisible Dick, who was on his way to play football when he bumped into something he couldn't see. It turned out to be a one-legged sailor named Peg Leg Pete, who was nice enough to give Dick a bronze Egyptian bottle containing a liquid that could turn one invisible for a certain period of time.

Overman figures that the odds of running into someone like Peg Leg Pete at a parking garage in Van Nuys are rather slim. He's then reminded of Invisible Boy, who had some kind of device that he stuck in his belt when he wanted to disappear. Where was Overman supposed to get such a thing? He is about to open the car door when he feels a tap on the shoulder.

"Hi, I'm Julie."

Julie is the breathtaking Asian girl from the waiting room.

"Feel like a cup of coffee?" she asks Overman.

One thing is for sure. He barely looked at the woman yet somehow she felt the vibe. The force is still with him.

"Don't you have an appointment?" he asks Julie.

"It shouldn't take long. I'll meet you at the Sensation Café in Encino in a half-hour."

So what if she's barely older than Ashley? What could it hurt to have a cup of coffee with the young lady? One could appreciate eye candy without necessarily sucking on it. Overman gives the thumbs-up and gets in his car. As he heads for the Sensation, he wonders why Julie picked the busiest, noisiest place in the entire valley. They had a nice outdoor patio but it was always so crowded that you could barely hear the person across from you. And the place was full of hotheaded Israelis, from the owners to the wait staff to the clientele. For what possible reason would this Asian chick want to immerse herself in such a scene? It's all part of the adventure, Overman reminds himself. Experience the moments and if you still have questions afterward, ask them then. It wasn't a bad way to live, undoubtedly far more satisfying than the studied fearfulness that had always been Saul and Irma's bread and butter.

The patio of the Sensation is filled with smoke as Overman takes a seat. He doesn't think smoking is allowed but the Israelis have a way of getting around red tape. Overman surmises that circumventing county health laws was small potatoes next to surviving a world that pretty much wanted you dead. The waitress, an adorable Sephardic brunette named Lina, asks if he wants something to drink while he waits.

"Just water for now. Drinks when my guest arrives," Overman smiles.

What exactly was he going to say to this guest? Naturally he would kick it off with "Why did you want to have coffee with me?" She would answer that some nebulous thing about him spoke to her; he would then feel flattered and go on to enjoy his incredible good fortune. But where would that lead? What could the two of them possibly have in common? Perhaps a sexual escapade was the only thing that could save them from having to make awkward conversation. Just as he realizes what a lame rationalization this is, he sees a vision in terror that thankfully has yet to see him.

Rita Rosenfarb is on her way into the restaurant with the book club sisterhood in tow. He knows that if she spots him she will make a scene, publicly castigating Overman as the lowlife who ruined her husband and decimated her marriage. Not a moment to waste, he quickly skips over the patio fence and runs to the parking valet, who is understandably confused since Overman arrived barely five minutes ago. Overman gives the guy an uncharacteristically generous tip to shut up.

As he peels out of the parking lot, Overman realizes that he has no way to get in touch with Julie. They hadn't exchanged cell numbers, assuming that was to come later at the café. He doesn't even know her last name. Overman suddenly has the bright idea to call the Vision Center, have them contact Julie and tell her to meet him at a place in Sherman Oaks instead of the Sensation. But when he gets the doctor's office on the phone, the answering service explains that the staff is out to lunch and won't return till two. Since it is only noon, this means he has no way of getting in touch with her. He can either go back to the Sensation and face the music, or stand up Julie.

"Excuse me, sir. Did you want to leave a message?" the answering service asks.

"Yeah. Would you leave word that Ira Overman needs the office to call an Asian patient named Julie to tell her that he had an emergency and had to leave town?"

As feeble as the move might seem, Overman is convinced that anyone who had endured a Rita Rosenfarb tirade would do exactly the same were they in his shoes. What was it about these Rosenfarbs? It was bad enough that he could never shake Jake, now it seemed as if he was forever doomed to be pestered by Rita as well. Another thought occurs to him. He can call the restaurant and ask to speak to Lina, the waitress. He can tell her to have Julie meet him in Sherman Oaks. But the more he thinks about it, the less he wants to waste this young girl's time with an invitation that goes nowhere. He leaves Lina the same message for Julie that he left with the answering service, resigned to never knowing why this stunning Asian chose an Israeli hangout for their foiled tête à tête.

When Julie finally does enter the Sensation, she lets the hostess know that she is there to meet a man named Ira. The hostess refers her to Lina, who explains that Mr. Overman had to leave town unexpectedly. The waitress, however, has offered up this information a bit too loudly, within earshot of Rita Rosenfarb.

Rita looks at the gorgeous Julie, then back at the waitress. "Did you say Ira Overman?"

"Do you know him?" asks the poor, unsuspecting young woman.

"Do I know him? I hate his fucking guts!"

And she's off. Rita's rant, packed with hoary gems like "A used car salesman who alienated his entire family" and "He fucks young waitresses at Jerry's, now he's fucking Asian schoolgirls," sends Julie and most of the patio fleeing to their cars. The book club table is asked to vacate the premises, after which they agree to read "Dealing with Anger" by Sally Livingstone as their next selection.

Overman is heading back home when he decides to take a detour and do some apartment shopping. While he was still clueless as to where and how he would earn future dollars, money had taken on an increasing sense of urgency. Surviving a possible relapse at the eye doctor's office and emerging unscathed from a potentially lethal Rita Rosenfarb attack pointed to the tenuousness of his situation. Things were going well now, but his luck could run out tomorrow. Overman wasn't about to let it expire on Wilton place, next-door to the stool sample analyzer.

He decides to house-hunt in the valley, which is both close to work and suggests a certain modesty of which Saul and Irma would have heartily approved, provided their son had an actual income. As it was, he would have to ask Big Dave to float him a small loan, further entangling himself in a relationship he had pledged to untangle. True to Overman's prediction, upon getting the call, Dave couldn't have been more accommodating. From where he stood, Cavanaugh Foster's star employee deserved a nice two-bedroom in a secure building.

Overman puts a down payment on a place in Colfax Meadows, walking distance to the office. When the day came that he was able to bag the hard money business for good, he would still be in a quiet, tree-lined neighborhood where a hero of modest means could go about his business in relative obscurity. The landlord says he just has to review Overman's application. Once approved, he can move in at any time. Overman is jazzed. He can have his daughter over for dinner. Shabbat even, if that continued to float her boat. Perhaps he could even patch things up with his son and be able to entertain Peter and his girlfriend on their breaks from college. It was an odd thing, this yearning for normalcy. Here he was, with the ability to have epic sex and will things to happen, but what was he getting off on? Finding a clean apartment where he might be able to host a Shabbat dinner. He concedes that he is living the textbook definition of "thinking small." But as cliché as it might sound, how could anyone operate on a grand scale before cleaning up one's own mess? And Overman still had plenty of garbage to get rid of.

Driving back to Wilton Place, an uneasy thought overtakes him. As impossible as his friend Jake Rosenfarb had become, the fact was that he had been installing window treatments quite contentedly until that fateful night at Jerry's when Overman spilled the beans. Had he been satisfied with whipping Rosenfarb's ass on the tennis court without further discussion, Jake just would have gone home pissed off. But by opening up and sharing his other experiences, he had caused Rosenfarb's life to unravel. Granted, had Jake been a different kind of person, he might have been able to be happy for his friend. But Overman knew the kind of personality he was dealing with when he laid his cards on the table. His momentary lapse in judgment had perpetrated the wholesale destruction of an admittedly troubled marriage.

For better or worse, Jake Rosenfarb had been his best friend. Who else was he supposed to confide in? Nancy and Stan? His uptight elitist GNT brother? His kids who weren't speaking to him? Hal Steinbaum? At the time, Rosenfarb was his only option. And now, even though the blame cut both ways, Overman felt culpable for his friend's demise. Although he had quite enjoyed the game of successfully ducking Rosenfarb, and the bonus of getting the silent treatment, he knew it could not go on forever. Sooner or later he would have to figure out a way to help Jake get back on his feet without allowing himself to be dragged down in the process. Overman wondered if this might be the ultimate test of a true superhero.

As he opens the door to the Wilton Place apartment, he is bombarded from all sides by cooking smells. The confluence of Middle Eastern, Mexican and Filipino doesn't entirely hang together, a fitting metaphor for Overman's tenure in this building and until recently, on the planet. As he surveys the dump he has crafted in his former self-image, he makes the decision to throw away nearly everything, donating the few pieces of furniture that might be of value to someone on the brink of homelessness. He heads for the kitchen and starts filling trash bags. Overman is struck by how many worthless things he has saved. A brand new unopened box of floppy disks? Was there anyone alive who would be able to make use of such a thing? Perhaps there was a country so poor that it only had antiquated DOS computers, yet had citizens literate enough to know how to use them. He dumps the disks in a cardboard carton alongside a bunch of obsolete wires with ninepin connectors.

The sifting through and disposing of his things produces a sense of accomplishment as Overman reduces a life to its essentials. But there is also sadness as he lingers over the meaning of what has been saved. For every trash bag filled, there was a photograph of Nancy and him happy and in love. For every chipped plate and bent fork there was a Father's Day card that Peter and Ashley had made for him when they were young and deluded.

"Best Dad in the World" read the crayon drawn flap of a card from ten years ago. That would have made Ashley eight, Peter eleven and Overman in his last year of working as an agent. A new crop was taking over the business, and he was out there schmoozing seven days a week just to try to stay afloat. While the motivation might have been to support his family, Overman was barely a father at that point, much less the best.

After spending nearly an hour poring over everything from his Bar Mitzvah album to the Writ of Divorce, Overman decides to switch gears and fill up a bag of clothing giveaways, starting with the Steinbaum Mercedes white shirts. Unfortunately, closets and bedroom drawers were also time-consuming diversions. As he reaches way over to pull out an ancient corduroy suit, Overman spots the tuxedo he wore to his wedding. When he was in the business, he continued to use it for industry functions, once having it stained by a piece of Rhea Perlman's tiramisu that mistakenly landed in his lap. Of course the strongest memory it evokes is of the wedding itself, hosted by Nancy's parents at Leonard's of Great Neck, the premier wedding and Bar Mitzvah factory in the known universe.

As Overman remembered it, Leonard's had been too ostenta-
tious and showy for Saul and Irma's tastes, but they weren't paying
so they bit their tongues. Saul spent the entire reception combing
for gatecrashers because he had heard that Leonard's had a reputation for attracting strangers seeking a free, kosher-style meal.
All a person had to do was put on a nice suit and he could go from
ballroom to ballroom saying he was from the other side of the
family, all the while filling up on bad egg rolls and soggy cocktail
franks. Ira was sure the stories were apocryphal. Why would anyone go to those lengths for such sub-par fare?

Saul would have none of it. "Are you on the bride's side or the
groom's?" his father grilled each guest suspiciously, proceeding to
cross-examine them until he was convinced they weren't there to
rip off anyone else's *kasha varnishkas*. The senior Overman considered this his contribution to the wedding since he hadn't kicked
in anything financially. The most unfortunate consequence of his
vigilance came with his decision to mimic Gene Hackman in "The
French Connection," pinning the bride's mother against the wall,
cop-style, and barking: "Do you pick your feet in Poughkeepsie?"

As he remembered the important parts of that night, Overman could not deny that he felt happy and hopeful, excited about
the life that was about to unfold for him and his young bride. Not
even the best man who pretended to forget the ring could take
away from this. It was Jake Rosenfarb's one sorry attempt at a
sense of humor and you had to cut the guy a little slack.

If sifting through hopes dashed and opportunities missed
was depressing for some people, it was downright devastating
for Overman, probably because the sheer number of them had
been so staggering. It feels as if he has been going through the
effects of someone else, reviewing a life that could not possibly
have been his. If it *was* his, how could it have turned out this way?
Granted, things appeared to be on the upswing, but to have gone
from that innocent, blissful night at Leonard's to the bleakness

of Wilton Place was almost unfathomable. He decides he's done with cleanup for the evening, shoving aside a box of old '45's and plopping down on the couch.

After a few minutes cursing a movie on TV with Bruce Willis (an ex-client who fired him just as he was starting to get big), Overman goes to the computer to check for emails. There is something from Janie Sweeney Leeds with the subject line: "Where They Are." He clicks it and reads her letter.

> Dear Ira,
>
> I have done some more thinking. Attached, please find a list of names, addresses and phone numbers obtained through various Internet searches. Perhaps they are not all up to date, but I seem to have located everyone involved and as much information on them as I could gather. Let me know if and how you would like to proceed.
>
> With deep appreciation,
>
> Janie

Overman clicks on the attachment and finds a thorough breakdown on the rest of the Lakeview Seven. While he himself had compiled ample data on General Merkowitz, the status of his troops was breaking news to Overman. Seth Hammer had apparently been married for twenty-eight years and ran his own dental practice in Hempstead, Long Island. Dennis Geoghan was a divorced, retired cop who moved to South Carolina to open a Bed and Breakfast, Mike Herzog a personal injury lawyer in White Plains, New York and on his third wife. Tony Saldo had six kids and owned a body shop on the South Shore; Kevin Royce was a gay English teacher in Portland.

From the looks of it, the rape of Janie Sweeney had not inspired any of the perpetrators to become career criminals. On paper at least, they had all evolved into productive members of society. Could there be any point in reminding these men of youthful transgressions carried out nearly forty years ago? He could tell that the answer had become a resounding "yes" for Janie. And it had been 100% his doing.

If Overman could miraculously channel the abilities of Rosenfarb's comic book heroes, he would surely know how to orchestrate an appropriate resolution. But he was at a total loss. Did Janie want a face-to-face apology from each one of her assailants? Perhaps personal letters would do the trick. At the other end of the spectrum, might she only be satisfied with out and out retribution? Before making any sudden moves, Overman needed to know exactly what she was seeking from this. His sense was that Janie might not even know the specifics herself. Although he had never "officially" been raped, Overman was certainly familiar with what it felt like to be violated. Whether one was dumped for another by one's spouse, unjustly terminated by an employer or assaulted by a bunch of high school drunks, the victim just wanted the wound to go away. The ultimate fantasy would be that if one could somehow go back in time, the entire incident could be erased, providing the possibility of a fresh start. Unfortunately, time-travel is as far from Overman's wheelhouse as the ability to become invisible. At the moment, the only consistently successful tool of his trade has been willpower, and it's anyone's guess whether that could be of use here. Overman returns the email, thanking Janie for the information and letting her know that while he continues to study the data, her next task will be to define her expectations. He, in turn, will begin to formulate some realistic options, unwavering in his belief that helping her through this is the worthiest of causes.

Before turning in, Overman performs what has come to be the semi-conscious nightly ritual of googling Glorietta Zatzkin. Lo and behold, thirty-two days into the process, he finds a picture of La Zatzkin in her current fifty-five year-old body. She is at a

Temple Emmanuel Hebrew School reunion to which Overman had apparently never received an invitation. Of course he never contacted anyone from the temple when he moved to California so there was so reason to expect one. Yet Overman was a man who had been brought up to feel offended at the slightest provocation and no superpower was ever going to take that away from him.

He is led to other reunion pictures, some of which feature the famous shit-eating grin of Marty Merkowitz. Overman hopes that Janie hasn't seen these online as they could only inflame her. After further examination, Overman concludes that the photos had just been posted minutes ago by Glorietta. He can't believe how much she looks like Estelle. Were his father alive, Saul would be creaming all over his computer monitor, assuming he had been convinced that computers were not some kind of fad. Glorietta has put on a little bit of weight since their night of stoned out passion thirty-five years ago, but most of it seems to have gone to her already formidable Estelle-like chest. She is smiling and happy, perhaps enjoying a respite from the grief she must be living on a daily basis since the death of her husband. Overman decides that he is definitely going to get in touch with her. Now that his life is moving forward, he feels no trepidation about revisiting the past. In a way, he *has* gotten to time-travel, slowly re-educating former non-believers in the value of Ira Overman. More importantly, he has begun to recognize that value himself.

Overman gets in to work early, a small gesture of thanks to Big Dave for graciously fronting the down payment on the new apartment. Rather than narrow his options, Overman has decided to embrace his role as usurer's apprentice while keeping an eye on his heroic future. He also feels himself becoming less resistant to the sidekick concept. Everybody needed input, and his case, there were major decisions that would have to be made regarding goals, direction and moral choices; an intelligent sounding board could prove invaluable.

On the surface, it hardly seemed that a man who charged his clients as much as seven times the prime interest rate would be the best choice to give ethical advice, but nevertheless, Dave projected a decency that moved Overman. Plus, there was the fact that Texans knew how to Think Big, and mapping out the future required someone who could visualize the big picture. He was confident that should he bring the boss into his circle, Dave wouldn't *noodge* and whine about every little thing like Jake Rosenfarb. And now that Dave actually knew Rosenfarb, he might also be able to advise Overman on how to put the shattered window man back together.

Dave bursts into the office like an otherworldly lightning bolt, proclaiming to the heavens that he has had a Come to Jesus moment. Suddenly, the state of Texas seems five times more immense than it was when Overman left work Friday evening. The lender explains that his good pal Jay Firestone arranged a blind date between Dave and the twenty-two year old porn star of "Squirtz," which resulted in the two spending the entire weekend together.

"She washed away all my troubles," Dave exclaims. "I'm in love with Juicy Jones!"

It occurs to Overman that a man on the rebound, in love with a woman who uses her vagina as a hose, might not be the best pick for that intelligent sounding board position. Still, he does not want to make any snap judgments.

"Dude, this girl is the best thing that ever happened to me!" Dave cries gleefully. "She can pick up a strawberry with her asshole."

"Sounds like love at first sight," Overman replies, his sarcasm lost on Dave.

The big guy proceeds to build on his enthusiasm with an offer to set up his best employee with one of Juicy's friends, whose specialty just happens to be fellating two penises at the same time. Overman respectfully declines, thankful that he hadn't prematurely spilled the beans and brought Dave into the fold.

"I'm telling you, Ira. There's nothing better for a man who's down on his luck than rough sex. Not that I'm saying you're down on your luck —"

"I appreciate that, Dave."

"Now your friend Rosenfarb — that's a different story altogether."

"What do you mean?" Overman asks.

"He made me swear not to share this with you, but I feel terrible for the guy. He's had a mental breakdown and he can't work. Meanwhile his wife threw him out and his son is a diaper head in some Hare Krishna-ass cult. Very sad."

"I'll bet he blames me for everything," Overman says.

"Actually, no. He blames himself for not being as strong as you are. He's convinced that you have some kind of superpowers or whatnot."

"Sounds like he could use a little Juicy Jones," Overman muses, trying to change the subject.

Dave abruptly turns serious. "Juicy is spoken for, Ira. However I'm sure Rosenfarb would like her friend."

"I'm not entirely certain that the answer to his problem is a multiple cock sucker," Overman offers. "But I *would* like to help the guy."

"Wasn't he the one you said you were going to bring to our investor dinner?" Dave asks, suddenly focused on business as opposed to his new girlfriend's bodily fluids.

"Yeah. That was before I knew he had hit the skids."

"So you're kind of screwed coming and going on this," Dave notes. "Now you've got to dig your friend out of the gutter and find five potential funders instead of four."

"Don't worry," Overman assures him. "No matter what else happens, I will deliver five prospects to you."

"What else would happen?" Dave asks pointedly, Overman realizing that he has no answers as well as no prospects.

"Nothing specific. But suppose, just hypothetically speaking, you fired me. I'd still find you five people for the dinner, because I'm grateful for all your support."

"Why would I ever fire you?" Dave asks, mystified. "You're like a son to me."

"I'm ten years older than you are," Overman blurts out, tired of Dave infantilizing him.

"But you're a baby in the loan business," Dave clarifies. "My job is to parent you into becoming the lender we both know you're capable of being."

Dave pats him on the back like he's a five-year-old. Overman segues into going over the boss's calendar for the day. He is scheduled to be in the office all morning, followed by lunch with a funder at the Olive Garden and meetings out of the office for the remainder of the day.

"Cancel all my afternoon appointments," he instructs Overman. "I'm going to watch Juicy get waxed."

Once Dave leaves for lunch, Overman sets about putting some wheels in motion. He will begin with a call to Janie. No doubt she was on the edge of her seat, eager to hear his plan for bringing the rest of the Lakeview Seven to justice, be it symbolic or otherwise. In truth, Overman has no idea how to do this, but posits that hearing her calm, gentle voice will once again inspire him to brilliance.

"Hello, Ira," the voice on the other end whispers. She doesn't seem happy to hear from him. She sounds tired, bordering on weepy. It turns out that Janie no longer has the luxury of thinking about how to clean up the past because something terrible is happening right now.

"What's wrong?" Overman asks, hating the idea of anything else bad intruding on the life of this lovely soul.

"Garvin had a massive stroke last night. I'm at the hospital."

"Is he going to be okay?" Overman asks, visibly upset.

"It's bad," Janie sniffles. "He doesn't know who I am." She goes on to explain that Garvin will need intensive therapy and has, at least for the moment, lost most of his language.

An English professor stripped of his words. Could it get any crueler than that?

"I want to come visit," Overman says.

"You don't have to, Ira. Garvin has family. His brother and sister live in the area."

"You're going to need as much support as you can get right now," Overman replies, though he has zero experience in the support game.

"It's okay. I'll be fine. But thanks," Janie tells him.

Overman senses that as much as she appreciates their new friendship, she has her hands full and doesn't need the pressure of one more person around.

"Okay, but if you change your mind, I can be there on a moment's notice," Overman lets her know.

"Thanks, Ira. The nurse is calling me. I'll be in touch."

After Janie hangs up, Overman takes a deep breath and reflects on the random spitefulness of the universe. The Heavens do not seem to reward lives well lived or worlds rebuilt in the face of terrible hardship.

Overman was at a loss for how to capitalize on the new strength he had acquired. As he thought about it, he recognized that aside from Janie, there were no functional adults in his life, certainly no one with whom he could discuss his options. On the upside, his less lofty ambitions now seemed entirely achievable. He was excited about moving into the new apartment and fixing it up to look respectable. But there was no denying that Overman wanted more. He didn't need to fly, but he still wanted a chance to soar. The man who had for so long been dismissed by so many ached to feel connected to things, people, deeds. Yes, he was making progress with his daughter, and there might be another stunning babe in a doctor's office drawn to him for reasons she didn't understand, but he was miles away from the deep human bond he so desperately craved. He would be willing to give up any hope of superpowers for something that had proved equally elusive: Overman wanted to know what it was like to love and be loved back.

Overman stands at the Ventura Boulevard address pulled from the file Big Dave has compiled. It is a sleazy adult motel in the West Valley, the current home of Jake Rosenfarb. The light is on in room 202 and as Overman walks up the stairs, he hears the sounds of "Jeopardy" blaring from the television. Rosenfarb always loved trivia. In a way, the window man's whole existence had been an homage to it. But who was Overman to judge the shallowness of a life? He had been there, done that as well as anybody.

He positions himself so he can see through the crack in the curtain. There is no Alex Trebek-loving hooker present, rather a slew of empty pizza boxes and soda cans surrounding what looks like a street person. Overman takes in this frightening image, knowing that while his desire to do the right thing has brought him here, he has no plan of attack. Would Rosenfarb be satisfied and turned around by a simple apology? Does Overman need to get him out on the tennis court and deliberately throw the match to lift his friend's spirits? Would he accept a cash donation to help him get back on his feet? As much as Overman hates the idea of diving head first into this pool, he is convinced that the direness of the situation demands a response. And the bottom line is, if he doesn't save Rosenfarb, who will?

An older man and a young, heavily made-up Latin girl climb the staircase, arm in arm, shooting Overman a "what the fuck are you doing here?" look before entering room 204. It's a safe bet that they have not shown up to watch the Double Jeopardy round along with their next-door neighbor. Overman tries to ignore the loud giggling coming from their room and concentrate on the task at hand.

He bites the bullet and knocks on the door, but Rosenfarb doesn't move or even register a reaction, choosing instead to shout at the TV: "What are the Punic Wars?" A louder knock produces the same non-reaction. Overman opts to stay the course, figuring that sooner or later the show must end and most likely before that, cut to commercial. Perhaps then the down-on-his-luck window man would snap out of his trance and open up. Overman waits patiently through shouts of "What are the fallopian tubes?" and "Who is Mort Sahl?" when Trebek announces the upcoming Double Jeopardy, which of course will be preceded by a commercial. Surely Rosenfarb could be diverted from an ad for carpet shampoo.

Overman knocks again, this time calling out: "Jake! I need to talk to you."

Rosenfarb looks toward the window, shrugs and goes back to his TV. Overman thinks about breaking down the door. It would be a whole lot less dramatic and noisy if he could will the thing open, but his mind has yet to be able to move inanimate objects. He has another idea. Maybe Rosenfarb still has his cell phone. A true salesman couldn't live without a phone, even once he'd stopped selling. Of course he would see that it was Overman calling and could elect not to pick up. But it was worth a shot.

Just as Overman finishes dialing the number, the door opens and out steps Jake Rosenfarb, wielding an empty ice bucket.

"What are you doing here, Overman?" he sneers.

"You know who I am. That's great," Overman replies, relieved.

"Why wouldn't I recognize you? Excuse me. I need ice."

Rosenfarb shuffles down to the end of the all, then shuffles back with his full tub.

"Did you come for the loan money or to ask my forgiveness? Either way, I can't help you."

"Can I come in, Jake? I want to talk to you."

"Knock yourself out," he mutters, entering first without bothering to look back at his guest.

"Jake, I'm worried about you," Overman announces, shoving a pile of dirty clothes off a chair and sitting down.

"That's very sweet. Snapple?"

"No, thanks, I'm good."

"I'm glad you're good, Ira," Rosenfarb shoots back sarcastically, as the Double Jeopardy round comes on.

"If you want to watch the rest of the show, I can wait," Overman says, remembering how much Jake loved being on the business end of deference.

He also knew, however, that Jake was equally fond of one-upping, whether it be at work, tennis or deference.

"I'm pretty sure I know how it ends," Rosenfarb replies, shutting off the television set. "So what is it?"

"I want to help you."

"Who says I need help?"

"Look at you. Look at this place."

"Rita threw me out. As you know, I'm a little strapped for cash."

"Jake, you stopped working. You harassed an eye doctor. You stalked me. What is going on with you?"

"I was tired."

"So that made you go crazy?"

"I didn't go crazy. I just hated my life. It didn't make any sense, so why should *I* have to make sense?"

"You always said you enjoyed being your own boss," Overman reminds him, trying to accentuate the positive.

"In theory it's great. Then you work all those hours trying to make people happy, but no matter what you do, they're never satisfied. You pack up and go home and instead of a peaceful refuge, it's more demands."

Overman understood completely. "I'm sorry it was so tough on you."

"Then when I saw what happened to you, I saw an opportunity. I thought I could help you and shake up my own shitty little world."

"Jake, I didn't even know what it was I had. I'm still learning."

"When you rejected my offer, I had nowhere else to turn."

"I didn't realize that not becoming my sidekick would be so traumatic for you," Overman tells him.

"Neither did I at the time," Jake replies. "You got any more powers since we last spoke?"

"Not really. I tried to teleport like Nightcrawler, so far without success."

"Nightcrawler. Tell me that guy's not a *meshugenah*," Rosenfarb sighs, as if he knows the man personally. He goes on to say how impressed he is that Overman's so familiar with a relatively obscure superhero.

"I've been doing my homework," Overman explains, sharing a few choice Invisible Dick anecdotes before breaking down and popping open a Snapple.

"You look good," Rosenfarb tells him. "The truth is, you're figuring it out on your own. You didn't need me."

Overman studies his face and concludes that Rosenfarb's statement was heartfelt, uttered with respect rather than rancor.

"It's a day-by-day process," Overman says. "I'm still not sure how or why it started, if or when it's going to end. All I know is I want to use what I have to do good things."

"Spoken like a true superhero," Rosenfarb smiles. "Remember though, having these powers also means you're susceptible to becoming a villain. You have to be careful not to fall for that bait."

"Jake, I have no interest in being a villain. The first order of business is to get you back on track."

"That's nice of you, but I'm not sure what track I want to be on. Nothing means anything to me anymore."

Overman knew of one thing that would mean a lot. "What if I could bring Jonathan home?"

Rosenfarb sprang to attention as if struck by a cattle prod. The mention of his son changed his whole body language.

"What are you talking about, Overman? You really think you could get my son back?"

"I'm not saying it's a lock, but suppose I could? Would that make a difference?"

As Rosenfarb nods, a lifetime of sadness oozes out of his soul. Overman has heard it said that the worst thing parents can experience is having a child die before they do, but there was something equally tragic about parents with a living child who has cut off all contact: he is known by others, even has casual acquaintances, but he remains unknowable to them.

"The day he left was the beginning of the end," Rosenfarb explains. "Suddenly Rita became all about fancy jewelry, cosmetic surgery, bathroom remodels with douching toilets. It seemed like nonsense to me, but I felt like I needed to give her whatever she wanted because of what she lost. It finally got to be too much."

Overman thinks he sees a tear in Rosenfarb's eye. He shoves a pizza box aside and sits down on the bed next to him.

"You think if we got him back it would repair the marriage?"

"Who the fuck knows with Rita?" Rosenfarb answers. "But separately or together, at least we'd have our son again."

"I don't know how much I can do, but I might as well give it a try, right?"

"Thank you, Ira."

"I'm going to need your assistance."

Rosenfarb is aglow. While the offer has gone unnamed, he is in effect being given a chance to audition for that pot of gold at the end of the rainbow: the Sidekick Position. And better yet, if it goes well, he will be the one to reap the biggest reward.

"Where is the cult based?" Overman asks.

"In the mountains outside Santa Fe. My understanding is that it's one of those big compounds where they grow their own spinach and shit."

"Are you available to go to New Mexico next week?" Overman knows the answer but wants to appear respectful.

"I can leave now," Rosenfarb shoots back.

"I have a few things I need to take care of first. Maybe you can help me out with them."

"Whatever you need," his friend nods. "Jake Rosenfarb, at your service."

"Don't try to lift that," Rosenfarb admonishes him, swooping in to pick up the TV himself and carry it down the two flights of stairs. "I don't want you to waste your strength on inconsequential things. That's what I'm here for."

In fact, Rosenfarb proves to be a gifted and enthusiastic mover, packing the trunks of both their cars with such efficiency that they are able to complete the entire job in two trips. A lifetime of *schlepping* blinds had produced a knack for organizing that Overman had never been able to master. Rosenfarb explains that this is really the whole point of his involvement: to complement the hero's skills, bringing something to the party that the main attraction is unable to provide.

Overman knew the unspoken eventuality: that the new apartment's second bedroom would be occupied by Rosenfarb until he got up and running. But what the purported hero couldn't get over was that Jake hadn't begged for it or *noodged* at all. In fact, he hadn't even mentioned the idea. Perhaps the real Jake would make himself known at any moment, but regardless, Overman considered the possibility that if he had the ability to change so dramatically, perhaps so did Rosenfarb.

"Where do you want the computer?" Rosenfarb asks, holding up the tower.

"Just put it down in the living room. I haven't figured out where everything goes."

Rosenfarb does as he is told, cheerfully, but not obnoxiously so. They finish the job before lunch, the work having proven to be both seamless and stress-less. As a thank you, Overman tells Rosenfarb he'd like to take him out for something to eat. He decides to run a test on Jake, asking Rosenfarb to pick a place for lunch. In the past, this had been a sure-fire recipe for disaster. Rosenfarb would be in the mood for Mexican but halfway there, suddenly feel like Chinese. They'd sit down at the Chinese place, it would smell funny to him and they'd be out the door on their way to the deli. Generally, it took about fifty minutes from the time he picked the place to the moment you landed at your final dining destination. Just how insane would he be this time?

Without revealing his choice, Jake has Overman drive to the West Valley, past the motel where he still has some of his things. Overman suspects that Jake is pointing him in the direction of a high-end steakhouse, angling to get the most bang for his buck since he knows Overman is picking up the tab. Once again, Rosenfarb surprises. He commandeers them to a mini-mall in Canoga Park where he points to a Vietnamese deli called Da Nang Sandwiches.

"I want to introduce you to *Banh Mi*," he tells Overman. "In case we ever wind up working in that part of the world."

Two high-end *Banh Mi* sandwiches set Overman back less than eight bucks. He is impressed with both the quality of the food (basically a sub with fresh chicken and Asian vegetables) and the unlikely frugality of Rosenfarb's choice. Rosenfarb says that the last few months have taught him that you can cut back and still live well. He admits this is not quite as doable when you're flat broke, so he's extremely grateful for the free chow.

As they sit at one of the two tables listening to the owner and clientele converse in a language they don't understand, Overman bides his time, wondering when Rosenfarb is going to ask for the next favor. He's already resigned to giving Jake the second bedroom, but certainly there must be more on the agenda.

Instead, Jake asks Overman about his life. "How are the kids?" He inquires about Nancy and for the first time in over twenty years, does so without reference to her vagina. He talks about Rita and the deep hole that was left in their hearts when Jonathan stopped speaking to them. Much like the old Overman, he seems to have hit rock bottom, but unlike him, he lacks the tools to do anything about it.

"It's not like I expect to be a superhero. But I'm sure you didn't expect it either," he tells Overman.

"I'm technically not a superhero," Overman replies, wanting to set the record straight. "I've simply turned my life around and can do things I never imagined possible."

"I don't want to quibble over the fine print. My point is, I don't have what you have and I'm not exactly sure how to get out of the ditch I'm in. But springing Jonathan from those diaper heads would be a helluva start."

Overman agrees. "I think it would inspire you."

"Inspiration would be nice," Rosenfarb agrees.

"But I'd rather have cash," is what Overman expects the next line to be. It doesn't come.

Rosenfarb starts to reminisce about the past. How on the day he and his family moved into the Zatzkin house, it was if a pall had been cast over the men and boys of Melvin Terrace. The legendary Estelle and Glorietta had been a ridiculously hard act to follow. Overman tells him about the death of Glorietta's husband and Rosenfarb is appropriately solemn. Testing the waters further, Overman goes on to say that he has been in touch with Janie Sweeney.

"She was a nice girl," Rosenfarb replies. "Very quiet, as I remember. The family moved away all of a sudden and we never heard from her again."

Overman had just assumed his friend knew all about the Lakeview Seven. True, he had left the party early, and the incident had been hushed up afterward for fear of prosecution, but still, this was Jake Rosenfarb, whose nose had a time-share in everyone else's business.

"Janie always seemed like one of those girls who would get more beautiful once you got to know her," Rosenfarb says.

That was Janie to a T. Overman had only found that out recently, but Rosenfarb had picked up on it even way back then.

"Anything wrong?" Rosenfarb asks, sensing that Overman is lost in thought.

Overman is conflicted. He wants to talk about Janie and his dilemma regarding the Lakeview Seven, but still, did it make any sense to share this with someone fresh off a nervous breakdown? It made no sense. Despite that, Overman blurts out the whole story, followed by his quest for justice and his respect for and admiration of Janie. When he is through, he looks up at Rosenfarb for a reaction. Rosenfarb is somber and contemplative as he ponders his response. Overman tries to *utz* him along. "Jake, do you think I'm crazy to want to dig this up after all these years?"

"You're asking me to judge crazy?"

The man had a point.

"Look, Ira. We know what happened was wrong and that nobody paid a price for it. People just went about their lives. As a regular person, this saddens me. As a superhero who could actually do something about it, you feel obligated to stand up for justice. A perfectly natural and commendable reaction." Rosenfarb goes on to cite three Marvel and two DC comic books where superheroes witnessed similar personal injustices and acted upon them. It is obvious to him why Overman is leaning in this direction.

"Isn't this different than a comic book?" Overman asks, hoping to highlight the importance of the real world.

"It's completely different," Rosenfarb concurs. "Because you, my friend, have got Jake Rosenfarb to help you get it done."

Overman's head starts spinning. What has he wrought? He had worked so hard to create a distance between them and now he has willfully re-opened the door, inviting all things Rosenfarb to muscle their way into his personal space. But in truth, Rosenfarb's insanity has thus far been more measured. He is genuinely grateful to Overman for coming to the motel and attempting to

rescue his son. For this he is willing to accept his hero's ground
rules, whatever they may be. He is there to serve.

Overman reports for work the next day, wanting to check up
on Big Dave before departing for points east. He and Rosenfarb
have slated their New Mexico trip for the weekend, but if things
should get complicated and they have to stay longer, Overman
will call the boss and deal with it from there. When the cowbell
rings, Dave marches in with his new squeeze, Juicy in tow and
announces that the two of them plan to be married as soon as
his divorce comes through. They are hopelessly in love, eternally
bound by a passion that takes them to a higher plane, according
to Dave. Juicy Jones nee Lois Czyzyk was a high school dropout
from Elkhart, Indiana who entered the porn business at seventeen,
spent the next five years searching for her niche in the trade, finally
discovering female ejaculation as her God-given calling. Currently
at the top of her game, Juicy is confident that her career will have
a longer life span than the majority of porn stars because of her
unique talent, the only caveat being if the well should literally run
dry. To that end, the x-rated diva has devised a comprehensive
program to keep herself moist, encompassing everything from diet
(lots of ripe melon and avocado) to soaking in bath oils twice a
day, to making sure she inserts something between her legs every
three and a half hours. She explains to Overman that if a penis is
not available, a vibrator or cucumber substitutes quite nicely.

"That's very practical," he notes, trying to be encouraging.

"Thank you," she replies, eyeing a thick, long flashlight on one
of the file cabinets.

Dave has gone back into his office to start working the phones.
Overman must admit that while his boss's new relationship may
not have been meticulously thought out, the thrill of it has energized him. Dave begins dialing up a storm and reeling in takers, a
lender on fire. He'll need as much business as he can get to pay off
Divorce Number Three and the rest to invest for Number Four,

which is a lock as far as Overman is concerned. He can only pray that Dave has the sense to insist on some sort of pre-nup the next time around. The "higher plane" analogy, however, did not bode well for Dave covering his ass.

After Juicy finishes telling Overman her life story, which is mercifully brief, she joins Dave to keep him company while he makes his phone pitches, rewarding him with some brisk, callisthenic fellatio for foreclosing on a car wash in San Antonio. Dave winds up spending the entire day in the back room, emerging only for a quick trip to the bathroom and to send Overman out to get his beloved's lunch of choice. (What else but Jamba Juice?) He doesn't seem in the least bit perturbed when his employee asks to go home at five. There is nothing urgent for Overman to do, but he has been in the habit of sticking around until Dave leaves, a chance to prove his loyalty while at the same time sharpening his Internet research skills.

As Overman arrives at his apartment building and climbs the stairs to the second floor, he is greeted by the pungent aroma of garlic seeping out from one of the doors. To his surprise, he discovers that the irresistible smell is coming from his own kitchen.

"Wash up. Dinner is ready whenever you are," announces a flitting, aproned Rosenfarb. The table has already been set, the domesticity of the scene alarmingly legitimate-looking.

"Since when do you cook?" Overman asks, even more incredulous that Rosenfarb is cooking for him.

"I always played around in the kitchen. That is, when Rita let me. We've got garlic roasted chicken, mashed potatoes, and braised carrots."

"Sounds great," Overman nods, impressed and curious, as always, as to what "braised" means. He goes to his bedroom to change into something comfortable, only to find that while he has been at work, Rosenfarb has arranged and organized his entire wardrobe. Socks and underwear are neatly folded in the top drawer; slacks and shirts hang symmetrically in the closet. The room has the fresh, lemony smell of a recently cleaned hotel room. Overman pauses to consider whether Rosenfarb is auditioning for the role of sidekick or wife. In truth, Nancy had never been that neat or orderly, so on some level Jake Rosenfarb was a step up.

The food is simple, but delicious, the conversation uncharacteristically productive. As Rosenfarb lays it out, he intends to earn his keep by running all the day-to-day aspects of life that a superhero shouldn't have to be bothered with. In addition to the shopping, cooking and cleaning, Jake will be in charge of the calendar that keeps track of whatever heroic deeds were on the docket. Right now, New Mexico has been blazoned into the books. He has reserved airline tickets for early Saturday morning, one of which is completely refundable in case Overman decides to attempt another teleportation. They are also booked into an inexpensive motel about thirty miles from the Swami Guptananda compound in the Sangre de Cristo Mountains. Rosenfarb has compiled satellite photos of the area and printed out various game plans based on rescues previously performed by other superheroes.

"It looks like a lot of reading, but I can summarize it for you, if you prefer," he explains.

"I think the main thing we need to do is figure out how we're going to get in there to see Jonathan," replies Overman.

"It might just have to be you going in," Rosenfarb informs him. "If he sees me, he'll resist. You'll have to get him out alone, then bring him to me on the outside."

"Assuming they let me see him in the first place. My sense is that these groups don't take too kindly to outsiders. Plus, what is Jonathan going to think when he sees me?"

"It's delicate stuff," Rosenfarb agrees. "Tell me. How good are you at shape-shifting?"

"I've never had the pleasure," Overman states. "I think that's strictly a comic book thing."

"Too bad. These swamis love their hot young chicks. If we could turn you into a blond with a nice full rack, you could walk right in."

Cooking him dinner was one thing, but Rosenfarb imagining him as a young girl with big breasts kind of crossed the line as far as Overman was concerned. "I'm really not comfortable with that kind of thinking, Jake," he informed his friend.

"Relax. You don't have to be a chick. You could be a cat or something."

"But I don't know how to shape-shift."

"And I'm not crazy about cats. If you happen to learn how to do it, reconsider the boobs."

"Jake —"

"I'm just saying — whatever gets the job done."

Rosenfarb rises to clear the table and Overman takes the opportunity to excuse himself. Having not spoken with Janie since she called about Garvin's stroke, he wants to touch base to see if there has been any improvement. He was sad for Garvin, who didn't deserve such a fate, and worried about Janie, who might well be left with a husband who no longer recognized her. And of course it couldn't help her mental state that a painful wound had needlessly been ripped open, courtesy of one Ira Overman.

He felt himself trembling as he auto-dialed the number from his cell phone. No answer, just a voicemail, recorded in happier times. Overman hated leaving messages during crises like this. What could one say in thirty seconds that didn't sound trivial? Leaving a long, concerned offer of sympathy was even worse. Few things are more irritating than a voice message that goes on past its welcome. Nonetheless, Overman must give it a go.

"Hi, Janie, it's Ira," he begins. "Just checking in, wanted to see how Garvin is. I'm going to New Mexico on Saturday, but you can call me anytime, day or night. I really want to know how he's doing. How you're doing, too. My love to both of you."

"My love to both of you?" Very un-Overman-like, in the historical scheme of things. The only explanation was that in his evolving state, he had been deeply touched by these people; moved by a relationship that while only experienced for a couple of hours, appeared to be the healthiest he had ever known. What he hadn't witnessed in the way of facts was filled in by looks and gestures, by the grace of a husband and wife who were not about possessions and fancy homes, but dealt in the true definition of real estate: living a life with meaning and valuing the real things that mattered. Overman had to wonder. In the event Garvin could never communicate again, what meaning could one find in that?

"Come get your parfait," boomed Rosenfarb's voice from the kitchen.

When was the last time he had a parfait? When was the last time he had even heard that word? Fittingly, it was at Jonathan Rosenfarb's Bar Mitzvah.

———————————————————

The plane trip from Los Angeles to Albuquerque is all business. The plan, as of now, is for Overman to drop off Rosenfarb at the motel outside Santa Fe and then continue solo to the mountain headquarters of the Guptananda Fellowship. Once there, he will attempt to gain admittance by politely expressing an interest in Hinduism and possible cult membership. ("Who's the leader of the cult that's made for you and me? G-U-P-T-A-N-A-N-D-N-A.") Should this prove ineffective, he will revert to Plan B, summoning every ounce of willpower in his arsenal to obtain an audience with the brainwashed son of a dopey sidekick. There were no guarantees of either ploy being successful, but at the moment, it's all he's got. Rosenfarb has been pushing the idea of Overman teleporting his way in even though he's heard, in specific detail, the sorry results of his friend's second stab at it. On the way home from work one night, Overman attempted to transport himself into the local Ross Dress-For-Less, purposefully closing his eyes while imagining a cabal of bargain hunters poking ravaging the lingerie rack. As hundreds of bras and thongs did an underwear dance in his head, Overman absentmindedly dropped his cell phone into the street. Rushing to retrieve it, he found himself face-to-face with five thousand pounds of screeching metal, barely managing to scramble back to safety on the sidewalk.

Rosenfarb's reaction to the failed teleportation: "Hey, the only way to get to Carnegie Hall is practice, practice, practice." He believed that it was only a matter of time before his friend rivaled the big guys with capes. "When Nightcrawler was starting out, he couldn't do an invasive teleportation worth shit. This is only the beginning for you and you've made unbelievable progress. Eat your sandwich."

Rosenfarb takes out a pair of freshly made turkey subs from his carry-on bag. "I'll bet you've never been pampered like this."

Overman had to agree. How odd was it to have Jake Rosenfarb be the person overseeing his welfare and anticipating his every need? He understood that his friend was grateful and would be eternally so should Overman rescue his son from the clutches of the swami. But still, there was something bizarre about how effortlessly Rosenfarb took to this sidekick position. Perhaps this was the role he was born to play.

When lunch is over, Rosenfarb lets his new boss know that he has not forgotten about the Marty Merkowitz and company situation. He has pooled his own research with Janie's and has a number of ideas as to where to begin. Overman tells him that all bets may be off due to her husband's condition.

"All the more reason why we need to take action," Rosenfarb says. "If the rest of her life is going in the dumper, we have the responsibility to make this part right."

"But I want her to feel good about whatever it is I do on her behalf," Overman asserts.

"And she will. She's not dealing with egomaniacs like The Justice League of America. She's got a sensitive team behind her. We are not going to do anything that makes her feel uncomfortable in any way."

Overman takes this in, amazed at how seriously Rosenfarb is treating all of this while maintaining a level-headedness that, until now, had been entirely absent from his being. "Thanks for your help, Jake," Overman smiles. "This bread is great, incidentally."

"It should be," Rosenfarb replies. "I baked it myself."

Overman tells his friend that while he appreciates Rosenfarb's interest in exploring the Merkowitz affair, they should probably concentrate on their work in New Mexico for the time being. Rosenfarb is happy to oblige. The last thing he wants is to overtax his superhero with unneeded stress. To that end, he refrains from asking Overman to "will" their curvy flight attendant into giving him her phone number.

"Why do you think Jonathan joined this group in the first place?" Overman asks Jake, thinking it a good idea to stay on point.

"He was rebelling against the life he saw us living, I guess. Now I'm doing the same thing. Funny, isn't it?"

"But would you ever cut off all contact from everyone close to you?" Overman asks.

"Maybe, if they disappointed me as badly as we disappointed him."

Apparently Rosenfarb saw himself and Rita as parental failures, too. Overman was lucky in that his kids had done well despite him. But who knows? Maybe Jonathan Rosenfarb was also thriving in his own new-agey way. Still, Jake and Rita's sense of loss was genuine, and they deserved one more chance to make their dysfunctional family whole.

As the plane lands, Overman checks his new cell phone to see if there are any messages from Janie. There are no voicemails, but there is an email of note. The subject line: "YOU ARE SO SWEET, HOW ARE YOU?" bodes well, given that the sender is Glorietta Zatzkin Feinman. Rosenfarb is very much impressed that Overman still has a connection to the female who inspired so much lust in so many. He asks his friend if he'd mind reading the missive out loud. Since Rosenfarb has been on his best behavior, Overman relents.

> Dear Ira,
>
> I just returned from traveling through Europe with a friend and was both surprised and touched to learn that you had made a donation in Fred's name. After a year of non-stop grieving, I wanted to try to get out of my own head and see a bit of the world. While I still think of him every day, I realize now that I do have the capacity to move on. And knowing that there are people in the world like you makes it a little easier. Thank you for your kindness and generosity. It would be great to see you again sometime. Do you ever get to Florida?
>
> Love,
>
> Glorietta
>
> P.S. Remember that night? Tee-hee.

"What night?" Rosenfarb asks. "And what's the 'tee-hee' all about?"

"Nothing, just an in-joke."

"You have an in-joke with Glorietta Zatzkin? That's incredible. Elastic-Man couldn't pull that off."

Overman had deliberately withheld news of the Zatzkin tryst all these years because he was certain Rosenfarb would grill him for the rest of their lives about details of her breasts and all points south. And even though there were considerable bragging rights

to be had, they hardly seemed worth the envy they would engender. But as Overman thought about it, he realized that unleashing
the previously guarded information could provide a window into
the staying power of Rosenfarb's makeover. How hard would the
sidekick press the issue? Would he begin to come undone, and if
so, how insane would he be driven by this mysterious tidbit?

"What's the joke between the two of you, if you don't mind
my asking?"

If this wasn't classic Rosenfarb prying, what was?

"She stayed over at my dorm one night at Columbia."

"And…"

"We, you know —"

"Holy shit. You fucked Glorietta Zatzkin? You got to feel
those things against you?"

"We were stoned…and drunk," Overman nods.

"That's enormous. Batman-level stuff. How could you keep
this from me, Ira?"

"The whole thing was a fluke. It was never meant to happen."

"An even better story. Do you realize how many guys would've
killed to be you? If you remember, Larry Lebowitz almost committed suicide because she broke up with him before he got to
feel her up."

"It was a long time ago. I'm sure Lebowitz is doing just fine."

"I heard he had a massive coronary. But on the mend."

"I'm glad." Overman had always sympathized with Lebowitz's frustration. He had come so close before woefully missing
the mark.

"I don't know what to say about this news."

"You don't have to say anything because it doesn't affect us
worth shit. The whole thing was a zillion years ago."

"I'm in awe of you, Ira. Don't try and take that away from me."

"Suit yourself. It's all yours."

"I mean, first I find out you're a superhero and now this. You
got any other secrets I need to know?"

"Just that we're the only passengers left on the plane. Maybe we should get off."

Rosenfarb looks to the front of the aircraft and sees that the flight crew is waiting for them to make their exit. He gathers his things and heads for the door, stopping to give the blond flight attendant his business card. "If you ever need window treatments, give a holler. I'd love to do your blinds."

Overman rides shotgun on the drive into Santa Fe as his side-kick has insisted on him preserving his energy. Rosenfarb's new-found admiration for his friend is palpable and slightly creepy, the window man shaking his head and smiling at him moonily every couple of miles.

"I'm really happy that one of us got to enjoy her," Rosenfarb announces. "Who knows? Maybe it's cosmic payback for me banging Nancy first."

"Who knows?" Overman echoes, failing to see the philosophical symmetry, but wanting to end this conversation as fast as humanly possible. The *noodge* door was starting to re-open.

"I probably should have said something a long time ago, but I'm sorry I had sex with Nancy before you did. Maybe if I hadn't gotten in there first, you two would've stayed together."

"I doubt it. You're giving yourself way too much credit."

"Touché," Rosenfarb laughs. They drive a few miles in silence, but the potent combination of curiosity and coveting is unable to contain itself any longer.

"So what were they like? Nice and heavy, I bet." The reference of course, was to Glorietta's generous endowments.

"To the best of my recollection, they were substantial in the weight department."

"Round or cylindrical?"

"Very round, especially for the kind of mass we're talking about." Overman decides to lay it all out on the table in an effort to pre-empt any follow-up questions. "Pink nipples, medium sized areolas, nicely groomed landing strip."

"Fantastic. What a coup. I'm happy for you, Ira. But I would be less than honest if I didn't tell you that I wish it had been me."

Rosenfarb always did excel at stating the obvious. "Jake, this was eons ago. We're grown men now with real lives. In retrospect, don't you think it's all a little silly?"

"We are each the sum of our parts," Rosenfarb reminds his passenger. "It seems to me that Glorietta Zatzkin was instrumental in shaping how we came to view women."

"Come on. We were young, horny guys and she was stacked."

"She was our goddess. The impossible dream we could never attain, but nevertheless taught us how to be men. Of course the icing on the cake for you was that the dream came true."

"If it makes you feel any better, she made sure I knew it was a big mistake. That it never would have happened if she hadn't been under the influence."

"That does help a little. Thanks."

They reach the Days Inn right off the freeway and check into a non-smoking room with two queen beds that reeks of tobacco. Rosenfarb pledges to address the issue with the motel manager while Overman heads off to take care of business.

"Good luck up there. Call my cell as soon as you know something."

"I will. Assuming I can get a signal. See you later."

Overman starts for the door when the all but broken window man calls out to him.

"Ira?"

"Yeah, Jake?"

"You're a great friend. You have no idea how much this means to me." Rosenfarb is genuinely moved, but Overman feels he must downplay the moment.

"It'll mean even more if I can pull it off. Later." Putting the Ford Focus in drive and peeling out of the motel parking lot, Overman is renewed by the brisk mountain air and the humbling big sky. As he winds his way north, taking in the dramatic picture of the light hitting the jagged, brown hills, he is struck by the feeling that anything is possible. Why shouldn't he be able to spring Jonathan Rosenfarb? So what if he lacked Superman's cape or a secret potion like Invisible Dick? He was still a man reborn, the same man who told Hal Steinbaum to "take a flying fuck" and never looked back.

Next to the stark beauty of its surrounds, the mountain town of Sorayò, New Mexico, was best known for a half-century of drug problems, encompassing everything from heroin distribution to property crimes, record rates of deaths due to overdose, and multiple large-scale federal drug raids. It was against this storied backdrop that Sri Guptananda nee Steven Yoder from Akron, Ohio, built his utopian community, melding tenets of Buddhism and Hinduism with good old-fashioned Woodstockian values. Yoder was an ex-hippie who had studied briefly with the swami Sri Chinmoy before breaking off to form his own sect. The Guptananda Fellowship, as he dubbed it, started with thirteen members, grew to over a hundred at one point, and was now down to somewhere around forty diehard followers.

Overman climbed State Road 76, looking for a dirt turn-off called New Pueblo Junction, which ended at a private road that had recently been, renamed Guptananda Gulch. The map indicated that New Pueblo was five miles north of the town center, but as Overman traveled back and forth over ten miles, he could find nothing. On his third pass through the village center, he decided to pull into the Wal-Mart parking lot to see if anyone could give him directions. He found it ironic that a town full of drug dealers, felons and sex offenders uniformly referred to the residents of the Guptananda Fellowship as "The Crazy Ones." Nobody knew how to get there but everyone told him to avoid the place.

"What's wrong with these people?" Overman had to ask.

"Niños de Diablo," answered an eighty year-old toothless man selling Indian artifacts out of a garbage bag, running away from Overman as if he, too, were one of the Devil's children. A mother with two young toddlers claimed they were cannibals who ate only women and vegetables. Overman didn't try to engage her further, thinking it best to move on to the normal-looking guy who had just purchased a t-ball set for his son. The man didn't know where the place was, but gave Overman his email address in case Overman found it. He'd like to take little Jimmy hippie-hunting sometime. The boy flashed his best Aspiring Delinquent smile, convincing Overman that the Sorayò Wal-mart was the wrong place to be seeking such information.

The gas station owner up the road is more helpful. He says that he has never had a bad experience with the Fellowship and has even visited the compound for one of their holiday feasts. "Nice folks, tasty beets," he recollects. The man explains that the reason the Pueblo Junction turnoff is so hard to find is that it has gotten overgrown with brush in the past number of years.

"Isn't it the town's or the county's or the state's responsibility to keep up the road?" Overman asks.

"Technically, yes. But since the town doesn't like the Guptanandas and they don't like visitors, it just kind of gets left the way it is and nobody says anything."

"Why don't people like them?" Overman feels he must inquire once again.

"Because the Fellowship folks keep to themselves. Anybody who lives in your town that don't want nothing to do with their neighbors is suspect, you know."

"But you said they open themselves up to visitors at holiday time," Overman reminds him.

"That's true. But it's their turf and there's no meat. People around here don't trust folks who don't eat meat. Plus, who wants to see guys in turbans at Christmas time?"

"Didn't the Wise Men wear headdresses?" Overman ventures.

"Sure, but they were wise, not kooks," the man explains. "Anyway, I don't think they're bad people out there. A little whacked out, but who isn't, am I right?"

"Probably," Overman says, feeling fortunate to have met the one semi-tolerant individual in town. "So how would I go about finding the road?"

The station owner explains that after the four-mile marker, you go exactly 5/8 of a mile and see a huge cottonwood tree on your right. On the other side of that tree is an unmarked road that has two Ponderosa pines on the left side. It doesn't really look like a road at first because there is so much brush on the ground, but once you pass the two Ponderosas you'll see a clear path up the mountain.

Overman thanks him and offers the man a ten-spot for his time, which he refuses.

"See if you can get me some of them beets."

Overman can't imagine they'll be serving him a vegetable medley once they learn of his mission, but should he happen upon the desired roots, he will be happy to bring some back.

The four-mile marker is half obscured by windblown trash and errant dust devils that have been stopped in their tracks by the shiny metal post. Overman re-sets his trip odometer and slows to 35 mph as he searches for the all-important cottonwood tree. He considers for a moment that the gas station owner is nothing but a beet-loving nut job who enjoys sending out-of-towners on wild goose chases. The fact that Overman couldn't identify a Ponderosa pine or a cottonwood if they bit him on the nose is perhaps of greater concern. But the guy said the cottonwood was big, so no matter what Overman saw at the 5/8 mile point he was going to pull off the road. As advertised, he comes upon a huge arching tree, its expansive limbs full of yellowing, diamond-shaped leaves. There is no road in sight, but sure enough, as Overman inches past the cottonwood he sees a sandy path full of low brush that should be the ticket. He turns right and bumps his way down the dirt clearing, which, even at 10 mph, is a grueling ordeal that makes him wish he had shelled out the extra fifteen bucks for a four-wheel drive. As the nausea starts to kick in, he briefly entertains the notion of parking the car and attempting a Hail Mary teleportation. He then realizes that even should it work, there was no guarantee of success on the return trip, at which point he would ideally have Jonathan in tow.

Seven miles in, there don't seem to be any dwellings or other roads in sight. Bladder shaken like a double martini, he pulls over to take a whiz. The quiet is near absolute, save for an occasional bird chirp that could just as easily be a robin as a crow, since he knows as much about birds as he does about anything in nature. Overman gets back in the car, drives another six miles and suddenly realizes that he is without water. Much as Jake Rosenfarb has elevated him to superhero status, he can't quite imagine Spiderman or Batman driving down a dirt road in a rented Ford Focus, faced with an irritated prostate and no way of obtaining liquids.

After three more miles, Overman grabs his cell phone, thinking it prudent to fill in Rosenfarb on his progress or more specifically, lack thereof. He's not surprised to learn that there is no cellular signal as the Sangre de Cristos are now enveloping him on all sides. Determined, Overman presses on, searching for any sign of life. He imagined that sooner or later, one of the Guptanandas would have to drive into town for supplies so perhaps he'll spot a westbound swami barreling toward him in a Ford F-150. A few minutes later, a bright orange object on the side of the road diverts his attention. Pulling over and bending down to inspect the item, he sees it is a silk scarf, possibly brand new, that must have recently been blown to the ground. Then, appearing out of the blue like some dusty southwestern Brigadoon, Overman notices a cluster of ramshackle structures off in the distance. He quickly pockets the scarf, figuring that attempting to find its owner would serve as a good introduction should he have indeed discovered civilization.

The Focus slows to 8 mph, Overman not wanting to miss the turnoff. 3/5 of a mile later there is a "private road" sign on the right. He cuts the wheel, heading for what surely must be the Guptananda compound. Overman doesn't know how it is possible for there to be a road bumpier than the one he has been on, but Guptananda Gulch Extension is the hands down bladder-buster of all time. The would-be superhero decides to hold it in, not daring to take the chance of alienating a soul by urinating on private property. He inches closer to the makeshift buildings, spotting an outhouse or two among them. Apparently, in his quest for enlightenment, Jonathan Rosenfarb has not only given up his family, but indoor plumbing to boot.

As Overman reaches the front gate, a hastily assembled hodge-podge of wood and chicken wire with a flimsy buzzer and speaker set-up off to the side, the sign posted in front of him takes him aback. What Hindu or Buddhist tenet could have inspired the words: "Trespassers will be shot. Survivors will be shot again." An anxious, queasy feeling overtakes him, but he has come an awfully long way to back out now. He rings the buzzer and roughly thirty seconds later hears a pleasant woman's voice greet him.

"Guptananda is Love, how may I help you?"

Overman has gone over many opening lines, but the "no tres-passing" sign has thrown him. "Uh, I think I found something that belongs to someone here. An orange silk scarf."

"Thank you very much. Orange garments are worn by our *Sannsyasin.*"

Overman has no idea what that is, but the gate opens and the dirt-encrusted Focus motors through. The woman with whom he had been speaking greets him warmly as he gets out of the car. She is young, white, maybe late twenties, wearing a flowing robe and a big-ass dot in the middle of her forehead. Her face lights up when he hands her the scarf.

"Sannsyasi Ajatashatru," she immediately proclaims upon inspection. "He will be so grateful to have it back. I'm Gita."

"Ira Overman. Nice to meet you."

"The *Sannsyasin* are our most respected monks so this scarf is very important to us."

"Glad I could be of service," Overman replies.

"Are you looking at my *bindi*?" she asks.

"Of course not. You can't see anything under those robes anyway."

"I'm talking about the mark on my forehead. The *bindi* is a reminder to use and cultivate spiritual vision in order to better understand life's inner workings."

"Wow. A whole lot more going on there than a big old dot," Overman counters, suddenly aware of how stupid he must sound.

The lame remark doesn't even register, Gita responding instead with the inevitable and only relevant question: "So what brings you all the way out here, Mr. Overman?"

"Well, I happen to really like Hinduism," he answers, making the dot retort sound like a dissertation on Schrödinger's Cat.

"I see. You drove all the way out here because you *like* Hinduism?" She isn't buying it for a second.

Almost unconsciously, Overman finds himself taking a completely new tack, introducing a premise that by all rights he should have thought of long before now. "Look, I'm not going to lie to you. I do like Hinduism. I mean, what's not to like, but —"

"You're really here because —"

"It's just so sad," Overman shakes his head. "I need to have a word with one of your members. He has a parent who is very, very sick."

This was actually a statement of fact. Although there were no physical infirmities, both Rosenfarb parents were two of the sickest people Overman had ever come across.

The smile suddenly disappears from the woman's face. "If I might ask, who is it you that you absolutely must talk with?"

"His name is Jonathan Rosenfarb."

Gita shakes her head. "I've only been in Swami Guptananda's grace for six months, but we have no one here by that name."

"I see," Overman replies, scrambling to keep the subject alive. "Do you think you might be able to talk to some people? Maybe check the files?"

The woman is ready to send him packing, which Overman clearly finds difficult to accept. He has put in too much effort to throw in the towel without a fight. But what are his options? He thinks for a moment, then goes to the one reliable move in his playbook: the move that has worked so magnificently for him time and again.

Gita looks up to see Overman staring into her eyes. "I wouldn't bother you if this wasn't so serious," he implores.

There is a long pause, Gita disturbingly poker-faced. Overman is sure all is lost when she finally opens her mouth to speak: "Let me ask around. Perhaps another resident will have the information you're looking for."

"Thank you so much," Overman bows. He is glad for the reprieve, but cognizant that he might well be witnessing the Hindu equivalent of "checking with my manager" at the dealership. It was possible that Gita would go in the back, stand in an empty room for fifteen minutes, maybe meditate or do some bullshit yoga, then return and apologize for not being able to find what he's looking for. That was the nice version. The R-rated Director's Cut might involve backing up the threats on the "no trespassing" sign with an AK-47 or two.

Overman waits by the car, looking for traces of human activity and/or automatic weapons. He is there forty-five minutes before Gita emerges to inform him that she is sorry, no one has ever heard of a Jonathan Rosenfarb. She then invites him to leave the premises, thanking him again for the scarf and cheerfully reiterating: "Guptananda is Love."

"Tons of love, I'm sure," Overman vamps, hoping to somehow delay being tossed out on his ass. "Hey, tell me what you think this means. I am positive that in a past life, I cooked an awesome Tandoori Chicken."

She stares at him blankly, Overman realizing that he has not helped his case since the Guptanandas are strict vegetarians.

"So nice to meet you, Mr. Overman. Drive carefully."

Gita saunters back to her shack, leaving Overman to ponder what else might be lurking on these grounds, how many sets of eyes might be peering out at him from behind bushes. The silence is the most frightening part. What if all the Fellowship members have been killed and are buried in a shallow grave somewhere on the property? What if the young, bindi-branded Gita now shares the compound with Guptananda, a couple of other concubines and thirty-six corpses? Overman is certain that the longer he lingers, the closer he will come to provoking whatever is hiding behind these decrepit walls. He turns the Ford around and drives about a mile before pulling off the road and parking behind some overgrown shrubbery. Recognizing that if something should happen to the car, he will be hard-pressed to get back to Santa Fe in one piece, he also imagines how he might feel if one of his kids were trapped in this God-forsaken place. The plethora of unsettling thoughts and images give him the impetus to set out on foot. Doubling back toward the compound in as quiet and unobtrusive a way as he can manage, Overman visualizes himself as a chameleon, subtly becoming one with the parched New Mexican scrub.

Aside from the abject fear pulsating throughout his body, it is a peaceful trek. The sound of the soft earth beneath him, the soothing tweets of unidentifiable birds, the spotting of two jackrabbits and a non-rattling snake: all lovely stuff if one isn't worried about being offed by an axe-murderer. A half-mile or so into the walk, he sees an opening. Literally. There is a small but discernible break in the barbed-wire fence surrounding the compound. Kneeling down to inspect the hole, Overman determines that while it is not anywhere big enough to slide through, the surrounding metal may be damaged enough to manipulate. Further examination reveals that the edges of the break are covered in rust and corroded, some of the fencing brittle enough to break off, the rest sufficiently malleable to bend back. Within minutes, Overman is slithering furtively on Guptananda soil, headed for a confrontation he would feel a whole lot better about were he the comic book brand of superhero as opposed to the Rosenfarb-anointed kind. He approaches what appears to be a former barn, a huge wobbly affair that looks as if it could be blown over in a heartbeat by even the gentlest of summer breezes. The flimsiness of the edifice makes it all the more mind-blowing when Overman peeks through the window and sees its contents.

Through the glass, staring him square in the face is the most spectacular collection of classic Bentleys the ex-Mercedes dealer has ever laid eyes on. He recognizes the massive but elegant 1960 S2, a '65 S3 Continental convertible with so-called "Chinese headlamps," and a vintage 1931 all-alloy 8 Liter two-door which, to Overman's recollection, was valued somewhere in the high six figures. He had learned all about Bentleys from Gene Cantalupo, the bottom-feeding pre-owned salesman who had somehow amassed his own personal fleet of them, and broadcasted their value to anyone who would or wouldn't listen. Doing the math in his head, Overman's ballpark appraisal of the swami's collection veers well into the millions. He imagines himself a superhero whose specialty is jump-starting and stealing vintage vehicles. Automotive Man wheels up to Cantalupo's door in the 8-Liter '31, bearing the news that in addition to his jump-starting prowess, he has successfully hot-wired Maricela Flores. The delightful daydream is short-lived, Overman remembering that he is not in the market for an English car, but a brainwashed son.

He slithers onward. A third of a mile up the road, he comes upon an even shabbier structure, a space one could not imagine being used for anything but feeding horses or scooping up their shit. Incredibly, it is filled with thirty or so men, women and children of various races, deep in meditation. In front of them, a turbaned white man with a graying blond beard leads the assembly in a guttural, droning chant. From the pictures Overman has reviewed online, the turbaned one can only be the infamous Swami Guptananda. Overman scans the group, but from this vantage point, is unable to identify anyone resembling the younger Rosenfarb. Creeping to the window on his left for a different view, he is suddenly and violently grabbed by two large bearded, turbaned men. Trying to explain that he has come in peace, the "Guptananda is Love" thing does not seem to apply in this particular instance. One robed follower pins him down while the other pummels him with a series of jabs and uppercuts. It all happens so fast that Overman is unable to summon any kind of power, will or otherwise. A disadvantage of being reborn in middle age was that he still had to work with middle-aged reflexes. Everything Overman had accomplished up until now, he had done with deliberation. The vegetarian attackers of the Fellowship had not afforded him such a luxury.

He awakens in some sort of storage room, surrounded by huge sacks of brown rice, lentils and dried peas alongside the familiar Kirkland bulk items purchased at Costco. Admittedly off-point considering his circumstance, Overman finds himself wondering if the most common link between Americans today is the shared experience of using Kirkland paper products. As he tries to sit up, he realizes that his hands and feet have been bound. Using both elbows for leverage, he manages to prop up his head on a sack of rice. He hears murmuring outside the door but is unable to make out any of it. The door creaks open and one of his assailants enters, Overman recognizing him as the man who held him down rather than the pummeler, which provides a small sense of relief.

"I'm sorry we had to be so harsh with you," the man says, in an accent that sounds either Indian or Mexican.

"Roger that," agrees Overman, wondering if his wise-ass retort will earn him another beating.

"There are bad people out there who want to destroy us," the man explains.

"I'm not one of them, believe me."

"Then why did you stay here after you had been asked to leave?"

Overman takes another stab at it, hoping for a more receptive audience this time around. "My friend is very sick and he believes his son is with you. I had to at least try to see him."

"But you were told he isn't here."

"That's true. But I felt I couldn't face his father unless I had determined that for myself."

"You trespassed on private property."

"And I apologize for that." Overman knows he needs a major maneuver here. "Might I ask your name?"

"Dhani."

"That's beautiful. Dhani, if you were estranged from your own son and learned that you were going to die, wouldn't you want to see him one last time?" Overman looks deep into the man's eyes. He might not have his strength but that didn't mean his willpower was gone.

"It is difficult to respond to your question, because my only family is the Fellowship of Guptananda," poker-faced Dhani answers.

"Fair enough," Overman nods. "Suppose then, that God forbid, Swami Guptananda was stricken gravely ill, and faced with the possibility that he might never see one of his most devoted followers until the next life." The reincarnation *schtick* worked much better this time around, Overman thought to himself. "Wouldn't he want to look in your eyes one last time, Dhani?"

"I would hope so," the man replies, gamely challenged by this hypothetical scenario.

"That's all I'm trying to say. Jake Rosenfarb is certainly no swami but he is a decent man who deserves to leave this earth with an ounce of dignity. Denying him a visit with his son would guarantee a cruel and painful exit. I know that is the last thing a holy man like Swami Guptananda would want."

As Dhani takes this in, Overman wonders if perhaps he has pushed it a bit too far by playing the death card, an out and out lie.

"I'll see what I can do," Dhani tells him. "Are you comfortable, Mr. Overman?"

"I'd feel a little better if you could untie these," Overman smiles, holding out his hands.

"I'm sorry, I don't have the authority to do that," Dhani apologizes, proceeding to walk out the door.

While Overman senses he has made progress, his confidence begins to erode as the hours pass with no movement. He notes that if his willpower had indeed had some effect on Dhani, perhaps it could also be used to untie his hands and feet. The aching ex-Mercedes salesman closes his eyes, convinced that the only way to escape captivity is by immersing his consciousness in the joy of freedom. The mobile tilt-a-whirl in Fresh Meadows, the intoxicating spell of the Zatzkin women, the watershed moment when his daughter began to see him in a whole new light. Yes, he was fearful and wounded, yet he felt his spirit begin to soar, his blood rushing with a strength and determination that belied his weakened frame. But was it enough strength to burst out of these bindings? Before he has the chance to find out, Dhani returns to the storage room with another follower in tow.

"I'm sorry I took so long," Dhani informs him. "But your request was debated at length by the *Sannsyasin*. This is Manavendra," he says, introducing his cohort, so similarly robed, turbaned and bearded that Overman can barely tell the difference between them.

"I guess the fact that there was such a long debate means that Jonathan is here," Overman replies, his newfound strength prompting his less than tactful pressing of the issue.

"Jonathan is not here," replies Manavendra, who affects a much sterner presence than Dhani.

"Then why would anyone bother to debate my request?"

"Manavendra should be able to help you," Dhani informs him. "I will see you at evening meditation, Manavendra."

"*Namasté*," Manavendra answers, clasping his hands together and bowing his head.

Dhani walks out the door, leaving Overman alone with the dour new guy.

Manavendra gets right to the point. "Here's what I know. Jonathan wants no further contact with his family."

"So he was actually on the premises at some point?" Overman asks, trying to nail down something.

"He was," Manavendra confirms. "He left three years, eight months and twenty-six days ago."

"Then how could you know what his wishes are now?"

"You wanted the answer, I gave it to you," is Manavendra's retort. "Will that be all, Mr. Overman?"

Something about that smug look gets to Overman. Also, the obsessive way the guy spelled out to the day when Jonathan Rosenfarb left the Guptanandas. What kind of idiot speaks in statistics like that? And then it hits him. Wasn't it Jake who in a moment of characteristic pettiness, pointed out that he had beaten Overman in tennis 232 sets to 1? This kind of mindless specificity could only be genetic. He takes a closer look at the haughty, robed one, suspecting that the answer lies under the bushy beard.

"Manavendra Rosenfarb?"

"I dropped the 'Rosenfarb' three years, eight months and twenty-six days ago. My surname is Guptananda now."

"Do you remember me, Jonathan? I'm sorry — Manavendra."

"I do. You're the used car salesman."

"Actually it's new cars and I don't do that anymore."

"My parents always used to put you down. They called you a hopeless loser."

"Can't say I blame them," Overman nods. "I had a lot of bad luck, made some unfortunate choices."

"I hated the way they talked about people; their callous judgment, always diminishing the value of others."

"Nobody's perfect, Manavendra."

"I'm embarrassed to tell you that I once heard them joking about how my father had sex with your wife."

"It was a long time ago, before we were married. We're divorced now, by the way."

"Mr. Overman, I'm sorry you have to live in a world so full of deceit and unhappiness. That is why I left for the welcoming and loving arms of the Guptananda family."

"Your father is not in a good place right now, Manavendra. His most fervent wish was for me to help find you."

"After the way he talked about you, why would you ever want to help him?"

"Because I know it's the right thing to do."

"How sick is my father?"

"Enough that he stopped working and your mother kicked him out of the house."

"She's even more unenlightened than he is," Manavendra snorts.

"Which is where you come in," Overman explains, not quite sure where he's going with this. "A visit with you could turn everything around."

"People don't change overnight, Mr. Overman."

"Please, call me Ira. Let's put our own prejudices aside and look at the facts. You remember the moment you became Manavendra, down to the exact day, correct?"

"Yes."

"So in a sense, you became a different person overnight."

"You can't compare my situation with theirs. I was fortunate enough to be in the presence of a powerful teacher who had the ability to transform me."

"And I'm saying that maybe you have that same power. Maybe we all do." This is sounding pretty good to Overman, like one of those interchangeable self-help books that simplify everything but nevertheless strike a chord with people.

"There are few who possess the gifts of His Holiness Guptananda."

"What would you say Manavendra, if I told you that I have that power?"

The former Jonathan Rosenfarb can't help but giggle.

"Ah. You laugh at me, much the way your parents did," Overman reacts. "Perhaps your enlightenment has not been so complete."

"I'm sorry, that was wrong of me. It's just that a car salesman comparing himself to the swami. I mean —"

"Excuse me but His Holiness Guptananda was a convicted drug dealer named Steven Yoder before he got into the swami business. I may have sold lemons, but I never got anyone hooked on cocaine."

"Guptananda repented when he was shown the light. Have you been touched by God?"

"I don't like to be touched by supernatural beings I don't know. But that's not the point."

"What is?" the young man asks, starting to become annoyed.

"That I'm aware of the things your father may have said about me in the past, but I have gained the power to rise above his pettiness. As well as my own. Are you powerful enough to do the same?"

Manavendra thinks about this for a second, then sighs: "Fine. Tell him I forgive him. Nice to see you, Mr. Overman. Ira," he corrects himself, starting for the door.

"I'm sure your dad will appreciate that. One last thing."

The young ex-Rosenfarb turns back.

"Manavendra. I think it's important that you see your father one more time, maybe the last time ever. We're staying in Santa Fe. Come back and visit for an hour, if only to show him how enlightened his son has become."

The young man looks down at the floor. "I can't do that."

"Why not?"

"It would be against the swami's wishes."

"What if I spoke to the swami?" Overman volunteers. "How do I speak to Guptananda?"

"You request a private session and one of the *Sannsyasin* will get back to you in a week or so."

"I don't know that we have a week, son," Overman replies, bending the truth in the interest of getting the fuck out of there.

"It's that bad?"

The storage room prisoner nods. "I know you'll do the right thing. You're a good son." Regardless of the transformation Overman had experienced, in this instance, Saul and Irma's tutelage had served him well. He had not forgotten how to play the guilt card.

The young Rosenfarb leaves him alone for what seems like hours. Overman fades into a woozy sleep as the bindings continue to chafe against his skin. He dreams he is watching a Lakers game on a seventy-inch television. The offense is cooking, Overman in awe of Kobe's no-look pass, followed by a three-pointer at the halftime buzzer. He applauds as the camera cuts over to the Laker bench. Sitting there, plain as day, in a front row, $3000 seat, is his ex-therapist Gary Sheslow, the shameless quack having craftily converted the fruits of the Overman divorce into a celebrity-style bounty. Overman is incensed, berating the helpless TV. He's screaming "Fuck you, Sheslow!" when the door to the storage room bursts open and a cult member he hasn't met before begins untying his legs.

"I wasn't cursing you," Overman explains. "Just dreaming about a guy who stole a fortune from me."

The cult member says nothing, efficiently removing the ropes from Overman's ankles and matter-of-factly switching them out for a nearby blindfold. Next stop, beheading? Overman wonders, thankfully not aloud. It would be a hell of a way to go, made doubly absurd by the fact that his demise would be in the service of one Jake Rosenfarb.

The blind Overman is being led down a dirt path by the blindfolder, who is either mute or just not big on conversation. Attempts at pleasantries about the weather and how the economic downturn might be affecting Guptananda membership go soundly unanswered. Overman is not sure whether he is being taken a long distance or walking in circles, just that no one wants him to know where he is. After what seems like at least a half-hour, he is led up the rickety steps of a building. Once inside, he hears a voice commanding the silent guide to remove the blindfold and return to his quarters.

Overman, now seated across from the cheesily regal Swami Guptananda, has been shuffled uptown, trading in the bare-bones plywood storage room for a pad that could hold its own with a swanky apartment in most metropolitan areas. The grass-roots Jonestown aura evidently did not extend to Guptananda's lair. Computers, wide-screen television with surround sound speakers, a dining room that appeared conjoined to a modern, stainless-steel kitchen: all had been imported to the Fellowship for the pleasure and comfort of its revered leader. A leader who didn't like intruders.

"Mr. Overman, is it?"

"Ira," Overman corrects him. "Pleasure to meet you, Swami." When Overman extends his hand, Guptananda points to a water-filled bowl with towels next to it. Overman washes and dries until he is suitable for shaking.

"They say you want to drive Manavendra to Santa Fe."

"That's right. To visit with his terminally ill father."

"We frown upon our members leaving. Exposure to evil puts their purity at risk."

"Jake Rosenfarb is not evil, sir. A dumb asshole maybe, but not evil."

"The secular world is evil, the Judeo-Christian world hardly better. I would assume Mr. Rosenfarb is an inhabitant of one such place."

"Actually, Jake kind of lives in his own world."

"I'll be blunt, Ira. If Jonathan leaves, how do I know he'll come back? Who's to say that you and your minions won't pollute and brainwash him?"

"First of all, I was never popular enough to have minions. Second of all, why don't we draw up some kind contract? We did it all the time in my last job."

"And if you should break the contract?"

"Sue me. You can probably afford a much better lawyer than I can," Overman cackles.

Guptananda is not laughing. "Ira, there's no good reason for me to sanction the exit of a loyal fellowship member."

Overman sees the window rapidly closing. "A father is very sick and needs to see his son, swami. I'm sure you understand that."

"I do. Many people are ill. On their deathbeds they suddenly regret their mistakes and try to correct them before passing. Of course this is impossible. Their best bet is to step it up in the next life."

Not the playbook Overman had in mind. "I'm begging you, swami," he pleads, "honor the last wish of a dying man."

Guptananda doesn't seem the least bit moved. "I'm sorry. I really don't believe that leaving here will be useful to Manavendra. Did you park on the premises?" he asks, getting up as if about to validate Overman's parking ticket.

Overman refuses to back down. "Swami, what if letting him go could get you something equally or even more valuable?" A vague, iffy plan is formulating in his desperate head.

"What would that valuable thing be?" the former Steven Yoder asks suspiciously.

"I'm not sure yet. Do you have a landline I might be able to use," Overman requests, assuming there is no cell phone signal even in the boss's headquarters.

"No landline, but you can try this." The swami hands him an expensive satellite phone, capable of dialing anywhere at any time.

Within seconds, Overman is talking with Maricela, asking her for an outrageous favor.

"Anything for Ira Overman, she replies."

Forty-five minutes later, His Holiness Guptananda is sitting in front of a computer monitor, poised to make the PayPal purchase of his dreams. The gorgeous, and kindhearted Maricela had gone into action immediately and used her wiles on Gene Cantalupo, persuading the dickwad to part with his 1923 Bentley TT Replica Three Liter Tourer at a rock-bottom price. Guptananda studies the screen, drooling over picture after picture of the pristine automobile, elated that one more of his coveted dream cars might soon join his collection. If Overman can make this happen, he is prepared to offer him just about anything he'd like, including a night with Gita, the gate woman. Overman, while oddly attracted to Gita's *bindi*, has far weightier requests in mind. As he goes over the list in his head, the swami clicks "send" and his payment is confirmed. His Holiness smiles broadly, moving in for a near Big Dave-like hug. Overman then goes on to lay out a short, but specific battery of instructions with which the swami is only too happy to comply.

Overman is the one smiling serenely as Manavendra Rosenfarb stares at his guru in disbelief. "It's really okay if I leave for a visit?"

"Absolutely," the swami responds. "Vishnu will always welcome you back into his arms. And as you remember, he is well endowed in the arm department," Guptananda chuckles.

The young Rosenfarb has never seen his swami chuckle before. It is more than a little disconcerting. "When do I have to be back?"

"Whenever it suits you," Guptananda responds, making good on Overman's second bullet point.

"I can go just like that?" He clearly doesn't know what to do with this kind of freedom.

"Of course you can. You're with Mr. Overman, a person I trust implicitly."

Rosenfarb junior is thrown for a loop. "I don't get it. Why him?"

"Because he had the power to do something for me that I couldn't do for myself."

"What's that?"

"That is between, Overman, me and Vishnu. *Namasté*, Manavendra." Guptananda kisses the young man on both cheeks and repairs to his bedroom for afternoon meditation.

Suspension be damned, Overman guns it to almost 70 mph on a road that should be traveled at 10. While realizing that being released with the swami's blessing allows him to navigate these roads without fear, he still wants to get out of Guptananda Gulch in a hurry. Until he remembers the Promised Land to which he's hurrying; that the pot of gold at the end of the rainbow is two thirds of a Rosenfarb family reunion. How ludicrous this might turn out is anybody's guess, Overman having learned long ago to approach all Rosenfarb encounters expecting the worst. What's more, the successful rescue would add rounds of unwanted ammunition to the Overman as superhero stockpile.

Four or five miles into the drive, it occurs to Overman that the young ex-Rosenfarb has not taken his eyes off him the entire way. Becoming the object of Jake Rosenfarb's moony stares had been peculiar, but being observed with wistful reverence by his turbaned, cult member son was a whole other kind of icky. Sidekick Jake saw himself as a junior partner, a position that came with responsibilities and demanded out-of-the-box thinking. Manavendra, on the other hand, while less obnoxious than his dad, was less motivated and needier, a person willing to give up his sense of self to serve a higher authority, even if that authority was an ex-convict from Akron.

"My parents never mentioned that you were a man of such power," Manavendra informs him.

"None of us knew I had it." Overman quickly switches the subject, embarrassed by the young man's obsequiousness. "Your father is going to be very glad to see you."

"How long does he have?" the son asks.

"Hard to say. With the right support around him, years I'll bet.

"I thought he was dying."

"I may have exaggerated. But he is really sick. In more of a mental kind of way."

"That's nothing new. How could it be otherwise given his lack of spirituality? Tell me about your relationship with God."

"We've never been close," Overman explains. "I have nothing against the Dude but honestly, I don't think he's all that crazy about me."

"On the contrary. He must regard you with great love and respect. To bestow gifts upon you that Guptananda himself has yet to achieve is truly awesome."

"Maybe it's got nothing to do with God," Overman poses. "Maybe it comes from planets, or sunspots, or standing in front of the microwave too long."

"How can you joke about such power?"

"Because it's not really important where it came from. What matters is how I choose to use it."

"That is deep," replies the young man. "To me it confirms that God has chosen you for a higher purpose."

"Fine. Let's run with that. It seems to me that there could be no higher purpose than to bring a family together. And since God is the one who chose me, that must be what He thinks."

Young Rosenfarb is suddenly quiet, unable to reconcile the idea of a father-son reunion with the spiritual life he has embraced over the last few years.

"There are always disagreements in families, but it's important not to lose these connections," Overman reminds him.

"Why?" the young man wants to know. "If your family led you down the wrong path and you worked hard to find the correct one, why would you ever want to return?"

The kid had a point. But Overman also saw the other side of the argument, having had considerable experience in this arena. "People make mistakes. A shitload of them, pardon my lack of holiness. Parents make horrible choices not because they want to, but because they don't know any better. The big tragedy is when they learn from their mistakes after it's too late to do anything about it."

"You're telling me that my parents are changed people?"

"Your father is. I haven't seen your mother so I can't speak for her."

"She's such a bitch."

An understatement if ever there was one, Overman thought. "All I'm saying is that people act the way they do for all kinds of reasons. But with the help and guidance of someone more en-lightened, anything is possible."

"Namasté," Manavendra answers, clasping his hands.

"Which means?"

"I bow to you."

"Are you happy on the compound, Manavendra?" Overman asks him.

"I am happy to be living a Godly life."

"Do you feel you might ever be able to live a Godly life some-where else?" Overman wasn't sure how this question would go over and is quite surprised when it elicits a big smile from his passenger.

"Are you saying what I think you're saying?" the young man asks.

"What is it that you think I'm saying?" Overman counters, careful not to introduce anything that might destroy the founda-tion he has carefully been building.

"Are you asking me to join your group of followers, Ira?"

"Huh?"

"Because I would seriously consider that as an option."

Overman can't believe what he is hearing. First the father wants to be his sidekick, then the son wants join his cult. No doubt about it, these Rosenfarbs were certifiable.

"I don't have a group of followers and I don't want one," Over-man explains. "I've got enough to deal with trying to turn my own life around."

"But you have so much to teach."

"Fine, if you insist. Lesson Number One: Make up with your father."

Eyes closed in meditation, Manavendra doesn't speak for the last ten miles of the trip. The young man registers no reaction whatsoever when Overman takes out his cell phone to call Jake, letting him know that they will be at the Days Inn momentarily. Assuming his position at the motel window, Rosenfarb eagerly awaits the arrival of the Ford Focus and the son who long ago abandoned him. Jake watches Overman pull into the lot and is about to rush downstairs when he sees the boy he Bar Mitzvahed emerge from the car wearing a turban. Even with the full beard and loose robe, he looks skinny to Rosenfarb, as if he had been abducted from Encino and banished to a cave in Tora Bora. Jake takes a minute to catch his breath and regain his composure, opting to hang back and let Overman bring his son upstairs.

Turban or no turban, as the door opens Rosenfarb has the urge to wrap his arms around his flesh and blood, but suddenly freezes, unable to follow through on his instincts.

"Special delivery," Overman says, figuring it couldn't hurt to lighten the mood.

"Hello, Dad," Manavendra deadpans.

"Jonathan!" Rosenfarb cries, now unable to control his emotions and bursting forth with a bear hug. "Come sit down."

Father and son awkwardly take seats at the table.

Overman seizes the opportunity to reinforce the trust he has gained from his escapee. "He's called Manavendra now."

"What the hell does that mean?" Jake barks.

"It means 'king among men'," his son calmly informs him.

"No argument there. Your mother and I always thought you were tops at everything. Especially archery. Remember that summer at camp when you won all those blue ribbons? And I think there was a red for a potholder you made —"

"Ira said you needed to see me. That you were suffering terribly."

"It's true. The shutter business is in the shitter."

"I'm not talking about shutters. I want to know what's going on with your health."

At this juncture Overman pipes in. "Why don't I leave the two of you alone to talk? I'm going across the street to get a cup of coffee. I'll be back in a half-hour."

"Take longer if you want," Rosenfarb responds.

Manavendra doesn't seem quite as excited by the prospect of facing his father one-on-one for an extended period of time. "See you in a half-hour," he tells Overman.

Overman is thrilled for the respite. These Rosenfarbs were a taxing bunch no matter the circumstance and one had to be grateful for any time away from them. He walks into the McDonald's, excited to drink mediocre coffee out of a Styrofoam cup. In a swell of spontaneity, he decides to spring for an apple pie and place another call to Janie. By the second ring he is already disappointed, sensing correctly that he will get her voicemail. This couldn't be good news. Perhaps she was camping out at the hospital, or a nursing home, or worse, making funeral arrangements for the beloved life partner it had taken her so long to find. Anything was possible. It bothered Overman to be so out of the loop. Even more frustrating was the realization that regardless of whatever power he had developed, in this instance he had come up empty-handed.

While Overman marked time, Rosenfarb and son faced each other at the motel table, the younger educating the elder on how he came to arrive at his current spiritual destination. Outlining each step of his enlightenment, he paused along the way to decry the suburban lifestyle, the dearth of values, the inherent flaws of a society based on consumerism.

"I just couldn't live like that any longer," he told his father, bracing for the obligatory lecture on the importance of money and achievement.

"Jonathan —"

"Manavendra —"

"Manavendra. The truth is, I don't disagree with anything you just said."

The son is naturally suspect. "But?"

"No buts. The world is fucked up. The best you can do is live right and treat others with respect."

"So you see something positive in the notion of spirituality?"

"I do," Rosenfarb answers.

"That is wonderful. Perhaps you would like to join me at the Fellowship for a while.

"I'm afraid I can't. The fact is, after I hit bottom I found my own calling."

"Which is?"

"Dedicating myself to the service of Ira Overman. You see, my friend has been given certain gifts —"

"I'm aware," the younger Rosenfarb tells him. "But he said he doesn't see himself as a guru."

"Guru-schmuru," Rosenfarb answers. "This guy's beyond that. He's a real-life superhero."

"A superhero?"

"As good as anything Marvel or DC ever came up with," Rosenfarb nods. "The man has important things he wants to accomplish and I believe it's my job to help him."

"He said he didn't want any followers."

The father bristles. "Son, there's something you need to know. Jake Rosenfarb has never been a follower. I'm a facilitator. Being an expert in the superhero field, I bring a world of hands-on experience to the table."

"I see. So it's just the two of you doing this?" the son asks.

"Yep. And the truth is, I don't even know how long I'll be in the picture. He's a modest guy who gets a little uncomfortable with the whole sidekick concept."

"I think it's good for him to have somebody around," Manavendra replies. "To help protect him, at the very least."

This gets Rosenfarb's wheels spinning. Perhaps he has unwittingly arrived at the inroad he has long sought with his son. "You're absolutely right about protection. But you know, sometimes I worry."

"For his safety?"

Rosenfarb nods. "You live with that swami. How many people does he have to protect him?"

"Maybe forty."

"See, now that's a strong number. With Ira, it's just me. I do what I can, but the truth is, I'm not such a young man anymore. Rosenfarb looks at his son for a reaction, but can't quite read him.

"I agree with you, Dad. You need help."

"But how am I going to get it? Where am I going to get it, Manavendra?"

The son's expression gives little away but somewhere in those glassy eyes, the father detects what he believes to be empathy.

Overman decides to split the difference and after forty-five minutes of Styrofoam bliss, climbs the stairs to assess how much damage could have possibly been done by two Rosenfarbs together under one roof. He has imagined any number of scenarios including Manavendra escaping and hitching a ride back to the compound, but surely that would have provoked a cell phone call from Jake. Since the phone never rang, perhaps there was reason to be optimistic. He puts the key in the door and crosses his fingers.

Jake has his laptop out and is sharing information with the now beardless, turban-less young man who informs him that he shall once again be known as Jonathan Elliot Rosenfarb.

"That's my son!" Jake crows, happier than Overman has ever seen him.

"Does this mean you're not going back to the Fellowship?" Overman asks.

"That's what it means," smiles the clean-shaven Jonathan, putting his arm around Jake. "I've decided to help my dad."

"That's fantastic," Overman responds. "I think the two of you will have great success re-building the window treatment business."

"Unfortunately, I can't help in that department," Jonathan explains.

Overman thinks he understands. Thanks to Overman's grand gesture of bringing father and son together, Jonathan wants to help Jake reunite with Rita and tweak the Rosenfarb family unit into something nominally functional.

Apparently this isn't the case. "I'm not interested in dealing with my mother right now," Jonathan tells him.

"Then how is it that you intend to help your father?" Overman wants to know.

"I'm going to help him take care of you. And strengthen the Overman brand."

Overman feels as if he is about to go into anaphylactic shock. Whoever invented the phrase "No good deed goes unpunished" must have had dealings with Rosenfarb ancestry.

"What exactly are you talking about, Jonathan?"

Jake answers for him. "The kid's a natural. Granted, he's not up to speed yet on his superheroes, but when it comes to stuff like ethics and spirituality, blah, blah, blah — look out."

"I really think it's important to have another body in your camp," Jonathan explains. "For security purposes alone."

"I don't have a 'camp,' Jonathan. I don't want a camp. My goal was to get your father back on his feet and help another friend, but once that's done, it's over. I'll figure out what I want to do with the rest of my life, how I intend to make money, and I'll be on my way."

"It sounds easy," Jonathan nods knowingly. "But my dad is right. You can't go it alone when you're trying to negotiate a world that isn't worthy of you."

Jake glows. "I told you, Ira, the kid's good."

"Do you have any special dietary needs?" Jonathan wants

to know. Apparently Swami Guptananda liked the occasional Twinkie after his brown rice and vegetables and one of Jonathan's responsibilities was to see that there was always a supply handy.

"Your father's been handling the food service unit quite nicely."

"Excellent." Jonathan turns to his father and asks him to draw up next week's menu so he can make nutritional notes.

"I suppose we should book our flights back to L.A," Overman offers dejectedly.

"Done," Jonathan tells him. "I've got a former Fellowship member picking us up at the airport."

"Did you promise him a job cleaning my underwear?"

"Not at all. He knows there's nothing available at this time. But I'm sure he'll be thrilled to meet you just the same."

He had opened the door and it had come back to bite him in the ass big time. A week ago, Overman was a man with no Rosenfarbs in his life. Now he had two who were rapidly becoming attached to him at the hip. Part of him wished Janie would call so he could duck both of them and get on a plane to upstate New York. He yearned to be watching her in the garden, miles away from the mini-cult that was forming around him. But for now, that didn't seem to be an option.

"We need to get you some new clothes," Jake tells his robed son.

"I don't require much," Jonathan says. "I'd be happy with just a blue shirt and some beige pants."

Of course this was exactly what Overman happened to be wearing.

three

cOntact

Not long ago, he was Overman the Pitiable Car Salesman, Overman the Failed Father, Overman the Perennial Loser. Now, according to his crack team of Rosenfarbs, he is Overman the Fucking Brand. As the plane heads for Los Angeles, father and son are planning and scheming in the row ahead of him, occasionally turning around to check whether he is comfortable enough. A strange turn of events to say the least. He has brought these Rosenfarbs closer to one another than ever imaginable, but to what end? They're behaving like high-powered executives in a multi-million dollar business, when they are, in fact, unpaid employees serving a $12-an-hour glorified file clerk. Small details like earning an income seem to have little interest for them. Jonathan called it faith. Jake tossed it off as subordinate to keeping an eye on the big picture.

Upon arriving at LAX, they are greeted by an enthusiastic, balding ex-hippie who introduces himself simply as Zabowsky. Apparently the overweight but not unhealthy-looking man dropped his first name after an acid-induced epiphany in the late sixties. Zabowsky is cheerful and deferential toward Overman, his good humor making a potentially embarrassing situation tolerable. On the ride back to Studio City, Overman learns that the driver was the Number Two man in the Guptananda organization until falling out of favor with the swami.

"What happened?" Overman wants to know.

Zabowsky shakes his head sheepishly. "He thought I was ungrateful. He slept with my wife and I wasn't happy about it."

"Believe me, Ira can relate to that," Jake jumps in. "Been there, done that, am I right?"

"That's really not appropriate," Jonathan admonishes.

"No biggie," Jake waves him off. "Right, Ira?"

Rosenfarb hadn't changed so much that he was ready to stop talking about banging Overman's wife. It was possible that the subject was so ingrained in him that its absence would leave a gaping hole in available topics of conversation. In truth, the wife-banging *schtick* barely registered with Overman anymore. It was the pained expression on poor Zabowsky's face that got to him.

"You were right to defend your marriage," Overman tells the driver.

"I don't know about that. Maybe if I hadn't gotten so pissed off, I'd still be married to Gita."

"She was your wife?" Overman asks, remembering the pretty girl-zombie and her *bindi*.

Zabowsky nods sadly. "She went back to New Mexico to live with Guptananda."

He elaborates that after she took off, his soul became so numb that he lost faith in both God and humanity. The substance of his life became nothing more than paying the rent, which he accomplished by offering himself as a jack-of-all-trades, doing the kinds of jobs people declined to do themselves.

"I've met a bunch of nice folks along the way," he says. "Little by little I'm starting to see the goodness in people again."

Overman took a shine to Zabowsky. Unlike the Rosenfarbs, the man had responded to his unfortunate circumstance with both practicality and an admirable work ethic. The Jake-Jonathan tag team were putting a lot of work into what they were doing, but "strengthening the Overman brand" was hardly anyone's idea of a legitimate profession. Certainly not Overman's. He felt like he wanted to reach out to the driver to do whatever he could to improve the forlorn man's lot. "I rent an apartment so I don't require a lot of handyman work, but if I find something I can throw your way, I'd be more than happy to," he tells Zabowsky.

"And I'll be there for whatever you need, sir. Of course, I wouldn't take a dime."

What the hell was he talking about? Overman wondered. And then he realized: it was that pesky worshiping thing. As sweet and likable as Zabowsky came off, he was a born follower just like the Rosenfarbs and saw in Overman an opportunity for some first-class groveling.

"If you won't take money, I won't hire you," Overman answers. "I don't expect people to do things for me for free."

"Of course you don't," Zabowsky beams. "That's what makes you special."

Overman knows it's an unwinnable argument, so he shuts up the rest of the way home. Zabowsky unloads all the bags, insisting on carrying them upstairs and rejecting all manner of remuneration. He reminds Overman to think of him should he need any additional staff down the line. Overman nods politely, wondering how any adult man could exist in such a submissive state. Even at his nadir, Overman had been pissed-off, bitter, sad, desperate, but never submissive. To his way of thinking, submission was a rung below suicide in that it necessitated bringing in another party to squeeze the self-worth out of the submitter. Offing oneself was clean, a one-man show. Other people might get hurt, but it didn't require anybody else to behave like a pig.

Zabowsky is barely out the door when Rosenfarb announces that he needs to go grocery shopping. Jonathan assures his father that he will be there, guarding their superhero/guru with his life.

"Don't you think you guys are being a little overdramatic?"

Overman asks. "Hardly anybody knows who I am. So why would they bother to do anything to me?"

Jonathan jumps in. "You can't be too careful. You could be liquidated at a moment's notice. Superpowers require super security and super vigilance."

"And that's without reading any Fantastic Four," Jake beams at Overman. "It's all instinct with this kid. I love it."

Jake is off to Trader Joe's. Overman sits down to watch CNN while Jonathan ogles his new guru.

Never has a person been as anxious to report to his $12 per hour job as Overman was that Monday morning. The previous night's dinner with the Rosenfarb Security Force had been a joyless, bombastic affair in which father and son proposed various Mission Statements, one more preposterous than the next. As he observed them elevating their pointless busywork to an endeavor of earth-shattering importance, Overman suggested that perhaps a formal Mission Statement wasn't necessary: he knew what he had to fix and that's all there was to it. Jake and Jonathan said they found his naiveté both charming and refreshing; that his simplistic but direct approach spoke to his undiluted greatness as a hero. Despite that, just like his forbears, from the Green Hornet to Swami Guptananda, Overman would need a clear message and devoted minions to help push it through. To the Rosenfarbs' way of thinking, it was incumbent upon the brain trust to nail down the message before the hero could convert it into action.

Driven to escaping the apartment as early as possible, Overman enters the gym at 6:30 A.M, diving into a vigorous upperbody workout followed by a crafty ducking of Detective Carla's ass-waxing diatribe. He arrives at the office feeling blessed to have Cavanaugh Foster as a place of refuge. When the cowbell rings and Dave walks through the door minus the porn star girlfriend, Overman is further excited. Perhaps while he was off in New Mexico, the Big Man came to his senses.

"Morning, Overman," Dave whispers, without any of his usual élan.

Overman suspects the worst. Juicy has dumped him on the heels of his wife leaving him and now the man has been reduced to loan shark rubble.

"Everything all right, boss?" he asks the hulking Texan.

"Ira, you and I need to have a chat," Dave answers solemnly, taking the seat opposite Overman's desk.

"Did I do something wrong?" Overman wondered if he had inadvertently made some enormous career-ending mistake.

"No, you didn't, son. You have been the most exemplary employee I have ever hired."

To Overman's knowledge he was the only employee Big Dave had ever hired, but that was beside the point.

"Ira, I don't know how to say this, but I've decided to branch out from the loan business. I need something more out of life than begging for capital and then having to foreclose on the poor douchebags who can't pay it back."

"I thought you loved what you did," Overman replies sincerely.

"This field has rewarded me beyond my wildest dreams, I can't deny that. But I've found something potentially even more fulfilling. And lucrative."

"That's great. What are you going to be doing?"

"Spreading my wings. I'll be working among young, vibrant people. Not that I have anything against being around you —"

"No offense taken," Overman assures him.

"I'm going to be a film producer, son. Instead of Juicy working for other companies like Vivid and Wicked, we're going to finance the productions ourselves, retaining all worldwide rights and profits."

A muted "wow" is all Overman can seem to muster.

"I'm telling you, Ira, this is what I was born to do."

Cheesy squirt videos where actors got paid by the hour to be covered in vaginal fluid? Everyone had a calling, Overman supposed.

"Congratulations, Dave, that's wonderful news."

"Thanks, son. I see a bright future for Cavanaugh Foster Films. Very bright."

It seemed only fitting that the two fictional upper crust Brits were going to accompany Dave to the world of porn. A natural progression, Overman reasoned, the transition from hard money to hard cock a shrewd career move.

"Are you going to close down the office?" Overman naturally inquired.

"No, this will continue to be my home base. But I won't be doing loans full-time. I know I promised to be your mentor. It kills me to let you down."

"You're not letting me down. It's your business, your life. You need to do whatever makes you happy."

At which point, Dave motions to Overman to stand up so he can hug his protégé. "Should I start looking for another job?" Overman asks, as Big Dave wrings the oxygen out of him.

"There's no need for that," Dave replies. "I just won't have as much time to devote to your lending education. And the film division is just starting up, so we don't have any positions there yet —"

"One day at a time." Overman assures him it's all good.

Dave is beyond grateful. The talk of diversifying the company naturally raises the matter of loans that need to be paid up, the Rosenfarb loan, of course, being the greatest concern to Overman.

"Is the window guy gonna be able to come up with the cash?" Big Dave wants to know. "'Cause I'd hate to have to take his house from him."

"I'm sure his wife wouldn't be too keen on that either," Overman adds. "Rosenfarb will get it together, don't worry."

"If you say so, I know it's true," Dave smiles, disappearing into his office to call Juicy's favorite director of photography about filming her next liquid extravaganza in 3-D.

Overman was sure Jake Rosenfarb didn't have a clue as to how to get his hands on fifty grand in two weeks. More alarming was that he didn't seem concerned about it. Was Jake's recent change of attitude and nascent partnership with his son all part of some devious Rosenfarb scheme to get Overman to pay off the loan using superpowers? Overman didn't think so, but the Family Rosenfarb, with its well-documented history of lunacy, was capable of anything.

Understandably fearful about what awaits him at the apartment, Overman's senses are on full alert for alarming sights or smells as he climbs the stairs. Opening the door, he finds cold cuts and bread on the table and both Rosenfarbs planted on the sofa, watching an infant's brain surgery on the Discovery Channel.

"Hello, Ira," Jake barks. "We'll sit down to dinner just as soon as they stitch up the head."

"Great close-ups of the cerebral cortex," Jonathan pipes in, telling Overman that this is the first TV he's seen in over five years.

Overman says there's no rush. He wants to go change anyway.

"I decided not to cook since it's going to be a working dinner," Jake shouts out as Overman heads for the bedroom.

A working dinner? What the hell does this mean? They were obviously taking their idea of an Overman business empire very seriously, viewing themselves as hard-working executives with too few hours in the day. Select matters required the type of attention that necessitated their being discussed after hours. Never mind the fact that Overman was the only one with a job and these guys spent the whole day lounging around the apartment. The Rosenfarbs perceived themselves as consummate professionals, mimicking whatever it was they imagined professionals did.

Overman's place is at the head of the table, his two associates eagerly flanking him. Jake elects to open with "I know you like corned beef. Would you like me to make you a sandwich?"

"Not necessary. I can do it myself," Overman assures him.

"Jonathan's into all that vegetarian shit but I figured it might be a long night, we need meat. Am I right?"

"Why is it going to be a long night, Jake?" Overman feels he must ask.

"We've got a lot of ground to cover. These things take time."

Jonathan nods in agreement.

What in God's name were these people talking about? Certainly not the fifty grand Jake owed and his plan for paying it back.

As Jonathan makes himself a cucumber and carrot sandwich on wheat, his father formally introduces the topic at hand.

"Ira Overman in 'The Adventure of the Lakeview Seven' featuring Janie Sweeney and Martin Merkowitz. Also featuring Seth Hammer, Dennis Geoghan, Kevin Royce, Michael Herzog and Anthony Saldo."

He seemed to be turning this regrettable chapter from Overman's life into a comic book slash radio play slash movie. For what reason, Overman had no idea, but he had been around long enough to know that there was idiocy afloat.

Jake continues. "In this adventure, Overman seeks justice for a young rape victim whose attackers suffered no consequences for their odious actions."

"It's a really exciting adventure," Jonathan interjects.

"Guys, this isn't a comic book or a TV series," he reminds them. "Why are you talking about it like it's some made up story?"

"Made up or not, Ira, all stories have a narrative that can be played out any number of ways," Jake explains. "It's up to us — mostly you, actually, how the tale gets told."

"Please be a little more specific," Overman insists.

"Of course," Jake signals his son to dim the lights.

In between bites of fatty but tender corned beef, Overman is treated to a PowerPoint presentation on each member of the Lakeview Seven: his current professional and personal status along with the Rosenfarbs' dual assessment of whether the man had made any moral progress in the ensuing forty years. The Rosenfarbs' judgments of a person's behavior seemed like tenuous criteria for doling out retribution, but Overman was enjoying his sandwich, so what could it hurt to watch their little show?

The PowerPoint presentation begins, naturally, with Marty Merkowitz, whose trajectory from rapist to Silicon Valley entrepreneur has followed a uniformly ruthless path. Distrusted by his peers at Stanford Business School, he went on to leave a trail of bitter ex-wives, burned ex-partners and grown children who hated him. His current wife was nearly twenty-five years his junior and had recently given birth to twins who were primarily cared for by nannies. Merkowitz's philanthropy was widely recognized as a calculated ploy to spruce up his less-than-stellar reputation in the business world. Even those who took the money knew it was somehow tainted or "Merkowitzed" as some chose to call it. Accessing his years of decorating metaphors, Jake likened the charitable Merkowitz to pre-finished hardwood flooring, expertly finished on its exterior, with an inside composed of cheap fiberboard.

"A despicable individual," Jonathan cries out. "While we haven't found evidence of any other sexual assaults, the man seems to have grown even more hateful since the incident."

Jake nods his head. "This is the kind of person most people would not object to seeing 'go away'."

"Are you suggesting we put a 'hit' on Merkowitz?" Overman gasps.

"Calm down, Ira. I'm not suggesting anything until you finish watching the presentation."

And on it went. By all accounts, Seth Hammer the dentist seemed to be a good father and upstanding citizen with no record of attempting to gas and fondle any of his patients. He had served on the PTA, run his son's Boy Scout Troop, bought his wife a new diamond ring for their twenty-fifth anniversary. The only dirt they were able to dig up was that he played keyboards in a geezer garage band with other dentists and that a few of the younger hygienists might possibly be groupies. If so, Overman was happy for Hammer. Anyone who spent thirty years looking into mouths and breathing germs deserved payback. Having cute hygienists watch you play rock and roll hardly seemed adequate, but it was something.

Geoghan the ex-cop had been wounded twice in the line of duty, the strains of the job having taken an irreparable toll on his marriage, which ended in divorce when his kids were still young. Later, after investigating a home robbery invasion in which a man was brutally murdered, Geoghan wound up marrying the widow and adopting her three kids. They were now happy and productive, running the Willow Springs B&B in Asheville, S.C. Both Rosenfarbs seem to be impressed by Geoghan's successful rehabilitation, but do their best to hold back their opinions until Overman weighs in.

Kevin Royce came out of the closet in his junior year at college, meeting his live-in companion of almost thirty years at the University of Oregon graduate school. He and his partner are devout churchgoers who perform regular community service for their diverse congregation.

"I never would have suspected that one was queer," Jake offers, the absence of political correctness surprising no one.

"Queer is a derogatory term, Dad," his son informs him.

"I apologize. I have nothing against fags."

In truth, Jake was tolerant of all kinds of people. He just didn't know how to speak to or about them.

Next up was Mike Herzog, the personal injury attorney. Overman figured there was bound to be scandal there, what with society's penchant for frivolous lawsuits. As it turned out, Herzog's only infraction was his wife's displeasure with the amount of time he spent on the golf course. Jonathan pointed out that according to their research, the relationship always improved with the onset of winter, suggesting that the couple truly enjoyed each other's company.

Last in the group was Saldo, the body shop owner. Tony had always had his hands full making ends meet, trying to support his large family through economic downturns and the constant onslaught of cheaper competition. According to the Rosenfarb stats, in thirty some-odd years he had hired a hooker on two occasions, starved for the sex he wasn't getting from his pregnant and/or exhausted wife. Aside from those brief dalliances, Saldo had been a good husband and an exemplary father. He brought two of his sons into the business only after pleading with them to go to college so they might have better lives than their dad's. Saldo Auto Body was known for its quality work and Tony Saldo was regarded as a quality guy.

As Jonathan turns the lights back on, Overman compliments both Rosenfarbs on their thorough detective work. Father and son are aglow, overjoyed to have won their "leader's" approval. As always, Overman finds their adulation revolting, but knows it is a waste of time to argue.

"So it all boils down to Merkowitz," Overman says, cutting to the chase.

"In terms of who stayed a villain, absolutely," Jake concurs. "If the Lakeview Seven minus Merkowitz have become the upstanding individuals we think they've become, it should be fairly easy to extract five apologies that would satisfy Ms. Sweeney-Leeds. Adding in yours, that's six out of seven."

"Merkowitz, of course, is a whole other ball of wax," Jonathan concedes.

Overman doesn't know where to start. First and foremost, he hasn't heard from Janie, who is dealing with a horrendous reality in the present. "You know, guys. I just don't want to bother her with this right now," he tells father and son.

"We're on the same page," Jake assures him.

Jonathan nods. "Our first choice is a plan that won't involve her."

"We've found a way to bypass the entire apology phase," Jake explains. "Yet once the plan is put in motion, it will yield a satisfying conclusion, leaving Janie with no thoughts of her unspeakable ordeal."

Overman can't imagine what crazy line of attack these two

have put together. Whether he wanted to or not, he was going to find out. "Lay it on me, guys."

Jake smiles and presents Overman with six vintage DC comic books covered in protective shrink-wrap. "The answer lies within these pages," he tells his friend. "I'd like you to review the material so you can discuss our proposal from an informed point of view."

Overman sees that these comics all feature The Flash, long one of Rosenfarb's favorites. Overman hated comic books even as a kid, but now the Rosenfarbs expected him to study five of them before revealing their intentions.

"Look, guys, before we waste a lot of time, can you just give me the bullet points of what we're talking about? Besides," Overman reminds them, "my instinct is to leave it alone for the time being."

Jake shakes his head. "If it were my adventure or Jonathan's adventure, we might have to leave it alone. But we believe that if it were the Flash's adventure, he wouldn't need to. And since it's your adventure, you don't need to either."

"I'm lost," Overman throws up his hands.

"Okay," Jake relents. "I still want you to read the material, but since nobody reads anymore, I'll give you the general lay of the land."

"Thank you," Overman sighs.

"Here's the idea," Jake smiles. "Speed Force. We feel Speed Force would be the perfect thing for this adventure."

"Fair enough," Overman tries to stay calm. "What the fuck is Speed Force?"

This is like reciting the alphabet for Jake. "Speed Force is a force in the universe that lets speedsters travel at otherwise impossible speeds as well as do nifty tricks without being hindered by physics."

"What does this have to do with me?" Overman must ask.

"Dad thinks you have all the makings of a speedster," Jonathan chimes in.

His father elaborates. "Like you, Ira, the Flash had enormous willpower. But he didn't stop there. As he built on that power, he discovered the Speed Force, which allowed him to time-travel."

If Rosenfarb is saying what Overman thinks he's saying, he wants the former car salesman to solve his problem by going back in time.

"Bingo," Rosenfarb snaps his fingers. The concept here is for Overman to return to the party on that fateful night and see to it that the rape of Janie Sweeney never happens. This was beyond cuckoo, even for Jake Rosenfarb.

"What makes you think I'd possibly be able to do such a thing?" Overman asks.

"I just have a feeling," Rosenfarb responds.

"A 'feeling'?" Overman repeats. "Your scientific research has really paid off."

"You don't have to get nasty about it. Let's say you try and you're a total bust. Tell me, what have we lost?"

While obvious, it was probably the only sane thing Rosenfarb had ever said. It was a fact that if he should reach for the stars and fail, he, and ultimately Janie, would be no worse off than they were today.

"But if my dad is right, look at the payoff," Jonathan points out.

In this case, Overman was more comfortable with the probability of failure than the possibility of success. Even as a hater of science fiction, he had seen plenty of time-travel movies where changing events of the past portended disastrous effects on the future. He wasn't about to be the one responsible for changing the course of history, conceivably for the worse.

"So you think Janie being raped had some positive effect on the world?" Rosenfarb asks, point blank.

Overman couldn't think of one off the top of his head, but tried spitballing a workable argument. "Okay, how about this? Let's say it never happened and Janie's family never moved to New Jersey. She might have had a normal relationship with a boy in high school, married when she got out of college and never would have met Garvin."

"Who is on his deathbed and will leave her alone, maybe for the rest of her life, which could be another forty years," Jake reminds his friend.

"She loves him," Overman says.

Rosenfarb has no issue with that. "But think of all the opportunities she would have had to love had she not been brutalized into avoiding human contact for all those years."

"And the additional upside is that it puts the kibosh on the defining moment of Martin Merkowitz's venal existence," Jonathan adds. "There's a better than even chance that getting away with the rape shaped his whole personality."

"There's no downside here as far as we can see," Jake declares.

Overman finds himself pining for those precious, Rosenfarb-free months of his life. He can't help but think that if he were somehow able to go back in time, that blissful vacation would be the period he'd choose. Jake informs him that the first Flash achieved Speed Force by inhaling fumes from an experimental chemical mixture, while the next two Flashes were hit by lightning.

"Perfect!" Overman exclaims. "How about I stick my face in cyanide-laced gasoline while standing under a tree in an electrical storm? That should cover all our bases."

"Relax, Ira. We think there's a better way," Jake informs him.

"According to the texts," Jonathan plows on, holding up the six comic books, "the power has also been achieved by various surgical techniques."

"Great," Overman snaps. "You want to crack my head open like the kid on the Brain Surgery Channel."

"Ira, I must tell you that you're not behaving very superheroically," Jake admonishes him.

"And you're both deranged," Overman shoots back.

"Let's all take a deep breath," Jonathan suggests, channeling his Fellowship meditation and yoga techniques.

Overman watches as father and son close their eyes, escaping to some internal retreat for what seems like five minutes or so.

They emerge from their side trip obnoxiously refreshed.

"I love you, Ira," Jake announces, putting his arm around his friend.

"We both do," Jonathan chimes in, positioning himself on the other side.

Overman backs away. "I appreciate that, I really do. But I think you guys have fallen off the reality cliff here."

Jake begs to differ. "Before you make that kind of statement, hear us out. We're not saying you need surgery now."

"My frontal lobe's safe for the time being?"

"Yes," Jonathan smiles. "You see our theory is that you've already had the surgery you needed."

Jake elaborates. "After the Lasik you became a changed man with powers you never had before. We're thinking you may possess the Speed Force but don't know it."

"Wouldn't I know if I had it?"

"Not necessarily. Have you ever attempted to go back in time?"

"No. But who would?"

"The Flash, Max Mercury, Savitar," Jake answers, rattling off the first three comic book time-travelers he can think of. "All we're asking you to do is give it a shot."

"And how would I do that?" Overman can't wait to hear this one.

"Focus on that specific moment in your personal history," Jonathan instructs him. Maybe while you're lying in bed when it's really quiet. Call back every memory of that night, down to the minutest details. The premise is that if your mind takes you there, your body will follow suit."

"And you guys believe this will work because of what you've read in comic books?"

"Mostly what my dad's read," Jonathan corrects him. "I'm pretty new to the superhero deal."

Overman can't believe he's having this discussion. How could they honestly think that comic books could apply to real life? Jake points out that many would assume that Overman's recent accomplishments were only attainable by comic book heroes. Who else but Overman and possibly Batman could so easily bed Maricela Flores? So what prevented him from expanding on such talent?

He tells the Rosenfarbs that as much as he enjoyed their PowerPoint presentation, he'll need to give this one some more thought. Even in the unlikely event that he could make such a thing happen, why would he want to risk fucking with people's pasts, thereby jeopardizing their futures? The post-meditatively mellow Rosenfarbs accept his decision, re-emphasizing that they are conduits, there simply to provide all available data so their boss can make informed decisions. Overman thanks them and announces that he'd like to turn in early.

As far as the Rosenfarb camp goes, Jake is confident that based on the facts presented their superhero will seriously consider their proposal. Jonathan gets no sense of it one way or the other, attributing his lack of intuition to being a neophyte. Regardless of the outcome, Team Rosenfarb feels they can take pride in the thoroughness of their work and their unwavering devotion to a higher power than their own.

Closing the door of his eerily organized bedroom, Overman is anxious to get under the covers, watch some mindless reality show on cable, retreat to the mundane world from which he had ached to escape. The new world, promising though it was, came with its own set of headaches, the most grating being the deluded father and son sycophants. Crawling in between the freshly laundered sheets that Jake had meticulously ironed, he settles in for a rerun of "Dirty Jobs." This particular episode chronicles a prominent sewage processor, a giant in the field of "digested sludge" as it is known in the waste game. As dirty as the sludge guy's job might be, Overman finds it far more interesting than selling cars and certainly less stressful than being other people's superhero. Recycling was heroic in it's own way, he thought, and although he wasn't about to lobby for a career in sewage, watching the mechanics of it was a welcome diversion.

As the recycler explains the difference between raw primary sludge (fecal material) and secondary sludge (a living 'culture' of organisms that help remove contaminants from wastewater before returning it to rivers or the sea), Overman's cell phone rings. Looking at the caller ID, he is both pleased and petrified.

"Janie," he exhales, about to get to the "how are you?" when he hears her cries, aching, resonant and raw. Garvin had passed away in the Endicott night, his heart giving out despite numerous attempts to revive him. Janie tells Overman this news just as the TV show is warning of dangerous sludge-based health incidents such as respiratory complications, abscesses, cysts, and tumors. Reasonably sure that sludge was not responsible for Garvin's death, Overman switches off the set to concentrate on Janie.

"I'm so sad," she wails, Overman feeling her pain deep in his soul. "I'm empty."

"Why don't I come out tomorrow morning?" he offers, figuring it would be a help to Janie as well as a much-needed vacation from the Rosenfarbs.

"Please don't," Janie says, throwing him a little off guard. "Right after they cremate him, I'm going to Florida to spend a little time with my dad. In a few months or so, or whenever I'm ready, I plan to scatter his ashes at Watkins Glen. Maybe you could come out for that."

"Of course I will," Overman tells her. "Are you sure you don't need me to do anything right now?"

"I don't. Garvin's family is here."

"That's good." It hardly feels like the right time, but he is compelled to ask: "I assume you haven't given any more thought to what we had talked about."

"God, no," Janie says. "What happened forty years ago is the least of my problems."

"I understand. If you need anything call me right away, day or night."

"I will. Thank you, Ira. You're a good man."

After she hangs up, it occurs to Overman that in fifty-five years, no one had ever said those words to him. What's more, for the first time he actually felt like a good man. Somehow, in a life full of missteps, Ira Overman was making the transition from directionless blob to focused self, able to process empathy and somewhat adept at acting on it. He closes his eyes, sad for his widowed friend, but pleased that his own progress has allowed him to help her in some small way.

Sleep doesn't come easily. Overman tries to tune out the concept of two Rosenfarbs sharing his home as he wrestles with how he might continue to help Janie through her inconsolable loss. Until Garvin, she had never known the love of a man, never been touched with tenderness, her only connection with the flesh of another brought about by force. Perhaps having had such a kind and caring spouse would impel Janie to trust again and someday seek out another. The less positive take was that the only time she had opened herself up had resulted in a pain possibly more excruciating than the one which shut her down in the first place.

She was a fifty-five year old widow living in a small town in upstate New York with a job, a garden, two dogs, and a few years of memories to carry her to the end. Of course there were other things in life besides being in a relationship, but once one had accomplished it successfully, continuing alone had to be less appealing. Overman acknowledged that there would be other available professors at the university, but he sensed in Janie a reserve that might indicate a grim and solitary future. He couldn't know for certain, but it had also been Jake's first thought when he heard of Garvin's illness. And although Jake Rosenfarb was hardly a barometer for anything, something else he said kept replaying in Overman's mind.

"So you think Janie being raped actually had some positive effect on the world?"

Overman could still only think of one: the conspiring of events led her to Garvin, the love of her life. Was that worth the agony that led up to it and the pain that would ensue now that it had ended? No one could know for sure. But assuming for a second that Overman could crazily manifest the comic book-like power the Rosenfarbs were pushing, the thought of doing something that might sabotage those years of happiness seemed reason enough to abort the idea. Yet at the same time, it was fascinating to think what might be gained if one could prevent such an injustice from occurring. Who was to say that the benefits wouldn't be exponential? What if everyone involved, including Overman, became better and healthier people as a result of not taking part in Janie's rape?

Enjoying this brief interval between Rosenfarb onslaughts, Overman allowed himself a moment to fantasize, considering the various cause and effect scenarios of the time-space continuum. If he could indeed summon the ability to travel back to that moment and stop the group's brutal actions, he would, of course, be stopping himself, thereby changing his own history. That being the case, would the altering of this one event change the life of blunders that had led to his now welcome transformation? The variables were mind-boggling. If for some reason, the changed young Overman grew into a man with no superpowers, what would happen to the grown Overman who had visited the past to presumably tinker with the proceedings? Would he simply dissolve into thin air and assume life as a sixteen year-old once again, having to endure the agony of adolescence and his twenties yet a second time? A terrifying prospect, to be sure.

Against his better judgment and thorough dislike of the medium, Overman makes the decision to read the comic books the Rosenfarbs have provided, if only to satisfy his curiosity. It will be interesting to see how history is changed in these stories and whether it turned out to be beneficial in the long run. Overman also decides to do an abrupt about-face and play the swami card with father and son. As much as he hates being their "leader," establishing control and having them fear him is preferable to slinking around in their subservient presence. If they dote too much, the leader will reprimand them. It was the kind of boiler-plate guru-follower stuff Jonathan knew like the back of his hand and Jake could pick up quickly. Satisfied that he has gained some clarity, Overman decides to call it a night. He closes his eyes once again, images of Rosenfarbs and sludge dancing in his brain.

Devouring a four-course breakfast prepared by Jake and served by Jonathan, Overman has come to the table ready to carry forth his plan. When he informs them that this is a business breakfast, which he intends to conduct with maximum efficiency since he is due at the office in thirty minutes, father and son hop to attention. He can see in their eyes that they thrive on such assertiveness: the more forceful his commands, the more eager they become. They remind Overman of the Moonies from the sixties, their glassy-eyed obedience giving him an inkling of what it must feel like to be a self-proclaimed Korean Messiah.

"You both know I appreciate all you do," is the Overman kick-off line.

"Absolutely," Jake and Jonathan answer in perfect sync. There is, however, a look of terror in their eyes as they await what they perceive to be the "but," the hammer about to come down, the pink slips ready to be passed out. Overman had no idea that people who made no money could be this worried about being fired.

"Have we displeased you in any way?" Jonathan asks, reminding Overman of the Simple Son at the Passover Seder.

"I do find you a bit fawning at times," Overman answers honestly.

"We're so, so sorry," is Jake's answer.

"See, that's fawning right there. Cut it out. I want to talk about the Speed Force." He didn't really, but he liked the idea of keeping these two on their toes.

"What would you like to discuss?" Jonathan asks.

"Since this concept has its origin in comic books, I'm wondering how it might affect the safety of a real life person, specifically, me. I wouldn't want to try anything foolish that might permanently land me in another dimension where I'd feel uncomfortable, not knowing anybody and all." Did Overman actually believe he could time-travel? Not in the slightest. It was, however, great fun to see how seriously the Rosenfarbs were taking the whole thing. "I would also prefer that the Speed Force not result in my premature death," Overman tosses in for good measure.

"Of course not," Jake nods, "but if it makes you feel any better, in death you would become One with the Speed Force."

"I'm going to pretend I didn't hear that," Overman shoots back.

Jonathan clears his throat and makes his case. "The last thing my father and I would want is to put you in any kind of danger. We'd be prepared to shut down the entire operation before letting anything like that happen."

Overman didn't realize that there was an "operation" but he'd learned not to be surprised by any new policies Team Rosenfarb leaked out. "It's up to the two of you to see that there are no fuckups, you understand?"

"Of course," Jake whimpers.

Overman loved the reaction he was getting from the new aggressive posturing, for the first time taking pleasure in their treating him like a superhero. "I'll be home at five. To be continued."

"We'll be having organic wheat pasta in a chanterelle mushroom sauce," Jake nods. "If that's okay with you, of course."

"It's fine."

Overman is out the door, comic books in hand. Briskly striding the short distance to the office, he ponders the state of his finances. Adding up the trip to Santa Fe, rent, utility bills and Chef Rosenfarb's grocery budget, he was down to only a few thousand bucks, which he would burn through quickly in the days ahead. And there was still the matter of paying off Jake's loan, the big question being where these dollars were going to come from. Taking precedence over everything, of course, was the realistic longevity of the current living situation. Overman knew in his gut that if being a hero meant having to spend the rest of his life with the Rosenfarbs, he'd just as soon go back to selling cars or start a new career in sludge. Bossing them around was a hoot, but that would get old soon enough. What Overman really wanted was to find a way to benefit from the second chance he had been granted while at the same time live a normal, independent life, rife with possibilities and free of hangers-on. Yet even as he acknowledged how far he had come from the dog days of Wilton Place, it still felt like a tall order.

To Overman's surprise, the cowbell had been taken down, the office now filled to the brim with bodies and movie equipment. Big Dave and Juicy had apparently arrived hours ago and were in Dave's office prepping a scene for her upcoming release, "Soaking Brett." One of the crew explains that the movie's minimal plot involves a hard moneylender and his comely, no pun intended, secretary. The part of Brett is being performed by none other than Big Dave himself, whose mission is to bring a blazing authenticity to the part of the lender. Meanwhile, Overman can see that the cameraman and soundman in Dave's office have already been outfitted with rain slickers.

"Would it be okay for me to have a word with my boss?" Overman asks some guy eating a donut.

"Sure. We can't start shooting anyway till he's hard," Donut Man explains.

Overman taps on the door and peeks his head into Dave's office, getting an eyeful of the bootylicious Juicy and his flabby, naked boss, the latter not quite an audience-pleaser to his way of thinking. "Hey, Dave."

"Ira, welcome to my new world."

"And a fine world it is," Overman replies, for lack of a better response. "I was going to clean up some files, but I guess it's a little hectic right now."

"Nonsense," Dave fires back. "In a couple of minutes, the whole crew will be back in my office and you can go about your business."

"It shouldn't even take that long," Juicy smiles, as she coaxes limp Dave into a semi-upright position.

"Nice to see you, too, Juicy," Overman replies, in the interest of being polite.

She doesn't take the time to answer him, opting instead to orally ingest Dave's still semi-limp member. She starts to go to work when the donut guy runs in shouting: "Hey, save some of that for when we're rolling." Evidently Donut Guy is also the director. It is a glaringly low-rent production, Overman shuddering to think that this is the basket in which poor Dave is putting his eggs (and now sperm). Juicy, ever the professional, accomplishes her task in short order and the crew files into the back room, leaving Overman alone to deal with his chores.

The files turn out to need minimal organizing. He just has to revise the list of outstanding loans as two of them have recently been paid off. Finishing quickly, he has little else to do and casually starts perusing his pile of comic books. In between Big Dave's loud, nauseating moans, Overman manages to brief himself on the adventures of The Flash. Exceeding his rock bottom expectations, he finds himself intrigued by the similarities in their situations. It seems that Bart Allen, the fourth and current Flash, wants to live a normal life just like Overman does, but jumps back into action and summons the Speed Force because a dear friend needs his help. Yes, it is a comic book and The Flash's buddy happens to be threatened by lasers and pipes that emit poison fluid, but the analogy is not lost on Overman. Bart watching his roommate Griffin Grey writhing in pain was Ira Overman witnessing Janie Sweeney on her back being abused. The Flash might be dealing with evil super villains, but were they any different than Marty Merkowitz? Overman is also surprised to discover another parallel. Bart and Griffin both work in the automobile business, albeit on the manufacturing side. Suddenly, Rosenfarb connecting Overman with The Flash was starting to make a lot more sense.

He reads on, immersing himself in the characters of Valerie Perez (a Flash ally), the Black Flash (his arch nemesis) and the various former Flashes who are now One with the Speed Force. As much as sci-fi has always bored him, the underlying dilemma and motivation strike a chord. It all boiled down to injecting a dose of "good" into a poisoned and fucked-up world. Another universal theme in these comics was that spreading good required extraordinary commitment. One had to dig deep and unearth the maximum of one's capabilities, risking everything to carry out the task at hand.

Was this the bottom line? Overman wondered. Was the decision to use whatever power he had not a choice at all, but a moral obligation? Certainly there were great artists who were reticent about showing their work and made the decision to keep their paintings and sculptures to themselves. There were brilliant actors of the Garbo and Brando ilk who hated the public eye and eventually renounced their profession to become recluses. One could argue that like superheroes, they had gifts possessed by a chosen few and hence had a responsibility to share them with the world. They maintained, however, that regardless of their abilities, it was their God-given right to live as they pleased. Was this any different from Overman deciding not to get further involved and risk screwing something up? Unlike Griffin Grey who was in mortal danger and needed the Flash, Janie Sweeney had told Overman to back off. That being the case, why would he want to press the issue in any way, naturally or supernaturally? Before studying the Flash, he had scrapped the idea of moving forward. Now, in spite of the risks, the potential rewards of correcting a giant mistake and improving a life had been validated anew.

The door to Dave's office flies open, bodies pouring out like a fleshy, sweaty, "Night at the Opera" stateroom scene. When the soundman asks Overman if he has a mop, it becomes clear that Juicy has turned in nothing less than a tour de force performance. Dave emerges for a post-coital donut, apologizing to his protégé for spreading himself too thin. Overman assures him that there's no need to feel bad about anything. He is grateful for having had the opportunity to be taken under Dave's wing, and wishes him nothing but the best in all his endeavors.

"I owe you one, son. I owe you big time."

Overman can see that the Texan wants to move in for another of his trademark hugs, but given that the man has just filmed a squirt scene, Overman deftly backs away, explaining that he's coming down with a cold.

"Very considerate of you," Dave nods. "We wouldn't want to get Juicy sick."

As the crew packs up to move to another location, Overman learns that Juicy has a wardrobe change for the next part of the script, where she will be working her liquid magic on two unsuspecting escrow officers. Dave seems excited to put his producer hat back on and watch his fiancée perform with other men. He claims that "Soaking Brett" will break new ground, not only because it will feature the first three-way shot in an escrow office, but because Juicy will be working with real escrow officers rather than actors.

The man was certainly passionate about his new line of work. Overman wishes his boss good luck and spends the rest of the day tidying up the place, every now and then reviewing one of the Flash comic books that had made such an impact on him. Closing up shop at five, he walks down the stairs and peeks in the window of U Wash Doggie, scene of his first anonymously heroic good deed. Overman recalls that the feat was accomplished purely with fortitude, assertiveness, and a number 2 pencil, nary a superpower coming into play. As he starts the trek home, he recognizes that the U Wash Doggie incident recalled a simpler, less demanding time. His universe had expanded, now populated with people and situations that required much more of him.

Having excelled for so long at blending into the woodwork, this wayward son of faux holocaust survivors was now weighing grand concepts like courage, selflessness and the duty to serve the Greater Good. Still, he was steadfast in the belief that he didn't want to be Superman or Batman even if such a thing were possible. Their high profile antics generated far too much hoopla for his tastes. Let the guys in capes battle Lex Luthor and save Gotham City. Overman wanted no part of such showiness. In this respect he would always be Saul and Irma's son. The only act of heroism he cared about now was reaching out to a friend in need. This was not only relatable, but something at which he had already achieved a measure of success. In the plus column, he could cite his defense of Maricela to Hal Steinbaum, the donation in memory of Glorietta Zatzkin's late husband, his offer to let Jake Rosenfarb move in so he could get back on track, the rescuing of Jonathan, and of course, his apology to and concern for Janie Sweeney. None of these actions had produced earth-shattering results but they were all worthy causes, executed with the selflessness of a person for whom good deeds were second nature. There was no denying he had made considerable progress from those hellacious, zero-down days. The question now was whether he wanted to continue the quest for greatness at a cost that was unknown.

Flexing the new muscle he has come to thoroughly enjoy, Overman enters the apartment affecting a pissed-off pose, his M.O. being to throw the Rosenfarbs off kilter and keep them guessing. He knows that if he is too effusive about what he has gleaned from the Flash, Jake will spin out of control and try to send him to another galaxy or further. If the plan was to try and help Janie, it required nothing less than a sober approach. As cool as it might be for Jake to see a comic book come to life before his eyes, the fate of actual humans hung in the balance.

"You don't like the pasta?" Jake asks the taciturn Overman.

"It's fine, Jake." Overman chews deliberately.

"Hard day at the office?" Jonathan wants to know.

"No."

Father and son exchange glances, wondering again if they are teetering on the edge of expulsion from the Overman inner circle.

"Here's what I need to do." Overman announces abruptly. "I want to spend a little time with my son and daughter, just in case."

"Just in case what?" Jake asks, confused.

"Well, let's say I were to go somewhere and I couldn't come back. Or I came back and everything had changed."

Jake is beside himself. "You're going to try? Going back?"

"Sure."

Of course they think he means he's going to time-travel, but in Overman's mind, he might be going back to see Janie, or the Lakeview Seven. He really didn't know where he was going, but he knew that leading the Rosenfarbs down this path would at least buy him some time.

"Fantastic!" Jake bellowed. "Go visit your kids and as soon as you're ready, we'll send you on your way."

"It's not that simple," Overman replies. "There are still a lot of unanswered questions."

"Whatever you need, we're here to help," Jonathan responds. "As you know, my dad is an expert on this stuff."

Overman turns to Rosenfarb Senior. "What about stuff like: How are you going to pay back your loan? How are you going to get back your business? What's going to happen with Rita?"

"I'm not worried," Jake replies with a wave of the hand.

"But shouldn't you worry? If I disappear, what are you going to do?"

"First of all, you're not going to disappear and second of all, we've got it all figured out."

"Oh really?"

"Really," Jake confirms. "What do you think we do all day while you're at work? Sit around yanking our *schlongs*? We're at the computer, researching, pitching ideas, acting out every possible scenario in order to provide you, the superhero, and ourselves as your retinue, with all the tools for success."

Jake had suddenly gone from meek to belligerent, yet it wasn't the Rosenfarb of years past who would simply pester a person to death. This was a prideful Jake Rosenfarb, one who was not about to be belittled in his area of expertise. True, he had reached his wit's end with Rita and torpedoed a successful window treatment business, but that didn't take anything away from the work he was doing now. Overman had to admit that Jake was as diligent and dedicated a sidekick as any he had studied.

"I apologize if I've offended you," Overman tells him. "I'm just saying —"

"We know what you're saying," Jake cuts him off. "Go see your kids if that's what you need to do. We'll talk about the other stuff when you get back."

"So you're telling me you have a plan to pay back your loan?"

Jake smiles. "Have I ever let you down?"

"Plenty of times," Overman answers.

"Yeah, well you've let me down too. But I don't hold grudges."

Overman wants to tell Jake it's because he can't afford to, but realizes it would be rubbing salt in a wound his friend won't even acknowledge in the first place. Then, just as Overman feels waves of tolerance welling up within him, his finely tuned Rosenfarb radar detects a new blip on the horizon.

Jake brings out a beautifully wrapped gift box to present to his leader. "We were going to save this for a special occasion, but maybe it'll come in handy on your trip."

Jonathan is bursting with anticipation. "Try it on, just to make sure it fits."

"You really didn't have to do this," Overman reacts, meaning he wishes like hell they didn't do it. If they were giving something as simple as a shirt he didn't need, he could deal with that, but these were Rosenfarbs and with them there was no such thing as simple. As Overman opens the box, his theory is borne out, and then some. He finds himself staring at green and gold sequins, topped off by a sloppily stitched "O" in the center of the garment. Somehow, he should not be surprised that this day has come, but his jaw drops as he removes from the box a full-body super-hero costume, replete with cape, that has been made just for him. "Wow. I don't know what to say," Overman gulps.

"Beautiful, huh?" Jake beams. "Jonathan sewed the whole fucking thing himself."

The younger Rosenfarb flashes a bashful smile. "I learned my stitches and seams at the swami's, so I could make robes for him."

"Go try it on," Jake commands.

Overman does his best to demur. "Look, Jake, I'm not a su-perhero —"

"To yourself. To the rest of us, a whole other ball of wax. But hey, it's your call."

"I appreciate that."

"Still, the kid made it from scratch. Humor him and try it on."

"I really don't want to."

Jonathan starts to pout. Jake throws his hero a look that says this will never end unless you throw us this bone.

Overman can't believe he is even considering a wardrobe change. "If I try it on, will you leave me alone so I can go be with my kids?"

"You'll never hear another word about it," Jake assures him.

Overman emerges from the bathroom to wild applause, both Rosenfarbs blatantly unaware that they have fashioned a uniform so amateurish and ugly that should it be donated to a poverty-stricken child for Halloween, he would be too embarrassed to be seen in it. The color combination is awful, the shoulders uneven, the overall quality of the handiwork pathetic.

"Looks good," Jake crows. "It'll fit even better after you take off a few pounds. Pack it up in your suitcase just in case you need it."

Overman shakes his head, relieved that spending time with his children will afford him a much-needed break from these nutcases, who have just proven that their insanity knows no bounds. After changing back into civvies, he makes a quick call to Big Dave, which thankfully goes more smoothly than the costume fiasco. The moneylender slash producer slash porn star is cool with his protégé taking as much time as he needs to attend to family matters. He is also nice enough to describe, in detail, a scene they're shooting at the escrow office in which Juicy blows out twenty-one birthday candles with her high-pressure honey pot. Overman thinks that a break from Cavanaugh Foster might be a good thing as well.

As whacked out as the Rosenfarbs were, the truth was that Jake now had a better relationship with his son than Overman had with his. Peter Overman had always been an exemplary student, socially awkward but professionally ambitious. He had little patience for dilettantism and the fact that he viewed his father as the embodiment of it put a major crimp in the family hierarchy. Peter could find little reason to respect the man who had asked his wife to abandon a career of her own to raise their kids, only to crap out himself, spiraling downward into increasingly bleaker lines of work. Perhaps if father and son had bonded earlier in life it wouldn't have mattered how Overman earned a living. As Maricela had pointed out, her father drove a taco truck and his kids revered him. But there never seemed to be common ground for Ira and Peter, even a point at which they could meet halfway. Peter had no interest in sports. Ira hated video games. Ira would take Peter to his favorite burger joint only to have Peter suddenly declare his veganism. Peter would introduce his dad to a girl he was dating and Ira would respond by recounting some embarrassing story from his Peter's childhood. Overman had never meant to humiliate the boy. He was simply referencing the times when he and his son enjoyed each other's company.

As he dials Peter's cell phone, Overman wavers between wanting to get voicemail and hoping his son answers. He had thought about skipping the call and just showing up on campus, but a surprise visit could engender more hostility than Peter already harbored toward him. He wonders how much Ashley has told Peter about the changes she's seen in her father, conjecturing that if she had, it might mitigate some of the tension.

"Hello, Dad," Peter answers in the half-hearted monotone he has perfected over the years.

"Hey, Pete," Overman responds, knowing full well that no one ever refers to his son as "Pete." "I'm going to be traveling up your way."

"Why?" his son inquires suspiciously.

"I'm working on a couple of real estate deals in the Providence area," he answers, amazed by how effortlessly he can revert to bullshit mode. "I thought I might drop by and say 'hello'."

"When?" Peter asks, simultaneously wanting to put off the visit and get it over with as quickly as possible.

"I can be there Thursday afternoon," Overman informs him. "Maybe we can have dinner. Are you still dating Kendra?"

"Kiana. No, we broke up."

"I'm sorry to hear that."

"Why? She was a bitch."

"Sorry to hear that, too. Should I pick you up on campus?"

"Let's meet at Dominic's. Seven o'clock?"

"Sounds good," Overman responds.

Click. Peter never was one for extraneous conversation. It there was nothing more to say he saw no point in wasting verbiage pretending there was. It could be off-putting, but on the plus side, the boy seemed to be born with a sense of purpose. It would be interesting to see how he reacted once he discovered that his father, the man for whom he had lost all respect, had acquired a purpose of his own.

Whenever they were together, Peter's affect was abrupt and sour, exuding an almost curmudgeonly air of superiority. Overman couldn't help but wonder if Kiana really was a bitch or whether she was driven away by Peter's crankiness and rigidity. It saddened him to think that these character traits were likely a result of his own inadequacies in the human relations department. Then again, what about Nancy? Peter's mother radiated warmth and was as socially adept as anyone Overman knew. Why didn't their son inherit any of that? He supposed that you couldn't pick which traits you got from which parent. Overman tried to think of any positive qualities that he might have handed down to his children, but came up empty.

Going to the computer to book his airfare, he thinks about briefing Team Rosenfarb on the proposed length of his trip, where he's staying, etc, but then makes the executive decision not to, thereby avoiding the unnecessary comments, criticisms and windbaggedness that always proved so tiresome. His rationale was that since seeing Peter had nothing to do with Jake and Jonathan, there was little need for their input on the subject. Plus, since he had brought them back together, they should, by all counts, allow him to reconnect with his own son in peace. Not a minute passes before he hears Jake's voice from outside the door.

"Everything all right in there, Ira? You want a piece of sponge cake?"

"I'm fine, Jake," Overman answers, in awe of how the window man had so remade himself into a carb-dispensing *bubbe*.

Hearing Jonathan join his father at the door to assist in fretting about their superhero's well-being makes Overman just plain crazy, fueling his desire to beat a hasty retreat. Yet he bites the bullet and goes out to talk to them, filling in father and son on his plan to fly to Providence the next morning and stay at Marcy's Motor Lodge in Seekonk. The Rosenfarbs give their blessing, assuring him that they will hold down the fort and take care of business while he is gone. The fact that there is no business seems immaterial to them.

The flight from Los Angeles is blessedly uneventful. In between the bad Hugh Grant movie and the rank fettuccine that takes him back to a previous incarnation, he ruminates: If Ira Overman could have any life he desired, what would it look like? The picture that instantly comes to mind is as unrealistic as it is fraught with guilt. In Overman's fantasyland he is not a multimillionaire, making nasty, relentless love to Maricela while enjoying the Asian hottie from the doctor's office on the side. He is not destroying an opponent at tennis and crowing about his victory to the waitress with the plumped lips at Jerry's. In his reverie he is Garvin Leeds, smiling as his graceful wife plants sage and tarragon, wagging-tailed dogs beside her as she waters the soil.

While Overman is happy that his instincts seem to value depth over pure sex, he is nevertheless appalled to be having such thoughts. Though it was natural to be envious of the exquisite relationship Garvin and Janie shared, he felt sickened to have plugged himself in as a substitute with Garvin barely in the ground. He cuts himself some slack, mindful that it is only fantasy. He had dared to dream and this was what came out organically. Probing further, he realizes that his fantasy is based exclusively on what he had experienced over a two-hour time period. How could one draw meaningful conclusions based on such skimpy data? Who knew what displeasures, grudges, and flat-out arguments lurked in the corners of that bucolic world?

Before Overman knows it, the plane has landed and he is in a cab, bound for Marcy's Motor Lodge. It is already dark out and he feels as enervated as he would have had he teleported to Rhode Island. The prospect of sitting down with his son, the compounding stress of sharing a living space with two Rosenfarbs, the fate of Janie Sweeney and the Lakeview Seven all weighed heavily on him. He needed to lie down, clear the competing static in his brain, and regroup in the morning.

Between the concave mattress and the road noise, sleep proves elusive. Things aren't helped by the fact that his cell phone rings at 6:30 AM, courtesy of the Rosenfarbs, calling just to make sure he arrived safely and be their annoying selves. It is only after he's at the coffee shop, well into his third cup, that it dawns on him: Jake and Jonathan phoned at 3:30 in the morning their time which meant that they must have set their alarms to wake up at that ridiculous hour just to check in on their Leader. Their madness long ago confirmed, they never fail to outdo themselves, always finding some new sycophantic wrinkle to throw into the mix. Ordering a fatty bacon and egg combo he knew they would disapprove of, he feels liberated to be so many miles away from the toxic tag team.

Combing the galleries downtown seems like a relaxing way to fill the time before dinner, but before starting off, Overman wants to try touching base with Janie. Since it has been a while since she initiated contact, he considers the possibility that his concern has had a Rosenfarb-like effect on her. He shudders to think of his newly evolved self being viewed this way. He just knows that when Jake and Jonathan direct their worry toward him, it is a colossal pain in the ass.

Her cell phone rings twice and he is sure the voicemail is about to pick up when he hears the trembling, weepy sound on the other end.

"Oh, Ira." She starts bawling, her anguish bursting any levees of defense the recent widow might have previously erected. She is convinced her life is over, at least any life worth living. Overman reminds her of her teaching job, the university community, the house, the garden, the dogs.

"None of it means anything. Garvin was the only person I ever trusted. There's no point if he's not here."

Overman pauses for a beat, giving serious thought to what he so wants to ask but is afraid to. Then he reminds himself that fear was Saul and Irma's milieu, not his. "Janie?"

"Yes?" she sniffles.

"Do you trust me?"

"Well...yeah...I don't know...I'm sorry. I want to, but —"

"I understand," Overman jumps in, realizing that as important as it was for him to operate without fear, it had been a selfish question and its directness had made her uncomfortable. "When do you take off for Florida?"

"I postponed the trip. I just can't leave this place right now."

"That makes sense," Overman says. On the other hand, he suspects her getting away for a bit might be beneficial.

"I've been thinking though. Maybe I should just move to Delray and live with my dad and stepmom."

To mark time before agonizing through two more deaths while preparing for her own is where Overman's mind goes. It didn't seem like much of a life, a sad way to go out when all was said and done. Her brief dance with happiness had been so unjustly terminated. Having worked so hard to overcome years of psychological damage, she deserved as many great years with Garvin.

While acknowledging the awful hand Janie had been dealt, the thought of this still relatively young woman giving up seemed even more tragic to Overman. "Do you want me to go visit your dad in Florida with you?" he offers.

"No. It's nice of you to ask, but it's really not necessary."

"I know it's not necessary, but—"

"Thanks. I'm okay."

She wasn't okay, Overman knew. Janie had closed down all over again and this time she wouldn't have the will or the energy to risk any new relationships.

"Thanks for calling, Ira." She hangs up, leaving him with visions of this kind and decent woman sitting with her father and stepmother at bingo night, re-using old teabags, checking off the hours until it was time to master the mechanics of adult diapering.

The Rhode Island School of Design was a place he had heard about all his life, but the concept of a college that specialized in training creative people to become more creative was as foreign to a sales and numbers guy as crucifixes to a Jew. Of course he had represented talented entertainers during his career as a manager and agent, but their lives had mystified him as well. How did anybody have the confidence to perform or write and expect to make a living at it? And forgetting the money aspect, the mere act of exposing one's inner self to others for the purpose of being judged was unthinkable to someone like Overman. If he had been confounded by show business, serious art was even more bewildering to him. What giant leap of faith must it have taken for a Jackson Pollock to bet the farm splattering paint on canvas? It seemed to Overman that these people possessed a kind of divine *chutzpah* that allowed them to stand before the world naked and unashamed. Sure, there were countless drug and alcohol casualties among artists, but you found that everywhere. At least these folks had strived for something, attempted a life that transcended the corporate bullshit.

According to the weekly freebie guide they put in his motel room, the school had its own art museum that featured both a permanent collection and revolving special exhibitions. This would fill up most of the day until it was time to meet Peter. Plus, it would give him something interesting to talk about should his son be resistant to the rigorous demands of two-way conversation. It had been so long since they had spent time together alone that awkwardness was sure to be the tenor of the evening. But one couldn't worry about that, Overman told himself. The best approach was Pollock's: Go ahead and splatter whatever the results.

Overman enters an Asian gallery featuring nothing but a nine-foot wooden sculpture flanked by meditation benches. As he takes a seat facing the Buddha from whom apparently all other Buddhas and aspects of the universe flow, it occurs to Overman how far he has come from his days at Steinbaum Mercedes of Calabasas. While he does not join the various students and visitors in holy meditation, he fully intends to summon his own brand of deep thinking. Staring into the sculpture's eyes, Overman is struck by how much the Buddha resembles his ex-mother-in-law Ceil with the triple chin. As he remembers, Ceil was a deep thinker in her own way, having developed the theory that feeding her home-cooked brisket to the pigeons would somehow grant her a long and fruitful life. She was now ninety-one and thriving. Overman wondered how many pigeons had died young.

Wandering through the rest of the permanent collection, Overman admires the lush Monets and Manets, the buoyant Renoirs and rippling Rodins. He had accepted it as fact that he had not an ounce of artistic ability himself, undoubtedly because his parents discouraged him from pursuing any activity they hadn't deemed practical or an investment in future earnings. What good did it do little Ira to paint a tree or sketch a face? If he liked to look at plants, let him study botany. If he wanted to see people's faces, go be a dermatologist. Was it any wonder that he had been doomed to such a narrow existence, devoid of vision?

Overman moves on to the special exhibition, a collection of work from the late American photographer Harry Callahan. Most of the photographs are black and white, taken between 1940 and 1968, comprising street scenes, landscapes and portraits. Especially striking are the portraits, specifically those of the photographer's wife, Eleanor, his frequent subject during the period. She is sometimes clothed, oft times not, but in each case radiates a power that burrows its way to the Overman core. Eleanor is not classically beautiful, her face bordering on masculine in certain pictures. Her body is curvy but not taut, sensuous by virtue of the fact that it is real. Overman wonders what her husband thought as he shot these photographs. Surely he had studied the way the light hit her skin, how the flesh folded as she curled in different positions. He had obviously been fascinated by Eleanor, having photographed her through two decades. But somehow, it seemed to Overman that the power of these pictures must have increased a hundredfold with time. He was curious whether or not Callahan got to study the entire set toward the end of his life, and if so, how the totality of these images affected him.

Their effect on Overman was a combination of awe and wistfulness. This was not abstract art that might elicit a random emotional reaction or become the object of exhaustive intellectual analysis. It was not an ancient Buddha in whose presence one prayed or meditated. It was the document of a life lived, of a man and his partner, to whom he had stayed married for over sixty years. From the little information Overman could gather, Eleanor had spent most of her career as a secretary, pumping much of the money she'd earned into her husband's photography. But the facts weren't really the point. It was those images, that window into the place Overman felt a man should be at fifty-five. To have shared the deepest experiences with a magnificent, imperfect woman who evolved as you evolved. He now understood that having an Eleanor was all he ever wanted. Others besides Harry Callahan had been able to achieve that goal, but the building blocks had bypassed Overman. As he again looked at the close-up of Eleanor's bent arm resting on her forehead, Overman had one more epiphany. Perhaps he had been so taken by these photographs because as he looked at Eleanor, he saw Janie Sweeney.

Overman arrives forty-five minutes early in order to secure a table at the East side hole-in-the-wall that, according to locals, regularly has lines spilling down the sidewalk. As luck would have it, Dominic's is not crowded at all this evening and its sole server is happy to seat the enlightened but weary museumgoer at a small table by the window. Overman asks for a glass of their cheapest house Chianti in nervous anticipation of the reunion with his son. Since Peter is habitually late, Overman sips slowly so as not to incur the extra cost of multiple ordering. The wine isn't half-bad and does, in fact, take some of the edge off, soothing the guilt that engulfs him whenever he is about to see Peter. The combination of the father's culpability and the son's resentment always makes for a combustible encounter. But tonight could be different, Overman thinks. With the exception of a few mindless text messages from the "team," he has had a thoughtful, Rosenfarb-free day that has filled him with excitement about what lies ahead. The icing on the cake is the knowledge that whatever power lives within him is real, and not some comic book fantasy. It has manifested itself in the form of good judgment and emotional candor. If Peter wasn't able to ascertain that, then the problem was his — which of course Overman couldn't really accept, because he believed that Peter's issues were a direct result of his father's previous ineptitude.

"Another glass of wine?" the now frazzled waitress wants to know. More people have showed up and Overman will start to cost her money if he doesn't keep knocking them back.

"No, thanks. I'm good. Maybe a little more water." More tap water. They love that one.

"Sure thing," she frowns, traipsing off pissily to fetch her pitcher.

Overman starts to peruse the menu, finding it on the pricey side, but figures he'll be okay if he sticks to pasta or eggplant.

"When did you get here?" croaks the young but crabby voice that could only belong to Peter Overman. Overman the elder looks up from the menu to see his son staring at him nonplussed, as if waiting to be admonished for his tardiness.

"I've been here a while," the father says. "Just wanted to make sure we got seated. It's good to see you, Peter."

He shakes his son's hand, a more formal gesture than Overman would have liked, but he is reluctant to attempt a hug given the uneasy history between them. Peter sits down, burying himself in the list of Dominic's specials.

"Would you like some wine?" Overman asks his son, a convivial tip of the hat to the boy having recently turned twenty-one.

"No, thanks. I'll have some pot later."

The attitude was still intact. Peter always made sure to lead off with something incendiary to cause his father discomfort. But Overman wasn't about to buy into it this time around.

"Maybe we could smoke some together," he suggests.

"Yeah, right," Peter responds. Like he'd ever want to smoke dope with his dweeby loser dad. "So what are you doing here anyway?"

"Well, this afternoon I went to the RISD museum. Have you ever seen Harry Callahan's work? I love his use of natural light."

"I meant what are you doing in Providence? You said something about real estate deals."

Overman had completely forgotten the false pretext for his trip. "Oh yes. The real estate deals." What should he fabricate here, he wondered? A strip mall off I-95? Gutting a slew of row houses for gentrification? All of it seemed like a waste of energy. Needless, meaningless wordcrap and for what? What reason was there now to obfuscate a truth that warranted no embarrassment in the first place?

"There are no real estate deals," Overman blurts out.

"Why am I not surprised?" Peter smirks. "They all fell through?"

"No. There never were any deals."

His son nods knowingly. "So what's up then? Are you thinking of selling used cars here or something?"

"I never sold used cars, Peter. And the only reason I came to Providence was that I wanted to see you."

Before Overman can assess his son's reaction, Frazzled Waitress comes by with the water pitcher and asks Peter if he'd like a drink.

"No, I'm ready to order. Are you?" he turns to his father.

"I'm ready," Overman says, having settled on the dull but cheap penne with marinara sauce.

"I'll have the scampi," Peter says.

"That's excellent," smiles the server, who seems to like his taste much more than the father's.

Market price $27.95, Overman can't help but note.

As the waitress snatches the menus out of their hands, Peter looks around the room, fidgeting to avoid whatever is about to be thrust on the table.

"Peter —"

"What's with you, anyway?" his son dives in. "Ashley said you had goddamn Shabbat dinner with her, that you were funny and charming, and that all of a sudden you're trying to act normal."

Overman was pleased that Ashley had been communicating with her brother, even more so that she had heaped good reviews on her father. "I'm trying to change it up a bit," he explains. "I've decided that I want to be a better role model for my kids."

"A little late for that, don't you think?" Peter responds, chugging down his water.

"It may be. I just didn't want you to go through the rest of your life not having heard this from me."

"Heard what?"

"I fucked up big time. I know the kind of father I should have been and I'm sorry I didn't deliver."

"Okay," Peter answers, grabbing a piece of focaccia. "So now what?" He is so distant, so closed to re-imagining their relationship as anything positive.

"I guess that depends," Overman tells his son. "Do you want me in your life?"

"I don't know."

At least he was honest. "I can understand your ambivalence," Overman relents. "How about we just have dinner and not make any rules about anything?"

"Sounds good," Peter nods.

Overman celebrates getting through his apology by ordering a second glass of Chianti. This loosens him up enough to make his son more comfortable, which in turn propels Peter to order a large Italian beer. After a couple of swigs, he offers his father a scampi, a baby step toward the first real connection between father and son since the skeeball days of Santa Monica Pier.

For the first time in Overman's memory, Peter is volunteering information about himself as opposed to just answering questions. Evidently he is very excited about his legal studies, explaining, to his father's surprise, how he plans to forego the corporate route for a career in public interest law. That way, he can help protect the rights of ordinary citizens and make a difference in the world. Overman is speechless. From where had this zeal for social justice materialized? Certainly not from Peter's mother, who, upon hooking up with Dr. Stan, defined equality as being able to spend as much as her friends did at Tiffany's.

"That's fantastic," Overman complimented his son. "What made you want to go in that direction?"

"I guess I've seen a lot of people, you know, struggle," Peter answered, quickly looking away to ask the waitress for more bread.

Overman suddenly felt as if an anvil from a Warner Brothers cartoon had just come crashing down on his head. Those giant Acme numbers that flattened and knocked the life out of you only to have you inexplicably regain consciousness two seconds later. There was something about Peter's demeanor; the embarrassed look on his face as he tried to avert his father's gaze. Unless Overman had it all wrong, it seemed that he had been at least partially responsible for the career to which his son aspired. Not because he had taught Peter to value other people or instilled in him the principle of equality. Rather, it was because unbeknownst to Overman, Peter had observed his father's struggle and emotionally digested it. While the young man never showed any interest, it must have disturbed him to watch his mother flaunt her nouveau riche lifestyle while his father plummeted to lowly working stiff, stuck in a hole for most of his life. As unbelievable as the notion was, it appeared as if Ira Overman, the father for whom Peter outwardly projected nothing but antipathy, had touched him.

"So if you're not in real estate and you're not selling cars, what are you doing?" Peter asked.

It was a reasonable question, yet Overman felt he couldn't be totally forthcoming without squandering the good will he had finally managed to accrue with his son. "I'm re-evaluating everything," he answered obtusely. "I know that may sound vague, like some loser guy who keeps changing careers trying to make that one big score—"

"Aren't you kind of old to be starting over, Dad?"

"I am," Overman agreed, savoring the long absent sound of his son uttering the word 'Dad.' "But it took me till now to figure out what I really want."

"Well, whatever it is, I wish you luck."

"Thanks. Can I get you another beer? "Remember though," says Overman smiling, "you've got to save room for the pot."

This provokes a loud, spontaneous laugh from Peter, something Overman hasn't heard for over a decade. It's Nancy's laugh, deep and unbridled, the laugh he remembers from when they first met, when they were in their twenties and madly in love.

"Peter, I'm considering some big changes, maybe doing a bit of traveling. I just want to say that if something should happen to me, not that I'm expecting it will, I have a life insurance policy that should help out you and your sister."

"Where are you going, Afghanistan or something?" his son asks, deducing from the insurance remark that his father is bound for someplace dangerous.

"Nowhere that exciting," Overman assures him. "You just never know what might happen."

"You never know what might happen anywhere, anytime. You just have to live your life," Peter says.

Overman is impressed. It had taken him fifty-five years to learn that lesson. "Have you talked with your mother lately?"

"Last night. She and Stan are planning another cruise."

"That's great."

"Stan's an insufferable asshole. I want there to be socialized medicine just so that fucker stops enabling the pharmaceutical companies to rip people off."

"I had no idea you felt that way."

"Seriously?"

"Stan's a nice enough guy." Overman hated Stan, but he

couldn't see the point in further poisoning the relationship between Peter and his stepfather. Still, he was pleased that despite all that had gone down since the divorce, he and his son were now on the same page.

By the third Chianti, the waitress was a lot friendlier. After they ordered two desserts she was family, proceeding to sneak them free cappuccinos and limoncello. Overman and Peter wound up closing the place, relishing their time together as if it was their last, which, in turn, gave them the impetus to make sure it wasn't.

As they stumble into the crisp Providence night, Overman considers asking his son if he'd like to stay out a while longer, maybe hit the Mews Tavern and cherry-pick from their collection of two hundred scotches. Peter, however, has something else in mind, reaching into his pocket and producing the expertly rolled joint that is to be their nightcap. They amble south on Hope Street, passing such local landmarks as the Aqua-Life Aquarium Store (New Fish Arrival: the Red Scribble Discus) and the Tockwotton Home (Providing skilled nursing and assisted living since 1856). In his tipsy, about-to-be-stoned state, Overman finds all of it fascinating, the city of Providence worlds away from the harsh, in-your-face sunlight of the San Fernando Valley. Peter is leading them toward Indian Point Park, where they will be able to look at the lights reflecting off the water as the cannabis kicks in.

Sanguine about the gargantuan forward progress that has been made this evening, Overman feels the need to share. "You know, Peter, I'm really glad I came out here."

"Me, too," his son smiles. And then, as if from someone else's life, Peter makes the first move and hugs his father.

There was no way Overman could adequately express the potency of the moment to a person from a family with even quasi-normal relations. It wasn't a close or long or sentimental hug, but it was a crucial nod toward a rapprochement that could only strengthen the characters of both father and son.

The pot is much stronger than Overman remembers, Peter explaining that as in virtually every field, weed technology had advanced by leaps and bounds over the last thirty years. There was a greater plant variety available, and what with the advent of liberally dispensed medical marijuana, a highly educated consumer base. People picked and chose their weed much the way coffee lovers bought exotic, freshly roasted beans, relishing the discovery of a rare new strain as if they had unearthed a treasure that would transport them to a clandestine nirvana.

Taking a deep hit of the joint, an uncharacteristically unique thought occurs to Overman. "It's amazing. These days, there are more connoisseurs of obscure shit than anybody could ever dream of when I was growing up."

"People are better informed," Peter explains.

"Or, they're just more obsessed with minutiae. There are too many fucking choices. With everything. Water. Tap or bottled? Spring or filtered? Reverse osmosis filter or magnetic de-scaling? Who has the time for this?"

"Consumers are just trying to make educated decisions," Peter figures.

"But is it really important or is it just pretentious? So we can feel like experts on subjects most people don't have the luxury to give a rat's ass about?"

"Wow, you're really getting worked up. This Easy Rider is supposed to be a mellow strain."

"I'm mellow," Overman assures him.

He definitely isn't mellow. Passing his son the joint, his brain is exploding with the passion of his own ping-ponging thoughts, quick-cutting from what he owes on his electric bill to the picture of Big Dave's flabby gut, to the Fed printing worthless money and pumping it into a sagging economy, to the classic curves of Mar-

icela Flores's delectable posterior. This part of the marijuana experience had not changed for Overman. While many smokers seemed
to react to the drug by focusing on one subject or object, pot always
sent his mind spinning in a million different directions. Sensing a
hard-on in the making as he pictures Maricela, Overman opts to
address another of his stream-of-consciousness thoughts.

"So why do they call this place Indian Point anyway?"

Peter tells him that the park, at the confluence of the Seekonk
River and Providence River, takes its name from the maritime activity connecting Providence with the East and West Indies.

"The West Indies. Remember when your mother and I took
you to Jamaica? Ocho Rios, I think it was. We could have scored
some awesome strains of pot there, am I right?"

"I was four years old," his son reminds him.

Overman feels himself drifting back, retreating to the maudlin
view of his ignorant past. "That was a great time, wasn't it?"

"I don't remember it very well," Peter admits, dragging hard on
the soon-to-be roach.

"There was a calypso band," Overman tells him. "The leader's
name was Duke, or Doc, or something. He wore a big straw hat
and you made us buy you one exactly like it. After that, every night
you'd get up and sing along with the band, following them around
the hotel and strumming an air guitar. You never stopped smiling."

"Yellow Bird." Peter does remember.

At which point stoned-out Overman drifts back, once again
the bright-eyed young parent watching his babies frolic along the
shoreline. He softly starts to sing the tune, an old Jamaican folk
song rewritten in native dialect by three Jewish-American lyricists.
Peter is just gone enough to join in. Suddenly, two Overmans are
wailing at the harbor's edge, intoning to the Rhode Island sky their
very own West Indies connection.

This yields another outburst from the extremely buzzed Ira.
"It's true. It's all fucking true!"

"What's true?" Peter wants to know.

"In the song, when the bird's chick bailed, he could just fly away. I couldn't do that. I had responsibilities."

"Dad, it's just a song."

"Songs are powerful. The great ones tap into our deepest feelings." The pot had removed all the walls and filters that normally kept Overman's emotions in check. He began to tear up, sniffles growing into full-blown sobs.

"You still miss Mom, don't you?" Peter asks, gently putting his arm around his father.

"No, not at all. I miss that moment in time. And I feel like a fool because back then, I had no idea how special it was."

"Even if you did know, life would still move on. Maybe if you recognized it all along, you would have felt even worse after it was gone."

"I guess that's possible," tissue-less Overman admits, sucking in the errant snot.

"Are you going to be all right?" Peter wants to know.

"Yeah, I'm fine. I know it's hard to believe, but I'm great."

"Do you always cry when you're great?"

"I never cry. Then again, I'm never great."

This gets a laugh from both of them, the elder Overman realizing that *this* moment in time, this father-son pot-smoking bonding adventure, deserves family memory status on par with Ocho Rios and Santa Monica Pier. Perhaps it resonated on an even higher level because both parties were fully functioning, if temporarily wasted, adults. Never in his wildest dreams had Overman pictured himself and Peter sharing such a heartfelt evening. The only quasi-meaningful exchange he had ever had with his own father was in the nursing home as Saul was squeezing the last drop out of old age. The reformed Sanka addict had mellowed in his advanced years, the unspoken theory being that Irma preceding him in death had finally bought him some peace. One day, after Ira finished feeding him a bowl of cottage cheese, Saul took his son's hand and said: "Maybe you should have a life." When Ira asked what he meant by that, his father had already nodded out, going on to expire in his sleep that very evening. Upon later reflection, Ira interpreted the spontaneous outburst as Saul wishing his son a more rewarding stint on the planet than he himself had managed. While the final tally was probably a ways off, Ira was certain that his dad would recognize this night in Providence as a major Overman milestone, even though it had taken so long to get here.

Ira and Peter begin the long trek up Hope Street, Peter wanting to get back because he has an early class the next morning. When father drops off son at his apartment, they both voice approval of how well the evening went, vowing to make these get-togethers a more regular occurrence. As he watches Peter head through the door of his building, Overman feels a massive adrenaline jolt. He finds himself skipping down the street and headed for the Mews Tavern, primed to continue his personal celebration long into the night. He polishes off five 18-year single malt Glenlivets, the pot and liquor leaving him just reckless enough to turn on his cell phone and find the seventeen voice messages from Jake Rosenfarb.

One of the upsides of being stinking drunk and delirious was that it made dealing with the Rosenfarbs more like a mindless game of say, tic-tac-toe, than the drudgery it actually was. He knew that even though it was 4:30 in the morning on the west coast, Jake Rosenfarb was clutching his cell phone with the sweatiest of palms waiting for his return call.

"Ira Overman!" Jake shouts, with the enthusiasm of a hungry politician about to give a stump speech at the Tallahassee VFW. "Tell me everything, man!"

"Well, I saw Peter, it went well —"

"Happy to hear it. We've got a lot business to discuss, but I won't bother you with the details until you get back. When are you coming home?"

Suddenly a crazy idea occurred to Overman. Although he wanted to see Ashley again and this brainstorm put that at risk, his intoxicated state was getting the better of him. Perhaps a Flash-like maneuver was actually doable. "Maybe I have the power," he slurred into the phone.

"Of course you do," Jake assures him, not bothering to ask what power it is he's talking about.

Overman quickly clarifies. "You know, Jake, if I'm going to try this Speed Force *mishegos*, I'm thinking maybe I need some practice before diving into something as complicated as the Merkowitz mess."

"This is exciting. Very, very exciting. And a totally valid point, vis-à-vis not overreaching. I'm putting you on speakerphone."

"Overman is Love," Jonathan chimes in, having co-opted the salutation from his tenure with the swami.

"Hello, Jonathan. And never use that language with me again."

"I'm sorry. A thousand apologies, Mr. Overman," quivers the hopeless toady.

"Forget about it and call me Ira."

"The idea of a practice run is intriguing," Jake jumps in, eager to get back on point. "What are your coordinates?"

"Drop the Star Trek shit for a second," Overman snaps. "I don't know anything about coordinates."

"Fine. Give it to me in layman's terms."

"Here's the pitch," Overman begins. "What if I tried traveling back from here to say, the night I sprung you from that crappy motel?"

"That depends. Are you going to leave me there this time?" Jake laughs.

Overman hadn't thought of that but the notion was tempting. "Of course I'm not going to leave you. The point is how do I know I can even get myself back there in the first place? And assuming I can, is it realistic to think that I'd be able to spring you and return to where I am now without having to re-live the entire last month?"

"This is out of my realm of expertise," Jonathan defers. As if anyone could possibly know the answer.

"Look," Jake begins, as if he has handled this situation hundreds of times. "To my mind, there's no question that you're putting your best foot forward by not trying to bite off more than you can chew. It reminds me of the first time I installed motorized shutters in the Wood Ranch section of Simi Valley —"

Only Jake could compare a voyage through time and space to the mounting of window treatments. "What does this have to do with fucking shutters?" Overman must ask.

Jake is more than happy to oblige. "All I'm saying is, even though I knew the motorized shutters were a great product, it was my first experience with them so I told the client I would only do one room initially, just to make sure they liked it."

"What if I get stuck back at the motel?" Overman cuts to the chase.

"Worst case scenario, we see you in a month. Which won't be a month for us, incidentally, because we're laying low right here in the present. We get to see you tomorrow at the latest. It's win-win, baby."

"Unless, of course, something screws up. Here's my question. If I'm really in the past, how will I know I came from the future? Won't I just think that this is where I am, plain and simple?" He couldn't wait to hear Rosenfarb's detailed explanation of this one.

"Beats the shit out of me," Jake responds. "Do I look like a guy who has the Speed Force?"

"So if you don't know anything, why are you so sure I should try this?"

"Why? Because you've had a terrific record up till now and I have no reason to believe this will turn out any differently."

"I'd just like to say that I wouldn't think any less of you if you backed out," Jonathan pipes in, willing to throw his dad under the bus if it will further endear him to his God, Overman.

"Thank you, Jonathan," Overman replies, as if he cared what the younger Rosenfarb thought.

"Okay, Jake, I'll give it a go," he announces, the wine, pot and scotch having officially transported Overman to Rosenfarb Wackyland.

"Godspeed, Ira."

Jonathan offers up some Hindu meditation, leading into horrendous guttural chanting that becomes even more unbearable once Jake joins in.

"Guys, this is all very nice," Overman interjects. "I'll see you soon, Jake. In fact, I'll probably see you at the motel."

"Try not to scare me this time when you peek in the window."

"Try not to scare me by looking so pathetic," Overman counters.

"I'll see what I can do," answers Rosenfarb, suddenly the great compromiser.

The die has been cast and drunk/stoned Overman is ready to go forth. Prepping himself to relive a scene from his past, he suddenly wonders why on earth he would choose an episode that features Jake Rosenfarb. In theory, if he really is going to attempt such a huge undertaking, he can pick whatever experience he wants. The idea here is to see if he is able to successfully make this sort of journey and if so, is he *schtarker* enough to turn it into a round-trip? And should he arrive at his destination but happen to get stuck there, why shouldn't it be somewhere pleasant for heaven's sake? It was a fact that for all Overman's achievements since his surgical reawakening, he had barely indulged in self-gratification. So if there were a way to perform such a risky experiment that also made him happy, didn't he owe it to himself to explore such an option?

As Overman staggers down Hope Street toward his car, past the regal tower of St. Joseph's Church, he envisions himself back in Los Angeles, trudging along a noisy, smoggy, billboard-laden thoroughfare. There it is still light out, ninety degrees instead of fifty, brown hills in the distance rather than dark green ones. He

picks up the pace, singularly focusing on that west coast boulevard, channeling the deep satisfaction he had once received there.
He passes Arnold Street, seeing an older couple shuffle into a
quaint gray clapboard house, when he feels what must be a gale
force wind propel him forward. He feels as if his body has been
blasted from a cannon and falls to the ground. Opening his bleary
eyes, he is no longer on Hope Street in Providence. He has landed in what appears to be an elevator that looks vaguely familiar,
holding a paper bag of something. He is about to check out its
contents when the elevator door opens.

And there she stands, the hard-bodied angel of Steinbaum
Calabasas, smiling at him in the tight black tank top, just as she
had that fateful evening when he brought her the Grey Goose
and she bestowed upon him every beautiful, nasty thing he had
ever dreamed of in a sex partner.

"Hi," Maricela coos, giving him the identical kiss on the cheek
and full on hug, the wildflower smell even more intoxicating than
it was the first time around.

Overman is struck by how much harder he is this time, despite knowing the extraordinary outcome. As the lovely receptionist leads him to the apartment where boyfriend Rodrigo will
be chugging his beer on cue, Overman grasps the significance
of what is happening. If he recognizes that what's going on is a
replay, it indicates that he is Future Overman consciously paying
a visit to the past, as opposed to Future Overman becoming Past
Overman and unconsciously replaying a scene he doesn't know
has already taken place. This means he will be able to savor the
moment anew and then try to gather whatever strength he has
left to return to his point of embarkation.

One wouldn't think that knowing the endgame would make
it more of a turn-on than the original experience, but it had been
a long while since the first go 'round and Overman hadn't had sex
since. His excitement was uncontainable, all of his senses drink-
ing in this scrumptious paradigm of womanhood, feasting on the

tastiest buffet of flesh he would ever know. As he kisses every inch of her, Overman marvels at the way Maricela's tiny waist curves into her soft, inviting hips and rock-solid ass. This time it's all about savoring, and when Overman finally comes, he feels as if he has thoroughly lived inside this woman, filling her with a love that pours out of his soul as well as his dick.

Overman soon learns that like all great journeys, even time-travel must come to an end, this particular trip culminating with the cruel realization that the only place to which he has traveled is the curb where he fell and hit his head. He had re-lived history in his dreams, performed cunnilingus in the unconscious, and now he was being scraped off the sidewalk by two good Samaritans inquiring as to whether or not he'd like a lift to the local homeless shelter. He politely rejects the offer, thanking them for their help and asking directions to an all-night diner, where he will proceed to pump himself full of black coffee.

Certain that the destitute man at the other end of the counter looks far better than he does, Overman nevertheless regrets none of what has transpired this evening. As stupid as it may have seemed, expecting that he could transport himself back into Maricela's bed had resulted in the feeling of actually being in Maricela's bed. Dreaming he had the power to time-travel was the natural, albeit alcohol and marijuana-induced extension of the empowerment he felt from reestablishing a connection with his son. The fact was, rolling with the Rosenfarbs' take on his superhero-dom had cost him nothing but a few moments on the sidewalk and a scrape on his forehead. The trip to Providence had been time well spent, the only downside being that he needed to return to Los Angeles. He still had a job and a couple of rabid sidekicks to deal with.

Arriving back in Studio City and preparing to face the pair of father and son *bubbes*, Overman knows he must make a decision. If he tells them the truth, that his attempt at time-travel was an abject failure, they will respond by trying to buck him up, plying him with cheesecake while insisting that he will do better next time. The way Overman sees it, honesty will only motivate them to put together some ridiculous new superhero regimen designed to strengthen his time-traveling skills. The prospects are almost too frightening to imagine.

He enters the apartment to Rosenfarb squeals and hugs, Jake gearing up for the inevitable "So?"

Both Rosenfarbs wait with baited breath to find out the results of their superhero's experiment.

Overman steels himself and nods his head knowingly. "Visiting the past is awesome."

"You did it!" Jake crows. "I never doubted you for a second. And thanks for getting me out of that shitty motel."

"I didn't go to the motel," Overman informs him. "I decided to sleep with Maricela again instead."

"*Mazel Tov*, you bastard," Jake bellows. "You think I'll ever know pussy like that? Jesus, it's not enough you got Glorietta Zatzkin, now you get that hot Latina pussy twice?!"

Overman shoots Jake a look. His son is standing right there, for Christ's sake.

"I have nothing against your mother's pussy," Jake explains to Jonathan, as if such a statement would mitigate the previous one. "I just haven't seen it in a decade or so."

Jonathan is horrified to hear Jake talking like this, understandable in that it is the rare son who is eager to discuss his mother's genitalia with anyone, much less his father.

"So now you need to see Ashley," the oblivious Jake reminds Overman as he gets out the calendar.

"Shouldn't be a problem. No going back in time necessary for that one."

"That's true," Jake sighs. "Let's talk about after that. You feel you're ready for Merkowitz? I don't want you to push it."

"I may need to take it slow," Overman responds, wisely dampening the flames of the Rosenfarb fire.

"Understood," Jake agrees, Jonathan nodding in unison. "You have to go at your own pace. The important thing is that time travel proved to be a positive experience for you."

"Extremely positive," Overman declares. "I was tempted to stay where I was and spend the rest of my life getting deep-throated by Maricela."

"She deep-throated you?" echoes the ever-envious Rosenfarb.

"Sorry I brought it up."

At which point Jake turns to his son. "It wouldn't have killed your mother to learn how to do that, by the way."

Jonathan cringes, his revulsion well earned.

"Excuse me. I guess that swami made you all sensitive or something," Jake reasons.

Once again, the Rosenfarbs have energized Overman to get out of there ASAP. "Man, that time-travel stuff tires you out," he notes, feigning a yawn.

Excusing himself to recharge, Overman heads for his bedroom and grabs one of the Lakeview High School yearbooks, hoping that if he studies its contents, it will generate a sober kind of brainstorm. Flipping through the vinyl-covered tome, he takes a moment to appreciate the junior class's geeky headshots, noting that the kids who were considered cool looked even more nerdy in retrospect than the average, under-the-radar ones. He attributed this to a combination of liberal parenting and money. Jim Koslowski's parents didn't care how long his hair was so he grew it to pageboy length and accessorized the look with massive muttonchops. Steve Latham's dad was some big executive in the record business so he was allowed to wear Nehru suits, granny glasses and love beads. In a truly unforeseeable way, Overman was fortunate to be the son of Saul and Irma: two narrow-minded skinflints who took great pride in appearance and behavior that would never get noticed. To wit, the photo of Ira Overman was not dissimilar from the shot of Timmy Kaye or the one of Mark Beyer or countless others. They were all generic, pimply adolescents who would grow up to become doctors, lawyers, plumbers, and should the universe so conspire, perceived superheroes.

He turns to the "S's" and finds Janie. She is smiling, but not too broadly, her shoulder-length hair neatly falling on a simple black crewneck sweater. Her extracurricular activities are listed as "Lit Club, Honor Society, Young Poets." It is a picture of innocence and intelligence joined as one, an image suggesting nothing less than a bright future. What really stirs him, however, is the quote Janie chose. The other girls seemed to go for homilies like "Life is nothing without happiness" or "If you see someone without a smile, give him one of yours." Janie cited a line from the poet Wallace Stevens:

> *"I do not know which to prefer,*
> *The beauty of inflections*
> *Or the beauty of innuendoes,*
> *The blackbird whistling*
> *Or just after."*

Overman had more often than not leafed through the senior yearbook, by which time Janie had already moved. He had scanned the junior volume many times, but somehow this quote and its profundity had eluded him. Stevens's line was a simple thought that seemed to apply to so many things. What was better, pumping Maricela like a man possessed or the revelatory post-coital glow? They were each extraordinary in their own way. And it was valuable, though not altogether obvious, for a person to be able to recognize that you could get two acts of beauty for the price of one, so to speak. Then there was the whole other layer, the one that put the quote in context of Janie choosing it over all other possible sayings. A deep and serious thinker like her could easily have gone the Emily Dickinson or Sylvia Plath route, not to mention double-dipping into the Brontë well, having already done the research for her A-plus paper. Janie's choice was auda-

cious, yet hopeful, filled with appreciation for having been granted the gift of life. How had she imagined her future when she
picked Wallace Stevens? Would she experience her twin doses of
happiness from becoming a celebrated poet herself, or would they
come from being a wife and mother? Or did she foresee some
kind of combo platter? He hoped he would someday be able to
ask her that question.

Another question gnawed at him. What had Janie looked like
in her senior class picture in New Jersey? Could she have appeared anywhere near as composed? Would she even think of using a quote that buoyant after the less-than-beautiful experience
she had lived through at Lakeview? Overman had to wonder if
the corollary of the Stevens quote also held true. If one had suffered through something miserable, wasn't the aftermath a sepa-
rate misery of its own?

He hears the Rosenfarbs rustling outside the door, most likely
murmuring about whether or not to look in on the boss. He stares
at young Janie with longing, hungry to see her again whether it be
at fifteen or fifty-five. While Maricela had taken him to physical
heights he had never dreamed he could reach, Janie Sweeney had
been woven into the fabric of his being. As he fixates on the book,
his eyes glaze over, suddenly taken back to graceful, middle-aged
Janie harvesting her Endicott garden. She seems happier and
more self-assured than the one in the picture, due, no doubt, to
the addition of Garvin in her life. Now the only images Overman
imagines are sad and helpless ones.

As he continues to peruse the yearbook he is humbled by the
power of these ordinary pictures. Much like the Harry Callahans,
revisiting them so many years later only intensifies their meaning. With distance, one knows the fate of the subject in the photograph. Gordon Freitag from the chess club is smiling in the
headshot, but we know now that twenty years later, he gets cancer
and dies a horrific death. Jenny Lucas is the carefree homecoming
queen, unaware that in her first year of college her mother will be

in a fatal car crash. It strikes Overman that the smiles of the innocent are heartbreaking when viewed through the prism of history. He feels himself starting to well up with tears. He wants to
let go and bawl his head off, but knows if he does, the Rosenfarbs
will come flying in with homemade *mandelbread* to cheer him up.
Instead, he closes the yearbook and trudges off to the bathroom
to get ready for bed.

Overman barely tucks himself in and closes his eyes when he
feels an urge to study the Stevens poem in its entirety. He springs
out of bed, opens his laptop, and locates "Thirteen Ways of Looking at a Blackbird." It is a Spartan, but beautiful piece of work, the
last verse especially haunting:

> "*It was evening all afternoon.*
> *It was snowing*
> *And it was going to snow.*
> *The blackbird sat*
> *In the cedar-limbs.*"

Elegant, ambiguous, and frightening, Overman thought. It
was prematurely dark, snowing, and it was about to snow some
more. Yet the blackbird just sat there. Doing what exactly? Biding
his time, waiting for the right moment to make his move? Or just
submitting to the elements and getting ready to freeze to death?

The blackbird conundrum led Overman back to his own; how
could he be of help to Janie, and what made him think he'd be
better at it now than he was all those years ago? He tries to resist
rehashing the notorious night, but knows he is helpless to do so.
The more he attempts to block it out, the more detailed are the
images that come reeling back. Finally, not unlike the blackbird,
he gives up and just lies there, allowing the flurries of memories
to fall down as they see fit.

"Ira, don't you need a ride?" grates the strident voice of Irma Overman through the closed bedroom door. "We're supposed to pick up your friend, Jake."

"I'll be out in a minute," the boy responds. "I just need to finish studying this last page of homework." The subject currently under scrutiny was May Playmate of the Month, Sally Sheffield, bust: 36" waist: 24" hips: 35". His mother might be interested to know that the centerfold had studied at Wellesley College and had, for a time, lived on a *kibbutz* in Israel. On the other hand, Irma might not be as pleased to learn that the magazine belonged to her husband Saul, who apparently hid a substantial collection of Playboys deep in the pajama drawer of the armoire.

Ira takes one last gander at Miss May's ripe, creamy melons, then shoves the magazine under the bed, making a mental note to consider spending a summer in Israel. As he checks his look in the mirror, he pictures the Zatzkin women doing a mother-daughter spread for the June issue, thereby provoking dual father-son heart attacks.

Saul Overman drives him to Stuie Warshowsky's party with Rosenfarb in the back seat. Jake is doing his best Eddie Haskell, bullshitting with Saul about Dave Debuscherre having pitched for the Chicago White Sox before going on to be a star forward for the Knicks. Overman mulls over who might actually show up at the party, his curiosity focused on the English Lit class he took with Stuie, where drug dealer Robert Angarola sat in the back corner cutting his hashish stash into individual portions with a single-edge razor blade. This didn't seem like Hash Man Angarola's crowd, the event presenting itself as more of a sports and alcohol-oriented gathering. Two rows up from Angarola was one of the star students, Janie Sweeney, who always participated in class discussions yet was respected by her fellow students because she wasn't obnoxious about it and never sucked up to the teacher. This wasn't her crowd either. But more than anything, it wasn't Overman's crowd, because the only confirmed invitee who had ever said one word to him was Jake Rosenfarb. A sure lock for the guest list was one of the most popular boys at Lakeview, Marty Merkowitz. Ira's polar opposite, Merkowitz had single-handedly won last Friday night's game by grabbing a crucial rebound and dribbling all the way down court to score at the buzzer. Merkowitz was as slick as Ira was awkward, glib as Ira was tongue-tied.

Ira and Jake enter the Warshowsky house in time to hear Stuie announce to all that his parents are gone for the entire weekend. Rosenfarb dumps Overman on the spot, making a beeline for Sharon Kramer, who had previously intimated to Jake that her parents were out of town as well. It was astounding how uncomfortable Overman felt among this group of kids who were supposed to be his peers. As the Lakeview starting five broke into Irv Warshowsky's liquor cabinet, Ira marked his territory, hunching over the dip table.

"Do you think this is made with sour cream or cream cheese?" he inquires moronically of a buxom redheaded cheerleader named Debbie or Donna. She doesn't even bother acknowledging the question, darting off instead to greet Andy Lebensfeld, the reserve point guard who has just walked in the door.

Mouth stuffed with Wheat Thins, Overman looks up to witness the arrival of English Lit luminary Janie Sweeney. Everyone seems happy to see her, in marked contrast to the swell of indifference directed toward Overman upon his arrival. Merkowitz steps up to give Janie a hug and offers to get her something from the bar. She responds that she doesn't usually drink, but agrees to have just one. Overman figures that since she seems like such a nice person in class, she might actually be willing to have a conversation with him. He starts to make his way toward the bar to speak with her, but is intercepted by that world renowned King of

Poor Timing, Jake Rosenfarb. Jake has Sharon Kramer in tow and he needs Overman's help to get to the Promised Land.

"Ira, do you know Sharon?"

"Of course. How's it going, Shar?"

"I'm sorry," she answers blankly. "Do we know each other?"

"You were in two of my classes last year. Geometry with Corrigan and Biology with Alici."

"Right. Now I remember."

He's one hundred percent positive that she has no recollection of him whatsoever, but he can't get bogged down in being insulted right now.

"Sharon is a little worried about the World History final and she was looking for someone who might help her study," Rosenfarb explains, his concerned inflection masterful.

Overman considers offering his own tutorial services just to fuck with Rosenfarb but he knows he will never hear the end of it. "That's simple," he tells Sharon. "Work with Jake. He's an ace at history."

"Jake?" she turns to Rosenfarb. "Why didn't you say anything?"

"I don't like to blow my own horn," he answers, selling the false modesty that would become his trademark.

"Do you think you could study with me sometime?" Sharon asks, snatching up the bait.

"I have a bunch of clients during the week," he lies, "but maybe sometime on the weekend."

"That would be so great," Sharon beams, cozying up to him to help seal the deal.

Overman excuses himself to avoid throwing up. He's about to try and say hello to Janie Sweeney, but by the time he breaks free, Merkowitz is plying her with a gin and tonic. Ira wonders whether he should attempt to break into their conversation, but thinks better of it, sure that his social clumsiness would doom all chances of ever having a dialogue. Perhaps the best plan of attack would be to play it cool, let them talk for a while. The next time Merkowitz went to the bar, Overman would approach Janie, shoving Rosenfarb across the room if need be should the pest accost him en route.

At the moment, Janie seems enthralled with Merkowitz, so much so that she is completely unaware of Overman's presence. Realizing the futility of trying to engage her, he girds himself to mingle with some of the others.

"How's it going, guys?" Overman waves, oblivious to the fact that he has interrupted a weighty tête-à-tête between Mike Herzog and Seth Hammer.

"Fine," Hammer answers tersely but without annoyance.

"I'm going after her," Herzog informs Hammer, completely ignoring Overman as he looks toward the redheaded cheerleader.

"I hear she only goes to second base," Hammer says. "And only over the bra."

"Up till now," Herzog salivates. "I'll bet you twenty bucks I reach at least third tonight."

"How are you going to prove it?" Hammer wants to know.

Herzog has it figured out. "I'll bring you an RCH."

"Nice," Hammer nods his approval.

"What's an RCH?" Overman inquires, stupidly thinking his curiosity will ease him into the discussion at hand.

"A red cunt hair, you idiot," Hammer shakes his head.

"Maybe I'll bring you her panties, too," Herzog adds, as if trying to pump himself up for the conquest.

"Now *I* want her," Hammer says. "And I'd settle for an under-the-bra double, by the way."

"You can't touch her till I'm through," Herzog warns him. As Herzog stalks off to prey on the object of their mutual lust, Overman pegs them as hormonal powder kegs, ready to blow at the slightest provocation. How far would they go with the redhead? The possibilities were disturbing.

"Shame about that gang-bang in Pennsylvania," Overman blurts out almost unconsciously.

"What gang-bang?" asks the unsurprisingly clueless Hammer.

"An entire high school team got this chick right on the football field after a game," Ira explains.

"What'd she look like?" Herzog asks.

"Probably not too good after they were through with her," Hammer chuckles.

"The guys got caught," Overman tells them. "They'll probably be going to jail."

Hammer brushes it off. "Those things never hold up in court. They always figure the girl was asking for it."

As Hammer moves off to the bar to refill his glass, Overman notices Jake at the door helping Sharon with her coat. He waves good riddance to them, relieved to have Rosenfarb out of his hair, and free to take another stab at getting Janie's attention. Unfortunately, Janie's gaze is fixed on team captain Merkowitz and there's no way to break through. Now the two are walking toward the bar so he can have the next drink ready as soon as this one is finished. Overman sees opportunity starting to slip through his fingers. Not long afterward, Janie finishes her second drink and Merkowitz hands her another. He takes her over to talk to Herzog, who is, from the looks of it, fresh off a rejection by the redhead. After Janie takes a healthy swig of Gin and Tonic 3, Merkowitz whispers something in Herzog's ear. Herzog nods, moving off to find Hammer and Dennis Geoghan. Some sort of plot is being hatched. It is making Overman nervous.

As Merkowitz schemes, Overman utilizes the moment to finally sidle up to Janie in the hope of making contact. Eyes closed, she is gently rocking to the dopey strains of "Backfield in Motion." Janie is buzzed and happy, oblivious to whatever it is Merkowitz and company might have in the planning stages.

"Hello, Janie. Ira Overman."

"Hi, Ira," she smiles, radiating the distinctive warmth of the blissfully smashed.

"You know who I am?" he asks, caught off guard.

"You're Ira. You just said so."

Why was he wasting time with mindless bullshit? He was picking up a very creepy vibe and he had to tell her.

"Look, Janie, there's something I need to warn you about. I'm not sure about this, but I think that guy Marty Merkowitz —"

"What about 'that guy' Marty Merkowitz?" booms the voice of the devil himself, who has evidently finished his business and returned to further charm Janie. What was Overman supposed to do?

"Marty's a sweetheart, isn't he?" Janie swoons.

"*You're* the sweetheart," Merkowitz sleazes back, poised and ready for the kill.

Janie kisses him lightly on the neck, signaling that she has perhaps reached the necessary level of vulnerability. "I need another drink," she announces, guzzling down the last of G and T 3.

"I'll get it," Overman offers before Merkowitz gets the chance to, figuring he'll bring back straight tonic water and hope she doesn't notice. It's possible that one fewer alcoholic drink could make the difference here. As Overman steps up to the bar to pour, he looks up and realizes he's made a terrible mistake. Janie is on her way upstairs with Merkowitz, Hammer, Geoghan and a couple of others bringing up the rear. In spite of Overman's gut instinct and subsequent effort to stop something bad from happening, it appears to be out of his control.

Overman puts down the glass and rushes to the staircase, but as he starts upstairs, the ball players in between block him from Janie and Merkowitz.

"What do you want?" asks the lanky small forward Dennis Geoghan.

"I need to see Janie," Overman says, loudly enough that he is heard by both her and Merkowitz.

"You'll wait your turn like the rest of us," Geoghan whispers just a little too loudly.

Janie has heard him, but she's totally out of it. Merkowitz, however, demands to know what it is this little twerp Overman wants with her.

"Janie's dad is outside waiting to pick her up," is the first thing that pops into Overman's head.

"Why would your father show up so early," a concerned Merkowitz asks Janie.

"Who cares about that?" she answers, proceeding to shove her tongue in Merkowitz's mouth.

"That's our girl!" cheers Herzog, cupping Janie's ass cheek with his hand.

"I don't know about this," Merkowitz nervously tells the others.

"Tell him she'll be down in a few minutes" is Herzog's practical suggestion, after which Janie rewards him with a peck on the lips.

"Her dad's a big guy. Former Marine," Overman warns them.

"Former. And there's a lot more of us," the idiot Hammer chimes in, grabbing Janie's other cheek.

"Get the fuck away from her," Merkowitz commands his troops. "Time out."

"What's wrong?" Janie asks, as the disappointed crew starts to trudge downstairs. She tries to nuzzle Merkowitz's neck but he's having none of it.

"Get out of here. You're father's come to get you."

"I don't want to go," she whines, attempting another nuzzle.

"You're leaving, bitch," Merkowitz barks, grabbing her by the hand and yanking her downstairs. Overman follows, volunteering to help the girl find her coat.

Pleased that his Hail Mary had shaken things up, Overman knows the job isn't finished. Janie can barely stand as he helps her leaf through the pile of winter coats in the guest room so she can identify hers. And even though Merkowitz has given her up for dead, Overman still has to find a way to get her out of there before anyone finds out that there is no Marine at the door. Janie settles on a purple ski jacket with white trim. There's a better than even chance it's not hers, but who cares at this point? They head for the front door and slip out without anyone saying goodbye or paying them any mind whatsoever. That is until the moment

Janie realizes that her father is nowhere to be seen.

"Where's Daddy?" she shouts. "My father's not here!"

"He's around the block," Overman explains, trying to push her forward. He'll deal with the lie once they're out of harm's way.

But Janie isn't budging. Instead, she starts screaming at the top of her lungs. "Where's my father? You said my father was here!"

"He's around the corner. Just follow me."

At which point the door to the house opens revealing a royally pissed-off looking Merkowitz.

"He said my father was here, but he's not!" Janie shouts.

Merkowitz is furious. "You fucking loser. What the fuck is wrong with you, Overberg?"

"It's Overman," Ira politely corrects him.

Janie sees her opening and uses it to scurry back into the house, after which Overman finds himself staring at the shiny knuckles of Marty Merkowitz's fist.

"Now get the fuck out of here," the wicked basketball captain orders, proceeding to level him to the ground with one punch. Janie's would-be savior becomes dazed and limp as Merkowitz continues his attack with a volley of kicks, gleefully punting his throbbing prey toward the curb. Satisfied that he has thwarted the party's spoilsport, Merkowitz starts back toward the house, undoubtedly to resume the cold-blooded escapade that had been so rudely interrupted. An idea suddenly occurs to him and he signals to one of his lieutenants.

When Merkowitz disappears inside, a new hulking body appears in his place. Within seconds, Overman has been grabbed by Dennis Geoghan and yanked into an excruciating half nelson. Geoghan then orders him to his feet, pointing at the front door. Janie's foiled rescuer is fraught with apprehension as his captor steers him toward the stairs, aware that even if he can somehow manage to break free, he lacks the strength to reverse this whirlwind of malicious momentum. He is thrust into the master bedroom just in time to see Janie being lowered onto the mattress and Merkowitz unzipping his pants. Despite a Herculean effort, this rape will not only take place in front of Overman, but with his participation.

As his flashback ends, Overman notices that the rumblings from beyond the door have ceased, both Rosenfarbs tucked away to where they can do no harm. He is also aware that freeing himself to reflect on Janie's ordeal like the blackbird had reflected on the snow has revealed a long-forgotten but crucial detail of that night. While he had been steeped in regret and self-loathing ever since his involvement in the rape, what had been buried all these years was his courageous attempt to prevent it. Even though the effort had failed, it revealed a quality Overman never knew existed in his pre-Lasiked self. Saul and Irma had taught him right from wrong, but the concept of actually fighting back? Standing up for oneself or another person at the risk of bodily injury or worse, public ridicule? It simply wasn't in either of their DNA. Yet it was apparently part of his, even as a teenager. At fifty-five years old in a two-bedroom apartment in Valley Village came an enormous, life-changing realization: Ira Overman had defied his wiring nearly forty years ago. He had been imbued with the makings of a hero even then.

Overman is shaking with excitement as he absorbs the ramifications of this stunner. His futile stab at bravery had been erroneously self-interpreted as failure, nobility instantly forgotten as guilt and remorse set in. And since failure was the Overman default, from that moment on he went back to keeping his head down, returning to a life of ineffectuality. But the history books have been rewritten: Ira Overman fought for Janie Sweeney. He didn't just stand by passively. He did everything in his power to protect her. And now he is trying to be her hero for the second time.

Janie needs to know this. Overman picks up the phone, but stops himself. He realizes that while this has certainly been an insight of enormous magnitude for him, the forty year-old specifics might seem awfully petty to someone grieving in the present. He was reasonably certain she'd believe the story and appreciate his past efforts, but given her current state of mind, hearing the details would serve little purpose. It wasn't a Merkowitz apology, but a distant recollection that made Overman look better and feel better about himself.

A month ago, Overman might have been excited to share such a bombshell with Jake Rosenfarb, but now that father and son had joined forces to worship him, the forwarding of any information, no matter how insignificant, was a thorny proposition. Something as big as this could send them off a cliff, the upshot of which would be that they wouldn't die, they'd just come back more obnoxious. Overman decides to take advantage of the precious silence and attempt to get some sleep.

The next morning he arose at eight, prepared to act on the realization of the previous night, yet equally trepidatious regarding whatever it was the Rosenfarbs might have on the day's docket. Although Overman had yet to open his bedroom door, he was struck by how silent the apartment seemed to be. Most mornings, one could hear the patter of Rosenfarb feet scurrying about in anticipation of their superhero's every need. Perhaps they planned to take him out to breakfast, or some grandiose brunch they couldn't afford. Or maybe Jonathan had instructed his father to be extra quiet out of respect to the sleeping master. One way or another, Overman was determined to be rid of Rosenfarb nuttiness.

He turns the doorknob and peers into the dining area, witnessing what could only be described as an Eastern European tableau, a Pageant of the Jewish Masters if you will. Rosenfarbs Senior and Junior are sitting in silence at a table with enough lox, herring and whitefish to feed half the Diaspora. If Overman had to count, he'd guess there were three-dozen bagels in the various baskets, but the more significant news was that the Rosenfarbs weren't moving, much less eating. He wondered if they had become petrified like ancient redwoods in the same nonsensical way that Lasik surgery had changed him. No such luck. As Overman tiptoes into the bathroom, Jake barks that they are waiting for him.

Pissing for what seems like an eternity, Overman wishes he could piss longer to avoid having to join them at the table. As prepared as he was to put them in their places, a single interjection by Jake was all one needed to be rendered immobile by dread. Maybe a nice hot shower would revive Overman's motivation. On the other hand, it would only delay the inevitable. The sooner he faced them, the sooner he could shut down their nonsense and move on with his life.

Overman washes his hands and shuffles to the table in bathrobe and slippers. "Expecting a crowd?" he asks, eyeing the dozen or so whitefish heads staring at him with an expression that screams "*J'accuse!*"

"You didn't eat anything last night. We thought you might be hungry since you've had one meal in almost forty years," Jonathan explains.

Technically this might be true had Overman actually time-traveled, but it spuriously assumed that during Overman's time in the Speed Force he somehow lived through forty years of daily life without stopping to grab a bite. Only a Rosenfarb could muster this sort of logic.

"We hope you're feeling well today," Jake offers, trying to be on his best behavior.

"I'm fine," Overman assures him.

"You seem a little subdued," Jake throws in, unable to help himself.

"Jake, Janie just lost her husband, I still haven't figured out the Merkowitz problem, and you owe my boss $50,000 and have no way to pay it back. So it would stand to reason that I'm 'a little subdued,' as you put it."

"Yes and no," Jake counters, spearing a whitefish head that looks suspiciously like Madeleine Albright. "It all depends on whether you see the glass half-empty or half-full."

"Can I fix you a bagel?" Jonathan asks his master.

"No!" Overman snaps, grabbing a poppy seed and some chive cream cheese.

Jake takes a generous forkful of Madeleine and starts in on his thesis. "Ira, the truth is, no superhero has it easy. You're going to find your way, drop the ball here and there, but look at your stats so far."

Jonathan nods in agreement. "Impeccable. I'd put your winning percentage at roughly .867."

"I don't care about percentages." Overman hopes his lack of enthusiasm will shut them down at least long enough for him to digest his food.

No dice as far as Jake is concerned. "Were it not for the grace of Ira Overman, Jonathan would still be planting beets with the Guptanandas, doomed to a life of exile from his family."

Jonathan adds his two cents. "And if you hadn't rescued Dad from that scuzzy motel, he'd be living out of dumpsters, mumbling random questions to answers from an imaginary Alex Trebek. You've shined, sir."

"You got us back on our feet and for that we are eternally thankful," Jake caps it off.

"It was my pleasure to do that for you," Overman tells them.

"And as much as we appreciate it, we believe your success is far from over," Jake declares.

"In what respect?" Overman asks suspiciously.

"Ira, as you know, Jonathan and I have been working tirelessly on your behalf, exploring every avenue that might possibly be open to you."

"You've made me aware of that on many occasions. No matter how many times I told you it wasn't necessary."

"Ah, but it was, because as I'm sure you know, necessity is the mother of invention."

Jake Rosenfarb as Plato just wasn't cutting it for Overman.

"Ira, we know you're hesitant about your calling. That you'd prefer not to work in the limelight."

"I don't have a 'calling.' I just want to help Janie."

"Let's bookmark Janie and revisit that at a later date," Jake says. "We've got something very exciting set up. All you have to do is attend one meeting."

What kind of meeting? Jake might be smiling, but to Overman it sounded ominous.

Jake the salesman further stretches out the tease, informing his superior that this one meeting will "guarantee you and your associates a steady income for the rest of your lives, enabling you to pursue any and all of your dreams."

"By 'associates' I suppose you mean you two?" Overman asks rhetorically.

"Friends first and foremost," Jake assures him, "associates in the business world."

"We are not *in* the business world! We are not a business!" Overman cries out.

Jake explains. "We may not be a business, but the business world is about to reward us for all our hard work."

"And how exactly is that going to happen?"

"Two words," Jake replies. "Morgan. Schmeltzer."

Only Jake Rosenfarb would think of adding insult to last night's injury by combing through an ancient Overman address book. For what reason could Rosenfarb expect him to make contact with the sniveling little prick who got him fired from the talent agency and sent him plummeting into a life of polyester shirts and loss leaders?

"Are you trying to make me ill, Jake?"

"Not at all. We're going to complete the circle, don't you see?"

Overman didn't.

Jake turns serious. "Ira, what we're about to embark on is nothing less than the melding of Christ-like munificence with a stiff karmic ass-fucking."

He could quibble with Rosenfarb's choice of analogies, but that was secondary to unearthing whatever bizarre stew this madman had cooked up.

"Schmeltzer is a big *macher* at Disney now," Jake announces.

"I had heard that. Why would he want to meet with you?"

Jake explains that he and Jonathan had come up with this scenario quite a while ago. They began by calling Schmeltzer's office and dropping Overman's name on numerous occasions, which proved useless. Then Jake remembered that he had once installed swags and valances for a top director with whom everyone wanted to be in business. A casual mention of Christopher Nolan got them on the books right away, even though Rosenfarb's only connection to the guy was re-draping his media room.

"Just what do you expect to achieve here?" Overman asks incredulously.

"It's a pretty basic concept. At this meeting, we will synopsize your journey from nebbish to superhero. Afterward, we will offer the prick who threw you to the wolves the opportunity to pay you and your associates a bloody fortune to tell your story. You become a Disney legend, we collect our checks, goodbye and good luck, you move on to whatever else you want to do with your life." Rosenfarb and son smile in unison, waiting with baited breath for their proud leader's blessing.

The Rosenfarbs have become bona fide pimps. Apparently all that mattered to them now was taking their golden goose to market and peddling him to the highest bidder. Overman is tempted to blow off the father-son team with a volley of obscenities, but decides to go the less injurious route of letting them down easy. "Guys, I appreciate your entrepreneurial spirit, I really do, but your plan is well, naïve."

"How do you figure that?" Jake inquires.

"These people produce superhero movies all the time. They don't need to pay us to make another one."

"Ah, but they do," the senior Rosenfarb corrects him. "Because you, my friend, would be the only real life superhero the entertainment industry, or anyone else for that matter, has ever seen. If that's not a story, you can toss my testicles in a meat grinder."

"As fun as that sounds, I'm going to pass."

"On the meeting or the meat grinder?" Jonathan asks, just a little too seriously.

"Both," Overman confirms.

"You're not serious?" Jake looks like he's about to have a heart attack.

"Totally serious."

The younger Rosenfarb starts to sniffle. "I'll be all right," he assures them. "I went through a similar depression when Swami Guptananda told me I was incapable of having an original thought. Even though he said it was a good thing."

Jake puts his arm around Jonathan, assuring his flesh and blood that everything will be all right: somehow, some way, they will pick up the pieces and find a way to move on. It occurs to Overman that Jake has taken it upon himself to multi-task, assuming the roles of both comforter and victim. The bathos of the moment is something to behold, a command performance by a man who has been stymied in his quest to be the greatest sidekick who ever lived.

But then, like a Hebrew phoenix rising from the ashes, Jake Rosenfarb realizes that he has one last trick up his Nike Activewear sleeve. He knows his friend better than anyone on the planet so it would stand to reason that he might possess the key to the Overman Highway.

"Are you absolutely sure about your decision?" Jake whispers softly.

"I'm sorry guys," Overman answers, hating that he has any sympathy for these kooks.

"Ira, let me just remind you of one thing," Jake continues. You always told me that back in your Fresh Meadows days, waiting for the Dugan's Donut truck and the mobile tilt-a-wheel, your dream had been to unite with the Mouseketeers and become an upstanding citizen of the Magic Kingdom. Now, if you allow us to make you a Disney superhero, you will finally be able to take your well-deserved place alongside the legacies of Jimmy Dodd, Cubby and Karen, and the Almighty Annette Funicello."

Damn if Rosenfarb didn't know every angle. If there were a kernel of history, nostalgia or vulnerability to be mined for his gain, this son-of-a-bitch would find a way to get at it. The pre-Lasiked Overman would have bought into such an argument hook, line and sinker. What could be more perfect than the one-two punch of workplace retribution, followed by the fulfillment of an early childhood dream? But Overman is no longer that guy. There are different standards now and higher aspirations.

"Here's what I think, Jake," Overman begins. "Hypothetically, say I agreed to make a big deal. What would come with that money? Suppose they insisted I play myself in the movie? I'd hate that. Plus, I can't act. Then there's the small matter of me not really being a superhero. And what if they wanted to re-write my story and make me a gentile? None of us would be able to live with ourselves."

Jake, grasping at straws, insists that for every problem there exists a solution. "You owe it to yourself to run with it."

"No, I don't," Overman corrects him.

"But you're saying 'no' before you even hear the terms."

"I'm making the terms. For the way I live the rest of my life."

"A lot of thanks I get," Rosenfarb shrugs, accessing the guilt trip like it's a pair of comfortable old shoes.

"Thanks *you* get? I thought you were grateful that I saved you."

"I am. As you should be grateful that *I* pointed you in the right direction. Do you know how many hours I've spent trying to make your life better?"

"You cooked, you cleaned, you gave me some comic books. And I appreciate that, Jake. I do."

"That's all you think I did? Jesus Christ, Ira. You have no idea.

You want to hear what I was willing to do for you?"

"I don't know."

"I had it all planned out. Right after the Disney thing."

"I thought you said after the Disney thing it was done."

"Business-wise. But I still had plans for your personal life."

The guy was out of control. "What were your plans for me, Jake?"

"Turn toward the wall and cover your ears, Jonathan," the elder Rosenfarb instructs his son. Once he's convinced that Jonathan cannot hear the details, Jake spills the beans. "I was going to send you back to 1976."

"For what possible reason?" Overman has to ask.

"To have sex with my wife. I decided that since you had to live your entire adult life knowing your wife had been fucked by your best friend, so should I."

Overman can't believe what he's hearing. "Jake, that's insane."

Rosenfarb doesn't agree. "It's pure and simple, the right thing to do. Mind you, the year you nail Rita is totally flexible, but if you decide to go back and bang her in '76, you'll never see a finer ass on a white woman. Enjoy." Rosenfarb smiles as if he has just handed his friend the keys to his Ferrari for the weekend. Based on his enthusiasm, it seems he now considers Rita a done deal regardless of whether Overman accedes to the Disney meeting.

"Jake, I don't want to bang your wife."

"It's not a problem, really. I want you to."

Overman tells him that as much as he applauds the thoughtfulness of the offer, he doesn't need to take an eye for an eye at this point, or a vagina for a vagina to be more specific. Rosenfarb won't take "no" for answer. Overman is getting really agitated now. He had survived one traumatizing sexual encounter of which he wanted no part, now Rosenfarb was demanding he instigate another.

Jonathan decides to uncover his ears just in time to learn that the superhero has been ordered to pound his mother. He breathes verbal hellfire on his father for wanting to whore out the woman who gave him life. Jake yells back, explaining that it is nothing more than karmic justice, something Jonathan of all people, should know a little about. As they scream on, their blathering becomes white noise, piercing radio static that is impossible to decode. Overman can stand it no more. He cannot be in the presence of these people for one more second.

Cavanaugh Foster comes to the rescue once again, Squirt Video Central providing needed hiatus from the craziness. Overman finds the sound of the re-hung cowbell oddly comforting, a gentle reminder that the office's integration of pornography has not been at the expense of its down-home, loan-sharking roots. Even more welcome is the sight of Big Dave, who has come in early to re-write a scene from his latest production, "After the Flood," a pornographic meditation on post-Katrina New Orleans, shot entirely at an industrial park in Burbank. He explains that while he doesn't mean to denigrate the original writer (credited on the script's cover as "G. String"), there were motivation problems crying out to be addressed.

"I'm not saying that Juicy spraying every government official in the Lower Ninth Ward is a bad scene, I just want to know what in her character drives her to do it."

Overman is impressed by Dave's commitment to the art of storytelling. The fact that a coherent plot was rare and unnecessary in these kinds of movies had somehow eluded the big man, but why burst the bubble of anyone who had chosen to raise the bar? "Maybe Juicy feels sorry for the local officials," Overman offers. "Even though it's the federal government's fault for not acting sooner, the blame trickles down to the local guys and Juicy wants to ease their pain."

"Excellent!" Dave shouts. "You didn't tell me you were a writer, too!"

"I'm not," Overman replies, then fesses up: "Well, I did put together a few Direct Mail promos for the Mercedes dealership —"

"Aha. I knew it! What brings you in so bright and early, son?" Dave asks, going on to express his displeasure with a line of dialogue in the script. "Doesn't 'beaver' sound super-eighties to you?"

"It does. How do you feel about 'vuh-jay-jay'?"

"Kind of an airy sweetness to it." Dave pencils it in. "So what'd you say brought you in so early?"

"I didn't," Overman replies. He weighs how much he wants to reveal to Big Dave, then proceeds to divulge the whole Rosenfarb debacle, from their blind worship of him to their crass marketing schemes to the nightmare of sharing an apartment with father and son psychos. He also lets Dave know how concerned he is about Jake's loan and once again states his commitment to doing everything in his power to get it paid back.

"You're a fine young man, Ira," the mentor nods.

Overman thinks Dave might be tearing up, but these days, there could be any kind of fluid around those eyes.

"Don't worry about the loan right now. You just do whatever you need to do so you can live without being driven crazy twenty-four/seven. Remember, I told you I owe you one."

"I appreciate that, Dave. I really do."

"You're welcome to bunk with Juicy and me till you resolve your living situation."

"I don't know how she'd feel about that —"

"There's an extra room."

"That's very kind of you, Dave, but I'll be all right." How hygienic might that place be? Overman had to wonder. The room where they kept the sex toys and the icky rain slickers? Rosenfarbs or gonorrhea? What was the over-under on that one?

Dave types Juicy's last line in the movie, then stands to do a recitation: "Have no fear, brave soldiers of New Orleans. A brighter day will surely come. Until then, I flood each and every one of you with my abundant love."

Dave is swelling with pride. "I just came up with that this

second. Amazing, how the creative process works."

"Yeah, it's pretty interesting the places your mind can take you," Overman responds, Switzerland-like. At this moment, it strikes him that despite Dave's dubious writing talent, the man is perhaps the least delusional of anyone with whom he currently comes in contact.

Dave hits "print" on the computer, then announces that he must hurry over to the set with the pages. He can't wait for Juicy to read the new material. "Like they say, it all starts with the script. Later, son." The big guy flies out the door, leaving Overman to contemplate the silence and consider his next move.

"Is Mr. Merkowitz available?" he speaks into the receiver. "This is Ira Overman, an old friend."

Merkowitz's assistant puts him on hold for an obnoxious amount of time, then returns with the always reliable "What may I say this is in reference to?"

"I just want to touch base," Overman explains. "I wasn't able to attend the last high school reunion, so I just wanted to say how sorry I am about that and how happy I am that Marty's doing so well."

"That's very nice of you. Let me take your number and have him call you back."

"Great. I should be here for a couple of hours, then I'll be at a lunch meeting," Overman lies. "I really need to talk to him so it'd great if he could call me before lunch."

"I will be sure to relay that message," the assistant replies with a cheeriness reeking of insincerity.

Three hours of computer solitaire later, Overman places another call, learning that "unfortunately, Mr. Merkowitz has left for the day, due to his busy travel schedule." While unsurprising, it was no less annoying that Overman had seen it coming. He is about to turn off his computer and head to the gym when he takes a stab at looking for Merkowitz on Facebook. Perhaps going the Internet route and bypassing the secretary would yield better results than phone calls to the office. Also, Merkowitz would now be free to write to him if he preferred to use that form of communication to talking on the phone. Either way, Overman would keep his cell phone close at the gym, ready to intercept any kind of Merkowitz contact that might come his way. In a matter of seconds, he locates the now fuller, ever self-satisfied mug of the rapist-in-chief and shoots out a quick, friendly message, the icebreaker that is to clear the way for the real business at hand.

Driving east on Victory Boulevard toward the gym, he thought about what it was that he actually might say to Merkowitz should he finally get the chance. At this point, Overman was fairly sure that Janie wasn't looking for financial reparations. What she would appreciate, however, was a heartfelt written or spoken apology, taking responsibility for the cruelty of his youthful past and expressing remorse for the hurt it caused. The way Overman saw it, no one was going to be sued or held legally accountable, but it was only right that the score finally be settled and put to rest. The fact that there was nothing concrete to lose would surely put Merkowitz more at ease when Overman finally pitched the apology idea. Of course the "when" was predicated on a very important "if." It required that Merkowitz got back to him.

As Overman pulls into the gym parking lot, his phone starts beeping, indicating a new email message. He is naturally flabbergasted upon seeing that he has already received a response from the man himself, Martin Merkowitz. He quickly opens it and reads:

"Ira, I think I know who you are, but am not sure. Sorry to say I am really busy these days and don't have much time for reconnecting with my past. Hope all is well. MM."

That was it? Overman had finally made contact with the Major Domo, only to be unrecognized and blown off. A painless ending, Merkowitz must have surmised, clueless as to the caliber of the man he was ducking. Overman bristled at the thought of this terse email being the Grand Finale. Deciding to work out his frustrations on the elliptical trainer, his plan is thrown off from the get-go. Upon entering the locker room, Overman has the pleasure of seeing his ex-therapist step out of the shower.

"Ira!" Sheslow cries out, using his tiny swimmer's towel to dry a freshly dyed mane. "In all these years did you ever get your shit together?"

"I think I did, Gary. No thanks to you."

"I tried, pal," he counters, thankfully moving the towel to shield his genitalia, "but you resisted every piece of advice I ever offered."

He couldn't argue with that, but the relatively important detail Sheslow left out was that it wasn't very good advice. Overman starts to change into his own gym clothes, an ingenious diversion from pondering whether or not the shrink dyed his pubic hair, too. Putting on the "Jewcy" t-shirt given to him by Ashley, he suddenly felt ready for closure regarding the Sheslow chapter of his life. Overman turned to the self-important PhD, currently rubbing deodorant on his ass. "Gary, seeing how I was a pretty good customer for all those years, can I ask your opinion of something?"

"Sure. And then you can refresh my memory of what it's like to be ignored."

Overman notes the wit, but presses onward. "If someone you knew had been treated very badly, let's say even criminally, by someone almost forty years ago, and that person was never held accountable, is it worth bringing that to the surface?"

"Generally, no. It just dredges up bad feelings that ultimately never get resolved in a satisfactory way."

"So you think it's a waste of time."

"In ninety-nine percent of cases. On the other hand, there are your Nazi war criminals: cases where justice demands to be served. Are we talking Adolf Eichmann here?" He laughs.

Overman is not laughing. "Thank you, Gary. That is an astute comment and I intend to seriously consider it." He shakes the therapist's hand and heads off to the gym floor, feeling that he has, at last, gotten a little something for his money. Climbing aboard the elliptical trainer, Overman dives headfirst into the Sheslow thesis. Did Merkowitz fall into the ninety-nine percent or was he, for all intents and purposes, a teenage Eichmann, deserving of public rebuke and humiliation? The boy's venal action had not ended six million lives: it had seriously damaged one. He wasn't a Nazi, but on the other hand, unlike the Eichmanns of the world, he had never been forced to pay any kind of price for his violent indiscretion. Overman needed to decide: Would abandoning all hope of an apology be the best option in the scheme of things or would it be an undeserved free pass, allowing Merkowitz to be Mengele, free to hide out in style until his last breath? It was a puzzle that couldn't be answered in thirty minutes of cardio.

Moving on to do some leg work, he sees Carla by the free weights, in mid-yap with Bo, the wrestler. As Overman hoists the plates onto the rod of the leg machine, he identifies the conversation as work-oriented rather than bagel-related.

"He had been hiding out for months in a suburb of Omaha, but I traced him through a stolen iPhone," Carla explains to the wrestler.

"I wonder if you could find my first girlfriend from high school. I'd love for her to see the way I look now," Bo says. "I heard she's somewhere in the San Juan Islands."

"I can find anybody anywhere," Carla informs him. "All it takes is cash."

Overman's calf muscles barely worked, he nevertheless finds himself drawn to the free weights. Carla is now regaling the wrestler with private detective tales running the gamut from finding an abducted child in Palm Springs to tracking down a cheating husband at Kai Tak airport in Hong Kong.

"Ira, how are you?" Carla asks, having noticed Overman listening in.

The woman is a detective. She wasn't about to miss that. "I'm good, Carla. Real good."

"Have you tried the Everything bagel at Noah's? It may be better than the Everything at Manhattan Bagel."

The last thing Overman wanted was to let the conversation devolve into bageling. "I'm off carbs. But it sounds like your work is pretty interesting."

"I love it," Carla asserts. "Great job for an adrenaline junkie."

"Did I hear you correctly when you said you could find just about anybody?"

"I do a good job," she nods modestly. "Who are you looking for?"

Overman explained that he had already found who he was looking for. The only question was how to get to see him without trespassing or breaking and entering or doing anything stupid.

"Not a problem," Carla assures him. "Do you want to come into the office and talk about it?"

Ironic as it seemed, allowing himself to interact with one of these loony gym rats had given him the answer he'd been seeking to the Sheslow challenge. On some gut level, Overman was just not comfortable with Merkowitz being allowed to go the Mengele route as opposed to the Eichmann.

"I don't have a lot of money," he tells Carla.

"Is the person you're looking for in the U.S?"

"Silicon Valley," Overman says.

"No charge then, except for travel expenses."

"What do you mean? You're not going to do this for free."

"Sure I will. Hey, you're a friend."

Irony seemed to know no limits. This chatterbox of a woman, the one individual he had spent most of his gym time trying to avoid, considered him a friend; not just a casual acquaintance, mind you, but someone to whom she would offer her valuable services gratis. Overman is at a loss for words, more perplexed than ever by the inscrutability of people's true natures. Had he not overheard Carla's discussion with Bo, he would have gone on assuming that she was a shallow waste of time. He now knows that she is quite the opposite, and is moved by her kindness.

"Thank you, Carla." He gives her a hug, feeling her six-pack against him.

"You're welcome. What's the guy's name anyway? I'll do a preliminary search, then call you to book the appointment."

Overman sends both his own and Merkowitz's contact info to Carla's Blackberry and lets her finish her workout. Of all the discoveries he has made since his impulsive visit to the Clearview Vision Center, this unsolicited offer was the most unexpected. There had been no willpower or effort of any kind exerted on Overman's part. Carla's generosity suggested that human beings possessed an innate selflessness. Whatever the result of the Merkowitz affair, this moment would serve as inspiration for Overman as he traveled the road ahead.

He is barely out of the gym parking lot when it becomes clear that the generosity bug is contagious. The thought that pops into his brain is not a pleasant one, prompting the beginnings of a migraine, but he refuses to dismiss it. Upon further examination, Overman realizes that the course of action he is considering has less to do with his munificence than his own survival.

He rings the doorbell, expecting to be shot, punched, yelled at, or all of the above, but Rita Rosenfarb, decked out as usual in one of her Juicy Pilates outfits is, in fact, quite calm.

"Ira, this is a surprise."

"Hi, Rita. May I come in?"

"Not a whole lot going on here but suit yourself."

Overman enters, spontaneously setting a light tone for his visit. "This is pretty funny, Rita." He unzips his sweatshirt, revealing the "Jewcy" logo on his shirt.

Rita allows herself an oh-so-brief chuckle then reverts to all-business mode. "Sit down," she commands. "What do you want?"

"I have some good news for you."

"Jake is locked up?"

"No, Rita."

"I'm never taking him back, you know. Just so we're clear."

"Hey, it's your life."

"How much money is he asking for?"

"Nothing. But there is something he wants you to know." Overman recognized that he was taking a huge gamble here, but given the alternative, it seemed worth it. "We rescued your son."

"What? Jonathan's out of the ashram, or commune, or whatever they call it?"

Overman nods. "Freed from the clutches of the swami, back in Los Angeles."

"Oh, my God," Rita cries for joy. "How did it happen?" She's short of breath.

"Well, we couldn't send Jake into the cult because a parent would've spooked them. So I went in."

"You? You saved my son?"

"Well, yeah, kinda. I caught a couple of breaks, I found out the swami likes cars and I had this contact —"

Overman can't finish his sentence because Rita has thrown her arms around him and is hugging him for dear life. After considerable effort, he manages to pry himself free.

"Ira, I apologize for every bad thing I ever said about you," Rita sniffles. "How you were lazy, that you were a loser, wondering what any woman could ever see in you…"

"I appreciate that, Rita."

"What do I owe you?" She goes for her checkbook.

Overman stops her. "Rita, all I want is for the three of you to make amends. Jake is reconnecting with Jonathan and you need to do the same."

"What makes you think they want to reconnect with me?"

"They'll want it if I tell them to want it," Overman states confidently.

"Are you kidding?"

"No, I'm not kidding." He doesn't blink.

"Wow. The crazy thing is, I believe you."

"What would be really beneficial would be for you to meet with them and work with Jonathan to help your husband rebuild his business. Do you think you can you do that?"

Rita shrugs. "I don't know. I could try."

"Good. Jake also needs fifty grand to pay back the loan he had to take out after you emptied the checking account."

"Fifty thousand dollars?"

"This is your family, Rita. Certainly, he's spent that much on you."

"I'm so glad you didn't say 'spent that much on your tits alone.' Although it's pretty much true."

"Put your family back together, Rita."

"Jesus, you're like a whole different guy."

"A good thing, right?"

"Duh?"

"So long, Rita."

Her kiss goodbye lands squarely on his mouth, an odd sensation given their contentious history. Identifying the taste of Rita Rosenfarb's lip-gloss as some bastard form of vanilla, Overman returns to his leased Mercedes, filled with the hope of a better and less encumbered tomorrow.

Refusing to return any of Jake and Jonathan's forty-seven voice messages, Overman spends the afternoon and evening at the multiplex going from movie to movie for the price of one matinee ticket. He deliberately avoids the superhero stuff, opting instead for a Julia Roberts chick flick followed by a cheap slasher film and a Judd Apatow arrested adolescent comedy. None is as satisfying as the Hot-Dog-on-A-Stick that constitutes dinner. He thinks about calling Maricela, but instead goes back to the Cavanaugh Foster office where he will mark time with more solitaire before crashing on the couch. Just for peace of mind, he inspects all the cushions and turns them over before settling in for the night.

"You're in much better shape than you were a year ago," Dr. Abe Resnick exclaims as he finishes Overman's physical.

"I'm been taking better care of myself," the rejuvenated would-be hero tells him.

"I wish more of my patients realized they have the power to change their habits. What made you change yours?"

"Long story, but the important thing is, it worked."

"Amen," Resnick agrees, done prying. "I'll see you in a year."

Overman shakes the doctor's hand and heads out to Ventura Blvd, figuring he'll grab lunch at one of the many Encino eating establishments. He is barely out the door when he sees an appalling sight: Jake and Jonathan Rosenfarb are coming toward him, each with a crazy look in his eyes. Overman's instinct is to run like the wind, hoping to use his improved physical conditioning to outpace and lose them. He bolts west, but just as he is about to cross the street, the light turns red and he stops, taking a hard right north. Jonathan is young and quick, and Jake, while huffing and puffing, is giving his all. They are both hot on his tail. He is about to cross another street when that light turns red and the Rosenfarbs are literally steps away. Overman knows that if there was ever a time for superpowers, it had officially arrived. As Jake lunges toward him screaming, "Iraaaaaa!" Overman leaps into the air and in short order finds himself looking down on two Rosenfarbs.

It had been born of necessity. Against all odds, Ira Overman had pulled off the hands-down coolest superhero trick in the book. He was fucking flying. He wondered how many people were looking up in the sky, watching a fifty-five year-old Jewish man soar over Encino. He finds himself heading in the direction of Universal Studios and considers swooping by to entertain the tourists. Then he can swing west over to Steinbaum Mercedes of Calabasas and whiz on Hal from above. He nixes both ideas, choosing to soar higher toward the San Gabriel Mountains. He surveys the endless grid of the valley, the high-rises of downtown, the swells lapping the shores of the Pacific. At this moment in time, every facet of the world below seems nothing short of miraculous.

It occurs to him that flying has proved less difficult than procuring a satisfactory conclusion to the Janie Sweeney story.

In the midst of soaking in his spectacular, bird's-eye view, the cell phone rings, blasting him out of his fantastic, superheroic sleep. Dazed and somewhat befuddled, he is awake enough to be grateful that the Caller ID does not read "Rosenfarb."

"Hey Carla, what's up?" Overman asks sleepily.

"You're in luck. He's coming to Los Angeles."

"Merkowitz?"

"The one and only. Flying in tonight and staying at the Peninsula in Beverly Hills till the weekend."

"How did you —"

"Like I said, it's my job. I'm pretty good at it."

"Carla, I don't know how to thank you."

"Buy me a bagel sometime."

"Why not a dozen? Noah's, Manhattan, whatever you want. Thank you so much."

"No sweat."

As it happens, today's script pages are also in need of doctoring. Big Dave has arrived at Cavanaugh Foster to tinker with one of the film's early scenes involving Juicy and an assortment of exotic fruits. He explains that the scene as it is seems to lack a proper build, the action zigzagging from the pomegranate to the casaba back to the acorn-sized kiwi fruit.

Overman, as Big Dave's right-hand man, feels it his obligation to jump on the previously established Reality Bus. "Where would one even find fresh exotic fruit in a region dealing with the after-effects of a Category 3 hurricane?"

"By God, you're right," Dave exclaims, eager to attack the business of re-writing mangoes into a believable form of produce.

He thanks his employee profusely, after which Overman finally decides to cash in Dave's bighearted "I owe you one."

"Just tell me what you need, son. Your Lending Counselor is always there for you."

"I appreciate that. I really do," Overman lets the Texan know. As he lays out a beat-by-beat account of the Janie Sweeney story, not only does Big Dave appreciate its significance vis-à-vis his protégé, but finds in it a universality that demands his participation in the denouement.

"Whatever resources I have are at your disposal."

"Thank you, Dave." This time it is Overman who initiates the hug, fully prepared to sacrifice a few crushed ribs in return for his boss's kindness.

A woman of her looks and talent had graced many of the finer Los Angeles hotels, the Peninsula being no exception. It was, after all, a town where porn comfortably cohabited with mainstream. Squirtmistress Extraordinaire Juicy Jones had not only visited the Peninsula, but also had a personal relationship with the desk manager, Javier, having salsa-danced with him and his partner Michelangelo on numerous occasions at the El Floridita club in Hollywood. Dressed in the tightest white top she has ever worn and a black leather mini-skirt that barely covers her moneymaker, Juicy informs Javier that she is a friend of a friend of Marty Merkowitz. He looks at his notes and lets her know that Mr. Merkowitz is on his way from the airport. Juicy smiles and asks that Javier direct Marty to the bar upon his arrival. The desk manager winks, letting her know it will be his pleasure, and that he looks forward to the next time they get to dance "Casino."

Quietly, though certainly not invisibly, Juicy takes a seat in the bar, ordering an extra dirty Grey Goose martini and texting Overman with the pertinent information. He texts back, assuring her that he and his associate are in position to move in when the moment arrives. Juicy uses the down time to relax and enjoy her martini, all the while commanding the undivided attention of every straight and gay male in the place. Three Grey Gooses later, the rumpled, heavyset visage of Marty Merkowitz lumbers into the bar and begins scanning the premises for the unknown woman who has requested his presence. A smile and a nod is all it takes for him to identify the party in question and make his way over to the sofa where she has saved him a space.

"Ms. Jones?"

"Call me Juicy. Have a seat. Cocktail, Marty?"

"Sure," Merkowitz obeys, taking in Juicy with that familiar combination of curiosity and lust she knows like the back of her hand. "Dewar's rocks," he instructs the waitress.

"Lot of traffic from the airport?" Juicy asks considerately.

"It wasn't too bad." Merkowitz can't stop staring, finally forcing himself to address why he has been sought out by this knock-out of a woman. "Listen, I don't mean to be rude, but how am I supposed to know you?"

"You're not. You know my friend Dennis Geoghan."

"Dennis Geoghan? From Lakeview High?"

"He's a dear, dear friend," she smiles sexily.

"Wow. I haven't talked to Geoghan in years."

"I know him from New York. After he retired from the police force, he moved to South Carolina to run a Bed and Breakfast."

"Amazing. How'd he even know I'd be out here?"

"I'm not sure," Juicy replies, "Probably a social networking kinda thing. A friend of someone you know is friends with him, etcetera, etcetera."

"Totally wild," Merkowitz marvels, downing a generous gulp of the Dewar's that has been set before him.

"He said you were a big success and someone worth meeting,"

Juicy coos, going on to take a perfectly timed pause. "Was he right?"

"Depends on how you define success and what kind of guy you want to meet," he volleys back, lapping up the flattery.

"I've always liked powerful men. A weakness of mine, I guess," she giggles.

Merkowitz then sets about impressing the star of "Wet Sluts in Escrow" with his list of accomplishments and business acumen. Juicy plays the moment exquisitely, her pitch-perfect level of acting surpassing her award-wining turn in "Liquid Lunch."

"What I like about you Marty, is that you're not just a great business man," she smiles, sipping Dirty Grey Goose number five. "You're a great guy."

"Very nice of you to say, but how do you know that for sure?"

"I have incredible instincts."

"And incredible everything else."

"How do you know that for sure?" she bats her eyelashes. Merkowitz leans in to kiss her, Juicy melting into his arms as if she has found her Heathcliff, unable to resist his manly, diabolical charms. Merkowitz, in turn, seems oblivious to everyone else in the room, hands roaming anywhere they can find a home. Juicy is repulsed by the guy, which makes her performance all the more admirable.

"How about we have the next drink up in my room?" Merkowitz suggests, his palm now stroking her sweet spot.

"Sounds lovely," Juicy answers while gently removing his hand. "I just need to go to the Little Girls' Room and freshen up."

"Sure thing."

As Juicy heads off and Merkowitz signals for a check, Overman makes his precisely scripted entrance, planting himself in the film star's former seat.

"How're you doing, Marty?"

"Excuse me. Do I know you?" a befuddled Merkowitz asks.

"Ira. Ira Overman. The guy you blew off on the phone and Facebook. Remember me now?"

"No. I mean, I remember you called and wrote me. But who are you?"

"Lakeview High?"

"Yeah, you left that on your message. Wait a minute. Are you still friends with Geoghan? Do you know Juicy, too?"

Overman takes a well-timed pause. "I know Janie Sweeney. Ring a bell?"

"Janie Sweeney? Is she also from high school?"

"Very good," Overman nods. "Anything else you remember about her? And I'm not referring to her paper on the Brontë sisters."

"What's going on here? Look, I'm having a drink with someone."

"I promise, I'll be out of your hair as soon as she comes back. Do you remember much about Janie?"

"Not really. Wait a minute. Was she the quiet girl who hung out in the library?"

"Yeah. Except for that one night she hung out with you and the rest of the basketball team at Lakeview."

"Oh."

There is no doubt that Merkowitz's memory has come back with a vengeance.

"Do you have anything you'd like to say about that night?" Overman presses.

"Hey, we were kids — "

"She was a kid. And you took advantage of her."

"Look. That was like forty years ago — "

"And in those forty years, did you ever think to apologize to her?"

"I don't even know where she is."

"I didn't know where you were, but I made it my business to find you."

"You stalked me after all this time to bring this up? Are you crazy?"

"I don't think you, of all people, are in the position to name call."

Merkowitz is fuming. "Okay, I'm going say this one time and

one time only. I'm with somebody. Get out of my face."

"Juicy won't be coming back, Marty. She played her part. Now it's your turn." Overman turns to wave in Big Dave, who struts into the bar, video camera in hand.

"Bravo, Mr. Merkowitz. The authenticity of your animal desire was masterful."

"You filmed that?" Merkowitz shakes his head in disbelief.

"It was a fabulous scene," Dave nods. "Juicy played it so real."

Merkowitz grabs Overman by the collar. "You set me up for this? Why?"

"Because I need an apology," Overman informs him, Dave proceeding to pry the aggressor away from his protégé.

"You've got to be kidding," Merkowitz bellows. "Some high school chick begs to get banged by a bunch of guys who never gave her the time of day and you want me to say 'I'm sorry' forty years later?"

"I think it would be a good idea," Overman responds. "I don't think your wife or your various charities would enjoy seeing you canoodling with a porn star."

"I love that word 'canoodling'," Dave smiles as he holds up the camera, just in case Merkowitz is somehow still confused.

"She's a porn star?" Merkowitz cries out. "I knew she looked familiar."

"It's really your choice, Marty," Overman asserts sternly. "You'll decide how this all plays out."

While Merkowitz weighs his options, Big Dave resumes heaping praise on what he feels was the performance of a lifetime by the woman he intends to make his fourth wife. Overman, meanwhile, lays out the fine points of the deal, assuring the very public executive Merkowitz that should he agree to the terms, no charges will be pressed or money involved.

"So you just want me to say 'I'm sorry' on camera and you'll destroy what you just filmed?"

"That is the deal," Overman nods.

"As much as losing that scene hurts me," Big Dave pouts.

Merkowitz straightens himself up and brushes back his hair with his fingers. "Okay, boys. Roll camera."

Having squirmed with excitement throughout the six-hour flight, Overman is even more excited to arrive in downtown Endicott. He feels a sense of calm as his rental car passes through the landmark stone arch built by the now-defunct Endicott-Johnson Shoe Company, on which is carved the words: "Home of the Square Deal." Overman learned on his last trip to the Southern Tier that back in the forties, the Square Deal Plan was designed so that 20,000 E-J employees could afford to buy company-built homes, participate in profit sharing, and receive factory-funded health care. That utopian ideal having long gone the way of American-made footwear, Overman mused that had he indeed turned out to be a time-traveling superhero, able to re-write history, the Square Deal would have been worth preserving.

By the time Overman reaches the Leeds-Sweeney house, dusk has descended upon the Susquehanna Valley. Apart from random fireflies buzzing around Janie's garden, the still air is almost suffocating. Everything seems dead here, as if all creatures and vegetation that required oxygen had accompanied Garvin to the afterworld. Overman knocks, unsurprised when he gets no response. Maybe Janie decided to go to Florida after all, leaving the dogs in the care of a neighbor. Perhaps she went out for a bite to eat with someone from Garvin's family. Overman goes to peek in one of the windows and makes out what he thinks is the back of a human head at the far end of the living room. He taps on the glass, but the figure doesn't move. Maybe it's some kind of mannequin, used to scare away intruders while residents are out of town. Or perhaps it's a sculpture, propped on a chair for comic effect.

Curious as to Janie's whereabouts, but in no rush to leave, Overman ambles over to a wooden bench in the garden, across from the spot where he had watched Janie harvest her tomatoes. Closing his eyes, he can visualize every one of her graceful movements and hear Garvin's voice calling sweetly to his beloved. Then Overman, the man who has flown three thousand miles to help heal the woman he couldn't save, begins to recite:

"I do not know which to prefer,
The beauty of inflections
Or the beauty of innuendoes,
The blackbird whistling
Or just after."

If Garvin had been the blackbird whistling, maybe this was the "just after." Yet it seemed like reaching to interpret a good woman's suffering as beautiful.

It is a matter of minutes before Overman falls asleep on the hard wooden bench. Later in the evening, he is awakened by the slightly rough, yet gentle hands of widow Janie Sweeney, who has returned from supper at a neighbor's house. She ushers her weary friend inside, sitting him down amongst the treasures of her former life.

"Thank you for coming to see me," she tells Overman.

"I know you said not to. But I think I have something that might help."

"I'm glad you're here."

He follows her into the book-filled living room, noting that the mannequin apparition is, in reality, a large gemstone globe, evidently a present from Janie to Garvin on his seventieth birthday. As they settle on the overstuffed sofa, Overman can see that she is appreciative of his concern. For the first time, Janie is unafraid to address the giant hole that has been left in her life as well as the anger she feels toward the Almighty, in whom she had long placed her faith. The depth of their conversation touches Overman to the bone. The relationship he had sought to reinvent after nearly forty years has somehow produced a closeness he's never felt with anyone. A lovely and substantial woman feels safe in and soothed by his presence; comfortable expressing her grief with words, tears, even singing the songs that had defined the bond she shared with her husband. The old Overman would have put up a cinderblock wall in response to such an outpouring of emotion, but Overman Transformed wants Janie Sweeney to bring it on.

While he had never mourned the death of a spouse, loss had certainly not escaped him. Overman could look at the pictures of Janie and Garvin brimming with happiness and mentally replace those images with snapshots of his early years with Nancy, or of his young children frolicking on the Santa Monica Pier. The difference, he supposed, was that he no longer loved his ex-wife and had been able to reacquaint himself with his son and daughter in their burgeoning adulthood. Janie's earthly journey with her one, true love had been cut short with unbearable finality.

The two of them talk late into the night, traversing an array of subjects: Garvin's charming awkwardness with women, Janie's fear of spiders, Overman's failed marriage, his recently re-tooled relationships with Peter and Ashley. They flash back to high school, forward to their eclectic careers, back to Melvin Terrace Elementary and finally forward again to the present. In the course of their discussion, Overman is given many opportunities to bring up the DVD in his bag, but each time it seems like it would destroy the significance of the moment. The right time would eventually present itself, he figured. There was also the chance that there never would be a right time and maybe that was okay, too. As their talk intensifies, an unspoken truth is made obvious to Overman. The real meaning lies in the here and now, the "just after" where two imperfect human beings confront an undeserved fate with every ounce of strength and compassion they possess. Janie has been drawn into a merciless void and Overman must try to temper her anguish as best he can. He is keenly aware that he has no superpowers to assist him with this formidable task. The only answers he will be able to provide are the conventional, mortal ones he has learned in the course of his adventure.

As morning's light streams into the Endicott living room, Overman pulls himself up off the couch, rising to the smell of strong coffee and frying bacon. Janie enters with a set of towels, telling him that he can shower as soon as they're done with breakfast. She has plans for them today. The two friends devour their omelets and coffee, Janie taking the opportunity to inform her visitor that they are driving to Watkins Glen and they are bringing Garvin. Overman is honored that she's chosen to include him in her private ritual, but also realizes that he has never before participated in the scattering of a person's ashes. Jews were always buried, shoved in the ground as quickly as possible. The sooner for the mourners to get to the food, he supposed. Overman wondered what this alternative mode of acknowledging death would feel like, 180-odd pounds of flesh reduced to the contents of a coffee can. He remembered the dread he always felt at funerals, watching the casket being dropped into the ground, mourners adding their three shovelfuls of dirt to top it off. Perhaps there was something less gruesome about the Maxwell House approach.

Janie parks Garvin's old Ford Ranger just outside the entrance to Watkins Glen State Park, known for its picturesque waterfalls and dramatic rock formations. Reaching into the truck's bed, she grabs her backpack, inside of which are a couple of water bottles and the cremated remains of Garvin Leeds. Janie tells Overman that in the death business, these ashes are casually referred to as "cremains."

"Typical of the crass American culture," Overman grumbles, appalled that there was a stupid nickname for everything. The dead person wouldn't be bothering anyone anymore, wouldn't be taking up any space on the planet, why take away the dignity of the bits and pieces that were left?

The plan is to hike a mile or so in to the bridge at Rainbow Falls. There they will scatter Garvin from his favorite perch to the stream of water he held dear. Overman and Janie tread a path that follows a massive gorge, continuing past waterfalls and through various tunnels. At the halfway point, they reach the Central Cascade where the water seems to just drop out of nowhere at a ninety-degree angle into the valley below. The enveloping rock and greenery are foreign to Overman, the longtime California resident who had grown accustomed to the vastness of the west. Not that he was ever a nature lover. But he knew someone who was. No matter how far he had come, there was plenty of Saul and Irma still in there.

"This is the place," Janie announces, as they walk behind a waterfall, bound for the bridge where they will say their final farewells. Midway across the overpass, she unzips the backpack and removes not a coffee can, but a square brown plastic container, outside of which is taped a receipt describing the official cremains transaction: name, date of death, address of mortuary, state seal. She then takes two other items out of the pack: an empty biodegradable pouch made of hemp and a paper bag full of flower petals. As Janie snaps open the plastic box, she explains to Overman that she is going to combine the ashes with the flowers. After they are dropped in the water, Garvin Leeds and his homegrown white roses will decompose in unison, becoming one with the rocks, the moss and the rolling river.

Overman is to hold the pouch open while Janie pours Garvin in. Sadly, the moment isn't any less painful than the burial rites he has witnessed at cemeteries. They might not be handling a dead body, but they are dealing with an equally powerful end result. As Janie begins to pour, she instantly starts crying, the intensity of her weeping growing as she watches the ashes land in their organic receptacle. Some of her tears fall into the pouch, a profound addition to the mix in Overman's estimation. Surely, part of her must want to go with her husband, and now, in some small way, she gets the chance to. Overman offers his sleeve for Janie to wipe her eyes, which she gratefully accepts. She then ties the top of the pouch with twine and shakes it, making sure the petals, Garvin, and her deeply felt tears are inseparable.

Overman watches attentively as one half of the only couple he has ever admired descends into the fast-moving stream below. He gently pats Janie on the back, reminding her that she is not alone in her grief.

The drive to the airport is subdued. Janie expresses her thanks to Overman for his visit, but cannot bring herself to discuss what they have just experienced, or her vision of what lies ahead. Overman has many things he would like to say, but holds back for fear of upsetting her. He wants to tell her how angry he is that a man as complete as her husband now lies scattered in fragments so tiny they cannot possibly make an impact. He'd like to talk about the absurd phenomenon of a life disappearing into thin air, the finality of it all, the cruel concept of Never. Not only has a loved one left, he is never to return, his exit non-negotiable. Why was there no such thing as a comeback, if only a brief one? Why couldn't we all be Cher, returning to Vegas every decade or so just to check in with our adoring fans? While most of us weren't superstar entertainers, we still had friends and relatives who'd probably like to touch base with us every now and then. Why couldn't Garvin come back for, say, a holiday weekend engagement? Once a year wouldn't be asking all that much.

Overman would also like to recount for Janie some of the highlights of his momentous makeover. Who knows? The saga of the mad Rosenfarbs might cheer her up. On the other hand, it could just as easily send her into full-blown depression as she learned the depths to which the human race could sink. In a strange way, Overman was looking forward to seeing the Family Rosenfarb reconfigured upon his arrival in Los Angeles. Perhaps Jonathan's return had already begun to temper the sick relationship between needy Jake and overbearing Rita. Overman honestly wished them nothing but the best. In an odd way, he felt that the Rosenfarbs' whacked out response to his "superpowers" had accelerated his long overdue pilgrimage of penance and renewal. So in rooting for their future happiness, "he owed them that much," as Jake liked to say.

There is one final thought Overman would like to share with Janie. It is that much like her, he is beginning a new chapter, starting fresh with no road map in sight. He is ready to point out the parallel but thinks better of it. The last thing Overman wants is for the grieving widow to interpret this as a suggestion that they belong together. By the same token, he would love to ask Janie if she thinks they belong together. Yet if Overman had learned anything along the way, it was the importance of timing. Some questions would have to wait for wounds to heal and lives to be figured out. For his part, he knew there was still a fair amount of work to do.

Janie pulls up to the terminal and puts the car in park. She turns off the ignition and sighs. "Thank you again, Ira. This meant so much." She smiles, and as their eyes meet, Overman knows he is returning to California having won the greatest prize of all: he has earned this woman's trust. She reaches tentatively across the seat and they fall into each other's arms, Janie hugging him with a strength that defies her fragile state.

Overman is not anxious to let go but knows he must. "Take care, Janie," he whispers softly, kissing her on the forehead. "I'll call you when I arrive."

"Please do. I always get so nervous when someone I care about is on a plane. How do you feel about flying?"

"Flying?" Overman shakes his head. "No matter how many times I've tried, I can't seem to get the hang of it." He waves to her, smiles, and heads off into the terminal, Janie gazing after him as he disappears behind the sliding doors.

Acknowledgements

I would like to thank those whose keen eyes, advice and generous support helped me bring this project to fruition. Marley Sims, Elliot Shoenman, Allen Peacock, Eric Rayman, Susan Horton, Fred Rubin, Shari Foos, Roy Teicher, Neal Marlens, Billy Van Zandt, Brett Gregory, Tim Allen, Dwight Slade, Paul Harris, Christy Jacobs, Mark Morris, Robin Lamont, Stacey Miller, Nettie Reynolds, Jerry and Michelle Dorris, Rocky Lang, Joel Satzman, David Held, Bernie Kopell, Maria Berry, Dylan Berry, Hardik Vyas, Nancy Berk, Donna Cavanagh, Tyson Cornell, Julia Callahan, Rob Scheidlinger, Jim Ehrich and Rob Rothman. Thanks to the Ferber, Rogers and Lai families, and respect to the borough of Queens, the infamous island of Long, and the great, ever-mysterious Southern Tier.

Gratitude to the late Wallace Stevens, whose inspiring poem, "Thirteen Ways of Looking at a Blackbird" appears, in part, in this work.

BRUCE FERBER is an Emmy-nominated comedy writer and producer whose credits include *Bosom Buddies, Growing Pains, Sabrina, The Teenage Witch, Coach,* and *Home Improvement,* where he served as Executive Producer and showrunner. In addition to Golden Globe and Humanitas nominations, his work has received the People's Choice, Kid's Choice and Environmental Media Awards. Ferber lives in Southern California, with his wife, children, large dog, and assorted musical instruments.

Elevating Overman is his first novel.